# *The Daedalus Enigma*

# The Daedalus Enigma

*Waves of Darkness Book 6*

## Tamara A. Lowery

### Steele Rose Publishing

# The Daedalus Enigma

## By

## Tamara A. Lowery

1st Edition, Gypsy Shadow Publishing,2016 eBook, 2016 print

2nd Edition, Tamara A. Lowery DBA Steele Rose Publishing, 2024

Cover art, Copyright 2024 Fatima Saddiqa

Interior art, Copyright 2021 Tamara A. Lowery

talowery.wordpress.com

Published in the United States of America

ISBN eBook 978-1-956849-12-7

ISBN print 978-1-956849-11-0

# Table of Contents

# Dedication

To all my readers and coworkers willing to sacrifice their fictional lives to keep Viktor fed.

# Acknowledgments

I would like to recognize Susan Fox and Myfanwy Davies. They were the winners of the Red Shirt contest I ran at LibertyCon in 2015 before the 1st edition publishing of this book by Gypsy Shadow Publishing. Their surnames were attached to two unfortunate pirates in this book.
One has been added to Viktor's cadre of vampires.

# Author's Foreword and Warning

Each book in the Waves of Darkness series has contained a prologue section titled "Once Upon a Tide…." The purpose of this is to impart backstory about the primary character and/or some of the secondary characters and to set up some of the dynamics of their relationships and interactions. I try to make sure some element in the main story ties in with the prologue, even if I put it at the tail end of the story, as I did in Blood Curse (book 1).

Because of an idea suggested by one of my favorite BookTubers, Petrik Leo, I started including synopses of the previous books in the series at the end of each book to help readers refresh their memories of the story so far. I titled this segment "Here Be Spoilers." I started doing this in book 3, Silent Fathoms. I also wish to let readers who keep up with such things know that the official word count of The Daedalus Enigma minus all the fore and after matter is 93,223.

Now for the warnings. Pirates are not nice people, be they fictional or real life, especially real life. Vampires are by necessity serial killers.

I hope you enjoy my stories for the escapist entertainment they are intended to be.

# Once Upon a Tide...

A pregnant woman lay in the muck of a back alley in a small village. Torchlight flickered over her supine form and illuminated the bright blood erupting from her torn throat. The red, pulsing fountain pooled and mingled with her equally red hair.

A hooded and cloaked figure held the torch and leaned over to examine a dusty pile next to the dying woman. Light rain began to fall which caused the torch to gutter for a moment. The rain coupled with the blood gradually turned the dust, or more accurately ash, to mud. As it did, four elongated sharp teeth emerged to gleam in the torchlight.

"Interesting," the hooded female said. "The fangs survived."

She started a bit when the dying woman grasped her ankle. "Damn! You aren't dead yet?"

"B-belladonna, help m-m-meee." The woman's voice came in a faint burble. "W-water. Heal."

15

Belladonna shook her grip loose and stepped back out of reach. Even though she could see the blood flow slow, the prone woman's grip had been strong. "You should not have come to my territory, sister. I have always been free. I don't need your mate here. You knew he would follow you."

"Won't — leave — because — I'm — dead."

"We'll see, Marala."

Silence reigned as Belladonna watched her sister die. Finally, the blood flow stopped completely.

Belladonna shoved the lit end of the torch into the muck and left it there. Along her walk through the village back to the seashore, she dropped her cloak on the ground, as well. She walked naked to the end of a pier and dove into the salty water. Within moments her legs transformed into a shark-like tail, and she headed for the open sea.

Storms raged from one end of the Mediterranean to the other for seven months straight. Hurricane force winds crushed any ships that ventured forth. Enormous maelstroms formed where none had been before, and tidal waves drowned coasts which had always enjoyed moderate weather before.

Sirens did battle.

The male took the form of a great sea dragon. He raged against the female responsible for the murder of his mate. He cared nothing for the death of his unborn offspring, however. The three before it had been male, and he had slaughtered them at birth. He only cared about the pleasure his mate could give him.

Human females always seemed too fragile to him, although he found their flesh quite flavorful. They rarely survived long into the mating. Their bodies took too much damage well before he felt ready to finish.

No, only a female siren could hold her own with a male in the pleasure bed.

He determined he would have the one who'd stolen his mate from him. First, he would punish her insolence; then he would make her his new mate.

Belladonna took to land to avoid her foe. Although he could take human form as well, she knew the transformation took him considerably longer. She hoped to have time to hide.

She didn't anticipate the ambush. Five female vampires, all over two centuries old, pounced on her faster than she could react. She fought against them; a few gained vicious slashes from her talons. If there had been only two or maybe three, she might have escaped.

The siren was a match for nearly any vampire in strength and speed.

Apparently, her captors knew that and planned for it. They subdued her by sheer numbers.

Belladonna shrieked: a shrill ultrasonic and subsonic blast of sound. The vampires only hissed and growled. She realized then that these creatures were not vulnerable to such an attack which would've reduced them to mindless meat puppets, had they been human.

"Hold her steady!" A sixth vampire said as she stepped from the shadows. Silently, the others obeyed. Belladonna found she could not move.

The vampire stood before her and regarded her for some time before she spoke again.

"You are the siren responsible for the deaths of two of my kind seven months ago."

"I needed them to kill my sister. She tried to hide from her mate in my territory."

"Siren blood is deadly to my kind."

"I did not know that at the time."

"And now that you know?"

Belladonna tried to shrug but found the motion impossible while still restrained. "It matters nothing to me."

The vampire tilted her head and tapped her lower lip. "What to do with you, then? We cannot drain you for obvious reasons. You should be punished for your crime against vampires, yet —."

The siren held her silence. She allowed her muscles to go limp in the hope it would lull her captors into believing she accepted defeat. The ones who held her never moved or eased their tension.

"We will not kill you. You unintentionally did me a service."

"Oh?" Belle said. "You have an odd way of showing gratitude."

The vampire smiled. "You are an impressive predator; easily as crafty as one of my own. What say you, sisters; shall we initiate her into our sorority and make her a Daughter of the Dragon?"

Belladonna sneered. "I am already a dragon's daughter."

"Different type of dragon, siren," another of the vampires said. "I agree, sister; she should be one of us, since she did our job."

"Yes." The other four agreed.

"So be it." A small breeze buffeted them as she departed at blinding speed. Moments later, she returned.

In her hand, a branding iron with an intricate serpentine design glowed bright red, verging on white hot.

She bared her shoulder and showed the same pattern tattooed there; a dragon twined around a scythe. "Our marks are tattoos, but I do not believe that method would work on you. There is also the matter of capturing you again every few decades to renew the ink. However, I do know that your kind cannot fully heal from fire."

Try as she might, Belladonna could not squirm away. "Hold her firmly! I don't want the pattern marred," the lead vampire instructed.

The odor of burning flesh and screams of pain soon filled the night.

Hours later, the siren reached a secluded cove. The vampires had released her and vanished back into the night shortly after branding her. The burning pain on her shoulder blade made her left arm useless. She knew salt water would ease the pain and allow her to partially heal.

She also knew how dangerous it would be to enter the sea in her vulnerable state. Her adversary would sense her current weakness and use it to his advantage. The pain and wound severely hampered her ability to defend herself.

Even this cove, far removed from any human habitation, felt too exposed.

20

At that thought, a thick fog formed at the mouth of the cove. Belladonna eyed it with trepidation. Although she could do so, she had not called it. She scented the air, but the magic did not carry the flavor of the male she battled with.

Despite the aching pain in her shoulder it caused, she emitted a subsonic thrum to *feel* what lay hidden by the strange fog. Rather than a creature, the receptors in her sinuses told her a landmass had appeared where none had been before.

This puzzled her. She'd never encountered a magic like it before. She felt compelled to investigate.

To her relief, the blistered burn healed over to shiny scar tissue the moment she immersed herself to swim to the island. The fact she had to struggle with the swim frightened her, however. For the first time in her existence, her body failed to revert to its true form on contact with seawater. She didn't know if this was because of the unfamiliar magic or the fresh burn. She'd never had a wound caused by fire before, either.

Finally, she floundered to the mysterious shore. It took her a few moments to catch her breath: yet another new experience for her. She began to not like new experiences.

She spotted a glow over a low rise. Even though it signified fire, which raised an instinctive dread, she felt compelled to go toward it.

What she saw over the rise and down in the bowl-like depression made her try to turn around and flee. Some force held her in place. An ancient, dark-skinned man sat on a rock near a driftwood fire. He, too, seemed apprehensive about the flames.

"Come closer, girl," the old man ordered. "We have to sort out this little spat to two of you have been having,"

Belladonna shook her head. She moved her right hand to the new scar and shot a fearful glance at the fire.

"You will not be harmed, Belladonna. Come here," he said.

Against her will, she felt her feet move forward. Finally, she stood by an adjacent rock to the one the old man sat on.

"How did you know my name? Why did you give it to him?" She jabbed a finger toward the male siren standing opposite her.

"I am Zeke the Elder. I know quite a few things. If it will make you feel any better, he is Xandricus."

"You had no right to tell her that!" The male siren snarled.

"Quiet you," Zeke said. Xandricus opened his mouth to protest, but no sound emerged. He extended talons. Zeke pointed a finger at him. "Sit." He dropped unceremoniously to a rock at the command.

Belle took notice of the power display. She decided to be cooperative. She sat on the rock near her without coercion. She then turned a questioning look to the strange old wizard.

"Now then" Zeke said, "you two have caused quite a bit of chaos with your little lovers' spat these past few months."

"Pardon, Elder, but we are not lovers, nor have we ever been," Belle said.

He quirked up a corner of his mouth. "You speak respectfully, Belladonna. You learn fast. I know you are not lovers. I even know what caused this quarrel. However, I cannot allow it to continue."

He turned his attention to Xandricus. "Withdraw your claws, sea dragon. You have no need for them here."

The male siren obeyed.

"You arrived here on Hell's Breath first, so I will ask you first what you will accept to end this feud."

Xandricus glared at Belladonna. "She shall replace her sister as my mate. She shall submit to me and cede her territory to me," he stated his demands.

"No." Belle glared back at him. "I have always been free. I intend to remain free."

Zeke turned to her. "What will you accept to end this conflict?"

"He shall leave me and my territory in peace and never return."

"Unacceptable," Xandricus said. "My mate is dead because of her."

"That is not entirely true, sea dragon," Zeke corrected. "Your mate would not have entered her territory had you not slaughtered each of your offspring upon birth. She tried to hide to protect her unborn from you. Belladonna destroyed them both in the hopes of driving you out of her territory."

He turned his attention back to her. "Of course, that raises the question of would he have left you in peace if you had turned your sister over to him?"

She shook her head. "It is not in the nature of the males of our species. He would have tried to make me part of his harem and taken my territory. He would deal with any offspring in the same manner: if it were male, slaughter; if female, potential incest once she reached sexual maturity."

"Do you deny this statement, Xandricus?"

"It is my right as Dragon."

Zeke stared into his fire for several minutes. When he spoke, it held a tone of finality. "This is my decision. Belladonna shall cede her territory to Xandricus. He shall be bound to that territory and shall not expand it further."

Xandricus grinned and eyed Belle with a proprietary leer. His expression soon changed, however.

Zeke continued, "Belladonna shall retain her freedom and not return to her territory."

Xandricus frowned but said, "Very well, I accept."

"I do not!"

"You have no more say in the matter, either of you," Zeke declared.

The fog manifested and obscured everything from sight. Just as quickly, it cleared. Xandricus no longer could be seen.

Zeke looked square at Belladonna. She fumed but held her silence. She had not forgotten how powerful he was.

"You have your freedom, for now, siren," he said. "Do not bemoan the loss of your territory. The Mediterranean is small compared to the oceans."

"And if I try to reclaim it?"

"If you return to your old territory to reclaim it, you shall fall prey to Xandricus and be bound to him until his death. I will not permit the chaos the two of you caused to happen again."

"But I am free to swim and hunt in any other sea or ocean?"

"Yes."

She tilted her head. "Very well." She turned to walk away.

"Not so fast, girl; I'm not through with you."

She turned but wasn't quite able to hide her snarl of frustration. "You said I had my freedom."

"For now," he added the qualifier. "A day will come — I don't know when — that you will bind yourself to a male and will be bound to him for the rest of your or his life."

She sneered. "I have no intention of ever doing that, and if I ever find myself in that trap, I'll just make sure his life ends quickly."

He chuckled at her. When his laughter wound down, he said, "You say that now; but you'll sing a different tune when you finally meet the One. Now, let me see that nasty burn those vixens gave you."

Obediently but to her puzzlement, she turned to show him the brand. She felt an odd tingle as he waved his hand over it.

"What did you do?"

"Although it will feel like it, I did not remove it. I hid it. No one needs to know about it."

Before she could thank him, the fog manifested. When it cleared, she found herself alone in an unknown body of water. To her relief, her tail formed immediately.

She quickly dismissed the old wizard's forewarning. She would worry about that when the time came, if it came. For now, she needed to hunt.

Not until several millennia passed did she finally encounter the One of whom Zeke spoke.

Tamara A. Lowery

# Chapter 1

The *Incubus* approached Sapelo Island from the south. Bloody Vik Brandee and his crew had taken a prize just south of St. Augustine a few days prior. Vik planned to sell the stolen cargo when they reached Savannah.

The Grimm Reaper, Hezekiah Grimm, sailed the prize ship in tandem with the *Incubus*. Vik knew an agent in port who would buy the ship also.

The profit wasn't what Grimm looked forward to, though. His wife and their new twins awaited his return to Savannah. The boy and girl had been born while he'd been on this latest voyage with Viktor Brandewyne.

A raven fluttered down to perch on the railing near him. It bore a scrap of parchment in its beak.

"Lazarus?" he asked.

The bird cocked its head. Delicately, he took the scrap from it. It cawed once, dissolved into an inky cloud, and reformed as a large, sleek black cat.

*"Mrow."*

Grimm read the note. A wry grin spread across his face. He shook his head and laughed. "Aye, Lazarus; let Vik know we'll play bait."

The cat returned to raven form and flew off in the direction of the *Incubus*.

Grimm turned to his small crew and bellowed, "Prepare to pull ahead! Harris sails up the west side of the island, and the Captain wants us to play bait!"

A roar of raucous laughter greeted the announcement. The riggers swarmed aloft to adjust the sails.

Gradually, the *Hannah Marie* pulled even with the *Incubus*. As the pirate dreadnaught reefed her sails to reduce speed, Grimm's smaller ship passed between her and the island. Before long, they pulled well ahead.

The aft lookout reported sails on the landward side of the island as the *Hannah Marie* pulled north of Sapelo. At first, the other ship gave no intention of giving chase. Grimm knew better, however. He knew these waters almost as well as Viktor did. He grudgingly admitted the gradual improvement in Harris' tactics since Vik started this little game, years ago. Obviously, the man wasn't foolish enough to sail at speed through the shallower channel between the coastal islands and the mainland. Sand bars and shoals shifted often with the outflow of the Altamaha River and the tides and storms.

Once the *Georgia Belle* cleared the island and moved out to more open waters, she put on more sail. What started as pursuit of the *Hannah Marie*, however, soon turned to flight when the lookouts spotted the *Incubus*.

"She's taken the bait, Cap'n!" Jon-Jon shouted from the forward lookout. Viktor Brandewyne gave the nod, and his second mate yelled out, "Riggers set full sail!"

The sounds of sailcloth rippling out and pulled taut by the wind mingled with the calls of the rigging mates. The *Incubus* lurched forward, her copper clad hull slicing through the water.

"Damn! Did the fool finally grow a set?" Grimm watched the *Georgia Belle* bank around to face the *Incubus*. If he hadn't seen it with his own eyes, he wouldn't have believed it.

"Pull about, lads! Let's pen her in!"

Viktor frowned as he watched the *Georgia Belle* move about to a position of obvious challenge. His supernatural eyesight allowed him to see the crew of his prey clearly. He didn't recognize any of the sailors, but that didn't surprise him. Well he knew his periodic

31

harassments of the man coupled with Harris' personality, arrogance, and ineptitude made it hard for him to keep the same crew or mates from one voyage to the next.

What did surprise him was the absence of Harris' big floppy hat with its ridiculous, bobbing red feather. Nor did he see the man's face among those on deck.

"Lazarus!"

The cat appeared the moment he uttered the summons.

"Go search that ship. I want to see every face aboard her."

*"Mrrah!"* The cat transformed to a raven and flew to the *Georgia Belle*. Within minutes, Viktor saw through the creature's eyes what he needed to know.

"Mr. Jon!"

"Aye, Cap'n?"

"I want every man on that ship taken alive, if possible, especially the captain. I want him to tell me why Chadwick Harris is neither in command nor even aboard."

"You heard the man, lads: board and subdue!"

The battle lasted only five minutes. Viktor took the wheel and deliberately brought the *Incubus* within inches of ramming the *Georgia Belle* head on. Instead, he had his crew put out the large corkwood bumpers on the port side. The riggers reefed the sails, and Jon-Jon had men drop the sea anchors on the starboard side.

As a result, the *Incubus* slewed around much sharper and faster than a ship of her size and draft should have been able to. The two ships collided broadside. The bumpers and copper cladding prevented the larger ship from sustaining damage. The *Georgia Belle* did not fare so well.

The foremast of the smaller ship teetered then collapsed as the impact rocked it. By the time the *Belle*'s crew recovered their wits, pirates swarmed over to the rigging or dropped down to the deck. To add insult to injury, the *Hannah Marie* cruised to a slow halt at their other side and trained cannon and muskets on them.

Only a small handful of the *Georgia Belle*'s crew offered any sort of resistance. Jon-Jon had a few pirates use cast nets to subdue them. The rest of the crew surrendered without a fight.

Viktor slowly flew down to the deck of the *Georgia Belle*. He made sure his captives saw him do it. As a result, his men had to cudgel a few of the more panicked prisoners.

"Where is your captain?" he asked as he stalked around the crew of the *Georgia Belle*.

Several fingers pointed at one of the netted men. Viktor smiled and headed for him. The smile faded around the edges as he caught the faintest trace of a familiar scent.

"Thia?" he muttered.

The man the crew indicated as their captain started at the mention of that name. Viktor noted the recognition. His smile returned, but his eyes held cold fire.

"What is your name, sir?" He asked his captive.

"Captain Joseph Turlington," the man replied. "I take it you are the pirate known as Bloody Vik Brandee?"

"You seem well informed for someone not native to these waters. I am curious. How is it you come to be in command of this ship? What has become of Captain Harris?"

"I was ordered to take command of this ship and keep watch for you, as well as to warn any and all ships I encountered to beware of your ship."

"Indeed." Viktor gazed at him; the smile turned decidedly unpleasant. "You were ordered. So, you are Royal Navy."

Turlington remained silent but stood as erect as the net would allow.

Viktor continued, "You still have not said what has become of Captain Harris."

"I do not know. The day after I received my orders, he disappeared. It is assumed he fled Savannah."

Viktor pursed his lips and nodded. "So, he is still free; good."

Turlington blinked at him in confusion. "I was under the impression you had some sort of grudge against him."

Viktor laughed. "Hardly! Chadwick is one of my favorite sources of entertainment."

The pirates joined in their captain's laughter. They laughed even harder when Turlington asked, "In what way?"

Jon-Jon piped up. "The man fancies himself a pirate captain, yet he can't keep a crew more than two voyages, and he pisses himself every time the Cap'n catches him."

"Somehow, Mr. Turlington, I've a feeling you will not provide the same quality of entertainment," Viktor said. He circled the Navy man then turned his attention to Jon-Jon. "Mr. Jon, remove the net from this man. I wish a word with him in private."

"I have no intention of joining your crew, sir," Turlington stated flatly.

"I wasn't inviting you to, "Vik replied. "Lads, strip and scuttle her, no, belay that. Strip her and burn her. No sense in leaving a navigational hazard here."

The moment Turlington found himself free from the net he elbowed Jon-Jon in the gut. The tall, burly pirate doubled over in surprise as the air left his lungs. The Navy man brought his elbow down hard on the man's skull and dropped him to the deck, stunned. He bolted for the railing.

Viktor suddenly blocked his way. The vampire hovered just past the railing.

"Going somewhere, Mr. Turlington?" He reached out and grabbed the man by his shirt front. "Considering we haven't had our little talk yet; I find that rude."

Without further warning, he launched skyward taking Turlington with him.

Belladonna made herself comfortable in Viktor's favorite chair in his cabin. She'd returned from a successful hunt just in time to see the *Incubus* take the *Georgia Belle*. The sight made her smile. She knew Viktor was always in high spirits after an encounter with Harris, so she didn't bother to dress.

Viktor's appearance outside the bay windows of his cabin caught her a little off guard, as did the unknown man dangling in his grasp. She moved to the window casement and swung one of the multi-paned panels open. Viktor flew into the cabin and deposited his prisoner on the deck.

"That's not Harris," she said.

"What are you?" Turlington demanded as he scooted away from his captor.

"No, and you are not dressed, pet," Viktor replied. He ignored his prisoner for the moment, his attention riveted on the siren.

"Should I be?" She returned to his chair and lounged in it. She deliberately draped one leg over the chair's arm in a blatant display and gave him a coy smile.

He groaned appreciatively and gave her a searing look which promised much. Through the mental bond he shared with her, he said, *"Normally, I would say yes, but your state of undress does not seem to be a distraction to our temporary guest."*

She frowned and noticed Turlington barely registered her presence. Instead, the man's eyes darted about the cabin, taking in every detail and obviously looking for an escape route. She stood and sashayed over to the man.

"Aren't you going to introduce me to your guest, Viktor?" She pouted and ran her fingers down the man's chest. *"He reeks of that vampire bitch,"* she added mentally.

*"Thank you for your confirmation, pet,"* he replied in kind. Aloud, he said, "Belle, allow me to introduce Captain Joseph Turlington, late of His Majesty's Royal Navy. Mr. Turlington, this is Belladonna, a siren."

"Siren?" Turlington finally took notice of the naked red head. "You still haven't told me what you are."

"I am surprised you have to ask that, given how intimate you have been with the Lady Carpathia," Viktor said.

Belle noticed how the man stiffened at the mention of that name.

"I don't know what you mean, sir."

"Oh yes you do," Belle said with a sly smile. "He knows because we can both smell her on you. Granted, the scent is old; but you have bedded her. Her power hovers over your skin like a fetid mist, as well. I'll wager she fed from you and made you a personal pet."

"What are you talking about?" He looked at her as if she were speaking gibberish.

She blinked at him and gave Viktor a worried look. "He really doesn't know. She has altered his memory. He is not safe to keep around. She is older and more skilled in the use of her powers than you. She might be able to use him to spy on you."

"Trust me, pet; I thought of that possibility." He turned his full attention to Turlington. "You asked what I am, sir. I am a vampire unlike any other. The Lady Carpathia is a vampire as well, although of a different variety."

"What do you mean? That you are one of those blood-drinking walking dead that madman Westin was always spouting about? Why the Commodore even took that fool on is beyond me. At least he had sense enough to set him adrift later." Turlington blathered. "And how dare you besmirch the Lady's name by saying you are anything alike!"

"Enough." Viktor spoke the one word with power behind it. He grasped the man's jaw and forced eye contact. Within moments the vampire's eyes glowed bright green.

Belle watched with a vision she knew Viktor did not possess as the aura of Carpathia's power grew stronger around the prisoner's form. Powerless to stop it, she saw the man's eyes turn jet black and shine with an un-light. She could even see the female vampire's image superimpose itself over Turlington's body.

The vampire had taken possession of her pet.

Turlington/Carpathia captured Viktor's gaze. His eyes dilated to black pupils ringed by a thin sliver of green fire.

"Thia," he whispered. An almost tender smile shaped his mouth. Belladonna's heart wrenched at the sight.

"Viktor, my love; I have missed you so," Turlington/Carpathia said. She used her human puppet to embrace the pirate captain and pull him into a passionate kiss.

# Chapter 2

Viktor held Thia in his arms as they kissed. He hadn't realized how much he had missed her. He tasted blood. It held a smoky, honeyed flavor, and he knew it wasn't his.

Even though they still kissed, he heard her say, *"Only you can give me life, Viktor Brandewyne. Come to me in New Orleans. I need you."*

An unexpected, strangled scream broke the kiss.

Jealous rage engulfed the siren as she watched her master embrace the possessed man. She smelled the blood, felt Carpathia's power flare, and saw the vampire's trap spring to ensnare Viktor.

"No! You can't have him, you bitch! He's mine!" she growled. She plunged her talons into Turlington's heart and pulled him away from Viktor. The man let out a gurgling scream when she withdrew her talons. They shrank back to just fingers.

"And damned if I'm going to let you rise as a vampire and give that bitch even more access." She grabbed the pen knife from the desk and slit the heel of her hand. She then dribbled a few drops of her blood from the rapidly healing wound into Turlington's mouth.

In an instant, his damaged heart ceased to beat, and his eyes glazed over. Carpathia's aura of power around his body evaporated immediately. Siren's blood brought instant true death to vampire kind.

Satisfied Turlington would not rise as a vampire, Belle turned her attention back to Viktor. He stood with eyes open but plainly unaware of his surroundings. He reached forward, grasping for something or someone no longer there with a lost and forlorn expression.

A small amount of blood dribbled from the corner of his mouth.

"No. No, no, no, no," Belle said in horror. She stepped over to him and took his hands in hers. "Viktor?"

"Thia, where are you? Where did you go?" he said plaintively.

"Viktor, come back to me," Belle pled.

"Thia?"

She saw she needed to take drastic measures, ones which could easily end with her trapped along with him or with one or both of them dead.

She reached up to wrap her arms around his neck for a kiss; he did not bend down to her. She leapt up and wrapped her legs around his waist and kissed him fiercely. Instinctively, he held and supported her weight to keep his balance.

She tasted the blood in his mouth and knew it was not his. Faintly, she sensed Carpathia's presence in it.

She started to pull back to spit the blood out; Viktor finally responded to the kiss and returned it with passion at that moment. He carried her over to the bed and collapsed on top of her. The soft impact forced her to release her hold on him.

He stood up long enough to strip using his superhuman speed; then he was back on her.

Belladonna abandoned all coherent thought as Viktor held nothing back.

Carpathia sensed the siren's presence. It was too faint to give her any control over the creature, but something felt familiar. Recognition set in a split second before the contact broke.

Viktor's pet was the same siren she and her sisters had branded millennia ago; she saw through Turlington's eyes the unmistakable dragon and scythe design which marked the creature as a Daughter of the Dragon — and once again, the siren had unwittingly done Carpathia's job for her. Viktor's pet siren had just caused his death.

Viktor's full awareness returned in the midst of his lovemaking. A strange tingling sensation filled his mouth and washed down his throat. It spread throughout his body. His chest felt painfully tight, and he found it difficult to breathe.

When he finally could draw a breath, he roared out his orgasm.

Belladonna did not echo it. In fact, she remained limp and unresponsive. Blood trickled from two neat puncture wounds close to where neck met shoulder.

"Belle!" he cradled her body to him. He breathed a sigh of relief when she moaned softly. For a moment, he'd feared he'd killed her.

Then it struck him.

Her toxic blood had almost killed him, but somehow, he survived. It also completely freed him of Carpathia's trap. While he felt a pang of loss over that, he also determined that the ancient vampire better pray their paths never crossed again.

The *Incubus* had no need to recruit or replace crewmen at the time, so all the prisoners ended up in the larder hold as blood stock for Viktor and the six vampires who made up his cadre.

He ordered the body of Turlington burned with the *Georgia Belle*.

The *Incubus* and the *Hannah Marie* sailed on to Savannah.

Viktor met Grimm on the docks upon their arrival. He found his first mate directing his token crew to unlade the prize ship.

"Hezekiah, I'm sending Mr. Jon over to see to this. I've already sent a message to my agent to deal with him in the disposal of the prize."

Grimm frowned. "I usually handle these transactions. Is something wrong?"

Viki grinned and shook his head. "You never cease to amaze me, Hezekiah. All this time away and the first thing you think of once we make this port is business. I'd have thought you'd want to go meet your children and spend some time with your wife."

Grimm gave him a sheepish smile. "I didn't want to just rush off. Wouldn't look good to the men."

"Bilge. They think what I tell them to think. Of course, I've heard Jon-Jon owes Sniff a keg of rum because you didn't hie over to Celie's the minute your feet hit the docks."

"Serves him right." Grimm laughed. "He ought to know better than to wager with that rigging rat by now, anyway."

"Go check on your family, Hezekiah. Tell Celie I'll be around later tomorrow." He clapped Grimm on the shoulder.

"Thank ye, Vik. Console Maggie's girls on their loss of my services."

The two pirates parted company laughing.

Mother Celie led her foster son's friend to the addition on the back of her tabby shack. To any observers, the extra room appeared to be nothing more than a mossy overgrowth of live oaks. Long beards of Spanish moss completely camouflaged the sturdy tabby structure.

Celie tapped a spot with her walking stick, and the moss parted to reveal a door. Grimm nodded to her in thanks and entered.

He stood inside the doorway for a few minutes to allow his eyes to adjust. A sleeping form lay on the bed along one wall. A spill of dark curls masked her face. Grimm took a few steps toward his wife when a tinkling bell and movement near the foot of the bed caught his attention.

He walked over to the lidless sea chest and saw it had been made into a crib. Two good-sized infants lay in it and looked up at him with bright eyes. The bell sound came from a small jingle bell secured to the right foot of the little girl. She looked up at him and grinned; two tiny teeth peeked above the gum line of her lower jaw. The little boy scowled and gnawed on a small burlap pillow. The scent of cloves wafted up to Grimm.

"Hello there," he said. A gentle smile curled his lips.

The girl burbled and reached chubby arms toward him. Her tiny fists opened and closed. With a grin, he knelt down and picked her up. She cooed. As he stood back up, the boy let out a howl at being ignored.

He chuckled. "You'll get your turn."

Grimm grew very still. The edge of a blade came to rest below his right ear. A female voice he hadn't heard in over a year said, "Very slowly put her down and step away from the crib."

He kissed his daughter's head, knelt slowly, and placed her next to her brother. He brushed fingertips calloused by years of handling ropes over the boy's downy head.

The blade pressed into his flesh just shy of cutting. "I said step away from the crib."

He smiled with his back still to her. He knew he'd found a rare jewel in his wife. "Now is that any way to greet your husband and the father of your children, Mrs. Grimm?"

"Husband? Hezekiah?" The knife slipped from her nerveless fingers and dropped to the floor.

He turned as he stood back up and embraced her. He lifted her, and she wrapped her arms around his neck and showered him with kisses.

They both were laughing by the time she let him come back up for air. "That's more like it, wife," he said with a grin. "God, I've missed you, Brianna." He set her down and took a step back from her. "Let me look at you."

She shot him a sultry look. "I'll do more than that, Hezekiah Grimm." She unlaced the loose nightgown she wore, slid it off her shoulders, and let it drop to the floor.

Neither of them spoke much for the next hour.

Total silence swept over the common room of the Black Flag when Viktor entered. Most of the patrons knew him on sight; those who did not were quick to pick up on the fact he was thoroughly dangerous.

# The Daedalus Enigma

Viktor scanned the crowd, picking out new faces from the old. In this tavern where he spent his youth and learned his trade, he usually didn't get this much fear unless something was very wrong.

He strode over to a table that gave him a good view of the entire room, the exit, and the stairs. The chair still held the warmth of its previous occupant. The man had moved to another table the moment he'd seen Bloody Vik Brandee head in his direction.

Conversations resumed when he took his seat. Maggie, the owner, came out of the kitchen with a tray, a bottle, and two glasses. She carried this to the table. He smiled and nodded toward a chair. She set the tray down and sat.

"Hello, Maggie, pet." He pulled the cork and filled the glasses. "I have a feeling you have an interesting tale to tell me; one about Chadwick Harris, if my guess is right."

He noticed her blanch a bit.

"I do, Vik, but it might be better to save that conversation for a more private setting," she said after she gulped down her drink. "There are unfriendly eyes and ears here. The Flag might not be safe for you anymore."

"Is any place ever truly safe, pet?" he asked with a smile.

He tossed his own drink back, stood, grasped the bottle, and held his other hand out to her. "Upstairs, then."

She took his hand and stood. It alarmed him to see the terror in her eyes. Her hand trembled, and she almost tried to bolt. He raised her hand to his lips and looked her in the eye. Although her fear made it difficult to bewitch her, he did get her attention.

"You have nothing to fear from me, Maggie. I give you my word," he whispered.

She visibly calmed some and nodded. "Misty, take over down here for the rest of the day. I will be upstairs entertaining."

Grimm sat with his son in his lap. He kept the boy distracted while Brianna fed their daughter.

"Have you named them yet?" he asked.

"Not officially. It has not been safe to enter town to have them baptized," she replied. She lifted her daughter to her shoulder and patted the child on the back. In short order, the baby spit up on the rag Brianna had draped there for that purpose.

Grimm had rarely been around infants, and this alarmed him. "Is she sick? Do I need to fetch Celie?"

"No, she is fine. Celie taught me to do this after I feed them. She said they get a little air in their stomachs with the milk. If they don't burp, they will get colic and cry constantly." She laughed and wiped the baby's face. "I need to wean them soon. They are teething and tend to bite, especially *mon petit homme* there."

Grimm chuckled as he swapped babies with her. "Takes after his father, eh?"

"*Oui!*" She gave him a mischievous smirk and stuck her tongue out at him. He laughed harder.

His daughter yawned and stretched then blinked up at him with sleepy eyes. The tiny bell on her ankle tinkled and drew his attention. "This is pretty."

"It is also practical." He gave her a questioning look, and she elaborated. "She likes to climb out of the crib and crawl off."

"Oh, so you are a roamer, eh little one?" He smiled and stroked the baby's cheek.

Brianna surreptitiously watched her husband as he held his children. She saw how gentle and tender he was with them; yet it was obvious he was not afraid they would break or felt awkward with them. It made her glad they had found each other.

"I do have prospective names for them," she said softly. He looked up at her and raised his eyebrows. "Celeste and Sebastian."

He furrowed his brow and looked at his son. "Celeste is a very pretty name, but Sebastian Grimm doesn't sound quite right."

"It was my *granpere*'s name," she said defensively.

"I didn't say I don't approve, just not as a first name," he soothed. "How does Henry Sebastian Grimm sound to you?"

She cocked her head to the side as if thinking about it. After a while, she said, "Very well; but you must give our daughter an additional name as well."

"Fair enough; I've always liked the name Nicole. We shall call her Celeste Nicole Grimm to honor the friend you lost when we first met."

Brianna beamed at him. "*Je taime, mon amor!* Nicole was my *Mere*'s name also!"

"I did not know that." He laughed; pleased his choice gave her such pleasure. He felt blessed to have found such a wonderful mate.

Viktor sat on the edge of the bed and stared at Margery. She stood with her back against the wall and stared back; her scent soured by fear. Oddly, it did not fire his Hunger.

"Maggie, why are you so afraid?" He decided to be blunt and direct.

"You said you expected me to tell you about young Harris. I know you, Captain. Your calm means you are angry about it."

He grunted. Sometimes his personal tics worked against him. "I am not angry about anything, pet. I just want to know if you know what happened to him. That Navy bastard who was sailing his ship didn't tell me anything useful."

She grew so white he thought she looked like a drained corpse. "What have you done?" she whispered hoarsely.

"I took the *Georgia Belle* and disposed of the usurpers then burned it to the waterline. Why? Is that a problem?"

"Maybe; I'm not sure." She walked to the bed and sat down beside him. She still appeared to be in mild shock.

He took one of her hands and caressed it. At the same time, he rubbed small circles on her back in an effort to soothe and calm her. "Maggie," he said gently, "what has been going on here in Savannah since I left?"

She took a deep breath and let it out. "It's not just in Savannah, Captain."

"Vik," he corrected.

"Vik; all of the Colonies are on the verge of open rebellion. A storm is coming; a bad one. That British commodore who's hunting you is trouble. He's been back here every three or four months or has sent one of his officers, anyway, to get reports from the man he left on the *Georgia Belle*." She stopped and hugged herself.

"You are afraid of him." Viktor made it a statement. She nodded but did not look up at him.

"He likes it rough. He pays well, but he enjoys inflicting pain," she said. "I won't let any of the girls service him. I take that responsibility myself. I am afraid to refuse him, and I am afraid of what he will do if he ever learns of my part in Harris' disappearance. I don't think he really cares about it, mind you; but he would use it as an excuse to abuse me or my girls."

"Has my presence here put you at risk?" Viktor felt concern for the madam. He'd lost his virginity to her, after all.

Maggie gave him a wan smile. "I'm not sure. With Captain Turlington out of the way, perhaps not, but the Commodore does have other eyes and ears in this port."

Viktor caressed her cheek with the back of his fingers. As his hand moved down to her shoulder, she flinched.

She immediately apologized. "I'm still a little tender there. You just missed him by a couple of weeks, and the bruises haven't fully healed." She gave a self-deprecating laugh. "I'm not as young as I used to be."

"What did happen with Harris?"

"The first time the Commodore came in here, Harris was drunk. He whined and bitched about how you always go after him. The Commodore ordered his ship confiscated and used to patrol as bait for you. I had Harris kidnapped and shipped out that same night, both to save him from the King's justice and hopefully your wrath. His father is still powerful here, and I didn't need the trouble."

Vik hugged her and gave her a kiss on the cheek. "You did the right thing, Maggie. He may not believe it, but I do like the little shit. He's entertaining as hell. Thank you."

He felt the tension flow out of her. "I feel better about it now. Shall I fetch one of the girls to tend you?"

His smile turned wicked. "No."

Tamara A. Lowery

# Chapter 3

Mother Celie didn't turn around from her fire. Even though Viktor approached silently, she knew he was there.

"Supper's on the table."

"Your wards are strong tonight, Mother. Are you expecting company?"

"I'll explain later, boy. Right now, you need to eat. Hezekiah and his family will join you later; I'll let Lazarus and your siren in when they arrive."

"Belle is hunting, and I haven't summoned Lazarus."

"Go eat. We'll talk later." Her tone brooked no argument. Not once did she look at him.

He obediently went into the little tabby hut.

Viktor reached for the ladle to dish out a second helping of the rich seafood stew. He almost dropped it when an unexpected weight settled on his shoulder followed by a *mrrow*. He hadn't summoned Lazarus, nor had he sensed the creature's arrival.

The cat leapt to the table, sat, and gave him a quizzical look. Viktor frowned. His senses felt dull. He should have known Lazarus was there before he'd leapt to his shoulder.

On a whim, he tried to contact Belladonna through the link they shared. He found he had to concentrate very hard to reach her. He got a brief sense of confusion and alarm from her before the contact grew too muted.

He set the bowl and ladle down and turned toward the door. Celie came in followed by Brianna and Grimm. His first mate carried two infants.

The sight stopped Viktor in his tracks. He'd never seen Hezekiah Grimm look so happy and content. *No*, he thought, *I've never seen him at peace before*.

"You look lost, boy," Celie said softly. He looked down and saw her wizened face looking back up at him with a sad smile. "Sit down, and let's talk."

He hooked a stool with his foot and joined the others at the table. He wondered when they'd sat down.

"Captain, are you well?" Grimm asked, a look of concern on his face. He handed the babies, one by one, to his wife. Brianna bedded them down in a large woven basket crib. Viktor saw her glance between him and Grimm with a knowing look.

For a fleeting moment he almost lied; he decided in favor of honesty. "I'm not sure, Hezekiah. Something feels off. My perceptions and reactions are slow, even compared to when I was just human."

"Part of that was my doing," Celie said.

"You put something in the stew?"

"No." She shook her head. "I put a spell on your bowl. You will need to sleep soon. It will help you heal the damage you have done."

Vik frowned at her. "What are you talking about?"

"You drank blood tainted with another vampire's power, and you drank siren's blood."

"Mother Celie, surely you are wrong," Grimm said with alarm. "Siren's blood is instant death to a vampire." Brianna raised her eyebrows in surprise at the statement but kept silent.

Celie held up her hand to stop him. "Normally, yes, it is; but Viktor is different. I do not claim to understand it fully. His natural magic is wild and not completely predictable." She turned back to her foster son. "After you drank from your siren, how did you feel?"

"I would rather not say in front of Madam Grimm or the children."

Before Grimm could protest, Brianna stood and picked up the basket with the twins. "I need to get them to their bed," she said. She leaned down and whispered in her husband's ear then kissed his cheek. Hezekiah's eyes followed her with raw admiration when she left the hut.

Once the door closed, he said, "It's not like you to be bashful about whom you say what in front of, Vik."

"Brianna is a lady and your wife. She deserves my respect."

"Thank you for that. Now, what was so bad you didn't want her to hear it?"

"When I bit Belle, I had the most intense orgasm I've ever had in my life. I almost thought I *was* going to die. It never entered my mind until later what I'd done. Even immediately afterward my first worry was I had killed *her*."

Celie leaned back in her chair with her walking stick propped between her knees and rested her hands on its knob. She gave him a calculating look and smiled cryptically.

"I know that look, Mother."

"You've grown, Viktor. I approve."

A ripple of angry energy preceded the arrival of the siren. Belladonna burst into the room and snarled at the old marsh witch.

"What have you done to him?"

Viktor moved to Belle's side and ran a soothing hand down her arm. "Calm yourself, pet. I am unharmed."

She rounded on him. "The hell you are! I lost contact with you! Hell, I could barely hear you before that, and I can't hear you now! For that matter, how are you still alive? You bit me!"

He chuckled at her tirade. "Did you just now realize that, pet?"

"I —." She stopped and blinked at him. "Now that you mention it; yes. Viktor, what is going on?"

"I'm not sure. I hope Mother Celie can tell us."

Celie sighed and closed her eyes. Her smile remained in place. "Hezekiah Grimm, your wife is in need of your attention," she said.

Grimm looked at Viktor, the question plain on his face. Vik nodded at his first mate and cocked his head toward the door. Grimm stood.

Just before he stepped over the threshold, Celie added, "I have something important to discuss with you and Brianna in private later."

"I will let her know."

Celie opened her eyes when the door closed. She gave the vampire and the siren a long silent stare before she spoke again.

"As I told Hezekiah, your magic is wild, boy. I don't know its full scope or potential. I'd wager even old Zeke isn't sure. I do think I know what drove your actions, though."

Belle leaned forward. Viktor nodded; but the old witch knew her spell caused it more than his interest. Already, his eyes grew slightly unfocused. This didn't worry her, however. Her sleep and healing spell would ensure he heard and retained what she had to say.

"You have always had a strong survival instinct, Viktor. It led you to drink siren's blood to free you of the tainted blood you'd gotten. I do not know if it would kill you or not should you bite Belladonna again, but I would advise against it. Chances are this was a unique situation."

Viktor mumbled an incoherent response. His eyelids fluttered, and his shoulders slumped. Celie smiled at her foster son. What had started as dutiful guardianship had grown to love of and pride in her charge.

"Help him over to the cot, sea witch. He heals quickly, so he shouldn't sleep long. He will wake refreshed and invigorated with his senses back at full capacity." She stood and left the hut.

Viktor woke, immediately aware of a warm soft weight partially on him. He turned his head to see Belladonna snuggled up at his side on the narrow cot. He reached up and brushed a strand of crimson hair from her face. She gazed back at him with amber-gold eyes instead of sea grey ones.

"It's about time you woke up."

"How long was I asleep?" He didn't believe she was as irritated as she wanted him to think.

"Three hours; now let me up."

He smirked and opened his arms. "No one said you had to nap with me."

She stood and glared down at him. "I didn't intend to even lay down with you. You held onto me when I helped you onto the cot and didn't let go. Whatever spell she used made it impossible to wake you. The only way I could have freed myself would have been to hurt you."

He sat up, reached out and caught her hand, and brought it to his lips. "Thank you for choosing not to harm me, pet."

She snatched her hand back and glared at him some more. He smiled at her. He could sense her presence again through their link and knew she was no longer truly irritated with him.

"How do you feel?"

In answer, he stood, stretched, and yawned. "Refreshed."

"Good; I don't know how much time you wish to spend in port, but I've had a vision."

This surprised him. "I don't recall giving you a sacrifice."

"You forgot you offered me my fill of the prisoners?" She looked troubled. He didn't blame her. He had no such memory. Had that small dose of Carpathia's power really done that much damage?

"I must have been in worse shape than I realized, pet. I don't remember making the offer. You took it, then?"

"No; I only inspected them to make sure they did not carry Carpathia's taint, as well. They are clean. You need them for blood stock. I hunted to replenish my strength instead."

Viktor frowned. "How strong was the vision, then? Usually, you need a sacrifice from me to get clarity and accuracy."

"True." She nodded. "I only have a general sense of location. The Sister sensed me and tried to deceive me."

"Oh?"

"Yes, she projected a false presence and location. She pretended to be someone called Abuelita Mirabelita." She snorted. "She tried to focus me toward one of the old Spanish treasure ports south of Mexico, but that is not where she is, whatever her real name is."

He crossed his arms and leaned against the door jamb. "How do you know that is not where she is?"

Belle mimicked his posture and gave him a smug smirk. "Her magic has a distinct flavor I recognized immediately, and it is not found anywhere on this side of the world. She is somewhere in the Mediterranean, my native waters. Specifically, it tasted of the Aegean."

"You are sure of this?"

"Positive."

"I will have the lads begin arrangements to sail."

Tamara A. Lowery

# Chapter 4

"You should go with him, Hezekiah. He needs you," Brianna said, facing away from him.

"And you do not?" He walked up behind her and placed his hands on her shoulders. He gently kneaded the muscles. It mildly surprised him she was not tensed up. "We have two beautiful children, Brie. My place is here with you and them."

She turned in his arms and hugged him tightly. He grunted a bit. It never ceased to amaze him how much strength resided in her delicate form. He leaned down and kissed her; allowing his hands to explore and appreciate the lushness motherhood added to the curves of her body.

She giggled when he grew hard against her belly. When they broke from the kiss, she beamed up at him. "Husband, *je taime*, but I know you. Within two months you would grow bored and long for the sea."

"How could I grow bored with you, my love?"

"Not with me, silly man, with life on land, with domestication. To tie you to land would be as cruel as to cage a wolf. While the wolf would survive, a cage would kill the part of him which makes him a wolf. I will not do that to you, *mon amor*."

"How did I ever come to be blessed with such a wise wonderful woman?"

"You pirated me from other pirates."

A tap at the door interrupted them. Grimm growled in irritation but quickly hid it and answered the door. Celie stood outside patiently propped on her walking stick.

"Looks like I interrupted something," she said with a cackle and a pointed look toward his crotch.

"I was contemplating giving my children a little brother or sister."

Celie sighed. A look of sadness crossed her face. "You can't."

"What do you mean I can't? I am still a virile man, and Brie is still young."

"True; but she can bear no more children, Hezekiah Grimm. The twins were born early, and her womb was damaged during the birth." She held up a hand to forestall any comment. "This is beyond my skill as a healer. I might have been able to do something about it immediately after her labor ended, but it took all my skill and power to keep the babes alive. Their little bodies were not yet ready for the world."

Grimm hugged his wife to him. "Thank you for all you have done for us, Mother Celie. I see this as all the more reason I should stay here with Brie and the children."

Celie cocked her head to the side and peered at him. "Whether you stay or go is your decision, Hezekiah Grimm." With that comment, she turned and left.

He snorted.

Brianna looked up at him and asked, "What?"

"That was her way of telling me where my place is."

"And where is that?"

He looked down at his wife and smiled sadly. "She wants me to remain with Viktor. If *she* thinks he needs my help, he needs my help."

Brianna reached up and bopped him playfully on the back of his head.

"Ow! What was that for?"

"It is about time you saw reason. The twins and I are safe here. Go with your captain, you silly man."

"Silly, am I? C'mere wench! I'll show you just how silly I am not." He laughed and lifted her into his arms.

Grimm approached Viktor the next day at breakfast. He fixed a plate of chicken, gravy, and biscuits and sat down across the table from his captain.

"You look rested," Vik said and took another bite of food.

"Refreshed, aye, but Brie didn't give me much rest last night." Grimm tried one of the biscuits, and his eyes grew large. "Damn! These are the best I've had since we lost Mr. Trundle!"

Viktor grinned, not caring that his fangs showed. "Celie is still the best cook I've ever been fed by. She's sure to train your Brianna. You'll be able to grow fat and happy in your old age."

Grimm frowned in a mock pout. "Is everyone trying to be shed of me? Brianna refuses to let me stay. She insists I go back to sea with you, yet here you are trying to turn me into a land-lubbing country squire."

Viktor looked at his first mate, careful to keep his face neutral. "What would you prefer to do?"

"Bring Brie back aboard with me; but there are the children to consider."

He relaxed a bit. The thought had crossed his mind Grimm would want to remain with his family, and he'd tried to make peace with that if it had been his friend's choice.

"That is true. A ship is not the ideal nursery for infants." He took another bite of chicken. After he swallowed it, he said, "I'd like to see them, if I may. They were asleep yesterday, and I wasn't exactly at my most observant thanks to Mother's spell."

"Of course!" He watched Grimm's face light with pride at the thought of showing off his offspring. He saw a shadow of apprehension cross his first mate's face only moments later. "About the twins: they haven't been christened yet, and I think it's important to Brianna."

"Was she waiting for your return?"

Grimm shook his head. "No; the problem has been the danger of that damned commodore finding out who she is to me and where she is. I told her we took care of his man here, but she said Celie warned of other eyes in port besides Turlington."

"I'm surprised no one has come out here looking for her already. Your wedding wasn't exactly clandestine."

"Critchfield *did* the same day Brie gave birth. Celie kept her hidden; but the shock brought the twins early. Mother Celie says Brianna cannot have any more children now. She tried not to show it, but I can tell she is upset about it. She has been glum all morning."

Vik pushed his plate back and looked at his friend for a while. He wondered if having the children christened was more important to Grimm than to his wife. Although the man didn't show it in his body language, Viktor could almost smell his frustration with the situation.

He fished out a cigar and lit it with a small candle. He took a draw on it then exhaled the pungent tobacco smoke. "So, if I understand this situation correctly, it would be best if she was not seen travelling from here into town or back, since Critchfield already suspects."

"Aye."

"How much do you trust me, Hezekiah? More importantly, how much does she trust me?"

"Enough to ask you to stand as godfather to our children, Captain," Brianna answered as she entered the room.

The two men stood. Grimm pulled out a chair for his wife. Viktor moved around the table, took her hand, and brought it to his lips. He brushed her knuckles with his thumb and held her hand just a tad longer than was necessary. Giving his must sultry smile, he said, "I am honored, Madam Grimm."

He chuckled as he watched her eyes dilate and her face grow flushed; he even heard her heart and breathing speed a little.

Grimm gently put a hand on her shoulder and guided her to her seat. He shot Viktor a look of mock reproach. "Would you seduce my wife in front of me, Vik?"

Vik gave his most roguish grin. "Would you prefer I do so behind your back?"

"Stop it, both of you!" Brianna laughed. "What a pair of rogues you are!"

"Aye, love; that we are." Grimm leaned down and gave her a very thorough kiss. When he pulled back, he said, "I trust that will inure you to the Captain's charms."

"Oh, that sounds like a challenge, Hezekiah," Vik said with a wicked chuckle.

Brianna put her face in her hands and laughed until her shoulders shook. When she finally wound down, both men stood staring at her with puzzled and amused expressions.

"Do you feel better now?" Vik asked.

"*Oui, merci*." She nodded and smiled.

"Good." He sat back down and waited for Grimm to follow suit; then he said, "I have a plan which will keep your whereabouts safe from unfriendly eyes yet still allow you to have your children properly christened."

They both sat up and gave him their full attention.

Mother Celie emerged from the shadows after the trio left her tabby hut. Not even Viktor had known she was there.

She smiled and nodded. "Yes boy, you have grown. I am proud of you," she said to the empty room.

Under cover of darkness, Viktor flew Brianna and the twins out to the *Incubus*. He would never tell Hezekiah, but he enjoyed the sensations of holding his first mate's wife in his arms as she held tightly to the basket the babies rode in. He finally understood fully why Hezekiah had kept her locked in his cabin for the first few months after they'd "rescued" her from another crew of pirates.

He couldn't quite put his finger on it, but there was something about her that could lure even the most hardened salt from the sea.

Grimm watched as the vampire he called Captain levitated down to the quarterdeck of the *Incubus*. As

74

Viktor handed off Brianna and her precious cargo to him, he caught a brief look of longing cross his friend's face in the starlight.

"Thank ye, Vik. The preparations have been made at the church," he said. "Oh, and Mr. Jon and Mr. Bland assure me we'll be ready to sail with the tide tomorrow afternoon."

"Very good, Mr. Grimm. I'll see the four of you on shore in the morning. I have to go make my farewells to Maggie." With that, Viktor launched back into the night sky.

Grimm escorted Brianna to his cabin. She must have sensed some tenseness in him, though. "What is it, Hezekiah?"

"I'll tell you inside."

Once inside the cabin, she settled the twins in then turned a questioning gaze to her husband. He placed his hands on her shoulders and guided her to the bed. He sat down beside her with a serious look on his face.

"You are starting to scare me," she said, a note of worry creeping into her voice.

"He wants you."

"What?"

Grimm sighed. "I saw it when he dropped you off. I've known him for years, and I know that look. He wants you."

"But he is your friend; and I am your wife."

He smiled and caressed her cheek with his thumb. "And you are the most irresistible woman I have ever known, my love. Still, the fact you are *my* wife should be enough to save you from his attentions. If you were any other man's wife, he would have already had you."

She scowled at him, and her face reddened. "Do you think I am so easily had?"

"No! NO," he soothed. "I know you are not, Brie; but Viktor is Viktor. Given what he is, he can be very hard to resist. I do not believe he will act on this particular desire; but he does have moments when his self-control is not as adamant as you would think. Should it ever come to that, know that I hold you blameless."

She looked down at her hands and let him tuck her under his arm. With a sigh, she said, "I am glad you warned me; but at the same time, I wish you hadn't."

He lifted her chin, leaned down, and kissed her. "I know, love. I just didn't want you caught unawares."

The next day, Grimm brought his wife and children ashore. They took a hired carriage to the church, making a spectacle of it.

The christening went smoothly; and Viktor treated his first mate's family to a meal at one of Savannah's more reputable inns. Afterwards, they all returned to the *Incubus*.

The ship set sail with the tide.

That night, Viktor flew Brianna and the twins back to Mother Celie.

As she handed the basket containing the children to the old swamp-witch, she said, "Captain, please try to bring Hezekiah back to me safely."

Viktor took her hand and immediately noticed how she stiffened. He saw sorrow and a trace of fear in her eyes when he brought her hand to his lips. Not sure what caused her fear, he allowed her to pull her hand back from his grasp.

"You have my word, Madam; I will do my utmost to see your husband safely returned to your side." He bowed and took a step back. "I trust you to keep them safe, Mother," he said to Celie.

Without further delay, he launched into the night sky.

They sailed four days north along the coast before turning east to make the crossing. Viktor wanted to give any prying eyes the impression they were making for a New English port to deliver Grimm's family.

The reports he got back from Lazarus led him to believe the ruse worked and Critchfield's agents no longer believed Brianna was in Savannah.

Two weeks into the crossing, he noticed Belladonna seemed agitated. She'd holed up in her cabin and blocked her link to him. He decided to investigate.

"Pet, may I come in?" he asked and knocked at her door. He wanted her cooperation, so he figured this was the best approach.

After a few moments of silence, the door opened. He entered and closed it gently behind him. Belladonna sat with her hands in her lap, staring out the porthole. She remained silent even when he sat next to her.

After a few minutes of this, he said, "What is troubling you, Belle? This is not like you to stay cooped up in here."

He opened the link between them but did not push at her mental shields. He'd learned long ago she did not respond well to force or impatience.

The fact Viktor opened up to her but did not try to force his will on her caught Belle's attention. She could sense he really did care about what was bothering her. Wryly, she thought it a marked change from their relationship just a few short years ago.

She sighed and looked at him. "I am afraid."

He blinked in surprise at her. Clearly, he had not expected that answer.

"Of what, pet?"

"The search for this Sister will take us to a place I have been forbidden to return to — by Zeke, no less."

"Why would he do that?"

"To keep the peace. I once battled a male of my species who'd tried to claim me as a mate. The price of my freedom was the loss of my territory. If I return to the Mediterranean, he will be able to claim me, and I will be bound to him until his death. Zeke bound my ability to fight back against Xandricus."

She grunted in surprise when Viktor clasped her to him. She could sense both his frustration and his resolve through their link.

He buried his face in her hair and said, "I cannot let you go with me, then."

"But you don't know where to hunt. I only sensed she was in the Mediterranean. We still don't have her true name or where exactly to look for her," Belle protested.

He sat holding her in silence for a while. Finally, he said, "Your vision was not the result of a sacrifice on my part. You did mention her power tasted of the Aegean, but I understand she may not be there now. I remember how Dorada ran from my approach. Still, we are closer to her now. How many men would you need for a clear vision?"

Viktor only had to give up two men to the siren's appetite.

She returned to his cabin the next day, naked and wild-eyed. He ushered her in, alarmed she hadn't bothered to stop by her cabin for clothes. It meant the vision had been urgent or just that disturbing.

As soon as the door shut behind her, she asked, "How familiar are you with the seaways of the Mediterranean?"

"I personally have never sailed there; why?"

"Do you have charts or navigators who know that sea?"

"I'll have to check. Belle, why are you so distraught over this?"

She took a deep breath and let it out slowly. "I have to go with you, Viktor. She didn't bother to hide this time. She doesn't have to."

He frowned. "Is she that powerful?"

She shook her head. "Although her powers present a danger, you won't have to worry about them until you reach her. That will be the hard part. You'll have to sail through some of the worst ship-killing navigational hazards there are just to get to her island."

"What about this Xandricus you mentioned? I don't want to put you at risk, Belle."

"It is a risk I will have to take, Viktor. You will need my knowledge of these waters to make it safely to *Yia Yia* Circe. I'm not trying to reclaim my old territory; and if I remain on the ship, he may not even sense my presence."

He cupped her chin and studied her face. He saw uncertainty there but also determination. He leaned down and kissed her gently.

"I give you my word, pet; I will do everything I can to protect you if he presents a problem."

She said nothing but hugged him tightly. He held her and stroked her back soothingly.

"What does *Yia Yia* mean, and what specific powers do I need to prepare to deal with?" He asked both because he needed the information and to prevent Belladonna from lapsing into another period of glumness.

"It's Greek for grandmother. She has transformative powers. I would strongly advise against letting any of the crew go ashore or accepting any offer of food supplies from her."

He thought about what she told him and mused aloud, "So she uses food to weave her spells. The Elder's stone should help protect me, but it would not protect my men. I imagine she wouldn't hesitate to serve them up."

Belle looked at him sharply. "How do you know so much about her tricks?"

"I read, pet; remember?" He smirked. "Her name coupled with the magic you mentioned put me in mind of Homer's *Odyssey* and the witch Circe, although I grew up thinking it was pronounced ser-see rather than ker-key. If I recall, she turned most of his crew to swine and tried to trap him as her lover."

"Something like that."

"Then I shall remain wary."

He leaned over her and kissed her again. It was some time before either of them left the cabin.

82

# Chapter 5

Although Zach Brumble had never sailed the Mediterranean trade routes, he found detailed charts among the *Incubus'* wagoneer. The pirates had acquired them from the Brumble & Sons convoy they'd taken a while back.

Lockland Stoud, who'd joined the crew at that time, claimed to have sailed there. To hear the old salt tell it, there was hardly a port he hadn't visited. He suggested the ports along the Barbary Coast might be more welcoming to pirates than European ports; but he warned them the Berbers frequently took Christian slaves for the Ottomans.

Belladonna indicated Circe would be found among the Greek isles. Within two days, a general course was laid in.

The siren made sure to hunt before the *Incubus* reached Gibraltar. She knew she would be confined to the ship from that moment until it returned to the Atlantic.

A fully loaded slave ship sank in a sudden and unexpected storm shortly after it left the Azores. Belladonna fed well.

It amused Viktor how easily he could attain prey to feed his cadre's blood Hunger in the western Mediterranean. Simply by masking most of the gun ports they made the *Incubus* look like a merchant ship instead of a warship. That coupled with the obvious European lines of the ship made the perfect bait for the Berber corsairs.

The first attack came not long after they passed through the straits of Gibraltar. A small galley approached near dusk.

"Really?" Jon-Jon laughed when the warning shot came.

"Now, Mr. Jon, they've gone to all this trouble to bring my cadre their meal. The least we can do is heave to and invite them aboard," Vik said. "Besides, I don't want the sails all shot up."

"You heard the Cap'n!" Jon-Jon shouted. "Heave to!"

Viktor smiled inwardly as the corsair's ship pulled alongside. As a precaution against Circe's powers, he'd had Grimm give the crew a fresh dose of the "special" rum tainted with his blood. This put his bond with and control over the pirates at full strength. He used that bond to ensure the men left a clear path to the hold his cadre of vampires used as quarters. His vampires began to stir as the sun dipped below the horizon. He let them know breakfast was on its way.

Most of the crew of the corsair boarded the pirate ship and began to round up the crew as prisoners. Viktor permitted it. He'd purposely had most of the crew hide themselves to avoid raising alarms. He wished he'd been able to hide the guns from view inside the gun decks. He could see through Lazarus' eyes the number of masked guns and the easy surrender began to spook the corsairs.

Just when the attackers began to realize the trap they'd walked into, Viktor gave his men the signal to attack. Pirates boiled out of hiding places below decks. The vampires erupted out of the hold and spread through the ship at inhuman speeds.

Viktor snapped his bonds like strings and leapt into the air. He lit on the deck of the galley and fought his way through the remaining corsairs bare-handed. He only killed a couple, knocking out several more.

The sight of him ripping a man's head off took the fight out of his remaining opponents. A couple of his vampires joined him and took over, herding the prisoners off the galley and onto the pirate ship.

When he returned to his ship, he saw one of the corsairs emerge from the cabin area. The man forced a naked Belladonna out in front of him with a wicked-looking blade to her throat.

"Release my men, evil djinn, or I will kill your whore!" the man shouted in heavily accented English.

Viktor and every pirate on deck laughed heartily at him.

Before he could yell any further threats, the siren extended her talons and stabbed him in the leg. He screamed and dropped his blade. She grinned and turned on him.

The last thing he saw was the inside of her wide-open maw lined with multiple rows of needle-sharp teeth just before it engulfed his face. Even some of the pirates looked away as she bit the front of his skull off with a sickening crunch.

Five more corsair ships met the same fate by the time the *Incubus* reached Tripolitania and started its northeast tack.

Belladonna knocked on the Captain's door about a day out from the southern-most Greek isle.

"Enter."

She opened the door to see Viktor at his desk studying several charts. He glanced up at her and smiled. "Hello, pet."

She strode over to look over his shoulder. After a quick scan of the various maps, she pointed and said, "Those three are the ones you need. They look the most accurate. The others are either flawed or of the wrong portion of the islands."

"Thank you, Belle." He made quick work of rolling up the irrelevant charts and returning them to their oilcloth cases. He returned to the three charts she'd indicated and asked, "Can you pinpoint where she is on these?"

She looked at them more closely, flipping back and forth between them. Finally, she pulled one to the top and pointed at a blank spot. "She's there."

"There is no island marked there."

She just looked at him.

"Right; this is a Sister of Power we are dealing with. She must be very powerful to have kept an entire island hidden from map makers for centuries," he said with a resigned grunt.

"She is, but I've a feeling it has stayed uncharted because no one has returned from it."

"There is that." He looked the chart over again and smirked. "Let me guess, since no major navigational hazards are marked in that area, it is rife with them."

"Oh definitely," Belle said in confirmation. "They were set in place millennia ago and serve more to keep ships from reaching the Hidden Isle intact than anything else. Oddly, if I remember them correctly, getting away from the island is fairly easy. The tides and currents repel incoming ships but aid in sailing away."

"Then why did you say no one has returned?"

"Some were shipwrecked. Others fell prey to the Sister's traps."

"Hm." He stroked his neatly trimmed goatee and mulled the information over. "I shall have to proceed cautiously with her, then. We are currently well-provisioned. If you can guide us to the island safely, I will ensure the entire crew stays aboard. I'll have Hezekiah dole out double portions of the special rum. That should prevent anyone from disobeying the order not to go ashore."

"Good thinking."

"Now then," he said and sat back down, "shall we plot our course?"

Viktor found it mildly irritating the siren could not risk using her weather magic to help get the ship past the obstacles they faced. Still, he'd sailed for years without such aid, so it didn't upset him too much. He knew she didn't want to take the chance her powers would alert Xandricus to her presence.

She still proved useful without her magic. Use of her natural sea creature senses could go undetected if they were not unique to her species. They saved the ship from one hazard she had not foreseen.

*"Hard to port!"* Belle cried in alarm through the mental bond she shared with the vampire.

Viktor manned the helm while she rode the bow sprit to sound out the waters ahead of them. He spun the wheel to the left and the warship-turned-pirate responded. The riggers scrambled to adjust the sails so they wouldn't lose the wind.

*"What is it, pet?"*

*"Reef; it must've grown here during the time I've been banished,"* she replied. *"It has been a few millennia, after all."*

*"Of course."*

She ignored his snide comment. Instead, she continued to emit ultrasonic bursts along the reef they'd narrowly avoided. Finally, she found what she was looking for.

*"On my mark turn starboard and return to our original heading,"* she relayed to him. *"I've found an opening we can safely fit through."*

"Have the riggers make ready for another course change to starboard, Mr. Jon."

"Aye, Cap'n." Jon-Jon cupped his hands and yelled the order.

*"Mark!"* Belle sent the thought.

Viktor swung the wheel to the right, and the ship began its turn. Just then, the current changed. The *Incubus* rolled as the new current pushed it sideways. Cries rang out from the riggers at the sudden list.

One cry was cut short by a sudden crunch as a man fell and hit a spar on his way down. Viktor had to fight to control the wheel when he felt the blood bond break as the man died.

As the ship righted itself the wind carried it to the reef. Viktor saw the rogue current come through the gap in the underwater barrier. At least the wind remained in his favor.

"Mr. Jon, give me all the canvas we have! We've got to beat the current to get past the reef.

"Aye, Cap'n. Riggers, full sail!"

Swirls and eddies in the current made it a challenge to hold the ship on course. The siren continued to give him mental cues to keep the ship centered with the gap. The further through the reef, the stronger the current pushed against them.

Just before they'd finished the passage, the conflicting current weakened abruptly. The force of the following wind against the sails pushed the bow down to the waves at the sudden lack of resistance. A swell of seawater crashed over the bow onto the deck and soaked the siren in the process.

"Riggers furl topsails!" Viktor yelled. He sensed Belle's sudden alarm. They both hoped fervently she hadn't just been revealed to the male siren who wanted her.

*"Are you all right, pet?"*

Belladonna's mental tone remained resolute. *"I have to be. It won't be long before we reach the next hazard. I wasn't using any magic that would give me away, so chances are he didn't sense me."*

*"Let's hope so."*

They passed safely through the next obstacle, an uncharted maze of rocky pinnacles and arches, with the aid of Lazarus added to that of Belladonna. While the siren sounded out the channels deep enough to let the large ship pass, Lazarus took his raven form and scouted out which channels were wide enough.

Even so, the ship's design was the only thing which allowed them to finally pass out of the watery labyrinth. The hinged masts had to be lowered so the ship could pass under a rocky archway.

The next hazard came quickly. The tide turned, and multiple maelstroms swirled into action. The whirlpools threatened to drag the ship and the boats set to tow her back into the rocks.

Viktor ordered the mast raised and all sails set. The hinge and counterweight system let them do so rapidly. In minutes, the riggers swarmed up and unfurled the sails. The wind caught and pushed the ship away from the deadly eddies. She pulled the tow boats with her to safety with the exception of one.

One of the tow lines frayed against the rocks when the *Incubus* made a sharp turn in a tight space back in the rock maze. The force of the wind as it caught the sails snapped the damaged line. The pirate crew watched in helpless horror as the boat and the seven men on board rowed madly in a vain attempt to escape the whirlpools.

"Mr. Jon, take the wheel!" Vik yelled and launched into flight the moment the second mate had the wheel.

He flew toward the doomed boat and dove for the broken line. He managed to catch it, but the current threatened to rip it from his grasp. He flew close enough to the boat to give the line some slack, wrapped it around his waist, and knotted it securely.

"As soon as I pull, row like mad!" he shouted to the boat crew.

"Aye, Cap'n!" Mr. Bland called back. Viktor drew tension on the line, and Bland barked at his crew. "Row! Row with all ye've got! Yer lives depend on it! Now row, damn yer eyes!"

The men put their backs into it, and the vampire pulled with all his might. For a moment it looked like it would work — but only for a moment. The boat edged closer and closer to the rim of the whirlpool.

*"Viktor, use the current; don't fight it."*

*"What do you mean, pet?"* Even his mental tone showed the strain of his effort.

*"Turn the boat into the current and use it to sling them out of the whirlpool. It will work."*

He maintained tension on the line but increased his altitude until he was directly over the boat.

"Turn 'er to run with the current!" he ordered. He clamped down with his will when a few of the pirates started to protest the plan. Bound to obey their captain by the blood-tainted rum he used on them, they turned the boat around.

Viktor felt the boat jerk on the rope as it took up the current. He sped ahead to pull, as well. Just as the siren predicted, the boat shot free of the deadly eddy. He pulled it nearly to the ship before he freed the rope from his waist.

As the boat crew tied to the davit lines, Viktor returned to the ship's deck and strode over to Belladonna. Without warning, he embraced her and kissed her.

"What as that for?" She looked up at him in confusion.

He grinned down at her. "To thank you."

"You're welcome. We aren't out of this yet, though. That fog bank ahead surrounds Circe's island. There is some sort of ship graveyard concealed in the fog."

"Of course." He sighed, resigned. "Are there rocks or shoals to blame?"

"No; that's the odd part. There is a good deep draft there. My thought is they are the scuttled ships of those who've fallen prey to her."

He stroked his beard in thought. "How safe would the ship and crew be if I left them here?"

She blinked as if the thought hadn't occurred to her. She looked around using all the senses she dared. Finally, she turned back to him and said, "If they anchor here, they should be safe. It is far enough away from the whirlpools and the fog to not be at risk from them. Do you plan to fly in or take a boat?"

"Boat; I've a feeling I must pass through all of the barriers for the initial contact. If I fly to the island, she may view that as cheating. I want you and Hezekiah to come with me."

She gave him an apprehensive look. "That's awfully close to the water."

"You'll be in a boat, pet; and I'll fly you the short distance to shore, so you don't risk attracting *him*."

She shook her head. "It's not that simple. Those are my native waters. They call to me. Xandricus aside, it will put me far too close to temptation for my comfort."

Viktor reached out through the bond they shared. He seized her will and refused to let her move. When he felt her begin to panic, he released his mental hold.

"I apologize, Belle; I just felt it would be quicker to demonstrate I can keep you out of the water rather than argue it with you."

"Oh."

☠

The siren guided the two pirates through the fog-enshrouded wrecks. They soon realized getting the *Incubus* to the island would have been nearly impossible without damaging the copper cladding.

Once they neared the shore, Viktor lifted Belle into his arms and flew to well above the high tide mark. Grimm jumped out into the surf and pulled the boat up on the beach. Vik set Belle down and moved to help his first mate secure the boat so the tide wouldn't carry it back out.

When they turned to head inland, the vampire noticed how the siren looked longingly at the water. He sensed she was about to bolt for it. He moved to her before she could react and placed a gentle hand on her shoulder. The contact drew her attention away from the sea and strengthened the connection of their bond.

"No, pet; we need to find Circe."

She nodded her understanding, and her body relaxed as she drew strength from him. *"Thank you,"* she whispered mentally.

"I imagine that would be the place to start looking," Grimm said and pointed to a structure above the sea cliffs. "We just need to find a way up to it."

Since the fog ended abruptly a few yards out from the shore, they could see the beach they'd landed on was part of a cove. The cliffs surrounded it, and no path up could be seen.

A raven swooped down and fluttered in front of them for a few minutes, gave a harsh cry, and flew to their left. It disappeared around the end of the cliff face which cut off the beach in that direction.

Viktor closed his eyes, smiled, and opened them again. "There is a stairway cut into the cliff just out of sight."

Belle concentrated her senses on the area. "You'll have to fly us to it. The land ends sharply there, so we couldn't walk to it even at low tide. There is nowhere to tie the boat there, either. It would either drift away or be smashed against the cliff if we tried to use it to reach the stairs."

Grimm frowned. "Seems she intends for no one to be able to leave, if they can ever make it to her.

"Aye, it does; doesn't it," Vik agreed. He wrapped one arm around Belle's waist and pulled her tight against his side. He held his other arm out to Grimm.

"Wouldn't it be easier to take us one at a time?" the first mate asked.

"It would, but I can't trust her to stay out of the water. There's a male of her kind in these waters who would hunt her down if he sensed her. I don't have time to deal with him as well as the Sister."

"Makes sense." Grimm shrugged and let Vik embrace him, as well.

In a matter of minutes, they stood on the stairway. Viktor set his passengers down, and they began their ascent.

A half hour later, they stepped out of the crevice the stairs were carved into and onto a slightly rocky meadow. The path clearly headed for the structure they'd seen from below, so they followed it.

They topped a slight rise and saw several animals milling about. Wild pigs, a few lions, and some goats mingled in the meadow as if it were perfectly natural. One young boar raised its head and noticed them. The other animals ignored them for the most part. The boar trotted toward them. Grimm drew a blade and the creature stopped. It looked at them with an almost mournful expression and grunted and squealed as if trying to talk.

Viktor motioned for Grimm to put his blade away. The boar approached and nudged his hand then pointed its snout back the way they'd come.

Viktor bowed and said, "I understand your warning, friend. I am aware of the witch's wiles, however, and I have business with her which I cannot forego."

They proceeded toward the structure. The boar watched them go, shook its head and squealed, and returned to the other animals.

"How is it they aren't attacking each other or us, for that matter; and why did you talk to that one as if it could understand you?" Grimm asked, clearly confused by the unnatural behavior of the animals.

"If my guess is correct, it could understand me, for it once was a man," Vik answered. "Didn't you read Homer?"

Grimm shook his head. "I vaguely remember one of my school masters mentioned him, but I never had access to a copy."

"The next time we make Savannah, I'll see if Celie still has my old copy of *The Odyssey*. I'll have to check Jeorge's library for a copy of *The Iliad*. I've always meant to read it. Oh, here we are."

They stood before a broad, column-supported porch which appeared to wrap around the building. Ornate carvings decorated the portico. The place resembled etchings Viktor had seen of Greek temples.

A tall woman emerged from the door and stood on the top tier of the porch. She possessed a timeless beauty which would've made it impossible to judge her age had she been human. She wore linen so fine it was almost transparent draped artfully around her curves and held by jeweled brooches. Golden armlets coiled about her upper arms. Her dark hair formed an elaborate arrangement of braids and oiled ringlets. Jewel studded leather bands held it in place.

She smiled. "*I am Circe. Welcome to my home.*"

# Chapter 6

Grimm blinked in confusion. "What language is that? All I understood was her name."

"Greek," Belladonna answered. "She welcomed us to her home." She stepped forward and spoke in the same language Circe had used, mentally translating for Viktor. "*Greetings, Yia Yia Circe. I am Belladonna. This is my Captain, Viktor Brandewyne, and his first mate, Hezekiah Grimm. Forgive them for not addressing you directly. They do not speak Greek.*"

Circe pursed her lips but showed no other sign of irritation. The siren and the pirates waited patiently. At last, she spoke in heavily accented English, "Greeting Captain Brandewyne and companions. It has been some time since I've had to practice your tongue. Please, come in. I shall have refreshments brought. You must be tired and hungry after your journey."

Viktor bowed. "Thank you for your gracious offer of hospitality, *Yia Yia*, but my companions and I are required to fast this day."

Again, she pursed her lips. A small frown line appeared between her brows. The smile returned. "I understand. Still, I am sure you will want to rest after scaling the cliffs."

He allowed the faintest smile to curve his lips. "We came up the stairs."

A brief smirk flitted across her face. He could see she thought herself triumphant at last. "Then I will have guest rooms prepared. With no boat, you will be here some time." She turned to head inside.

Neither Viktor nor his companions moved. "Forgive me, *Yia Yia*, but we will be returning to our ship this evening. Our boat is secure in the cove."

She turned back sharply, a cruel smile on her lips. "Ha! You lie! The cliff is too smooth there to climb around to the stairs; and the surf would crush the boat into the rocks."

In answer, Viktor levitated a few feet above the ground. "I am not a mortal man, Circe. I have no need to lie about such trifles." He alit and drew gratification from the stunned realization on her face.

"You are the One," she whispered.

He inclined his head. "So I have been told, although I have yet to understand the significance of that title. All the other Sisters of Power I have dealt with either acknowledged it or tried unsuccessfully to disprove it. They just never saw fit to explain it."

102

*"She didn't need to know that,"* Belle told him through their bond. He gave no reaction to the criticism.

"Very well," Circe said as her smile returned, "you have successfully reached me. I am now bound to deal with you."

Viktor held up his hand. "Before we begin, I have something to ask you."

She blinked at him. "What is that?"

"Are you the Circe mentioned in *The Odyssey* by Homer, or were you named for her?"

Her face darkened with rage, and she launched into a tirade in Greek. Belladonna smirked as she mentally translated for Viktor. He carefully kept his face neutral. He saw no reason to let Circe know he could understand her. Grimm looked on with worry.

After the Sister wound down, Viktor gave a polite bow and said, "I meant no offense."

"Oh, I am not angry at you, Captain Brandewyne." Circe waved her hand. "I am angry at Homer for spreading the lies Odysseus told about me. I understood why my former lover lied. He didn't want Penelope to turn him out of his own house for his unfaithfulness to her; but that gossip-monger Homer didn't have to spread them the world over!"

Viktor smirked briefly. "If it is any consolation, I do not have a wife to lie to."

She gave him a sly smile. "My, my; handsome, educated, and unencumbered; are you sure you won't come inside and — refresh yourself?"

He chuckled. "It is tempting, but as I am frequently reminded, I do not know how much or how little time I have to complete my quest before my curse destroys me."

"I see." She pouted a little then turned her attention to Grimm. "And what of this handsome beast? It is rare for me to be in the presence of two such fine males at the same time. You could let him keep me company while you run my errand."

The first mate looked to his captain for some clue how to proceed. He saw a careful expressionlessness but detected a faint hint of pain in Vik's eyes.

"I am honored you would have me, Circe," Grimm said. "However, I must decline your invitation. I am first mate. Besides, I do have a wife, and I will not be faithless toward her nor lie to her. She is the mother of my children and the most precious thing in my life."

"This is true?" she asked Viktor.

Vik nodded. "It is true, Circe. You are the second Sister of Power to proposition him since he got married, and the second he has turned down."

She narrowed her eyes, still not convinced. "Who was the other one?"

"Clarissa, and she was naked the first time he saw her."

She looked at Grimm with a curious expression. Before he realized it, she stood close to him. He tried not to flinch, but the reflex proved too hard to overcome. She smiled and placed hands on his arms.

Her voice poured over him like dark honey when she spoke. "Odysseus truly loved his wife, too. All he could talk about was getting home to her. I took pity on him and helped him forget for a time. I couldn't stand to see him suffer so."

She snaked her arms around his shoulders and pressed herself against his body. She felt warm and soft in all the right places. He brushed his hands up her sides and to the arms that encircled him.

"Let me help you forget; let me ease your pain," she whispered a moment before she kissed him.

He did not return the kiss. Instead, he gently but firmly detached her from him and held her by the wrists at arm's length.

105

"No, Circe; I do not wish to forget Brianna or my children."

Her eyes widened as she looked at him. She ran her tongue over her lips. "How is this possible? No man has ever refused my kiss!" She paused then pulled away from him with a fearful countenance. "You taste of the Elder's magic!"

He nodded. "Aye, he gave me a portion of his magic to protect me so I may keep my Captain on course." He took a step forward, and she backed up a step. "You know the Captain is the One, therefore you know why we are here. He needs a portion of your magic. He has surmounted your barriers and avoided your traps. You are now bound to deal with him. Set the price you demand and stop these games, Circe."

Peripherally, he noticed even Belladonna looked at him with awe.

Circe pulled herself erect and squared her shoulders. A haughty scowl replaced her previous smile. "So be it. Beyond my dwelling is a labyrinth. At its center is a puzzle box. You, Viktor Brandewyne, will enter the labyrinth and retrieve the box. This is but the first part of your task. When you bring me the box, I will tell you what must be done next. You two," she pointed at Grimm and Belladonna, "will not go with him. This part is his alone to complete."

Viktor nodded to her and turned to his companions. "If I have not returned by sunrise, return to the ship without me. I will rejoin you when I can."

He held up a hand when Grimm started to protest. He turned and strode toward the far side of the building.

*"How the hell are we supposed to get back to the boat without him?"* Grimm thought.

Viktor smiled inwardly as he approached a large stone wall. Grimm had surprised him. He knew his first mate carried a small portion of Zeke's magic; but that was the first time the man had owned and exerted that power. Vik found Circe's reaction particularly gratifying.

He turned his attention to the wall. It curved away to either side and towered three times his height. From where he stood, it looked large enough to encompass a small town. No entrance readily presented itself.

He smiled, but it held little humor. Without summoning, he felt a familiar presence in the back of his mind.

"Lazarus," he whispered.

He closed his eyes and saw the labyrinth spread out below him through Lazarus' eyes. His friend and familiar hovered high above the maze in his raven form. This allowed Viktor to see that, although hidden and hard to spot, the maze had five entrances. It also had one obvious entrance that led deep into the maze but not to the center. It just ended in a closed loop which surrounded the center.

The view of the center of the maze revealed no puzzle box, just a small round courtyard with a stairway leading up to it from underground and what appeared to be a well which opened onto darkness.

At a thought, the raven dived down to inspect the well closer. The width of it would easily accommodate a man, yet it looked narrow enough to let him climb back up. Lazarus turned amorphous and drifted down into the darkness as smoke.

When he finally reached the bottom, he took his feline form. With now more sensitive eyesight, he looked around. He stood in a large round room with four doors.

Viktor could not see clearly while Lazarus remained a cat. Still, he sensed the raven would not be a practical form in this situation. He sent a mental message to his friend.

*"Mark a path for me."*

Within an hour, Viktor circumnavigated the outside of the labyrinth, and Lazarus returned to the sky. The vampire had located all the entrances, hidden or otherwise, but had not entered yet.

Circe strode up to him. "Have you given up already? Surely you found the way in. Why did you not use it?"

"I do not like to go in blindly. I found all six entrances. It has been my experience that the easiest or most obvious solution often proves to be false. I have decided which of the hidden doors I wish to take, so I shall be about my business now."

He left her side with inhuman speed. He caught the scent he searched for at the third doorway past the obvious gate. He turned and walked toward the wall. Just broad enough for him to pass, the hidden opening appeared to be just part of the wall. The illusion only failed when Viktor appeared to walk into solid rock.

He followed the pungent scent of cat piss through the winding, turning maze through multiple intersections and double backs. Eventually, he found a stairway to the underground portion hidden by the same kind of illusion used to hide the outer doors.

Once below ground, he saw only a curving corridor stretching into total darkness.

"Clever, Circe," he thought, "but not clever enough." He pulled out the milky crystal he wore on a silver chain. The Elder's Stone flared to life in reaction to the Sister's latent magic within the labyrinth. He shielded his eyes until the glow dimmed and stabilized.

He still followed the scent marks Lazarus left for him, but it helped to be able to see. He followed the curving corridor until it seemed to end abruptly. He soon discovered the inner wall ended before the outer wall. The corridor doubled back on itself. This pattern repeated for some distance at varying lengths with an occasional switchback along the outer wall rather than the inner.

He had no idea if he was getting closer to the center of the labyrinth or further away. He strongly suspected that part of his path passed below ground he'd already covered on the surface.

He encountered the first trap about twenty minutes after entering the underground portion of the maze. Rather than another switchback, a narrow door led off the curved corridor which appeared to continue on. In reality, the false corridor was a death trap, as evidenced by the ancient skeleton barely visible beyond the spiked bars which blocked the way.

The scent trail led through the side opening. Viktor encountered two more such traps. Both had already been triggered. He clearly saw cat paw prints in the dust on a slightly depressed stone in each barred room. He surmised Lazarus stepped on the trigger plates to release the bars and prevent him from walking into the traps. He sent a mental thanks to the creature.

He came to a sharp turn in the corridor rather than the now familiar switchback. From this turn the corridor ceased to curve but aimed straight toward the center of

110

the labyrinth. As he proceeded, the corridor grew wider. After ten minutes, he came to a fork in the path, not side by side but up and down. He faced two stairways and had to make a choice. He could smell the scent markings Lazarus left come from both stairs. However, the scent from the descending side smelled more pungent.

Viktor followed them down further into the ground. At the base of the stairs, the corridor continued on straight. He saw a faint trace of sunlight ahead of him and walked toward it. He almost stepped into the final trap.

A pit opened out before him. He could just make out a grid of long spikes pointing up from about thirty feet below. A very narrow ledge skirted the pit with regularly spaced niches in the wall. He doubted they were hand holds to make the passage easier.

He decided to fly across the gap. It looked too far of a jump for a mortal man, so he doubted he would trigger whatever came out of those niches. Even the glow of the Elder's Stone proved insufficient to light the narrow strips of darkness.

Once safely across, he alit and continued forward. About five steps away, he found the trigger stone. One cobble below his feet depressed as he stepped on it. He heard a click then several loud, hissing whooshes behind him. He turned and saw several spiked pendulum rods swing back and forth at various intervals. He hadn't noticed that the niches crossed the ceiling.

"So, this is not the way the builders expected someone to enter the heart of the maze, but they did expect it to be used as an exit."

He entered the large, vaulted room he recognized from Lazarus' earlier reconnaissance. He put the Elder's Stone back into his shirt and allowed his eyes to adjust to the column of sunlight which spilled from an opening just off center of the ceiling.

Directly across from him and to either side darkness gaped. The three doors were identical to the one he'd come through. In the dead center of the room stood a pedestal. On it rested a box-like form. He strode to it. Several odd-shaped crevices marred the surface, as if pieces were missing, which he suspected to be the case.

The box wasn't much bigger than the jewelry casket he kept his most prized possessions in. He picked it up and tucked it inside his shirt.

The stone pedestal the box had rested on rose a few inches, and a harsh grating sound came from both beneath his feet and from the surrounding doorways. He pushed the pedestal back down to its previous height. He immediately realized that had been the wrong thing to do.

Only his reflexes from spending most of his life on a ship kept him upright. A loud click from beneath the pedestal presaged sudden movement in the floor. A cloud of dust rose as concentric rings of the floor began to spin in opposite directions. Worse, bars began to descend, albeit slowly, in each of the four doorways. The fact each door looked identical helped the rotation of the floor make it impossible to tell which door he'd entered the room from. His only clue was the scent trail, but he knew how hard it would be to get past the death pit.

He looked up and saw his way out. Had he been a mortal man, this room would have been his tomb, but he was a vampire — and he could fly.

With that thought, he flew thirty feet up to the bottom of the well. As he ascended, he noticed multiple circular holes in the wall as well as suspiciously convenient stones jutting from the masonry. No doubt the stones triggered spikes or projectiles embedded in the holes. The designer didn't intend for anyone to escape with the prize. Luckily, he had no need to climb or use hand holds.

A few minutes later he emerged from the well. He landed next to the opening. As he'd half-expected, bars sprang up to block the way at the bottom of the stairs which led back into the labyrinth.

He just laughed and flew to the top of the wall. From there, he leapt from the top of one wall to another toward the only visible entrance. He crouched low to avoid being seen by Circe when he arrived at the last pathway within the outer wall. He hovered down to the path just around the curve, out of sight of the entrance. As a precaution, he maintained the hover just above the ground but moved as though walking.

The look on Circe's face when he emerged from the maze made his choice of how he returned worth it.

"How? It should not be possible for you to come out this way if you did not enter through this door."

"I found a secret passage." He reached inside his shirt and pulled out the puzzle box. "I believe this is what you sent me in for."

She took it from him and examined it. Finally, she nodded. "You have passed this portion of the test. This box was designed by Daedalus. Within it is what I need to return my magic to its full potency. It cannot be opened until all the missing pieces are returned to their proper places on it."

She handed the box back to him. "Long ago, the Elder ordered me to lock away this portion of my power. He then removed pieces from the box and disbursed them to five of my Sisters. You will have to visit them and meet their prices for the portions they hold. Once the box is reassembled, return it to me, and I will give you what you seek."

Viktor's eyes held a resigned tiredness.

"Of course."

# Chapter 7

The sea dragon felt the summons. He did not reply right away. Currently, he had a meal to finish.

Once a year, he visited this small fishing village on the northeastern shore of the Black Sea. For nearly a century the villagers had offered him a sacrifice in exchange for good fishing and fair weather.

He just looked at it as a free meal.

Xandricus pulled himself into the shallows of the sacrificial cove while still in his dragon form. The screams of the villagers' offering greeted him. He turned his monstrous head toward the sound and snuffed the air.

*"Another virgin,"* he thought in resigned disgust. *"Just once couldn't they give me a whore? At least that would make the sport a little interesting."*

Chained to the bluff at the back of the cove, the human female continued to scream. He contemplated screaming back and destroying her mind. He decided not to. He wanted some sport with her first, and he preferred a responsive female to a mindless husk.

He smirked when the sight of him taking his human form made her screams stop abruptly. He could still smell her fear, but it had changed from abject terror to the excited fear of an untried maiden faced with an unknown wonder.

Tall, muscular, graceful: Xandricus knew well the effect he had on females.

He brushed his blood-red hair back from his well-sculpted face and stalked over to his prey. She stared at him, mesmerized. He lifted the crown of flowers from her hair and tossed it aside. He had no interest in the dead plants. He then hooked his thumbs under the shoulder straps of the gauzy sheath she wore. Out of her sight, he transformed his thumbs into talons and sliced through the flimsy fabric. It slid down her form to puddle at her feet and left her bare to him.

He took a step back and looked her over. He liked the fact she was well-fed. She smelled healthy. He smiled and stepped in close to her. She leaned toward him, straining against her bonds. He did not release her, however. That would come later.

He lowered his face to hers to kiss her. At the same time, he reached down and parted her folds with his fingers. She jumped at the contact but soon began to moan into his mouth as he continued to explore her. He dipped one finger inside her and soon encountered the expected barrier of her hymen. Quickly, he extended that one talon enough to slice through. She yelped then gasped as he worked a second then a third finger into her. He twisted side to side then thrust in deep. When he pulled them out and brought his hand up to his face, his fingers dripped with her virginal blood and other fluids.

He licked them clean and savored the flavor. He had to admit, even though virgins tended to be boring as lovers, they tasted delicious.

Satisfied he'd stretched her enough to receive him, he slowly worked himself into her. He felt her spasm around him. She moaned; her eyes rolled back as she strained against her bonds to thrust herself deeper onto him. He smiled at her unexpected responsiveness. Perhaps she wouldn't be boring after all.

He lifted her knees to his shoulders for better access and began to thrust in earnest. Her moans turned to grunts and gasps. He lowered his face to one of her breasts and drew the nipple into his mouth. He played it with his tongue and lips until it swelled and stiffened.

She screamed as he thrust hard and deep to force past her cervix and into her womb. At the same time, he bit her nipple off and swallowed it. He drew more of her breast into his mouth and suckled at the wound.

He stopped thrusting but remained buried in her womb and allowed her to spasm and writhe around him. He expanded his mouth to its true size and let multiple rows of needle teeth manifest. He took her entire breast into his mouth and snapped his jaws shut.

Her screams took on a choking, gurgling sound.

He chewed slowly and enjoyed the mingled flavors of lust and terror. He did love breasts; it was a shame she only had two.

He resumed thrusting and increased his speed. He tore in and out of her womb until blood flowed freely down. Just as he poised to eat her other breast, he felt the orgasm wash over him.

He roared out his pleasure and reverted to his dragon form while still inside her. His sudden increase in shape and size ruptured her body and ripped it apart.

Once he could think again, he picked up the shredded remains of her body delicately in his claws. He sniffed it then tossed it into his maw.

He turned and glided back into the sea.

An hour later, he felt the summons again. He shared no bond with the witch; but he decided he would go see what she wanted. She could hold her own with him as a lover; and she always kept fresh meat around.

Xandricus took a couple of weeks to make his way to Circe's island. Hunting through the Hellespont and in the northern Greek Isles proved very good.

118

It surprised him to find the rocky maze and series of whirlpools completely gone. He'd been looking forward to trolling for fresh wrecks. Although he hadn't visited in several decades, natural erosion could not account for the drastic change.

No, this definitely involved magic.

As soon as he took human form and set foot on the stone steps he caught the scent. *She* had been here. He ran up the steps with inhuman speed. He found Circe in her bedroom.

"How long ago was she here?" he demanded.

Circe jumped, startled by his sudden appearance. "Who? What are you talking about?"

"Belladonna."

She frowned. "Why are you interested in some pirate's whore? I invited you here to aide me in the protection of my island, for which I intend to pay you well, not to talk about some little strumpet!"

He stared at her with a sudden realization of how much her magic had waned. He gave her a cunning smile. "Why do you need help to protect your island, Circe?"

"You know very well why, Xandricus. With the exception the ship graveyard, my rings of defense have vanished. I don't even have a fog to hide the wrecks.

There remains very little to keep my prey from escaping." She glared at him.

He chuckled. Her seduction skills never had been the best. Protection wasn't the only thing she wanted judging by her scent. He moved to loom over her, aroused by the advantage he had. He couldn't help but notice the effect his nudity and arousal had on her.

"Tell me what I want to know, and I will give you what you want, Circe."

She swallowed and looked up at him. She ran her fingertips up one of his thighs to his hip and rested it there. "What do you want to know?"

"Describe the female you say is just a pirate's whore. I want to know if she is who I think she is."

"She is about my height but a little wider in the hips, full-breasted, and her hair —." She paused, and he saw the pieces fall into place in her eyes. "Her hair was the same blood red as yours. Are you related?"

"Not yet, but she has sealed her fate by coming here. The Elder exiled her from these waters millennia ago."

"Why?"

"Her sister was my mate and with child. Belladonna killed her. By right, her territory became mine. She was warned; if she returned, she had to forfeit her freedom and take her sister's place. Now, how long ago was she here?"

Circe sighed and furrowed her brow. He could tell she didn't want to tell him. He gently cupped her chin and smiled down at her. "I give you my word, Circe; I will leave you satisfied and restore your protective fog. Just tell me."

"She left aboard a large ship shortly before I first contacted you a fortnight ago."

He frowned in confusion. "She is a siren. Why would she need a ship to carry her — unless; did she appear to be pregnant?"

"No, but I do not know how soon a siren would show. It takes a few months for a human," she answered.

"It takes nearly a year," he said. "The pregnancy lasts twenty months. Hmm; I wonder if she means to lure me out then have her mate challenge me."

Circe shook her head. "I don't think so. The man she was with is very powerful, but he is not a sea dragon. She seemed subservient to him."

"This is the pirate you spoke of?"

"Yes. His name is Viktor Brandewyne, and I believe he is the One foretold. He has a strong connection with the Elder."

121

"Then forgive me, Circe, but I need to be quick with you."

She placed both her hands about his waist and pulled gently. "There is no need to hurry, Xandricus. I have set him a task to perform. Given how quickly he solved and survived the labyrinth, I have no doubt he will accomplish it. Once he does, he must return here to conclude our bargain."

He grinned down at her with his true needle-like teeth. "Then I shall be waiting for him; and I will reclaim what is rightfully mine. You have your deal, Circe. I will take my time with you."

He extended his talons and shredded her garments.

A few days later, he left the be-fogged island and headed west. He intended to track Belladonna now he had her scent. It stood to reason if she had entered his territory, he should be finally free to go beyond it.

When he reached the Straits of Gibraltar, he soon learned of his error.

He tried to swim through the Straits to the Atlantic. Halfway through, a vicious current forced him backwards. He tried again with more force. He managed to get past the current but encountered an invisible barrier. He saw other sea life and some sailing vessels pass back and forth through the Straits freely, but he could not.

He roared his frustration.

Viktor had the *Incubus* put in at Tenerife before making the crossing. The pirates needed to take on fresh supplies. Apparently, word had spread among the Berber Corsairs to avoid them. It made for poor pirating.

He also wanted to give the crew some shore time. With his current quest before him, he didn't know when the next chance for it would come.

He decided to allow his cadre ashore, as well. None of the six vampires had been off the ship since they'd been made a few years ago. He still had plenty of blood stock for them aboard, so he knew he'd have no problem preventing them from feeding in the port town.

Since he'd gone to the Singing Mermaid the last time he'd been in this port, he decided to try out the Drunken Goat this time. The two taverns were run by the same family, but the Mermaid catered to a higher class of clientele than the Goat. The moment he walked through the door, he knew he liked the place.

"This place reminds me of the Flag," he said to Grimm.

"Aye, it does. Bigger brothel though, from the looks of it," the first mate commented. "Wonder if the food is as bad."

"Worse," Jon-Jon said as he pushed through the crowd headed for the bar.

"You should go to the Singing Mermaid if you're looking for a good meal, Hezekiah. I know they have excellent rum there."

Grimm shook his head. "The show will be here. I can endure bad food if I've got enough gin in me."

"The show?" Vik pretended he didn't know what the man was talking about.

Grimm chuckled at his friend and captain. He pointed toward one of the vampires as several of the wenches approached him, ignoring other patrons in the process.

Thomas Brumble looked to be at a loss over the attention the bevy of women paid him. Vik could hear several comments and compliments about the vampire's appearance: everything from his strawberry blonde hair to his unusual pallor. He sent a mental reminder to his young vampire to not reveal his fangs or feed; he also encouraged Thom to relax and enjoy himself.

Grimm spotted Zachary Brumble and waved for the navigator to join them. When he arrived at their table,

Grimm said, "Your brother looks like he's searching for someone to rescue him. Is it possible he's still a virgin?"

A shadow passed over Zach's face. "No, he's not a virgin; but his experience is very limited. He's probably afraid they'll be hurt because of him."

Viktor leaned forward and topped off Zach's glass. "I smell a tale behind that statement, Mr. Brumble. Please, share it with us."

Zach took a long pull on the glass before he spoke. "To my knowledge, Thom has only been with one woman, a girl really. Sybil was a chambermaid in our house. Thom was about fourteen, and I was already learning seamanship and training for my captaincy. Sam missed this episode, thankfully. She was visiting an aunt for a few months."

"Continue."

"You know how a lad's blood runs hot at that age. I think Sybil was about the same age as Thom, and she was a beauty. He grew besotted with her, and she with him. He was a pretty lad. Father did not find out about the situation until the girl got pregnant. He was livid with her and swore he'd turn her out in the streets for the whore she was."

"Thom came to her defense, probably the first time he ever stood up to Father. He revealed he was the sire and offered to wed her to spare her shame."

"Father flew into a rage. He would not stand for any of his children to marry beneath them, nor would he have a chambermaid bring shame to his family name."

"Thom told me later that Father didn't strike him as he'd expected. Instead, the old bastard beat the poor girl bloody in front of him and told him it was his fault she suffered."

"She lost the child and almost died. Thom told me about it when I got back to port. I tried to find the girl to offer her some sort of compensation, but she'd disappeared by then. Father had made it impossible for her to find work in Boston. She had no living family to ask about her whereabouts."

"Ever since then, Thom has been shy of women and completely celibate," Zach finished.

"Damn," Grimm said.

Viktor concentrated on the link with his young vampire. *"Thomas, your father cannot harm you anymore, nor can he harm any of these wenches. You are free to enjoy their pleasures, lad."*

Thomas looked at his captain from across the room with a questioning look. Viktor nodded and smiled. A new confidence seemed to shine in the young vampire's eyes as he turned his full attention to the bevy of females. Before long, he'd headed for the upper rooms with one of them.

"I think he'll do just fine, now, Mr. Brumble," Vik said with a smug grin. "Now, we need to decide on a course. I've got to revisit all the Sisters I've already dealt with."

"Of course," Grimm sighed. "Bitches can't make anything simple or easy, can they?"

"No. There are five pieces of a puzzle to be collected. Each one is with a different Sister. Four of them are in or around the Caribbean —."

"Four?" Grimm interrupted.

"Aye." Vik nodded. "Juma, the one who cursed me, is on Hispañola. Hopefully, she's not one of the ones holding a puzzle piece."

"So, that leaves Dorada, Gloribeau, and Venoma. Do you figure to visit each of them before heading south and through the Straits of Magellan to visit Clarissa and Rosalia?"

"Aye; and I'd like to get the most unpleasant one out of the way first. After Venoma, Dorada will be closest; then north to Glory."

"I'll plot a course as soon as I get back to the ship, Captain," Zach said.

Vik clasped him on the shoulder. "You can do it on the crossing, Mr. Brumble. For now, go find yourself a wench and enjoy this time in port. It may be some time before you get another chance."

# Chapter 8

At the midpoint of their crossing, Viktor sent Belladonna out to hunt. She didn't argue. Neither of them wanted Venoma to entangle the siren in her web of power again.

This move also kept the sister from detecting their approach and preparing a welcoming committee.

"I don't like it, Vik," Grimm argued. "She still wants you dead. Why risk facing her alone?"

"I will not risk my crew to her. I know where she is. I need you to stay with the ship and the crew. Your tie to Zeke will offer them protection from her creatures." Viktor rummaged through his sea chest while he spoke. Finally, he found what he wanted. "There it is. How did it get buried at the bottom?" He pulled out a sea bag and shook it out.

Grimm crossed his arms and leaned against the table. "I'd say it got buried because you haven't used it since the first time we went to see Rosalia."

"Hmph; it has been a while, hasn't it?" He began to stuff a change of clothes into the bag. After that, he put a couple of wax-sealed bottles of his blood-brandy mix. He settled them among the clothing so they wouldn't clank against each other. He put in the emerald encrusted cross he sometimes wore. Lastly, he put in Circe's puzzle box wrapped in a piece of oilcloth.

"Why are you taking bloody brandy and the cross?" Grimm asked as Vik tied the drawstring on the sea bag.

"I don't know how long this will take. The bloody brandy is for if it takes a week or so. The cross is to keep my Hunger in check if it takes longer." His eyes went out of focus for a moment. "Good; Mr. Jon has the small ketch ready to go. I want you to take the ship on towards the *Islas del Roques*. I'll rendezvous with you there. I would strongly advise against letting anyone go ashore on Dorada's island."

"Why not? Surely, she hasn't covered the whole island with gold vines."

"No, but she has some deadly traps, none the less. I slipped into Paella's dreams last night to spy things out." He leered. "She did her best to distract me."

Grimm blinked and raised an eyebrow. "How did you manage that?"

Vik chuckled. "I forgot I never told you about that ability. I learned with Angelique that I can consciously

130

enter and control the dreams of someone I've bitten. I must admit, Paella's gotten more powerful. I don't know if she's drawing on the Mermaid's Tear or if there has been a power shift between her and Dorada."

"You make that sound as if it's a good thing."

"I enjoy a good challenge."

"Mm-hmm; I'll be sure to remind you of that."

Vik laughed and clapped his first mate and friend on the shoulder. "I'm counting on it."

Viktor followed the Lesser Antilles south for about a week before he headed toward the South American mainland. He put in at the same beach he'd used when he'd first dealt with Venoma.

He pulled the ketch well above the high tide mark and secured it. He went so far as to cut some palm fronds and cover it to hide it from view from the sea. Wouldn't do for some passing sailor or fisherman to see it and think it free for the taking; never mind that was how he acquired it.

Once he felt satisfied with how he'd situated the boat, he took to the sky. He knew he stood a better chance of not triggering Venoma's power web if he stayed above the canopy until he reached her cave. He didn't want to give her an opportunity to make his approach difficult.

Venoma gnawed on the bones of her last victim. She knew she'd have to subsist on fruit soon. Man-flesh got harder to come by every year. Local tribes had long ago learned to avoid her mountain; and the Spaniards only cared for gold or gems, neither of which had been found there, mainly because prospectors had never escaped her traps.

She sensed a presence in her web — more accurately, in a place just outside her cave where her power web opened unexpectedly, as if unable to touch the source of the presence. This disturbed and confused her. The Elder never left Hell's Breath Island; and only his magic could disrupt her web like this.

Unless — the solution to the conundrum hit her just as she heard the voice outside.

"Venoma Noir, I know you are in there. I have business with you."

Rage, hatred, and a touch of fear roiled through her. What was he doing back in her domain? She'd begrudgingly admitted he could be the One. He'd passed the tests she'd set him and earned a portion of her magic. What could possibly bring him back?

Irritably, she emerged from her cave.

☠

Viktor resisted the urge to cover his mouth and nose. The stench of rotten flesh clung to the spider-like crone who emerged from the cleft in the rocks. The nearly meatless arm bone she carried confirmed his suspicions she was a cannibal. It bore obvious signs of gnawing.

Venoma waved the bone at him dismissively and said, "I have no business with you. You already took what you required and still left my powers crippled. Go away!" She started to turn back toward her cave.

"My apologies for interrupting your meal, but I do have business with you, Venoma. You have in your keeping an item I need."

He caught the brief flicker of fear in her eyes. It made him wonder if she didn't know about the puzzle piece, or worse, if she'd lost it. If she didn't know about it, he'd have no choice but to deal with Juma; and she hated him more than Venoma did.

"You have reached Circe." The old witch made it a statement rather than a question.

"I have. She set me to retrieve the pieces of a puzzle box scattered among the Sisters ages ago."

"Then you know such an item must be earned." She gave him a calculating look. "If I had been given warning of your visit, I could have had a task prepared for you."

"How much time do you need to get things ready?"

She regarded him silently for some time before she answered. "I will return to you at sunset tomorrow with the task I require in exchange for the puzzle piece in my possession."

She turned and squirmed back into the rocks.

"Of course," he sighed.

Viktor found a productive way to spend his night and day. Although he forbade Lazarus to join him, the creature let him "see" a merchant ship had anchored nearby and sent boat crews ashore to forage for meat and fresh water.

He made his way to the shore on foot. If Venoma sensed his movements she would think he'd gone to his boat to wait.

Viktor enjoyed the look of confusion on Venoma's face when she emerged the next evening. She obviously had not expected him to have company. Three men sat bound and gagged at his feet.

"What is this?"

He bowed and smiled. "A gift; a merchantman sent a foraging expedition ashore last night. I did a little

134

hunting and thought you might enjoy something a little fresher than what you had when I arrived."

He could almost see her salivate as she looked at the three bound men. "Have them stand."

He did as she instructed. The men eyed him with naked fear. He hadn't bothered to hide his true nature from them.

She stalked around them, and they soon forgot the vampire who had captured them. They stared at her with hungry lust. Viktor noted the scent of magic heavy in the air. She had bewitched them. He felt sure they did not see the grotesque truth of her form. She certainly didn't inspire lust in him.

"They look healthy enough. I thank you for this bounty; but do not think this will sway me to make your task any easier, Viktor Brandewyne," she said.

"I did not expect it to. As I said, this is a gift. Now, what is my task?"

She gave him her full attention with a cruel smile on her face. "Hidden within my cave is a crystal much like the Elder's Stone, but it is blood red and holds no special power. Find it and bring it to me."

"Very well." He took a step toward the crevice when she raised her hand.

"Not so fast. You will not enter my cave wearing the Elder's Stone."

He sighed and slipped the silver chain and milky crystal over his head and put it in his sea bag. "If you are thinking you can claim it for your own, forget such thoughts, Venoma. I've been wearing it for years now. It has imprinted to me; no one else can use it. I will need a torch."

She nodded. "There is an unlit one in a sconce at the entrance of the back tunnel."

# Chapter 9

Viktor removed his shirt to avoid tearing when he squeezed through the rocky crevice. He'd taken the precaution of coating his skin with a salve Belladonna had prepared for him. Poisonous frog slime covered the rocks.

The siren told him his curse should make him immune to any poisons; but since he was alive rather than undead, she'd used the secretion her skin produced when she was in her true form to make the salve for him — just in case.

Once inside the main cavern, he put his shirt back on and stood still for a moment to allow his eyes to fully adjust to the poor light. Once they did, he saw the floor worked alive with venomous creatures. Small but deadly spiders dangled from the ceiling.

He smiled grimly. He closed his eyes and concentrated. He planned to draw on the power of the Elder's Stone he had absorbed over the years. He did not allow himself to doubt it would work.

He opened his eyes and looked down. A clear bubble of space surrounded him. He took one step forward and

watched the scorpions, snakes, millipedes, and spiders
scurry to escape the edge of the invisible barrier. He
grinned and proceeded across the cavern to the torch he
was to use.

Venoma growled in frustration. Despite the pirate's
warning, she had dug into his sea bag and pulled out the
silver chain which held the Elder's Stone. As soon as she
brought the crystal into the open it flared to life. She
found herself forcibly flung against the bluff face; her
hand burned from the blast of power.

She thrust her power out through her web and
discovered another unpleasantness. Brandewyne no
longer needed to wear the crystal to use it. Her first two
traps had already been thwarted.

*"Never mind,"* she thought. *"He still has Arachne to
deal with; and she is deep within the mountain. He will
be too far from the Elder's Stone to draw on it for
protection by the time he gets to her."*

She turned her attention back to the three men.

Viktor came to another chamber at the end of the
tunnel. He faced three other tunnels. Two appeared to be
manmade. The one natural passage sported a thick barrier
of cobwebs. He put the torch to the webs and proceeded

138

that way. One thing he had learned from dealing with the Sisters: the easy way was usually false.

After some time and a few tight spots where he had to crawl through, he heard a rushing, roaring sound ahead of him. He still felt he was on the right course, though. He rounded a bend in the passage and lost his light source.

A trick of echoes had made him believe the waterfall was further away. The spray doused the torch almost instantly and plunged him into darkness.

"Damn!"

He stood still to try to allow his other senses to adjust and compensate. Unfortunately, the roar of the waterfall proved nearly deafening. Scent didn't vary enough to be of much help in the passage, either.

Just when he started to wonder if he had finally been trapped, he realized he could see something. At first, he thought his mind played tricks on him. The silvery sparks reminded him of those seen after a blow to the head or having shut his eyes too tight. Then he saw that the sparks formed a spidery thin trail.

It dawned on him quickly that what he looked at was exactly that: spider web, apparently with some magical properties.

"So that is what you've sent me to face, Venoma," he spoke into the darkness. "The strands don't extend the way I came, so the creature or creatures must just come here for the water."

He found the torch by feel and followed the spider strands until he was well away from the waterfall and could hear himself think again. It took him a few minutes to be able to get the torch lit again.

The flame made the spider strands nearly invisible, but at least he could see rocks without running into them headfirst. A few more feet down the tunnel and he saw it ended abruptly; but the webs grew thicker and gave the illusion that the tunnel continued.

He shifted the torch to his other hand and drew his sword. At this point, he considered both weapons. The sheer density of the webs in the cavern before him told him he faced either the largest spider colony he'd ever imagined or the most monstrous spider in the world. If a colony, fire seemed the best defense; if it was a monster, he definitely wanted his longest blade at the ready.

Dim light seemed to permeate the cavern. He risked a look upward and realized the mountain he stood in must have once been volcanic, and the cavern its main vent. A look down showed webs extending into the darkness.

A brief flash of red from the far side of the volcanic chimney caught his eye. He tried to focus on that area, but the webs made it difficult. He caught the flash again in a slightly different spot. This time he allowed his eyes to lose focus a little. Rather than try to make out a shape, he concentrated on sensing movement.

The next flash seemed much closer. Finally, he made out where, or more precisely, what it came from.

A semi-translucent spider with a body the size of a large goat and legs that easily spanned eight feet made its way toward him. Multiple eyes flashed red in its white head. A greenish fluid, most likely venom, beaded at the points of its massive mandibles.

Viktor smiled grimly. Centered among the spider's eyes glinted the red crystal Venoma had tasked him to retrieve.

"This is what I get for saying I love a challenge."

At the sound of his voice, the great spider sprang nearly half the distance between them. He found a niche in the stone to secure the torch in and tried to levitate. He couldn't move from where he stood, not even a step.

He risked a glance down to see his booted feet encased in webbing up to the ankle. Hundreds of tiny white spiders swarmed there but seemed unable to move further up his legs.

He looked back up just in time to see the giant spider land directly in front of him. It reared up on its back two sets of legs. He raised his sword, ready to do battle; then he hesitated.

Before his eyes the spider transformed into a beautiful woman. She stood before him naked and smiling with her arms outstretched. Her eyes glittered darkly, and several multifaceted rubies studded her forehead around the red crystal. Her white silken hair spun out behind her to join with the great webs of the cavern.

*"What is your name?"* she asked.

He recognized the language as Greek and replied in kind, grateful he'd gotten Belladonna to teach him on the crossing. *"Give me your name, and I will tell you mine."*

*"I am Arachne."*

*"Viktor Brandewyne, at your service."* Without warning, he thrust his sword through her head from just below the jaw.

In an instant, she became a spider again. Her legs flailed wildly then contracted and wrapped around him. Though her mandibles waved mere inches from his face, his sword kept her head too far back to bite him. Still, venom dripped from them. Some landed on his shoulder. Pungent, acrid smoke rose as the acidic fluid dissolved the fabric it stained and burned the flesh beneath.

He screamed at the unexpected pain.

Nausea and dizzying disorientation passed through him. The muscles in his shoulder twitched, and the creature's head slid down his blade to dip closer to him. He felt as if her weight nearly doubled. He could barely keep her mandibles from making contact with his skin. More venom dripped on him and intensified the pain until it felt like the stuff was burning a hole into him; she bent her terrible head toward his chest. The thought of what would happen if it made it through his flesh and into his viscera helped him rally his strength somewhat, and he managed to force her head a little further from him.

Whether partially in response to his actions or to her death throes, her legs tightened more about him. The stiff, chitinous spines on the foot segments which allowed her to navigate her webs so deftly pierced the skin of his back. He fought to keep from letting the fresh pain drive him closer to her bulbous body. At least they didn't burn like the venom.

He vaguely noticed his feet began to grow numb and the numbness seemed to creep upward. His legs felt heavy. He risked a glance downward to see she had expelled thick, quickly hardening web silk from her spinnerets. He was now encased up to his knees, and the tiny spider minions seemed to draw the silk ever tighter about him.

He gritted his teeth and twisted the blade of his sword. Her mandibles spread wide and quivered even as her legs drove their spiny ends deeper into his back.

Finally, they stilled, and the life faded from her multiple eyes, he drew the dagger he kept sheathed at the nape of his neck. Careful not to touch the venom which still dripped from her fangs, he used the smaller blade to pry the red crystal from her head.

He had to release the sword to sheath the dagger or risk dropping either it or the crystal. Once he had them secure, he retrieved his sword. Greenish black ichor dribbled from the spider's body. He would burn his ruined clothes once he got back to his boat. For now, he needed to concentrate on getting free of the carcass and out of the mountain.

Had he been human, it might have already been too late. Although the tiny spiders could not get past the protection of his portion of the Elder's Stone's power, the sphere of which seemed to have grown much smaller. They could, however, roam freely over the body of their mother. Just in the time it had taken to retrieve the crystal, they'd begun to encase Arachne's carcass in spider silk, and him with it.

He pulled his dagger again and hacked at the legs which encircled him. It took all of his unnatural speed and strength, which the exposure to Arachne's venom had weakened considerably, to stay ahead of the spiders. He felt the air grow close and hot within the cocoon of

144

the spider's embrace. He wondered for a moment if he would suffocate and lose consciousness before he could escape. Already, he felt light-headed and felt himself succumbing to a growing weakness.

Finally, he got free enough to get his arm through the silken tomb to reach the still-lit torch. He put the flame first to the thick webbing which held his feet in place. It burned hot and fast. His boots protected him, but they would need replacement. The flames also burned away the four great spider legs which pierced his back. Of course, they also burned the fabric of his clothes and blistered his back. He kept his boots on, but discarded the tattered, scorched remains of his shirt and breeches, glad he'd packed extra.

He thought about setting flame to Arachne's carcass but figured it might be too wet to burn directly. The volcanic chimney needed to be cleared for his escape anyway, so he tossed the torch into the heart of the webs. They caught quickly.

He ran back up the corridor to just past the first bend. He heard a sizzling sound then a loud pop. Shortly after that, a blast of heat followed by a *foomph* hit him.

Cautiously, he peered around the edge of rock.

The charred spider lay on its back, its remaining legs curled in. Blackened gooey bits clung to the rock around it where its abdomen had burst open. The brighter light coming from the chimney allowed him to see and let him know his escape route was now open.

☠

The look on Venoma's face when he flew nude, save for the ruined boots, from the mountaintop to her cave made it worth it. When he held out the crystal, she nearly spat with rage.

"Keep it! That is what you came for. Now go away!" She stalked off to her cave without further word.

He wanted to ask her about Arachne, but doubted he'd get any answers from her. The screams of a man emanated from the cave and confirmed the Sister's foul mood.

Viktor tucked the crystal away in his sea bag, retrieved the Elder's stone, and put it back on. He pulled off his burnt, fouled boots and put on the change of clothing he'd brought, hissing as the fabric pulled on some of the blisters and ruptured them. With a determined grimace, he pulled out one of the bottles of bloody brandy and just broke the neck off with his sword hilt. He drained the bottle quickly and felt the venom and fire burns seal themselves with new, whole flesh. He flew to his boat.

# Chapter 10

"Sail approaching!"

Grimm raised the spyglass in the direction of the lagoon entrance. He focused on the small craft headed toward them and smiled.

"'Tis the Captain!" he called out to the crew. A raucous cheer went up from the pirates. Fifteen minutes later, the boat pulled alongside the *Incubus*.

"What happened to your boots?" Grimm asked when Vik returned to the ship barefoot.

"Ruined 'em; had to burn my way out of thick cobwebs then got giant spider guts all over them."

"Sounds messy. Were you able to get the puzzle piece from her?"

"Aye." Viktor showed him the red crystal. Only then did he notice some odd notches carved into one of the facets. "Interesting; I wonder if that's a clue to how the pieces will fit together."

Grimm shrugged. "Probably won't know until you've got more of them. Belle hasn't returned yet."

Vik grunted. "Good; she doesn't get along too well with Dorada or Paella. In fact, it would probably be best for me to go ashore alone." He left out the fact the young woman's dreams held warnings of deadly plants other than the golden vines.

"Aye," Grimm's voice brought him out of his thoughts. "Even if you hadn't ordered no one was to go ashore, I would have kept the crew on board. Stopped at a small fishing village on the main not far from here. Heard horror stories of vines grabbing fishermen and ripping them apart."

"That sounds like Dorada. She's not too fond of men except for how they can serve her. How are our supplies?" He changed the subject.

"Fairly decent. We've been here a couple of days; and the fishing is good. Drink is starting to run low, though."

"I want to make for New Orleans next. I don't know how long this will take here. How far north can we make it before we need to resupply?"

"Tortuga if we don't take any prizes on the way."

Vik grinned. "I'm about ready for a good bit of piracy. Hunting should be good this time of year, too."

"Aye, it should. Here's hoping we can leave this lagoon soon."

☠

Viktor took the time to wash up, get fresh clothes, and tidy up his goatee. The lack of footwear marred the final effect, but he'd only had the one pair of boots. He felt sure he could guarantee he could keep the Sister's attention on other things than his feet.

He wasn't positive but given the amount of control Paella had now in her dreams, he suspected there'd been a power shift.

Once he felt satisfied with his appearance, he returned to the deck then took to the air. *"Why risk the jungle defenses when I can just fly over them,"* he reasoned with himself. As he'd expected, no one looked up as he flew over the village. He decided to land in front of what looked like a large ceremonial building.

The moment his bare feet touched the ground, vines sprang up around him. They waved and writhed wildly but were unable to touch him.

"You are not welcome here," a feeble voice croaked behind him.

He turned to find an old crone supported by a pretty black-haired girl with emerald green eyes. He barely recognized the crone as Dorada. What puzzled him was that the child had a stronger aura of power than the old woman. The child also bore a trace of his scent.

*"Abuela Carina, who is he? He has the same eyes as I do,"* the girl spoke in Spanish.

*"He is your padre, chica."* Dorada/Carina switched to English. "Why are you here vampire?"

He smiled and bowed. "I have business with you, Dorada."

She held up a hand. "You have no business with me, nor I with you. Begone."

"Oh, but I do. You have something I require."

"She has nothing you require, for she is no longer *la Madre* Dorada. I am, *mi amor*." The voice came from behind him.

He turned to see the young woman he had known as Paella. He raked his eyes over her form and liked what he saw. "Motherhood suits you."

"Send him away, girl!"

Paella/Dorada ignored the old woman. "What is it you seek, Viktor Brandewyne. I seriously doubt you came back just to visit."

He gave her his most charming smile. "And what if I did?"

"A pointless question; I heard you say you had business with me." He detected a slight hurt tone in her voice.

On an impulse, he stepped toward her. The vines sprang high between them, but he sensed no surge of power from her.

*"Don't you hurt my Mami!"*

He turned to face the child and recognized his own ferocity in her. He smiled with pride. *"You are brave and bold, little one. I give you my word I intend your mother no harm."* He spoke in Spanish, unsure if she understood English.

*"Victoria put your plants away. I am quite safe with your father. Take Abuela Carina inside now,"* Paella/Dorada said with a firm but gentle tone.

The vines withdrew back into the earth.

Paella/Dorada drew his attention back to her. "Walk with me, Viktor. We have made many improvements since last you visited."

"So, I see." He offered his arm, and she took it. "This village is quite impressive seen from above."

"Above?" She stopped and looked at him.

"Aye." He grinned roguishly. "I have learned how to fly, pet."

"You can really fly? So that is why I did not sense your approach."

He stepped in very close to her. Nothing impeded him this time. "Do you trust me, pet?"

"No; you are a pirate and a rogue." She tried to make her voice sound haughty, but he could sense her desire.

"Then you are a wise woman," he whispered by her ear. Without warning, he swept her up into his arms and took to the skies. Her squeak of alarm and strong grip around his shoulders gratified him to no end. He'd been without for longer than he liked, and she felt wonderfully soft and warm in his arms.

He kissed her passionately, and she returned it with equal fervor. When they finally broke from the kiss, he said, "Look down on your domain, Dorada. You may never get another chance to see it like this."

She turned her head and gasped. "It is beautiful! Is that your ship? It looks so small from up here."

"Yes, it is." He laughed. He noticed her grip tightened. "Are you ready to go back down?"

She nodded and scrunched her eyes shut. "Just don't drop me."

"I won't."

He set them back down on the spot he had launched from. Once her feet touched solid ground again, she smiled up at him.

"That was both terrifying and exhilarating! Thank you. Now what is it you need from me?"

"I have been charged to find pieces of a puzzle box. I was told that the puzzle pieces had been disbursed among the Sisters."

She gave him an astonished expression. "So that is what that thing is. It has been passed down from mother to daughter for generations. I never understood why. It is pretty, but it holds no magic."

"What do you want for it?"

She bit her lip in thought for several minutes. When she smiled, it grew distinctly sly and calculating. "Two things: first, I want a drop of your blood for a ritual I wish to perform; second, I want you to lay with me tonight."

"Before I agree, what will this ritual achieve? I have not forgotten how the two of you tried to enslave me before." He held up a hand to stop her answer and added, "Remember, I can smell a lie, pet."

"I would never lie —."

"You are lying right now." He grasped her chin but did so gently and raised her face to look her in the eye.

He did not try to force his will on her, and he saw in her eyes she recognized that. "Let's not be enemies. Deal fairly and honestly with me, and I will do the same with you."

She searched his face for some time. "You have grown, Viktor. Just a few years ago, you would have been furious by this time.

"Aye; something I have learned from dealing with the Sisters is patience and how to hold my temper. Dorada was the first I found. I have visited five more since then."

"I give you my sacred word as a Sister of Power that the rite I need your blood for will not enslave or ensorcell you in any way."

He felt the power in her words and knew she was bound by them. "Very well; I agree to your terms: a drop of my blood and a night in your bed in exchange for your portion of the puzzle box."

She beamed up at him. "Carina should be asleep by now. It is time for you to get to know your daughter, Victoria."

Viktor allowed her to lead him inside the building he'd seen the previous Dorada and the girl disappear into. Moss covered the dirt floor and flowering vines crept along the walls. Dim sunlight filtered through the latticework of the roof. It took him a moment to realize small panes of glass had been fitted into the rooftop to keep the rain out. A rattan chair sat at the back of the room with a curtain partition behind it.

Paella/Dorada moved to the chair and sat down. She called softly for her daughter. *"Victoria, come out here please."*

Obediently, the girl came out from behind the curtain and stood behind her mother's throne. She peeked out with a shyness she hadn't had before. Viktor squatted down to be closer to eye level with her.

*"Hello, Victoria. Has your abuela been telling you stories about me?"*

She nodded as she eyed him warily.

*"You don't have to be afraid of me. I promise I will never hurt you or your mother."*

She looked up at her mother for confirmation. Paella/Dorada nodded. *"Your father is a man of his word, mija. He might do bad things; but he does not break promises."*

Victoria stepped out to face him, no longer timid. She studied him with a silent, appraising look. Her little face looked so solemn he had to fight not to smile or laugh.

*"Do I pass inspection?"*

"*Si.*" She nodded then caught him off guard with a hug and a kiss on the cheek.

He hugged her back to keep from falling as a rush of power spread through the contact. He could tell from Paella's reaction she had not expected father and daughter's magic to react to each other.

As the power ebbed, he released the child. She stepped back and rubbed her arms. "You carry the power of the Elder's Stone within you, *Papi*," she said in clear English.

"Victoria, how did you learn, no, when did you learn that language?" her mother asked with a note of worry in her voice.

The girl looked at her. "Just now from *Papi*. His magic is strong."

"Your magic is strong, too, little one," Viktor said. Before his eyes, the girl grew nearly two inches. "Did you know she could do that, Paella?"

"No; she has never grown so fast, although she has had the gift with plants since before she could walk."

"*Si*," the child confirmed. "I stopped *Abuela's* vines from killing Samantha when I was only two and a half harvests old. She had pretty hair as gold as *Madre's* tears." She gave him a pensive stare and said, "Samantha said she was looking for you; that you had taken her brothers."

156

He realized she must be talking about the Brumble girl. It impressed him she'd been able to track him to this island. "Yes, I took her brothers prisoner to punish their father. He hurt a friend of mine a long time ago. They are part of my crew now."

"Will you give them back to her if she finds you?"

"Unfortunately, I cannot. They are pirates now. If they went home, they would be imprisoned and hanged."

She scrunched up her face at him. "Their *papi* is mean if he would do that."

"Yes, he is."

"I know! You can take Samantha with you! Then she could be with her brothers." She beamed, proud of her solution.

Viktor chuckled. "My cat, Lazarus, would like that very much. He has met her, though I have not, and he likes her."

"He must be a smart cat."

"Very much so."

Paella/Dorada smiled at the interchange, but her eyes held a heat for him alone. "Victoria, don't talk your father's ear off. Go make sure *Abuela* Carina is sleeping; then you may go play. I need to speak with your father alone."

The girl nodded obedience but looked at him and said, "I want a little brother I can keep this time."

"Victoria Auna!" her mother cried in shock.

Viktor's grin matched his daughter's, though he managed to keep his fangs from showing prominently so as not to frighten her. "I will see what I can work out with your mother. Now mind her and scoot."

His chuckle followed her from the room.

# Chapter 11

Paella moved to him with a lusty smile on her lips. He allowed her to embrace him and pull him down for a kiss; but he did not abandon himself to her passion just yet. The flux of magic from her kiss proved a pale shadow of what he'd experienced with their daughter. That had caught him off guard; this, he was prepared for.

Paella didn't seem to notice the difference, however. She nestled up close and smiled up at him. "Mmm, I have missed you, Viktor."

He smiled back down at her. "Business first, pet. I am still curious about why you need my blood. I also need to warn you about what we will do later."

She frowned. "What sort of warning? We have been together before."

"Yes, but you were just Paella then. Now you are *la Madre* Dorada, one of the Sisters of Power. There will be magical repercussions of our joining. It will be a long time before you will find any mortal man's attentions satisfying again; I am not bragging. I merely state personal experience."

"What kind of personal experience?" She continued to frown and pulled back from him a little.

"I have been with another of the Sisters, Gloribeau. An entire city felt the power rush. For months afterward even the most skilled whores seemed boring."

She sighed and smiled sardonically. "I asked. Thank you for being truthful. I shall return the favor. I need your blood to raise my power to where it would have been had Victoria been a male child. My role as Dorada came at the horrible price of the sacrifice of my first-born son. Unfortunately, my first-born was female."

"It has happened before," she continued. "The daughter will be a more powerful Dorada than the mother. That along with the Mermaid's Tear," she fingered the large opal encased in gold filigree about her neck, "is why I am more powerful than Carina was. Your visit provides me with a rare opportunity, however. A drop of your blood will provide the magical boost I would have gained from the son I had hoped to get by you."

Viktor digested this information. "I begin to have second thoughts about our night together. I have no wish to give you another child if there is a chance you will murder it to advance yourself."

She shook her head rapidly. "No; I only had to sacrifice my first son to inherit the mantel of Dorada. If there had been any other way, I would have taken it. I

160

had no choice. When the time came, the magic took me and used me. I still mourn my son."

"You mean you were a puppet?"

"Yes, exactly."

He reached out and stroked her cheek. Some of his past experiences with his Hunger gave him insight to how she must have felt. Even though he was still with him as Lazarus, Viktor still mourned his friend Jim Rigger. The Hunger had been on him, and as a new vampire he had to obey the impulse to feed. Jim had been the only acceptable source of blood at the time.

Jim had been the closest Viktor had ever come to having a brother.

He leaned down and kissed her gently. "I have done things I was powerless to stop as well, pet. There is regret, but there is no shame."

She buried her face against his chest and whispered, "Thank you."

He stroked her hair and held her until she regained her composure. Once he felt her calm, he stepped back, lifted her chin, and smiled. "Now, shall we get your ritual out of the way so I may pay the second part of your price?"

She blushed and nodded. Although she tried to sound aloof, her voice betrayed her emotions. "*Si*; how is it you are the only man who can make me forget myself and my station?"

He gave her a rakish grin which made her blush harder. "Because I am a rogue and see you as a woman first and a Sister of Power second."

Viktor felt grateful the ritual needed to be private. It also required both of them to be naked. Not that he minded if anyone saw him *au natural*; he just didn't care for an audience when he laid with a woman unless he intended to make an example of her.

He suspected Paella/Dorada didn't want her followers to know she wasn't as strong as she could be.

She'd led him to a secluded glen in the jungle. Moonlight and starlight filtered down through the canopy of trees and vines. Soft, thick moss covered the ground.

She directed him to stand in the center of the clearing then began to work him until he grew hard.

"I thought we had to perform your ritual first, pet." He chuckled lustily.

"This is part of it. The blood offering must come from your manhood, where it is most potent," she explained. When he flinched, she added, "I only need a drop, remember. You'll barely feel it."

Even as he steeled himself, the sight of her holding an obsidian blade triggered memories of her predecessor. He felt sure it was the same blade the previous Dorada had used to commit human sacrifice to regain her magic. She'd castrated a man, bled him out, and fed his corpse to her carnivorous vines.

Paella/Dorada made a tiny nick on his tip just as he started to grow soft. The stinging, brief pain galvanized him and almost brought him. He gritted his teeth to fight off the release.

She held the blade up to the night sky and chanted a seemingly simple spell. He saw a single drop of his blood glisten on the edge of it. She plunged the blade into the earth. The mossy ground cover rippled as a wave of magic burst out from the spot. They heard it whisper out through the jungle.

Dorada's back arched in an orgasm when the power wave returned to crash into her.

Viktor couldn't hold back anymore. He lifted her in his arms and took them to the ground. He plunged himself deep within her warm folds and allowed her spasms to bring the release he needed.

He barely gave her time to catch her breath. One of his gifts, even as a human, was the ability to perform again quickly after an orgasm. He leered down at her and said, "Tonight this is your bed, and I am already in it."

Her moans and screams accented the storm of magic which tore through the island for the next few hours.

Viktor lay on his side propped up on one elbow and watched Dorada breathe. Sweat covered them both. The jungle air had grown rather muggy during their lovemaking. He debated taking her again when an odd sound intruded on his consciousness.

"Do you hear that?"

She started to shake her head "no" when she caught it, too. She instantly recognized it. It called to her power.

"The plants are screaming!" she gasped. "Something is very wrong."

"Perhaps we should get back then." He stood and offered her a hand. He saw vines had interwoven into a chamber around them. The latticework all but shut out the moonlight even as he looked up. "Dorada?"

"This is not my doing. The vines answer to another. They are not responding to my magic." A note of panic tinged her voice.

He looked around and saw the walls of their prison grow closer by the minute.

Carina reeled from the bombarding waves of magic she'd endured for the past few hours. She'd awakened with the first wave and now felt drunk from them. It took her a moment to realize when the ordeal stopped. It had nearly driven her mad.

Once she felt sure the assault had ended, she acted quickly. It took her mere minutes to concoct the soporific potion. She then called the child to her.

Victoria answered the summons, fully alert and invigorated by the magic. Carina looked at her granddaughter; but in that moment, she only saw the child's sire in her. She determined to go through with her hasty plan. Viktor Brandewyne's bloodline would serve hers not inherit it.

Viktor noticed although Dorada's clothing had been swallowed up by the vegetation, his still lay untouched. He smiled grimly in realization. He'd taken off the Elder's stone to keep it from interfering with Dorada's magic. Whoever had usurped that magic was also powerless before the stone.

He fished it out of the pile of clothing and put it on. He tossed his shirt to Dorada and climbed into his breeches.

"Can you sense where you need to go?"

She nodded. "Back to the village. We need to hurry."

"Hold on." He wrapped one arm around her and pulled her to his side.

"Don't try to cut the vines. It will make them attack," she warned as she wrapped her arms around his neck.

"Heh, couldn't anyway. This is one of the rare times I didn't bring a blade with me." He held the Elder's Stone above his head and levitated toward the vines interlaced overhead. As expected, they opened wide around them and allowed them to leave the living chamber.

The flight to the village was short. What awaited them filled him with a cold rage.

"Victoria!" He wasn't sure if he or Dorada cried out their daughter's name. The child did not respond.

Carina stood naked, covered in strange markings drawn in blood. At her feet lay the limp form of the girl. A long gash down the child's forearm glistened in the moonlight.

Viktor moved to attack the old witch; a warm hand on his bare arm stopped him. He looked at Dorada and saw a stony expression on her face. Power tingled across his skin where she touched him despite the presence of the Elder's Stone. He realized this was her fight more than his.

"Carina, what have you done?"

"I could ask you the same, girl. I felt you let him corrupt your magic. His seed shall not inherit our bloodline. I have taken back the power of Dorada."

"Taken?" Dorada laughed at the claim. As she spoke, vines sprang up around Carina's feet. Tendrils curled around her toes and ankles and around the unconscious child's limbs.

"*Si*, taken. My spell will draw the magic and life-force from his whelp and transfer it to me." The old woman wore a triumphant and mad grin.

Dorada shook her head and allowed a single golden tear to fall. "Carina, you have sealed your own doom." She turned her back on her mother.

Behind her, the golden tear soaked into the soil. The vines crept higher up Carina's legs. A look of alarm crept over her face. She started to push at the vines, and they wrapped around her wrists. Try as she might, she could not free herself.

"Paella, child, what have you done to me?" she cried out in panic.

Dorada did not turn to face her. "You have done this to yourself, Carina. I am *la Madre* Dorada. Your time passed. Your womb is barren. Besides," she finally turned to look at her mother, "you of all people should know stolen magic will eventually turn on the thief."

Carina screamed as the vines' growth surged. They grew into her lower orifices. In minutes, the vine in her womb extended her belly as if she were pregnant. The skin stretched and split. Her blood marred the markings she'd made with Victoria's.

Her body writhed as another vine worked its way through her digestive tract in reverse. It finally emerged from her mouth, effectively cutting off her screams.

At that point, a shimmering layer of gold began to cover the vines. Terror shone in her eyes as she realized the full extent of her destruction.

As the golden vines began to desiccate and digest the former Sister of Power, Viktor noticed they also entered the wound on his daughter's forearm.

Dorada stopped him from ripping the child free. "They will not harm her. They merely return what was stolen from her. Watch."

To his amazement, clear, glowing fluid oozed from the vine into the bloody gash. He watched as color returned to her cheeks, and the wound slowly closed. Before long, only a thin golden line marked that the child had suffered any kind of wound.

The vines unwound from Victoria's body and gently lifted her to a standing position. Her emerald-green eyes fluttered open and closed again. She yawned and stretched. When she opened them again, she smiled at her parents. "*Mami, Papi*! I had a bad dream." She ran to them and hugged their legs.

Viktor reached down and patted her hair. He noticed the raven locks were now shot through with golden strands.

"Sadly, it wasn't a dream, my sweet," Dorada said as she knelt to embrace her daughter. "*Abuela* Carina tried to steal your magic." She pointed to the corpse.

Carina's bare bones hung held together by the golden vines. The jumbled knots where her abdomen had been gave the whole thing the look of a macabre organic sculpture.

"*Mami*, may I have one of your gold tears?" Victoria asked.

"Of course." Dorada smiled at her daughter's request. She allowed a single, shimmering drop of gold to gather at the corner of her eye and let the girl wipe it away.

Viktor watched, curious, as the child walked over to her grandmother's remains. She spoke a few syllables he could not understand and reached up on tiptoe. She frowned, unable to reach the skull.

He stepped to her and asked, "Would you like a boost?"

*"Si, gracias."*

Gently, he lifted her by the waist until she could reach her target. She pressed the golden drop in the center of Corina's skull. Viktor set her back down.

The tear took on a life of its own. In minutes it spread to coat the entire skeleton.

"Now everyone will always know what happens to those who betray *la Madre* Dorada," she said. In that moment, they could see the formidable Sister she would become.

"Zeke is going to have his hands full with her. I wonder how many holes he will put in my ship for it," Viktor muttered.

He returned to his ship with a carved piece of moss agate. He placed it in the same locked chest in which he stored the puzzle box and the red crystal he'd won from Venoma.

# Chapter 12

Belladonna headed straight for the captain's cabin the moment her tail transformed back to legs. She knew Viktor preferred she stop by her own cabin to dress any time she returned to the ship. Her current mood did not incline her to obey that edict.

She also didn't knock.

The sight that greeted her stopped her in her tracks. Viktor stood nude at the wash basin with a drying cloth in hand.

"Shut the door, pet," he said and bent over to dry his legs. Only then did she realize she had been standing there for a while. Irritated at herself, she did as he'd asked. The fact that the manner of her entrance didn't seem to bother him further irritated her.

"Damn you, Viktor. You know why I'm angry with you, don't you?" she growled.

"I do. I owe you no apology or explanation." He finished drying off and sat down on his bed. Then he surprised her. "But I will give you an explanation. Paella is now Dorada. Sex was part of her price for the puzzle piece."

She, in turn, surprised him. "Idiot, do you think I care about that? You shared power with her! You made her stronger!"

He blinked at her, obviously confused by her ire. "Why would you care about that?"

She pinched the bridge of her nose and sighed. "I keep forgetting for all your growing power you are so very young." She looked up at him and let him see the worry which underlay her anger. "You will probably be called to account for that by Zeke. It may not amount to much, but you have disrupted a delicate power balance."

He snorted, and she glared at him, ready to launch into a tirade. His words stopped her. "I already know Zeke won't be happy with me. I just didn't know that would be an issue, as well."

"What do you mean?"

"Dorada will need the power boost I gave her just to deal with our daughter. The child's power is already frightening."

Belle's eyes widened in amazement. "You mean your offspring will —."

"Will be the next Dorada?" he finished for her. "Yes; I just hope he doesn't sink my ship for it."

She sat down next to him, flabbergasted. He placed an arm around her shoulder and caressed her arm. She found it comforting but also arousing. The fact he remained naked did not help.

"You are impossible." She chuckled.

In response, he leaned into her and nuzzled her hair. She felt his free hand brush lightly up her thigh at the same time he made a rumbling hum in her ear. Gooseflesh rose under his fingertips.

Several hours passed before either of them uttered a coherent word.

Viktor heard the siren stir and glanced over at the bed. He watched her stretch and yawn, unaware a soft smile curved his lips.

She sat up and looked around tensely. He saw her gradually relax once she realized where she was. She frowned at him.

"You are still angry at me, pet?" His voice held amusement.

"You're dressed."

He laughed at her grumpy petulance. 'I have been up and dressed for a couple of hours now. I thought I'd let you sleep."

She stood and padded over to him. She leaned over his shoulder where he sat and looked at the charts in front of him. He felt her arms wrap around his neck and her warm softness press lightly against his back. Her hair brushed the side of his face.

"Where are we going next?"

"New Orleans, but I'd like to do some pirating along the way. I thought it best to sail between Cuba and Hispañola. The shipping is fairly active there this time of year."

"Jeorge," she sighed disgustedly.

"Aye, I'll have to deal with him, as well. We've a long voyage from there to Tierra del Fuego, and I begrudge the delays he will cause as much as you do, pet. He can be a tedious creature."

"That is an understatement." She snorted, straightened, and strode over to the window.

When she opened it, he asked, "Going for a swim?"

"Yes, I need to hunt again. Bedding you takes a lot of energy."

His chuckles followed her out the window.

Hunting proved very profitable once they reached the stretch of sea between Cuba, Jamaica, and Hispañola.

174

Viktor and the crew of the *Incubus* found themselves flush with trade goods, rum, victuals, and captives for the vampires' larder.

When they came upon a slow packet ship on their pass through the Florida Straits, Viktor almost decided to just pass it by. A quick scout of the ship by Lazarus changed his mind.

"What approach do you want to use, Captain?" Grimm asked during their strategy session.

"Keep most of the lads below and mask the guns. I want her to think we're just a large merchantman. We'll signal to exchange mail with her. I'll take the ship personally, so there should be no need for battle if we don't spook them."

Belladonna crossed her arms and leaned against the liquor cabinet. "What or who is aboard that you don't want to risk battle damage to?"

He smirked at her. "You are too clever, pet. There is a teacher we encountered while searching for a dodo egg. I'm surprised to find him on this side of the world, but I suspect his destination."

"Then why take the ship? Has he wronged you? We've supplies enough to make New Orleans."

"Oh, I bear him no ill will. However, if he seeks what I think he does, he'll stand a better chance of finding it and surviving with us than alone. Besides," he pushed back from the table and stood, "the ship carries Oriental silks and three women among the passengers. The lads could use some sport, and the silks will entice Celine and Angel to take the wenches on after we finish with them."

She just raised her eyebrow at him and snorted.

"Welcome aboard, Captain Leland. I must say I'm glad to see old Brumble trying to make a comeback. That ship must've taken up most of his savings. I hope it works out for him," the captain of the *Bellatrix* said by way of greeting. "Imagine pirates will think twice before attacking your ship."

Viktor smiled at his unsuspecting host. "Aye, she is formidable. She's been mistaken for a warship a couple of times. Tell me, Captain Jones, how fair the Colonies? I've only recently been recalled to these waters from the Indian Ocean."

"Of course, won't you join me in my cabin?" Jones grew suddenly cautious but tried to hide it.

"Lead the way, sir. I'll have my mate see to the mail exchange. We're bound for New Orleans."

"Oh." Jones pulled up short. "That is our destination as well. There's really no need to swap mail, then."

"Very well; the lads will be glad. We've rather a lot."

They continued on to the captain's cabin. Once the door was secured behind them, Jones turned to the man claiming to be Leland. "Tell me, sir; do your loyalties lie with the Crown or the Colonists who seek independence?"

"My loyalties are to my crew and myself, sir. I've little stomach for politics of any flavor."

Jones laughed nervously. "You almost sounded like a pirate, sir. Personally, I've no love for the Crown. They tax trade nearly to bankruptcy and offer little protection from brigands. Since the war in the Colonies began, some call it a rebellion and others call it a revolution, trade has been sorely restricted. Boston is blockaded, as are several other ports."

"I see. Well, I am well-versed in blockade running."

Jones poured two glasses of port. He gave Viktor a crafty smile. "I always suspected old Brumble was into smuggling."

"One turns a profit where one may." Viktor smiled back and made direct eye contact with Jones. The emerald glow of his eyes reflected in those of his victim.

"I am afraid I have not been completely honest with you, sir. My name is not Wayne Leland, nor am I in the employ of Brumble & Sons, although his sons do sail with me."

Jones laughed. "You are quite the wit, sir. Next, you'll be telling me you are the notorious Bloody Brandee."

"Damn, you are a clever bastard." He grinned wide enough to show fangs and released just enough of his hold on the man to allow a natural reaction. "Viktor Brandewyne, at your service, sir." He gave a mocking bow.

Jones paled and sat down hard. "Heaven help us," he whispered. "The stories of what you'd become are true."

"If you mean a vampire, then aye." He took a sip of the port and looked at the cup. "Not bad." A glance at Jones prompted him to add, "Drink your port, sir. You look too pale."

Obediently, the man downed his drink. The alcohol brought a flush to his face after drinking it so quickly. Shakily, he asked, "What do you plan to do with us?"

Viktor walked over to him, clapped him on the shoulder, and smiled down at him. "I feel generous today, Mr. Jones. You and your crew are free to go your way — just as soon as your passengers and those bolts of silk you're carrying are delivered to my ship." As an afterthought, he said, "Tell your crew pirates have been rumored to hunt the seas north of Cuba lately. You are sending the passengers and cargo on with me for their safe transport. I want you to head east after our transaction is complete."

Jones gulped in fear and nodded. "Of course, sir; th-thank you for sparing us."

Jean Beaujoulais recognized Viktor immediately. He looked askance at Captain Jones and noted the fear behind the man's smile. He'd thought the captain's joviality seemed a bit forced.

The moving of the cargo and himself didn't bother him so much. He felt it nice to get a bit of adventure before he left the world. In fact, if it hadn't been for Brandee, he never would have left his home to travel to the New World. He had hoped to see the private library the pirate had mentioned an acquaintance in New Orleans having.

Still, it troubled him to see the three young women travelling on the same ship being bundled over to the pirate vessel.

Careful to use the name Captain Jones had introduced him by, Jean approached Viktor. "Pardon me, Captain 'Leland,' may I have a word?"

179

The pirate raised an eyebrow at him but nodded and moved away from the bustle and over-curious ears. "It is good to see you again, *M'sieur* Beaujoulais. I surmised by your presence here you seek that collection I mentioned. I thought a personal escort and introduction might gain you safe entrance."

"I do appreciate that, sir, and you are correct about my goal. However, it troubles me you are taking these young women, as well."

"*M'sieur*, we are pirates. My crew has needs which have been denied for some time now."

Jean gave him a worried frown. "I fear for their survival, Captain." He still kept his voice low. "I have heard nightmare tales of *'demoiselles* taken by pirates and used so roughly they died."

Viktor nodded his understanding and patted the old man on the back. "Fear not, *m'sieur*. They shall be treated gently. The crew knows not to damage them or over-use them. I've some friends in New Orleans who will take them in and give them employment, if they so desire; or they can go their own way when we make port."

"The same friend with the library?"

"No." Viktor laughed and shook his head. "Jeorge's interests lie elsewhere. Celine and Angelique are a couple of the finest madams in all of the Colonies, and I've had most of them."

Jean sighed and shook his head. "Oh, for your youth and energy." He looked over at the women as they and their belongings were being carted to the pirate vessel. "I suppose there are worse fates. Captain Jones took quite a hefty sum to smuggle them out of Charleston before the fighting spread south."

Viktor smirked. "I may have to have a word with him about that, since he is handing them over into my care. Mr. Brumble will help you carry your things over to the *Incubus*." He gave a nod to the navigator and strode over to the packet ship's captain.

"*M'sieur* Beaujoulais, I did not expect to see you here," Zach said. "The Captain wants me to help you with your things."

"*Bon, bon*; but you might want to get some help. I brought a large portion of my books. My successor as school master had his own set of texts and some literature." Jean smiled at the look of resignation on the young man's face.

"Hey, Charlie! I need a couple of lads to help. Some of this is going to be heavy," Zach called.

"Aye, Zach! I'll send 'em right over."

Tamara A. Lowery

# Chapter 13

The vampire Guillaume met Viktor at the dock. Vik didn't find this surprising, since he knew Jeorge had assigned him as the pirate-turned-vampire's escort and to keep an eye on him while in his city.

"Guillaume; good to see you, man." He genuinely liked the local vampire. It didn't take him long to pick up that something was wrong, however. "What is it?" he asked low enough for only Guillaume to hear.

"I am forbidden to say why; but you should go." The vampire's gaze darted about nervously, as if looking for some watcher.

He shook his head. "Can't; I have business in this port which cannot wait. I need to pay my respects to Jeorge and then be about it. I also have someone to introduce to him, a former school master interested in his library."

Guillaume's eyes lost focus for a moment then cleared again. "He will receive you and your guest."

Viktor half-bowed. "Give him my thanks."

☠

He caught the scent a split second after the door opened. He hadn't expected *her* to be here. He whispered to Guillaume, "I think I know why you said I should go. *She* is here."

A brief flicker of fear in the vampire's eyes confirmed it.

Viktor's irritation grew, but he kept his expression nonchalant. He didn't fear Carpathia; but he didn't trust her, either.

He followed Guillaume to Jeorge's receiving room. Jeorge sat on the smaller chair rather than his customary throne. Instead, the Lady Carpathia occupied that place of eminence.

Viktor's breath caught despite his resolve. She wore her long black hair loose. Her eyes glittered like black diamonds in her ivory face. A white silk robe trimmed with black and red embroidery draped around her petite form and accented the curves of her body. He knew that body intimately, and a part of him ached for it despite her betrayal.

He recovered quickly and bowed at the neck, politely but not submissively. "Lady Carpathia; Jeorge."

"Captain Brandewyne," Jeorge said with genial neutrality. Vik wondered if he'd picked up on the tension.

Carpathia remained silent but nodded at him; her face a mask.

"I didn't see the *Lorelei* in port. Did you send Wormy off on an errand, or were you trying to hide your presence, Thia?" He decided to put her on the defensive.

Rather than answer him, she looked at Guillaume. "What is this one's name, Jeorge?"

"Guillaume, sired by Jerome."

"Ah, I remember Jerome. He was a troublesome one. Are you rebellious like your sire, Guillaume?"

He stared at the floor and said, "I have been told I am, my lady."

"Look at me when addressing me." Her voice held ice.

He looked up at her. Viktor saw him tremble in absolute terror.

"That is better. You were ordered not to speak of my presence here to anyone."

"I did no—."

She cut him off. "You tried to send our guest away. Why?"

"He is my friend." Anger colored his words, and his back straightened in defiance. "I know what you are, my lady, and I know why you seek out certain vampires."

"Oh; and why is that Guillaume?" She gave him an amused look, as if he were a puppy that had tried to imitate its human.

"You destroy them. You have a reputation for being relentless, and you have never failed to take down your chosen target. I fully realize had he heeded my warning it would only delay the inevitable."

"Then why bother with a warning?"

"I don't want to watch him die by your hand."

She stood and moved to stand in front of him. With a smile, she placed a hand on his cheek as if about to kiss him. "Fear not, Guillaume; you will not have to. You should never have presumed to know my mind or purpose."

Without further warning, she pulled him down into a kiss.

Viktor heard him utter a muffled scream and watched in contained horror as the vampire's body withered and shriveled. In a few seconds, nothing remained of Guillaume but a dry husk. Carpathia released him and let his body fall to the floor. It crumbled to dust upon impact.

She spared Viktor a glance and smiled knowingly. He cursed himself for letting her see his momentary fear.

Then he saw she turned her attention to Jeorge. He frowned. "He has not wronged you, Thia. Leave him alone."

"Oh, but he has; and he knows it, Viktor. He did not send word of your existence once he learned your true, unnatural nature."

Viktor laughed harshly. "I am no more unnatural than anyone else in this room."

"*Au contraire*," Jeorge said. "You are vampire, yet you are not undead. You walk in full daylight. You can eat human food. To a true vampire, that is very unnatural."

"Well put, Jeorge," Thia said. "I suspect there are some other oddities you have failed to reveal to me. You have had more dealings with our dashing pirate than I have, though I dare say not as intimate."

"He has far more power than one so young should have; so much so he frightens me. I admit I am unsure what the outcome would be, should he ever choose to challenge me."

She stared at him with an air of disgust. "If anyone is to be feared here, it is I."

Jeorge bowed his head. "I failed to inform you of his existence in a timely manner, my lady. I accept your judgement and your punishment."

Thia laughed, and a shiver ran down Viktor's spine. His status in this port depended on the outcome of this encounter. For a brief moment, he contemplated just taking her head and being done with it; but that course could cause more problems than it would solve.

"Dear Jeorge, you are too valuable here to destroy you. Still, you must be punished for your dereliction." She cast about the room, eyed his entourage, and tapped her lips with a manicured fingernail. Finally, she pointed at one of the vampires. "You, come here."

The blonde female approached her. Viktor recognized her as Memnette from his first encounter with the vampires of New Orleans. He saw naked terror in her eyes.

Carpathia placed a hand under Memnette's chin and forced her to meet her gaze. "What do you know of Viktor Brandewyne?" Power breathed through her words.

Memnette never spoke a word; but a keening moan passed her lips as her tormentor continued to pour power into her. Viktor silently contacted Belladonna to ask her about this. The siren let him know their enemy was stripping the information directly from the blonde vampire's mind.

He broke contact just in time to catch when the flow of power between the vampires reversed. Blood poured from Memnette's orifices, and her body collapsed in on itself; and still the earsplitting sound continued. The keening ceased only when the vampire lay reduced to a handful of blond hair and clothing lying in a puddle of thick black goo.

He barely had time to register the brief look of pain on Jeorge's face before Carpathia turned her attention to him. Viktor did not want her to touch him after what he'd just witnessed.

Her skin almost glowed from the power she'd just absorbed. Yet, the look she gave him was one of awe that bordered on fear. "You were able to hold a two-hundred-year-old vampire in thrall? How is that possible?"

He shrugged. "No one ever told me I couldn't."

She reached for him, and he stepped back. She frowned, a glimmer of hurt in her eyes. "Don't you want me, Viktor?"

"You know I do, Thia; I just don't trust you. Don't forget, the connection we shared briefly went both ways. I am fully aware of why your master sent you to find me."

Undeterred, she approached him again. "You also know of my deeper intentions. I give you my word I will not use my powers against you in this port."

189

He let her touch him and instantly regretted it. Her cool fingers against his skin brought back a flood of memories. Of all the other women he'd been with, only Belladonna could rival the place Thia held in his affections. Knowing she really had been sent to kill him, something he'd know long before Guillaume voiced it, made it hurt that much more."

He reached up and grasped her wrist gently but firmly. With some effort, he pushed her away from him and held her there. "No."

"You can't hide from me, Viktor. Your Childe is here. I can track you through her. I can use her to make you come to me."

He felt his eyes go hard and cold. He could even see their glow reflected on her ivory-white skin, giving it a greenish hue.

"Threatening Melanie is not a wise way to try to entice me into your bed, Carpathia." He felt her push with her power, and he pushed back. True fear shone in her eyes as he held her motionless with his will.

"Forgive me, Jeorge, but I fear Melanie is no longer safe here," he said but never took his gaze from Carpathia. "Melanie, go to the *Incubus*. My cadre will take you in and protect you. You will obey Hezekiah Grimm's orders and instructions until I return to the ship. Do not feed on the crew. Your sustenance will be provided."

190

Without a word, the young vampire fled the room.

Viktor felt Thia fight against him. He began to wonder how much longer he could hold her. "I will have to disappoint my friend who wanted to visit your library, Jeorge. It was not my intention that you lose any of your kiss; but you will understand if I do not offer to replace them."

Jeorge gave him a barely perceptible nod, out of Thia's line of sight, he noted.

"Stay," he told Carpathia. Without further preamble, he left. Once outside the house, he took to the sky.

Lady Carpathia remained motionless for a full hour after the pirate left. Jeorge remained with her but sent all the other vampires away. He didn't want to put any more of his kiss at risk once she broke free of Viktor's hold.

He did send for a couple of humans from his private cellar. He made sure that only the healthiest were sent up. He just hoped the meal would appease her wrath.

While he waited for her to recover, he pondered what had passed between her and Viktor. She'd mentioned a deeper purpose than the pirate's execution. A brief bond between them had been mentioned. Had she broken it; or, more frightening, had he? The fact the pirate had been able to enthrall the second most powerful vampire in the world led Jeorge to believe that Viktor had broken free from her.

He began to suspect Carpathia hoped to use Viktor in some way to overthrow her master and rule in his stead. He carefully kept this thought from his face. If she suspected he suspected her motives for not killing the pirate outright, she would destroy him.

Carpathia seethed with impotent rage. Viktor had seen her fear of him and his power. Worse, he had proved without a doubt he was more powerful than her— in front of witnesses.

She held no worries that Jeorge would try to use the knowledge against her. He knew well what the price for attempting to do so would carry. She planned to destroy any of his vampires who'd been present just as soon as she regained the ability to move.

What she could not fathom was how a relatively infant vampire could hold *her* in thrall.

For that matter, how was he still in existence? She felt him die when he drank the siren's blood; yet he'd stood there all too real and viable. Could it be she had finally met an intended prey who could not be destroyed? Was that why her master feared him enough to send her after him?

She needed to mend the rift between them somehow. If she hoped to survive, she needed to ally with the vampire she believed would emerge victorious from the inevitable confrontation between him and her master.

*Tamara A. Lowery*

# Chapter 14

Viktor found Celine waiting for him when he arrived at the brothel she and Angelique ran. She intercepted him in her charms and potions shop downstairs from the brothel.

"Granny wants to see you first thing in the morning."

"Good; that will make this a little easier." He took her hands and raised them to his lips then gave her a sad smile. "You need to increase your wards and do not accept any clients between sundown and sunrise for a while, pet."

"Jeorge has broken his agreement with you?"

He felt some relief she understood the warning. "No; but he has a guest far more powerful than him; and she is not very happy with me right now."

Celine paled and swayed a bit. "I knew I sensed a great dark power for some time now. How strong is she?"

"She and I are close to evenly matched."

"Wait; are you saying you are more powerful than Jeorge?"

"I am. He admits he fears me. I sent my daughter to my ship to protect her from Lady Carpathia." He had to catch her as her legs gave out beneath her. "Celine? Are you well?"

She trembled in his arms and shook her head. "Do not speak that name in this place. To do so is to give her power."

"I didn't know. I will be more careful, pet. Shall I carry you, or do you think you can walk?"

The Creole madam took a shaky breath and let it out. "I can stand. Go on up, Captain. I need to set special wards. I will fully close them after you leave. Please have Angelique invite you in when you return."

He understood her caution. Although he'd never required an invitation to enter anywhere, to cross a warded threshold without proper invitation would shatter the wards. She didn't want him to leave them vulnerable like that.

"You have my word." He bowed then turned for the staircase.

"*Merci.*" Celine set to gathering the items she needed from her store's inventory to set the wards.

At dawn, Viktor stepped out of Celine's shop. He instantly felt the wards she'd set slam shut behind him. A small, rebellious spark in his nature urged him to turn around and put those wards to the test. The moment passed.

Even as he stood there, he felt the glow of magic mute and blend with the ambient magic which permeated this port city. If he didn't already know the wards were there, he could have walked into them without suspecting their presence until they triggered. He smiled at Celine's skill and cleverness. Had she not hidden the wards, they would have served more as a challenge than a warning to Carpathia.

One thing he knew about the ancient vampire from his brief but intimate connection to her: she wouldn't hesitate to force lesser vampires to destroy themselves against the wards until the defenses were worn down enough for her to break them.

As he took to the air and flew toward the bayous, he fervently hoped his business with Gloribeau could be finished before dark returned.

Movement caught his eye when he alit on the supply dock. He looked around expecting to see Gloribeau but instead saw a gangly-legged youth with a shock of raven hair disappear along the catwalk to her stilt house. The lad appeared to be carrying a cane pole and a string of fish.

"It couldn't be —."

Viktor climbed the ladder to the catwalk and made his way to Glory's.

The aroma of food cooking greeted him when the Sister's house came into view. The cane pole leaned against the side of the shack. Even though he knew she expected him, he knocked at the door rather than barge in.

The boy opened the door. Viktor looked down into his own eyes looking back up at him. He marveled at how much the lad had grown in the relatively short time Glory had looked after him.

The boy seemed similarly stunned to see an older version of himself.

"Don't stand there gawping at each other," Gloribeau ordered as she came into the room from a rear door. The food aromas followed her. "Come in and sit down, Viktor Brandewyne. Get to know your son, Robert, while I finish cooking breakfast."

He nodded and stepped across the threshold. She turned and went back to tend the food. His eyes followed her movements with memories of shared passion and a reawakened longing.

When he'd first encountered Granny Glory, she had been the oldest crone he'd ever seen. After he'd helped her regain the portion of her magic which had been stolen by an ancient demon, she'd taken on this young, voluptuous form. He'd had the privilege of sharing her bed once and had been lucky or favored enough to have survived the experience.

"You are my Da?"

Robert's question drew his attention back to the boy.

"Aye, lad; I am."

"Granny says you are a pirate and a vampire, but not like the ones who tried to take me away from her."

Viktor's face darkened with his rage. Jeorge had agreed to leave the boy alone. "When did vampires come for you?"

"I don't remember it well. I was little."

"Jeorge only sent the one pair. His curiosity got the better of him. I dealt with them and made sure he got the message not to send any more," Glory said as she returned to the room. She set two platters down on the table. One held fish; the other held eggs scrambled with some sort of greens. "Now, eat. Then we'll discuss business."

The boy wolfed the food he dished onto his plate. Viktor smirked as he savored his own portion. He'd been much the same way at that apparent age.

Robert appeared to be in his early teens, but Viktor knew him to be only a few years old. Had the boy been human, he would barely be past the toddler stage. Apparently, merfolk had very short childhoods.

"That was delicious. Thank you, Gloribeau," Viktor said and pushed his plate away from him.

"Robert, clear away the dishes and go clean them. There's some leftover fish in the kitchen for you." She waited for the boy to leave before she looked at Viktor. "He is in danger here."

"I thought you said you dealt with the vampires."

"Not from them, at least not while he remains here." She stared him in the eye. For a moment, his surroundings faded completely from his perception. He felt the lure of her body, and his own responded to it. She broke the spell just before his lips could find hers.

"He is in danger from me."

He blinked at her. Why had he never picked up on it before? "You are a succubus."

She shook her head and sat back to give them both some distance from the other. "Not quite, although some of my powers are similar. I can drain a man's life-force through sex. That is one of the reasons I only shared my bed with you once. You can draw energy the same way. Our powers cancel each other out in that respect; but we would both become addicted to and obsessed with each other. Your son is fast approaching the point in his development where he will need to find a mate."

He quickly grasped what she hinted at. "I need to take him with me when I leave, then."

"There is something you must do first. Once you have, I will send him with you as well as give you the item you came here for."

"I'm not even going to ask how you know what I'm after." He chuckled and shook his head. "What is my task?"

"Deal with the Dragon's Daughter. Until she has been eliminated or neutralized, Robert will not be safe outside of my protection. She will hunt him down, just as she was sent to hunt you down."

He sighed and pinched the bridge of his nose. "It can never be easy, can it? You know she presents a special peril to me."

"I know she was sent to hunt you down and kill you."

"And yet here I sit. I know it too, but I also know why she hasn't tried to kill me yet. She knows I fathered

Robert after I became vampire. She is convinced I can reawaken her long dead womb and give her a child."

Glory frowned at him. "She has been dead for millennia; why would she want a child?"

"She wants freedom from her master. She wants ultimate power over all vampire-kind. She believes a child by me will give her the power she would need to accomplish those goals," he stated.

"Then you realize the danger. Why have you not dealt with her already?"

Viktor heard the reproach in her voice and answered honestly. "I love her."

She sat back and stared at him. She remained silent for some time. He patiently waited out her scrutiny.

Finally, she asked, "Have you had her blood or she yours?"

"I have only had her blood by proxy. I dealt with one of her human puppets, and she possessed him during the encounter. Belladonna's blood freed me from her spell. She has tasted my blood but has never bitten me. She wounded me slightly with a blade during our first encounter. Again, Belladonna helped me free myself. We made love, and I forced our combined magic into Thia. It made her body quicken briefly to life and it rejected the blood."

202

"You are one of the few beings who can still surprise me, Viktor Brandewyne. You are the only vampire ever to survive siren's blood."

"I think it is because she and I are linked."

"Quite possibly. Will you be able to do what needs to be done concerning this vampire?"

"I must. It will be hard; but it must be done."

*Tamara A. Lowery*

# Chapter 15

Belladonna picked up on Viktor's dark mood shortly before he arrived back at Celine's. She expected him to storm into the brothel bent on destruction; thus, it surprised her when she felt him call Angelique to the shop on the street level.

A short time later, he stood in the salon filling the room with a thunderous presence.

"How bad is it?"

"I have to eliminate the Dragon's Daughter then agree to bring Robert back with me." He stomped over to his favorite chair and dropped into it hard. His hand went absently to the humidor nearby and fished out a cigar.

Belle crinkled her nose. She'd never cared for the pungent tobacco smoke in enclosed spaces. Thankfully, Viktor didn't light the thing yet.

"You've known you would have to deal with her eventually, and I don't think you're that upset with the idea of returning Robert to his natural element. He should be close to mating age by now."

His look of incredulity caught her off guard. "He should just be past needing diapers. I have never seen a child grow so fast."

She laughed at him. "Viktor, he isn't human. Merfolk mature quickly as a matter of survival, males especially so. Just as with sirens, adult males are rare, and they will kill male offspring as soon as they find them. It is not easy for the females to hide from their mates."

He grumped at her, bit the end of the cigar off, spat it out, and lit the thing with the oil lamp. After a few deep draws on the burning tobacco, he blew out a long stream of smoke and said, "I still have the problem of eliminating Her as a threat. She and I are not exactly on speaking terms right now. Even if we were, I seriously doubt she would negotiate; nor would I trust her word."

Belle leaned against the wall and crossed her arms but raised one hand to tap her lower lip in thought. Viktor continued to smoke.

Suddenly, she stopped and straightened up with a wicked grin.

"What?" he asked.

"Have you had your mates report yet?"

"No; I came straight here."

"Jon-Jon mentioned the night watch had a female vampire, not Melanie mind you but one spouting tremendous power, try to come aboard last night. Your cadre forced the humans below deck and refused to grant her entry. They said she threw a tantrum and destroyed some very valuable cargo in a nearby warehouse."

"You think it was her?"

"Very possibly; she definitely wants to see you."

"And she can't board my ship without invitation, even though I am a vampire."

She nodded and her grin grew wider to reveal her true needle-like teeth. "I think I know a way to trap her, because as much as I'd like to kill her, that would be too risky."

"Too risky? Why?"

"She was sent. If you kill her, the one who sent her will know and send something worse. If you imprison her, that problem can be avoided."

"What would keep her from alerting her master to her imprisonment?" He sounded skeptical.

"Aside from her pride, the kind of prison I have in mind will block her from communication with her master. He may eventually check to see why she isn't responding, but I believe you'll be more than ready to face him by that time."

☠

They enlisted Celine's aide in obtaining what the siren needed to prepare the trap. Viktor, Grimm, and Jon-Jon carefully removed the mirrors from the ceiling of the main bedchamber of the brothel. Belladonna gathered holy water and powdered silver from the potions shop.

The pirates carted all of that out to the *Incubus*. While Grimm and Jon-Jon covered the windows of the captain's cabin with the mirrors, Viktor and Belle mixed the silver and holy water into a paste. They used their superhuman speed to paint between the joins of every plank and board in the walls, ceiling, and deck of the cabin.

They purposely left the door jamb free of the paint and only painted the edges of the solid door. Belle explained it would allow their prey to cross the threshold only while the door was open. For this same reason, she painted the inner handle.

Lastly, they hung heavy drapes to hide the mirrors from immediate view and drilled out a small knothole in the wall shared with the cabin boy's berth. This hole they left free of the special paint, as well.

When asked about the purpose of the hole, the siren realized Viktor still remained unaware of a very important ability their prey possessed.

"This is all about smoke and mirrors."

"Smoke and mirrors? What do you mean?"

"Have you ever noticed how Lazarus is just a smoky blob for a few moments when he changes form?"

He nodded. "Yes, and sometimes just before he appears when summoned. Are you saying she can do that, too?"

"I am. It is a rare talent among vampires, but I deduced she possessed it when I retrieved Robert from her cabin aboard the *Lorelei*. I could smell and sense her presence nearby, but the cabin door and the porthole were the only openings of any size for a solid body to pass through. However, the ceiling seemed lower than that of the passageway, and a few of the beams seemed widely spaced but showed no sign of being hinged."

He reached out and brushed a strand of hair away from her face and cupped her cheek. She saw wonder and pride in his eyes. "I keep forgetting how very clever and intelligent you are, pet."

For a moment, she forgot what they were talking about as he leaned in and kissed her.

The sound of Grimm clearing his throat brought them back to the present. "That's all well and good, lass; but you still haven't explained what the bloody hole is for. If this is supposed to be a trap, why leave her an escape?"

"The hole is the trap, Mr. Grimm, or rather the entrance to it. We just need some kind of container she can't escape from for her to flee into," Viktor said with a brief glance at the siren.

She gave him an almost imperceptible nod to confirm his reasoning. "And I have just the container."

"Go fetch it, pet."

Once she left the cabin, Viktor turned to his first mate. "Hezekiah, I'm going to need your help to seal the trap. Belle has a bottle of silvered glass. I want you to be the one to hold it to the other side of the hole."

"I'm more than glad to help you, Captain. I just don't understand why me in particular."

He clapped the man on the shoulder and smiled. "Other than Belle or I, you are the only one with the necessary speed to cork the bottle before she can escape. I have to be in here as bait. Belladonna's magic is too easily detected, so she won't even be on board. None of my cadre can handle the silver. It has to be you."

"I hope I am fast enough. Are you sure we'll only need to cork the bottle? Cork is spongy. She might be able to seep out through it," Grimm pointed out.

"I've still got some holy paint. I'll treat the cork with that."

Grimm stood and thought about it. "Right; it sounds like a good plan to me."

"Good man!"

*Tamara A. Lowery*

# Chapter 16

A very nervous Melanie accompanied by Thomas Brumble, returned to Jeorge's house about an hour after sunset. Viktor chose Thomas to escort her because he was the only vampire in his cadre with a respectable upbringing.

"Child, what brings you here? I thought your sire felt it wasn't safe for you," Jeorge asked, receiving them in the foyer mere moments after they'd entered.

"Captain Brandewyne sent me with a message for Milady. He sent Thomas Brumble as my escort."

"Brumble, isn't that the name the Captain introduced himself to you as?" He eyed the young vampire.

Thomas bowed. "Yes sir; I am the unfortunate whom the Captain impersonated to gain access to this lovely creature."

"Why child, I believe you have gained an admirer. Tell me, *M'sieur* Brumble, why do you call yourself an unfortunate?"

"I and my brother have been called to pay for our father's sins. Had he not been such a cruel bastard to all

213

who serve him, even we were not spared from his cruelty, I might have lived out my life as an honest sea captain and trader. Instead, I have been conscripted to piracy and eternal servitude to my Captain and my Hunger. Life used to be simple."

"A man who valued his mortality, what a curious creature." The female voice came from a side room and was soon followed by Lady Carpathia.

Thomas and Melanie turned to face her and made their obeisance. "Milady," they said in unison. They held their bow and curtsy as she circled them. Thomas remained motionless, but Melanie's form trembled at Thia's presence.

Finally, Thia stood in front of both of them. When she placed a hand under each of their chins, Melanie flinched a little. Thomas remained calm.

"You may rise."

They obeyed but kept their eyes respectfully downcast.

"I must say, Viktor has shown excellent taste in offspring. You are not what I would expect of a pirate, but then, you were conscripted as you said."

"Yes, milady."

She turned her attention to Melanie. "You may calm your fear of me, child. As your sire stated, harming you

214

would not serve to gain his favor or cooperation." The younger vampire visibly relaxed. "That is better," Thia continued. "Now what is the message Viktor sent me?"

"He wishes to apologize for his show of temper and to invite you to his cabin where he may make his apology properly and in person."

"Why could he not do so here?"

"Forgive me, milady," Thomas said. "The Captain does not like to perform to an audience. He thought the privacy of his cabin might be better suited to your needs."

She laughed, a sound that made all present shiver in mixed pleasure and fear. "Very well, I will accept his invitation. However, first I require a meal and entertainment. Jeorge, send for three of your healthiest stock. You all will dine with me. You and I will have one apiece; these younglings will share one."

He inclined his head to her. "It is done, milady. What manner of entertainment do you desire tonight?"

Her smile grew decidedly wicked, and Melanie felt her gaze like a smothering weight on her very being. "I should like to see how the dear captain's offspring perform together; after they have fed, of course."

"Perform together? Forgive me, milady," Thomas said, a confused frown on his lips, "I was trained in seamanship, not in the arts."

Melanie sent a silent cry for help to Viktor. She knew exactly what kind of performance Carpathia meant, and she knew the vampire's current mood to be very mercurial.

A thankful tremor went through her as she sensed him reach out to her companion.

Thomas' eyes widened briefly, and she thought he would have blushed if he'd already fed that evening. "Oh! That kind of performance; but Miss Melanie is a woman of breeding, not a common trollop. Why would you wish me to shame her like that?"

Jeorge laughed. "Did he tell you to say that?"

"No, sir; it is my honest sentiment," Thomas replied.

"It is very similar to what your Captain said the night he turned Melanie."

Carpathia stalked over to the younger vampires and circled them. She stopped in front of Thomas and trailed a delicately manicured finger down his chest to the waist of his breeches. She hooked the finger into the garment and looked up at him with sultry eyes. She gave a little tug and was rewarded with a groan from him.

# The Daedalus Enigma

"As I'm sure Viktor can tell you, even a noblewoman enjoys a good fuck, Thomas. Are you a good fuck?"

Melanie watched as his body straightened and his face took on an expression that made him resemble her sire. He reached down and removed Carpathia's hand from his clothing. When he spoke, she heard Viktor's voice come from his lips.

"Leave the boy alone, Thia. He is inexperienced. I, on the other hand, know exactly what I am doing."

Thia smiled. "I thought you might be eavesdropping, Viktor. I am impressed with your ability; I will leave Thomas alone now. He'll be of no use to me for a few hours anyway, once you leave his body. You really should leave it now and feed; or you will be too weak to receive me, as well."

He bowed over her hand and placed a kiss on her knuckles. "I will await you in my cabin."

As he sat in a nearby chair and abandoned Thomas' form, she turned her attention back to Jeorge. "I have decided to forego the entertainment. I will depart as soon as I've fed."

"As you wish, milady. Ah, dinner has arrived."

Melanie waited for the two older vampires to select their victims; then she took the remaining human by the

217

hand and smiled at him. The frightened man quickly fell to her gaze and visibly calmed. She led him over to where Thomas sat limply.

"Do you think you can eat?" she asked.

He managed a weak nod.

She brought the human over to him and held the victim's wrist to his mouth. She frowned when he could barely open his mouth. Clearly, he didn't have strength enough to bite. Part of her screamed for her to drink the human and just leave Thomas where he lolled; but he'd taken merciless taunts from the rest of the Captain's cadre for shielding her from their advances. She refused to let him languish at Carpathia's mercy.

Quickly, she tore the human's wrist open with her thumbnail and forced the blood which spurted out into her companion's mouth. At first, blood oozed from the corners of his mouth; then she saw his throat work as he swallowed the sustaining liquid.

When he regained enough strength to grasp the man's arm and feed in earnest, she released the human and licked the blood off her hand.

All too soon, she heard Carpathia declare it was time to escort her to the Captain.

# The Daedalus Enigma

Viktor greeted his guest and his young vampires at the dock. Thomas' rapid recovery pleased him as much as the youngster's ability to hide it from observing eyes.

He offered Carpathia his arm; she took it. Her power vibrated down his arm and threatened to overwhelm him. Careful not to let it show in his demeanor, he forcibly reminded himself this creature had been sent to hunt him down and execute him.

The fact she had an ulterior motive to use him to unseat her master from power did not help her case in his eyes. He valued his personal liberty above nearly everything, and he'd be damned if he'd let her get away with trying to use or manipulate him.

He kept his eyes on her but said, "Melanie, pet, take Thomas back to his berth then go to Mr. Kerns for something from the larder. He'll see you get a proper meal." He turned his full attention to Carpathia. "Join me, milady? I would like to make my personal apology and discuss your plans concerning me. I think we can come to some sort of understanding."

"Lead the way, Captain Brandewyne."

Just before they reached his cabin door, she observed, "Your pet siren does not seem to be on board."

"Given how territorial and prone to jealousy she is, I thought it best to send her out to restock my larder. She will not return with her catch until sunrise or later." He opened the door.

She looked inside. "You covered your windows? I thought you were immune to sunlight."

He gave her his most wicked smile. "I wasn't sure how long we wanted to take. You are powerful enough to stay active after sunrise, I'm sure."

She chuckled, and he couldn't suppress a shudder. "Oh Viktor, you naughty boy; will you invite me in?"

He stepped through the door and bowed to her then extended his hand. "Lady Carpathia, please come in."

She stepped across the threshold, and he closed the door. When he turned back to her, she had already crossed to his bed and shed her dress in transit. She lounged back on the bed and gave him an inviting look.

He groaned in appreciation of the sight and almost went to her right away. Memories of the feel of being inside her body washed over him, and his body reacted to the call of hers. He managed to hold himself in check, though. He could not afford to let her get her hooks in him again.

When she glanced over at the draperies, it gave him the respite he needed. "Morning is far away, Viktor. Let us make love in the star light."

He chuckled and pulled the cord which opened the drapes. At the same time, he shielded his eyes a bit. The Elder's Stone sat propped in a candlestick. The light from its reaction to her magic flared and reflected in the mirrors which covered the windows.

Carpathia screamed in pain. Her skin began to smolder in the light. Viktor felt the force of her magic drop drastically about the same time the light faded back to just what emanated from the candles and oil lantern.

He finally saw completely past her glamour when he saw her reflection. A shriveled, mottled, creature that barely resembled a woman lay on his bed. She looked like the embodiment of Hunger.

Some deep part of his soul cringed, not for the hideous sight before him, but for being forced to reduce her to such a state. He truly did love her, even seeing her like this. He allowed her to see the very real pain in his eyes. "I am sorry, Thia; I had no choice. The knowledge of your betrayal is the only thing which gives me the strength to do this. I love you, but I will *never* serve you or your cause."

She shrieked and rushed at him in rage. "I will do what I should have done the first time I met you! You will die for this!"

He stood his ground and let her claws tear at his shirt. He'd prepared for this reaction. A smirk curved his lips when she uncovered the emerald-encrusted golden cross.

She gave a blood-curdling scream as she pulled back the blackened claw the blessed object had reduced her hand to.

She flew about the cabin frenzied. He could see the terror and panic on her face as she began to realize the nature of the trap.

"Ha!" she cried in triumph. She'd found the unpainted knothole.

He watched as her body dissolved into smoke and poured through the hole. "Now, Mr. Grimm!" he cried the moment the last bit of smoke vanished.

# Chapter 17

The next morning, Viktor flew back into the bayous taking the silvered bottle with him. He landed at the supply dock but found no one there to greet him. Even the flambeaux stood unlit.

He wondered briefly if he should have paid Celine a visit in order to send a message to Gloribeau first. Still, the Sister had done nothing to impede his approach. He knew she stayed aware of all goings on in her territory. By her own admission, she was the oldest and most powerful of her kind.

He mounted the ladder to the catwalk and made his way to her stilt house. Robert answered his knock.

Viktor almost felt like he was looking in a mirror. The lad had grown and aged in the short time to the appearance of a youth on the cusp of manhood. He still hadn't filled out or sprouted facial hair, but otherwise he was a perfect image of his father at about the age Viktor had captured his first ship.

"Hello Da."

"Robert." He nodded at his son then looked past him into the structure. "I have done what Gloribeau required of me. Where is she?"

A look of pain crossed the lad's face. "She told me to wait here for you. She said it wasn't safe for her to be around me; she left. What did I do wrong?"

Viktor stood stunned by the question. Although he'd sired several children over the years, he'd never taken on a parental role with any of them. He had no idea how to comfort a child. Even though Robert appeared to be in his late teens, Viktor knew he was only about four years old.

"You have done nothing wrong, lad. She spoke to me of this; I just don't think she expected it to happen this soon. She has hidden to protect you from her magic."

"I don't understand. She taught me about magic. Why would hers be dangerous to me?"

"Let's go in and sit down; I'll try to explain it to you." Vik sighed.

Obediently, the boy did as told. Viktor sat opposite him and fervently wished he had some rum on hand. He decided for a blunt and honest approach to the subject.

"How much do you know about what you are, Robert?"

"I know my mother was a mermaid and that you are my Da and a vampire."

"But you are not a vampire." The boy shook his head, and Viktor continued, "You are a merman. Because of that, you have matured much faster than a human child."

"How much faster?"

"You've grown in four years to a point a human wouldn't reach until sixteen."

Fear shone in the boy's eyes. "Does that mean I'll grow old and die as quickly?"

Viktor shook his head and smiled. "No, I don't think so; but we can ask Belladonna when we get back to my ship. She'll know."

Robert seemed to accept that and got back to the subject; a trait Viktor recognized all too well. "Does my rapid growth have something to do with Granny Glory's magic being dangerous to me?"

"Yes; you are close to the stage where you will discover mating. If you are anything like me, you'll like it a lot and want to do it as often as possible. Part of Glory's magic is to feed on that kind of energy. You are powerful enough to survive her for a while, but she is addictive. I have been with her once, and I yearn to be with her again; but I know it isn't safe for either her or me to let that happen again. We both feel it best you never get a taste of her that way."

Robert gave him a thoughtful look as he digested the information. After a few moments, his eyes lit up. Viktor lifted an eyebrow.

"You will take me to the sea? I want to go swimming! Granny never would let me swim here." The last comment was followed by a pouting frown.

Viktor laughed and clapped his son on the back. "I may even jump in with you, lad! Can't remember the last time I enjoyed a good swim. Now, go on to the supply landing and wait for me. I need to find Gloribeau and finish my business with her."

The boy wasted no time heading out the door with a grin.

Once Robert was out of sight, Viktor circled around to the back of the stilt house. As he'd suspected, another catwalk manifested. He followed it to a deep pool on an isolated hammock of land. The last time he'd gone down this catwalk it had led to another stilt house.

The water of the black pool mounded. A form rose to the surface and Gloribeau, eldest of the Sisters of Power stepped onto the end of the catwalk.

226

Viktor had to clamp down hard on his will in order to keep from taking her right there. She gave him a sad smile.

"You handled that well with Robert. I am impressed."

He nodded in acknowledgement of her praise. He tried to take a step back and found he could not bring himself to do so. "Your lure is almost overwhelming, Glory. Is this why you hid from the lad?"

"In part, yes. His magic calls to mine; more so, because I have tasted yours. With both of you so close, it is hard for me to control it. I have never had a need to dampen it before."

"Then I will keep this brief and have myself and the lad out of here."

"You have dealt with the Dragon's Daughter?"

He nodded and pulled out the silvered bottle which contained Carpathia's essence. "She has been contained. The silver blocks her powers."

She took the bottle from him and looked it over. "I see you treated the cork with silver, as well. That was wise." She looked up at him. "Tell me, what made you decide to entrap her rather than kill her?"

"I acted on Belladonna's advice. This also keeps Thia's master from sending more hunters for the time being."

"Yes, he made her; he would know if she perished." She saw the look he gave her. "Oh, I know her master. I have not met him, but I have seen him in my scrying; all of the Sisters have." She turned her attention back to the bottle. Without warning, she flung it into the pool.

A few moments passed; then it rose back to the surface. A fountain of black water lifted it up, and Gloribeau retrieved it. Viktor saw black muck now covered it and gave it a pottery appearance. The only silver still visible formed a dragon and scythe pattern identical to the tattoo which identified any member of the order of the Daughters of the Dragon.

By the time she handed it back to him, the new covering reached the hardness of stone.

"No blow can ever break this now, and only the one who corked the bottle can uncork it. Keep this with you, Viktor Brandewyne. You will have need of it in the future. Now gather up your son and go."

She turned and stepped back into the pool. She disappeared beneath the surface without so much as a ripple to mark her passage.

Viktor had to use vampiric speed to return to Glory's stilt house. The catwalk began to vanish beneath his feet the moment he turned away from the pool.

He peeked into the dwelling to make sure Robert hadn't returned. The boy wasn't there, but a sea bag and sealed letter lay on the table. Neither had been there before.

Viktor picked up the letter and saw it was addressed to him and had a lump in it. He slipped it inside his shirt, hefted the sea bag, and headed to the supply landing.

Robert looked up as Vik descended from the catwalk. Once down the ladder, he tossed the bag to the boy, who deftly caught it.

"Where's your boat?" Robert asked.

"Didn't bring one. Loop that drawstring over your shoulder and hold onto my waist."

The boy did as told, but confusion filled his eyes. He gasped as Viktor launched into flight. His grip tightened briefly when they rose above the treetops then relaxed some.

The father looked down to see a grin and eyes alight with delight and wonder on his son's face. He felt a matching grin spread on his own.

"Here we go!" Vik whooped and soared toward the open water sparkling in the distance.

All too soon, the flight ended. Viktor alit safely on the quarterdeck of the *Incubus*.

# Chapter 18

Stunned silence greeted them from some of the latest additions to the crew. They hadn't known about Robert's existence. Even the pirates on deck who had known of him showed shock at his arrival. The last time they'd seen him, over two years ago, he'd been a toddler.

"Is that Robert?" Grimm asked as he approached the pair. "Damn, he's grown! Looks a lot like you did back when old Billy Black talked me into signing on with ye, Captain."

"Who are you? You look familiar," the boy said.

"Robert, this is Mr. Grimm, my first mate."

"Hello, Mr. Grimm."

"Welcome aboard, lad. Last time I saw you, we took you to live with Granny Glory. You'd only started to walk. So, you've decided to join the crew?"

"Granny sent me away. Da says she wants to protect me from her magic now I'm nearly old enough to mate."

Grimm shot Viktor a look the vampire could easily read.

"Hezekiah, take him to settle in with the crew. I need to go talk to Belle."

The first mate nodded. "Aye, 'tis best to get that done quickly." He turned his attention back to the boy. "Come along, lad. Let's find you a berth and introduce you to the crew. After that, we'll see if there's anything good to eat in the galley."

"Oh, I hope there's some fish!"

As his first mate led his son off, Viktor reached out along his bond with the siren. After a moment's concentration, he knew she would meet him in his cabin.

"How much do you know about the merfolk?" Viktor hit her with the question the moment she shut the door behind her.

Belle didn't hesitate. "Nearly everything there is to know; why?"

"Do you know how fast their young develop?"

She thought about it for a few moments. "Hmm, gestation for a mermaid usually lasts fourteen months or so. They have a live birth rather than lay eggs. The young usually reach sexual maturity at about ten years old."

"So, he's aging faster than normal, even for a mer," he muttered distractedly.

The comment piqued her curiosity and attention. "Are you talking about Robert? How much has he grown, and what has Glory said about it?"

"She sent him back with me. You can see for yourself."

"He's here now?"

Viktor gave her a look of worry and suspicion. "You didn't know? I'd have thought you'd have scented him by now."

"With that rancid troll in the rigging, it's a wonder I can smell anything. Your damn cat's piss would be an improvement over that stench!" she said with a growl.

He laughed. "Aye, Sniff does seem a bit riper than usual. Perhaps I should insist he bathe."

"Make sure he uses soap and burns those rags, too." She shuddered with revulsion. Viktor's laughter held a tone of malicious glee.

Once he'd sobered, she asked, "Why did Glory send him back? She's only had him a couple of years."

"Like I said, he's growing faster than normal. Even Grimm said he looks like I did when I first became a captain. I was only seventeen."

Belle felt her eyes go wide. "That could be a problem."

"Aye, I'd a feeling you'd say that. Did you know Glory can feed on sexual energy?" She saw he watched her carefully when he asked that.

"I suspected, but I wasn't sure. Some of our powers are very similar. So, she sent him away to keep from fucking him."

Viktor winced, surprisingly. "Aye."

"I give you my word to control myself, but I need to see him as soon as possible." Even as she made the promise, she hoped she'd be able to keep it.

"Grimm is showing him around. I'll send Jon-Jon to fetch him."

Viktor sat at his desk with a glass of blood-brandy mix. He sensed Jon-Jon's approach to his cabin a few moments before the knock came. Belladonna leaned back against the front edge of the desk facing the door. He noted she'd been careful not to block his view.

"Enter."

Jon-Jon pushed the door open and ushered the young merman in. Robert's attention still rested on the hulking, tall, tattooed pirate escorting him.

"What happened after the alligator pulled Da under?" the boy asked enthusiastically.

"Mr. Jon, what wild tales have you been spinning?" Vik barked with a tone of amusement in his voice to let his second mate know he wasn't really put out.

"Just tellin' him about the adventure old Granny Glory sent you on."

"Da, did Granny really used to be a scary old woman?" Robert held a look of disbelief on his face.

"When I first met her, she was the oldest looking thing I'd ever seen; she is still scary, though."

The boy nodded his agreement on the last statement; then he finally noticed the siren. He peered at her as if looking through her. He sniffed the air; a slow, almost leering smile spread on his face. Viktor recognized it as an echo of his own smile.

Belladonna stiffened and gripped the edge of the desk hard enough to make the wood creak. Viktor silently reached out to her along the blood bond they shared. *"Easy, pet,"* he thought at her.

*"I will not be able to stay aboard as long as he is here,"* came her mental reply.

"Who are you?" Robert asked. He'd move closer while the vampire tried to calm the siren. He reached out a hand to touch her. Vik could swear he looked taller.

"No!" Belladonna moved with inhuman speed to the window casements. Everyone present caught a glimpse of her true, needle teeth and golden eyes; then she dove out the window.

"Well, that was unexpected. Are you all right, lad?" Viktor saw his son wore a hurt expression.

"What did I do wrong? Am I that repulsive?"

Jon-Jon grinned and clapped him on the shoulder. "You were too pretty for her, lad; and you look too much like your da."

Viktor smiled at his son. "You've done nothing wrong, Robert. Belladonna left because she was frightened she might hurt you." He knew it was only half the truth; but the boy didn't need to know she also feared further enslaving herself.

Robert cocked his head and seemed to consider his father's words. "Is her magic the same as Granny's? They smell similar; but she smells salty. I like it."

"Aye, they are similar in some respects. She was also afraid she'd be tempted to eat you. You are a merman; she is a siren. Your mother's kind are her favorite prey. She didn't want to hurt you, because you are my son."

This revelation seemed to jog the boy's memory. "Oh, I just thought of something I overheard Granny mutter to herself."

"What was that?"

236

"She mentioned something about magic not being enough; that I'd have to learn how to defend myself against the people and things which would hurt me."

"She mentioned something like that to me, as well, when I took you to her after your mother died. You are of a size to learn now. Mr. Grimm, Mr. Jon, and I will teach you how to fight as well as basic seamanship."

The boy's face lit up. "Thank you, Da!" He ran to Vik and hugged him about the waist.

Viktor felt a strange expression cross his face as he awkwardly returned the hug and patted his son on the head. A glance over at Jon-Jon showed the large pirate giving intense interest to a chart tacked to the wall.

When Robert released him, Viktor smiled down at him and nudged him toward the door. "Off with you, now."

Jon-Jon turned and waved to the boy. "C'mon, Rob. Have I told you about the time —."

The door closed and muffled the pirate's words. Shortly, a burst of laughter rang out. Viktor smiled and shook his head.

He reached out to the siren through their bond. *"Are you all right, pet? I felt your panic."*

He let out a breath he hadn't realized he'd been holding when she responded. He'd half expected her to block him out.

*"I had to distance myself or break my vow to behave."* Her mental voice came clearly, which meant she was still close to the ship. *"Dammit, Viktor; his pull is almost as strong as yours. I couldn't let him touch me. If he could bewitch me as a babe, he could completely enslave me now."*

*"What do you suggest I do, Belle? I can't take him back to Glory, and Celie has her hands full with Hezekiah's wife and twins. I damn sure wouldn't trust Paella with him, either."* Frustration began to grow in his tone.

Silence came from her end; but he sensed she was merely giving the matter serious thought. Finally, she replied, *"He needs to join his own kind. He'll reach sexual maturity in another month or two, going by what I sensed from him. I will hunt up a mermaid pod for him to join. The tricky part will be to herd them to the ship."*

*"Thank you, Belladonna. My mates and I will do our best to teach him how to defend himself in the meantime."*

Belatedly, Viktor remembered the letter Glory left for him. He'd set it in the cupboard shortly after coming

238

to his cabin, but he'd become preoccupied with the matters concerning his son.

He retrieved it and poured another cup of his blood-brandy mix. He sat back in his chair and broke the seal on the letter. As he opened it, a small carved piece of jet tumbled into his hand.

A small sense of relief washed over him. The business with Carpathia and Robert had distracted him from the main purpose of his visit. He felt grateful Gloribeau had not forgotten. That would have meant another trip into the bayous to correct the oversight.

Given Glory's state when they parted, he had serious doubts about his ability to leave her presence again.

He shook those thoughts off and concentrated on the letter.

*Viktor,*

*For your sake, you should not return to my bayou for a long time, probably at least a decade. You are too much of a temptation to me right now.*

*Power balances are shifting, and you are the pivot point. It would be wise for you to refuse the beds of any of the other Sisters. They all sense the changes and will try to use you to tip the balance in their favor.*

*You cannot allow this.*

239

*The time for us to diminish has almost come at last. For you to do what you were born to do, it must be so. Soon, you will discover this purpose.*

*Know that you will always have my love and friendship.*

*Gloribeau*

He sat in silence for some time. Finally, he downed the contents of his cup, folded the letter carefully, and put it and the puzzle box piece in the locked chest alongside the puzzle box and the pieces he'd gotten from Venoma and Dorada.

Over the next three weeks, Robert became the favorite of the entire crew. He learned every lesson put to him with amazing speed. His reflexes were as uncanny as those of his father.

Jon-Jon soon found himself outmatched at wrestling the lad. Robert learned quickly how to avoid or wriggle out of holds. He even managed to pin the larger man a few times.

Viktor and Grimm took turns teaching him to fight with edged weapons. Both proved able to hold their own, but by the third week, Robert's skill had improved enough to present them with a real challenge.

# The Daedalus Enigma

Viktor relished sparring with his son. The boy's skill, speed, and reflexes made him proud in a way he'd never felt before about any of the various children he'd sired over the years.

☠

"Ho Sniff! A word with ye!" Grimm hollered up into the rigging.

The putrid, overripe aroma of unwashed pirate preceded the legless rigger by several feet. Grimm fought not to wrinkle his nose. The stench proved enough to purge any guilt from his mind for what he was about to do to the man who once saved his life.

"Ho, Mr. Grimm, what be the word?" Sniff asked as he dangled just above the deck. His leather prosthetic nose hung by its strap about his neck. A patch covered an empty eye socket. A single bright hazel eye peered out from the grime that covered his bald, toothless head.

Grimm gave a single nod and said, "Captain's orders."

Two of the larger members of the crew wearing scarves over their lower faces stepped up and grabbed Sniff by the arms. They took the struggling man toward the hatch nearest the galley.

Sniff managed to crane his head around to see where they were headed. Jon-Jon stood by a large metal tub filled with steaming water. The giant of a man held a scrub brush and a cake of soap. Sniff bean to scream, curse, and struggle in earnest.

"Acid; it's acid, I tell ye! Don't put me in there! There'll be nothin' left of me but me bones!"

"Strip him," Grimm ordered.

"Got all we can do just to hold 'im, Mr. Grimm," one of the masked pirates said.

"Lemme go, ye rank bastards!" Sniff yelled and squirmed. If he'd had whole legs, he might have had leverage enough to get loose. Grimm had to admit his friend was a ferocious fighter.

"Sniff, enough! You reek to high heaven, man. The Captain has ordered you bathed. Now stop resisting or I'll be forced to cut off your rum rations."

"Mr. Grimm, I thought ye were my friend."

"I still am, you lout. I spoke out against keelhauling you to let the barnacles scrape off the worst of the filth first."

Sniff made a sour face at him as Jon-Jon cut the rigger's rancid rags off. "Thank ye so much. I'd rather be drowned than boiled alive."

Grimm held his hand up in a staying motion just as they were about to dump Sniff in the tub. "Don't put him in the water —."

"Oh, thank ye, Mr. Grimm!"

He cut his friend's excited relief short. "Put him in like that and you'll have a tub of mud within minutes. It takes too long to heat that much water. Just use the dipper to get him wet; then use the brush and soap on him. If we run out of water before he's clean, we'll just lower him over the side to rinse him off. Shouldn't kill too many fish that way."

Screams and curses followed Grimm as he turned and headed for the helm.

Viktor turned from teaching Robert how to read weather signs to smirk at Grimm. "Sounds like it's going well."

"As well as can be expected. Never met a man that dead set against a bath." Grimm chuckled. "Mr. Jon already knows to burn the rags and give him fresh. Had to cut 'em off him."

Vik laughed and walked over to the rail to look down on the quarterdeck. Robert followed. "Don't take it so hard, Sniff! Belle requested you be bathed."

"Well, if that be the case, Cap'n, I'll let 'em scrub me pink for the lass," Sniff called back.

Viktor sensed the relief from the three pirates on scrub duty.

"Da! He's enormous! Will mine get that big?" Robert blurted at the sight of the naked rigging rat.

Vik and Grimm both burst into hearty laughter. Viktor clapped his son on the back and grinned. "Probably not, son. Very few men can match Sniff in size. I admit I don't."

"Aye," Grimm said with tears of mirth in his eyes, "the shame of it is the good Lord gave such a magnificent gift to a man few females would willingly touch."

Jon-Jon hollered up from the quarterdeck, "We've got him as clean as we could. We'll lower him over the side to rinse off."

Viktor nodded his assent and watched as Jon-Jon slipped a rope harness around Sniff under his arms. The three scrubbers then helped the legless man over the rail at the cargo net/ladder.

About that time, a dissonant keening sound began to grow to starboard. Vik looked in that direction and saw a frenzied churning headed toward the ship. Figures jumped in the surf as if fleeing from whatever formed a single wake behind them.

He sensed a familiar presence at the edge of his perception. *"Welcome back, Belle. I see you found some mermaids."* He let a wry tone color his mental voice.

*"Have the boy strip. Legs transforming to a tail while wearing pants is uncomfortable,"* came her terse mental reply.

"Da, what are those? They sound frightened."

"Mermaids, and they are. Belladonna is chasing them. She is their natural predator."

Robert seemed to grow agitated at that. "Can't you make her stop? What if she catches one?"

Viktor looked at his son and sighed. "Robert, one of the reasons we've taught you various types of fighting is so you can protect yourself from predators like sirens, not just against humans. Belle herded these mermaids here for you to join them. I don't know if she'll take one as prey or not, but if she does, she will kill and eat the mermaid. It's what she does and what she is."

He saw the torment in his son's eyes, and a small part of him wished he could shield the boy from such harsh realities. He puzzled briefly over that impulse. It was very unlike him. In the end, he shook it off. Robert was about to enter a very perilous environment. Better he should see the dangers for what they were, if he were to have any hope of surviving.

Viktor satisfied himself with knowing he'd given the young merman the tools and knowledge he needed to face what he had to.

He watched as Robert's torment changed to determination. The mermaids had nearly reached the ship. "You say the siren is bringing them to me, Da?"

"Aye."

"Then I have to protect them. They are mine."

Viktor grasped his son by the arm and let him see the pride and approval in his eyes. "You'll want to shuck out of those clothes. They'll only be a hindrance in the water."

Robert nodded his understanding and stripped off the shirt and breeches. He moved quickly to the rail, climbed up on it, and dove over the side.

Apparently, some of the mermaid pod had approached submerged and much faster than Viktor thought. Several surrounded Robert shortly after he surfaced; their fear of the siren forgotten. The rest of the pod joined them and surrounded the ship.

He saw no sign of Belladonna.

He felt grateful none of the mers started to sing or cavort. The fact Grimm had doled out portions of the special rum helped. Viktor had ordered the precaution in anticipation of the mermaids' arrival. The liquor tainted with his blood kept the pirate crew in line and ensured none would fall prey to the mermaids' lure.

"Oi, me lovely! I've got somethin' y'can nibble on!" Sniff's voice rose from near the water. He'd forgotten Jon-Jon still had the rigging rat lowered over the side to rinse him off.

Vik went to the starboard rail and peered over. He and Grimm, who'd gone to investigate with him, grinned at the sight. A golden-haired mermaid had wrapped her arms around Sniff's neck and impaled herself on his cock.

A few moments later, Belladonna surged from the water, buried talons into the side of the ship, and wrapped the other taloned hand around the mermaid's throat. Viktor saw the mermaid's body grow rigid; then the siren flung her prey up over the rail onto the quarterdeck.

"I will not have your spawn contaminating my food supply, troll," Belle growled at a terrified Sniff. She then swarmed up the net ladder hand-over-hand. By the time she reached the rail, her tail had reformed into legs.

She swung over to the deck and landed nimbly next to the mermaid. None of the pirates dared approach the pair. Terror painted the mermaid's features, yet she uttered no sound and remained motionless.

Belladonna crouched over her but did not touch her. Instead, she held one hand above the mer's throat and the other over her abdomen.

Viktor saw the siren had retracted her talons, and he felt the unmistakable tingle of a spell being cast.

Suddenly, the mermaid shrieked and doubled over in pain. The siren stepped back, leaving a clear path to the railing. The mermaid moved surprisingly fast and dragged herself to the rail and over it. A trail of bloody slime marked her path.

Belle, her features fully human again, turned and stalked up the stairs to the bridge in all her naked glory.

Viktor knew since he shared a deep mental bond with the siren, but Grimm had to ask. "Why didn't you eat her? I thought mermaids were your favorite prey."

She shot the first mate a look of pure disgust. "I wasn't about to eat that one; Sniff had his cock in her."

"Have the riggers aloft, get Sniff back on the boat, and let's weigh anchor. It's a long voyage to Tierra del Fuego," Viktor ordered.

# Chapter 19

Lazarus soared in raven form several hundred feet above the sea's surface scouting for prizes. It took a lot to keep the crew of the *Incubus* fed, healthy, and preferably wealthy.

He'd already reported two potential prizes just north of Cartagena. As he headed east, he felt a familiar presence. He altered his course slightly north to investigate.

A few hours later, he spied a lone ship below him. He circled down for a better look and recognized the lines of the *Shining Star* right away.

He sent the image to Viktor and heard his mental chuckle and reply. *"Enjoy yourself, Jim. These two will have us busy for a while."*

With his captain's blessing, he glided down to the deck of the ship. Sure that no one could see him, he transformed from raven to black cat.

He picked a perch atop some casks netted down to the deck to observe the activity aboard the ship. It gave him a clear view of most of the quarterdeck, the aft castle, and the fo'c's'le. It also kept him out of the way of the sailors. He'd learned some time ago about keeping his tail and paws out from under foot.

He scanned the activity, hoping for the odd finger amputation. All it took was someone a little careless with a line or too much slack and a sudden burst of wind. If he could just procure a tidbit of human flesh, he could use it to take his human form and pay Samantha a visit that night.

It surprised him to see her on the quarterdeck. She sat on a coil of rope facing him. In her hands she held a marlin spike, which she used to meticulously separate the cords of the end of another rope.

She wore a shirt and breeches and kept her golden hair short, but he could tell she no longer tried to hide her gender. For that matter, he didn't recognize most of the sailors on board. He guessed the captain had changed out the crew before allowing her to reveal her true identity.

On impulse, he leapt down and padded over to her. She didn't notice him right away, so he began to bat at the loose strands from the rope end. The ploy succeeded in getting her attention.

"Scamp! Stop that," she said with a laugh. When she tried to pull the rope free, he bit into the end and tugged. She put down her marlin spike, picked him up by the scruff of the neck, and tugged on the rope. "Let go!"

250

In response, he held on tighter and purred. She tried to pry his jaw open. He released the rope, wrapped his forepaws around her wrist, and bit her finger gently. He made sure not to pinch or break skin, and he kept his claws sheathed.

His purr grew louder as he tasted her skin. He released her from his jaws, licked her hand, then rubbed his face against it. She laughed and cradled him in her lap.

"Who is this fine fellow who's so demanding of attention?" a male voice asked with a note of amusement.

Lazarus opened his eyes to see who dared interrupt his pleasure. In seconds, his ears laid back, his pupils dilated, and his fur stood on end. Smiling down at him was a man who could have been his double when he was still human.

"Ow!" Sam's cry of pain brought him out of his stunned state. Quickly, he retracted his claws from her arm and licked the wounds clean. He gave her an apologetic *murr*.

She stroked his fur and said, "It's all right, kitty. Britt didn't mean to startle you."

He leaned into the petting and looked back at the strange man. He wondered why that name sounded so familiar to him. He found it eerie to look at his own face without the benefit of a mirror. Who was this man?

"I don't recall seeing this one before," Britt said and reached a hand down.

Lazarus tensed, prepared to claw or bite, but the man held his hand with the back toward him rather than trying to pet him. Curious, he stretched his neck and sniffed at the appendage. Samantha continued to stroke his fur in a soothing manner.

A burst of images flashed through his head at the scents he got from the man: a small boy, a dead woman, a man dragging an older boy away. It took him a moment to sort the information out enough to realize the images were memories, painful memories.

He turned and tucked his face against Sam's stomach.

"I'd almost swear he was the little thief who stole my locket; but I haven't seen that cat in a few years. He can't be the same one," she said.

"What locket was that?" Britt picked up the rope and Sam's marlin spike and continued where she'd left off.

"It had miniatures of my brothers. I wish I still had it. I don't want to forget what they look like." Her voice took on a sad, tired tone. "It was all I had of them."

"You miss them, don't you." Britt made it more a statement than a question.

"Those are ready to splice now. Do you remember how I showed you?" She avoided answering.

He nodded and picked up the rope she'd prepared earlier. Methodically, he began to braid the two ropes together. "I still miss my little brother. Sometimes, I wish I could go back in time and save him and my mother."

"What happened to them?" She sounded grateful for the change of subject.

Lazarus listened more out of contented complacency with the attention he was receiving than out of any curiosity. Although, the similarity of subject matter to the faint memories Britt's scent had triggered did pique his curiosity a little.

"The same she-vampire who turned my father killed them when I was very young. She must be very, very old and powerful, even though I know what happened to my mother and Jimmy, I haven't been able to remember it properly. I still have the false memory she imposed on me."

Lazarus gave Britt his full attention. The memories grew stronger and began to make some sense to him.

Sam stopped petting him for a moment to point at the work her student was doing. "That will be less awkward if you hold it overhand instead of underhand. If you don't mind my asking, what do you remember about it?"

"Thank you." He adjusted his grasp on the ropes and continued splicing. "And no, I don't mind. My memory is of my father coming in from sea and accusing my mother of whoring. He shoved her away, and she struck her head on a shelf corner. I remember blood pooling beneath her body, then my father dragging me away from her and my five-year-old brother. He said Jimmy was a bastard and son of a whore." He stopped and just stared into the distance for a few moments.

"That is a horrible memory to have."

He continued to just stare at nothing. When he spoke, his voice had a sad, haunted tone to it. "Could it be she told the truth when she said father had created the lie of blaming her to absolve his own guilt?"

Sam looked at him with a puzzled expression. "What do you mean?"

He looked at her. Lazarus saw unshed tears glisten in his eyes. "When she took my father, she said she'd never met either of us before. The more I think about it, the more her words ring true. Why would she feed on my mother and brother but let my father and me go? In tracking her, I have encountered several instances where she'd targeted a family. She never left any survivors."

Lazarus wriggled to let Sam know he wanted down. He hopped over, reared up on Britt, and rubbed his head under the man's chin. At the same time, he took in the man's scent. Now he had no doubt Britt was the brother he'd forgotten he had.

He also determined he would hunt his father down.

"Oh, so you like me now?" Britt chuckled and rubber behind the cat's ears. Lazarus rewarded him with a rumbling purr.

"So it would seem," Sam chuckled.

Britt's scent changed, and he took a deep breath, held it for a moment, and let it out. Lazarus sat back and looked up at him, curious. The man set down the rope work and reached for Samantha's hand. Lazarus laid his ears back.

"Miss Brumble —."

"How many times do I have to tell you? Call me Sam or Samantha."

Britt got a determined look on his face and started again. "Miss Brumble, I owe you my life. You have been kind, patient, and understanding to me. I feel I can talk with you about anything without judgement or you thinking me mad." He took another deep breath. "Would you do me the honor of being my wife?"

Lazarus sat, stunned. He'd planned on acquiring some human flesh so he could transform into a man and bed Samantha. Now he didn't know whether to feel glad he'd discovered long lost family or jealous his brother wanted his woman.

The next words he heard left him feeling crushed.

"Yes! Oh yes, Britt!" Sam gushed; then she paused, and her smile faded a bit. "On one condition."

Britt's face fell a bit. "There is very little I can think of that I could ever deny you, Samantha."

"I will continue my search for Viktor Brandewyne and my brothers. I am afraid you'll have to take me without a dowry. What's left of it I intend to use to ransom Zach and Thomas."

"Fair enough. I cannot ask you to abandon your brothers no more than I can abandon my mission to hunt down and destroy vampires."

Sam smiled at him and took his hand in hers. "I suppose the next step is to talk to Captain Bainbridge and ask him to do the honors."

George Bainbridge looked at the two young people before him. They stood giving him hopeful looks in return. Lazarus skulked in the shadows unnoticed.

Bainbridge sat back and folded his hands on the table. "Not that it would sway you, Sam, but I seriously doubt your father would approve this match."

"Of course, he wouldn't. It does nothing to further his fortunes except offer the possibility of heirs, should my brothers not be found. Britt is also aware that I am dowerless, for all intents and purposes," she said defensively.

Bainbridge held up his hands and chuckled. "Belay the broadside, lass. I was just pointing out the obvious. Personally, I've been watching the two of you, and I wondered when you would come to me with this request. I believe you are well matched."

Sam hugged him impulsively. From the shadows, Lazarus laid back his ears and growled. This drew Bainbridge's attention.

"Isn't that the cat you think stole your locket?"

"He certainly acts like him, but I don't see how it's possible. I haven't seen that little thief since the locket went missing. In fact, this is the only black cat I've seen on the ship in some time. He must've sneaked aboard at the last port."

"Hmph," Bainbridge grunted. "Dare I hope this turn of events means you are finally ready to settle down? You've still enough left to establish a well-appointed homestead and start a family."

Sam gave him a stony stare.

Britt spoke up with a firm tone. "Miss Brumble's determination and strength are what drew me to her, Captain Bainbridge, not her family's wealth. As you pointed out, we are well matched; and our quests do overlap. I hunt the kind of creature this pirate is reported to be. I know the vampire's weaknesses and how to exploit them, as well as how to defend against their powers and tricks."

Bainbridge smiled. He'd expected Samantha's reaction. Young Westin's response had been just the one he would accept. Had the young man argued for her to quit the quest for her brothers, he would have counseled against the match. Sam had long ago convinced him she would not be swayed, and he fully supported her now. He felt she was truly a remarkable young woman.

"Excellent."

Britt blinked at him, and he had to laugh. "I was testing you, lad. I learned long ago she would not be turned from this path. I just wanted to see if you had figured it out yet or not."

"Oh."

Bainbridge rang a bell. "I imagine you'll want to say your vows as soon as possible."

The cabin boy entered. "Yes, captain?"

"Gregory, go to the galley and have the cook prepare a feast. There's to be a wedding."

"A wedding?" The boy looked over at Britt and scowled. "You plan to marry Miss Sam?"

Britt nodded. "I have asked, and she has graciously agreed to have me."

The lad got right in the young man's face. "You better not try to make her go home."

Sam laughed. "Don't worry, Greg; he won't. He will help me find my brothers."

"He better."

"Off with ye now, Gregory," Bainbridge said with a chuckle. The boy obeyed but continued to glare at Britt until he left the cabin.

Lazarus followed the lad to the galley. It troubled him that his brother hunted vampires. If Britt spotted the old scars on her thigh, he might insist she have them cleansed. He still remembered when Angelique had threatened to have herself cleansed of Viktor's influence.

Lazarus wanted to be able to continue to keep track of Sam.

At the first opportunity he had, he bit his paw and let some of the blood drip into the sauce for the meat being prepared. He almost got caught by the cook.

"Hie you! Get away from there or you'll find yourself in the crew's burgoo!" The man brandished a cleaver at him.

In defiance, he snagged a strip of the roast and ran off with it.

Once Sam and Britt lay asleep in their marriage bed, Lazarus coalesced from the shadows. He crept up to Samantha and rubbed his cheek against hers. He did the same to his brother then moved to the other end of the bunk.

Britt's ankle lay exposed. Lazarus bit down just enough to break the skin. As he lapped at the blood that beaded there, he found he had to concentrate hard to keep the man from waking.

His brother's will had almost been strong enough to free him from the vampire cat's influence earlier. With this bite, Lazarus ensured he would never lose his brother again.

When the bleeding stopped, he crept out of the cabin and returned to the deck. There, he transformed into a raven and took to the skies.

# The Daedalus Enigma

# *Chapter 20*

As the *Incubus* travelled further south, shipping tapered off, and villages and ports grew farther apart. The entire crew felt grateful they'd taken several prizes while still north of the Amazon delta. All the same, by the time they reached that point, Viktor put his entire cadre into a dormant state to conserve blood stocks. Water and game could be obtained down most of the coast; human blood could not.

Even with Belladonna's weather magic, it took nearly a month to reach Tierra del Fuego.

Belle found Viktor in his cabin. She knocked lightly on the door before she entered. He stood bent over his sea chest, rummaging through the clothing there.

"Do you think she'll like this? It should be small enough to fit," he said as he stood with a dress in his hands.

The siren shrugged. "I have no idea. She seemed as comfortable going unclothed as I am. Why are you taking her a gift?"

She saw a glimmer of worry cross his face before he answered her.

"My Hunger is growing. It is a slim hope, but perhaps a gift will spare me the time of a lengthy test or errand to obtain her piece of the puzzle box."

She sighed. "It is worth trying, I suppose. I wish I could do more with the currents along this coast. For some reason, my magic lacks the usual potency in these waters. That, paired with your increased Hunger, makes me wonder if we're on the wrong course."

He folded the dress and laid it on his bed. He fished out one of his heavier dress coats and shook it out. "That has occurred to me, as well. I'm glad I put the cadre to sleep. My blood-brandy mix is almost depleted."

She frowned at him. By her reckoning, there should have been enough to safely see them from Trinidad to Tierra del Fuego and back again. More and more, she wondered if someone or something deliberately worked against them.

As he put the coat on, he looked at her. "You are not alone in your worry, pet. I should have only gone through about a third of my stores. I've even tried rationing it, yet I find myself craving blood. Hunting is poor in these waters. I don't want to feed on the crew."

"Have you tried using the emerald cross?"

He pulled the blessed object out of his shirt. "That's why I'm not drinking right now, but I have to use it more sparingly than I have for the past two weeks. It has weakened to the point it only takes the edge off my Hunger."

"That is not good. Like you, I hope we can finish with Clarissa quickly and get back to more populated waters."

"Exactly."

"Lazarus, come forth."

Almost immediately, the black cat manifested on the railing next to the captain. Viktor reached over and rubbed between the cat's ears.

"I need you to stay with the ship, old friend. Clarissa is frightened of you a bit. If I need you, I will call," he said.

Lazarus leaned into the rub then hopped off the rail. He padded to some nested rope, stretched, yawned, and curled up on top of the coils.

Viktor chuckled and turned his attention to Mr. Grimm. "You should stay as well, Hezekiah. I'd rather she not be distracted."

Grimm grinned. "I'm just too damn pretty."

"Aye." Vik snorted. "You're also forbidden fruit. Wenches just can't seem to resist that."

"It is what it is."

Both men laughed. Viktor clapped his friend and first mate on the shoulder. "I'm only taking Darrow with me. Hopefully this won't take too long. We need to get back to where the hunting is good."

"Darrow? I take it he won't be coming back." Grimm gave his captain a knowing look.

"Probably not. I'd like to say otherwise; the man is a good rigger." Viktor suddenly felt very tired. It seemed like he'd been hunting for the Sisters and running their tiresome errands forever. He'd sacrificed so many; not just to the siren for her visions, but to feed his ever-growing Hunger for blood. For the first time, it bothered him.

Grimm must have noticed the change in Viktor's mood. He stepped in close to avoid being overheard. "Vik, are you well? You don't seem yourself." He spoke low.

"Just missing the times when things were simple, and all I had to worry about was which whore to spend my share of the latest prize on." He avoided looking directly at his first mate. He didn't really care if Grimm caught him in the lie; he didn't want the man to see his Hunger.

It surprised him when Grimm backed away with superhuman speed. "Your eyes are glowing, Captain. Will Darrow be enough?"

"He'll have to be."

Without another word, Viktor turned and summoned the rigger through the bond he maintained with all his crew save Grimm and Belladonna.

The siren had permanently bound herself to him long ago, when she bit a chunk out of his shoulder. Hezekiah carried a portion of the Elder's power. Viktor reasoned it probably rendered him immune to the control of the vampire blood tainted rum; so, he didn't bother trying to use it on him. Only once had the first mate given Viktor reason to doubt his loyalty; and that had been because of old Zeke's machinations, not Grimm's design or desire.

Considering the capriciousness of his Hunger, Viktor figured Zeke had made the right move to place someone immune to his influence and with both captain and crew's best interest in mind at his side. Hezekiah was one of the very few he would listen to or that he trusted.

Darrow arrived and gave his captain an expectant look.

"Bring that." Vik pointed at a loaded sea bag.

"Aye, Cap'n." He never questioned whether he should bring a sea bag, as well.

# The Daedalus Enigma

☠

The two walked inland for a day without any luck. Viktor didn't press the pace. In his experience, tired blood tasted flat, so he didn't want to wear his potential meal out.

The vampire knew they were being watched. He caught occasional glimpses of the natives. They always ducked out of sight whenever he turned to look directly at them.

Just before sunset, a large flock of birds put on an impressive aerial display. Viktor took that as a sign Clarissa knew of their presence. He determined to summon Lazarus to locate her if she hadn't shown herself by the following midday.

He and Darrow made camp in a hollow. The rigger managed to gather enough fuel for a small fire and got it started. They ate a meager meal of biscuit and dried beef. Viktor found it very unsatisfying, but he held his Hunger in check.

He found he had to compel Darrow to sleep. The man tossed and turned for an hour trying to get comfortable on the ground. He complained that it didn't move like the ship. Viktor fully understood, but he wanted his potential meal well-rested. He also didn't want Darrow to accidentally roll into the fire during the night.

The vampire stood watch the entire night.

☠

Darrow roused in the pre-dawn twilight. The movement drew Viktor's attention. He also felt his Hunger flare. He watched silently as his prey walked a short distance to relieve himself. He did not notice a rhythmic hum nor the small, darting form of a hummingbird.

"Darrow," he said quietly, yet his voice carried clearly.

The man looked back at his captain. Viktor released him from his power. Darrow's face registered confusion then fear, as Viktor allowed his prey to recognize the predator poised to take a life.

"Run."

All the color drained from Darrow's face. He turned and ran. Viktor watched him for a few minutes then began to walk after him. He lost sight of his prey behind a rise in the land. He wondered briefly if the man had tried to hide. The sound of his frantic heartbeat ceased to move away.

Once he topped the rise, Viktor saw why. Darrow stood dumbfounded in front of a petite, nude woman. He felt another hunger rise.

"Run lass! I'm done for. Don't let him catch you, too," Darrow pled with the woman.

Viktor picked up his pace. In seconds, he was on them. He shoved Darrow aside and went for the woman. Her blood carried a power which made her radiant to his vampiric sight. He took her to the ground and pinned her body beneath his. He had his fangs at her throat before she could speak. An odd vibration against his lips and a shrill, whistle-like sound by his ear caused him to pull back and shake his head before he could pierce her skin.

"I thought you wanted to see me, not drink me, Captain Brandewyne."

The words brought him to his senses. In an instant, his Hunger vanished. "Clarissa?"

She smiled up at him and wriggled provocatively beneath him. "For a vampire, you are very warm."

"That's because I am not dead." He got up off her and offered his hand to help her up. "My apologies; my Hunger has been high lately."

She took his hand and stood but pouted about it. He saw gooseflesh raised on her body, and her nipples had grown dark and rigid. A small sigh escaped him at the thought that he couldn't afford to indulge. He kept Glory's warning firmly in mind.

"What did you wish to see me about?" she asked.

269

He decided to get right to the point. "I am on a quest from your Sister, Circe."

"I remember her." Bitterness colored her tone. Given Circe's transmogrifying powers and Clarissa's ability to take bird form, he didn't wonder if there might be animosity between the two. It did not bode well for his quest here.

"She has set me to retrieve pieces of a puzzle box. She dispersed them among the Sisters. Do you have one of the pieces?"

Clarissa shook her head. "No; I have nothing to do with *her*. She tried to claim mastery over me once."

He pinched the bridge of his nose and laughed. "Of course; I was hoping I wouldn't have to deal with Juma yet but is seems I have no choice." He sighed and looked at her. "I brought you a gift in the hopes you would accept it rather than require some errand in exchange for your piece of the puzzle."

"An item I do not possess," she reminded him.

"Aye; I would like to offer it now as an apology for attacking you."

She tilted her head and peered at him. Her eyes grew bright with curiosity. "Let me see it."

He led her back to the campfire and dug the dress out of his sea bag. He shook the wrinkles out of the garment and held it up for her to examine.

Clarissa wore a small smile on her face as she fingered the fabric. "I accept your apology, Captain Brandewyne. Will you help me put it on?"

"Of course."

In a matter of minutes, he had the garment on her and laced up. He withdrew his hands and rubbed them after a tingly wash of magic rolled over them. Before his eyes a layer of iridescent blue-green feathers covered the dress. They shimmered and glinted in the light of the sunrise. He found it mesmerizing.

"My god, you are beautiful."

The words shattered the spell. Viktor looked over to see Darrow had followed them and now stood transfixed by the petite Sister of Power.

Clarissa smiled at the rigger. "Thank you." She turned back to the vampire. "May I propose a trade?"

Viktor hadn't expected this. Since she didn't possess a piece of the puzzle he sought, he'd figured his business with her was completed. "What do you wish to trade?"

"Nathan Trundle is not faring well here. Your man there seems strong and healthy. I believe Nathan would do better in warmer climes."

271

"Darrow," Viktor called to his crewman. He had to say it twice before the man roused from his besotted stupor.

"Aye, Cap'n?"

"Clarissa wants you to stay here with her. What say you?"

The man's face lit up like he'd just been handed his greatest desire. "Aye!"

Viktor chuckled. "It appears we have a deal, Clarissa."

"What's this?" Grimm muttered to himself. It surprised him to see two men, one of them clearly the Captain, return to the ship. As they got closer, he saw the other man was not the one who'd left with Viktor.

"Ho, Captain!" he called out when the boat bumped against the hull of the ship. "Is that Mr. Trundle?"

"It is, Mr. Grimm. Have one of the lads gather up Darrow's effects. I'll deliver them to him; then we can be off." Despite his words, Viktor climbed up the net ladder after attaching the davit lines to the small boat.

"I take it you didn't drink him after all," Grimm said to his captain when he arrived on deck.

272

"I almost did. Clarissa broke my Hunger's hold on me, but I don't know how long that will last. She took a fancy to Darrow and proposed a trade," Viktor replied.

Grimm looked over at Trundle and smirked. "Be nice to have a decent meal again. I'll let Hanks know to bunk with the riggers now. He's a decent rigger but a horrid cook."

"Small consolation for a wasted visit, though. She didn't have one of the pieces. That means I'll have to deal with Juma," Viktor grumbled.

Grimm had never met the witch who'd cursed his friend and captain. He knew Viktor well, though, and it bothered him how much resigned dread the man ascribed to that particular Sister of Power. A part of him wondered how much could be attributed to her actual power and how much Viktor had built up in his own mind. *I wouldn't be the first time Grimm had seen someone cripple themselves with unreasoning or unfounded fear.*

Wisely, he kept these thoughts to himself. "Do you want to continue up to Juchitàn or go back the way we came?"

Viktor stopped and stared down at the deck for a moment. Finally, he replied, "We'll follow the Pacific coast north. The winds should be favorable this time of year."

273

*Tamara A. Lowery*

# Chapter 21

The voyage north proved frustrating for the first couple of weeks. The pirates encountered only small fishing boats and local traders. Viktor felt reluctant to hunt in any of the villages and small ports. He knew they would have to return this way after he finished with Rosalia in Mexico. No short route back to the Caribbean existed from the Pacific coast.

At least the winds and currents didn't hinder their progress. Belladonna's magic had grown so weak, Viktor forbade her to use it to speed them along. She didn't argue with him about it. That alone worried him more than any amount of complaints or irritability from her could.

The siren spent much of that leg of the voyage sleeping.

The *Incubus* put in at Concepción to take on water and fresh supplies. While there, Viktor allowed the crew to spend a couple of days on shore. Concepción was the largest port they had visited since leaving Trinidad.

He still kept his small cadre of vampires dormant. Their blood lust would have to wait until a suitable prize ship could be taken.

☠

Grimm walked the quarterdeck and inspected the state the riggers had left the extra line in. He smirked and nodded to himself, pleased with what he found. He'd be willing to wager the motley crew of pirates could rival any Navy crew for discipline in regard to their seamanship and care of the ship.

It surprised him to see Jon-Jon and a few of the lads rowing back to the ship. They'd only been in port a few hours; hardly long enough to get their drinking and wenching out of their systems.

The tall, tattoo-covered pirate scrambled up the ropes to the railing, while the rest of the men in the boat hooked it to the ship first. Jon-Jon wore an excited grin on his face as he approached the first mate.

"Ho, Mr. Grimm! Be the Cap'n available?"

"I think he's with Belle right now. Why?"

"There's a prize to be had if we're quick; one with trade goods and treasure!"

That got Grimm's attention. "Tell me what you know, Mr. Jon."

"Three days ago, a treasure ship and one escort made port here to take on water and supplies, like we have. They're supposed to head on north to Guadalupe then strike west. They're carrying trade goods to use to get supplies and spices in the islands. Yesterday, a local crew of about fifty headed after them in a fast sloop."

"Aye, this is worth interrupting the Captain for. Wait here; no sense in him going off on both of us." Grimm grinned and added, "If this plays out well, you'll get an extra share."

He turned and headed below.

"Enter," Viktor called.

The cabin door opened, and Grimm came in and shut it behind him. The first mate must have seen some strain in his eyes. His brows furrowed, and he asked, "What is wrong, Captain?"

Viktor sighed and rubbed the bridge of his nose. "I can't get Belladonna to wake up, even using her bond with me. It's like Glory's swamps all over again, and I can't figure out why."

Grimm scratched the back of his neck, a look of puzzlement on his face. "Wish I knew how to help, Vik. How did you bring her out of it back then?"

"I returned her to the sea and fed her about six crewmen. I was hoping it wouldn't have to come to that again. We need the men." He pulled out a bottle from the cabinet, uncorked it, and took a long pull.

When he offered it to his first mate, Grimm asked, "It's not the bloody brandy?"

"No." Vik shook his head. "My supply is running low, and I'd like to save it for when I really need it."

Grimm took the bottle and had a good swig. "Damn, that's some good rum!"

Viktor took the bottle back, replaced the cork, and put it back in the cabinet. "That's one of the bottles I picked up the last time we were in Tenerife. Same stuff that Belle had that one time."

"Heh, I think I understand why she reacted the way she did, now." Grimm grinned at his captain. "I think the news Mr. Jon brought might help with our current predicament."

"What news?"

"A triple prize, if we get to it in time; a Spanish treasure ship with a single escort bound for Guadalupe, and a small local pirate in pursuit. The fat prize has three days on us. The pirate has one."

Viktor felt a predatory grin spread across his face. "Lazarus, come forth!"

*"Mrrow?"* The large black cat slinked out of the shadows, yawned, and stretched. He looked at Viktor expectantly.

"Call in Mr. Jon," Vik said to Grimm and scratched the cat's head.

Grimm left and returned shortly with the second mate in tow. "Ah, Mr. Jon, what can you tell me about the three ships we're after?"

"Treasure ship and escort are both galleons. Both are armed mostly with eight-pounders; maybe fifteen guns between the two, according to scuttlebutt. The lot chasin' 'em in a fast sloop only carry small arms and blades. Their plan is to pretend to be fishermen then board at night and cut throats."

"Well then, we'd best get to them before the locals do. I want all three crews for blood stock." Vik rubbed his hands together in anticipation. "Jon-Jon, go back and make sure the lads know to head back now."

Jon-Jon grinned at him. "Figured you'd want to go after this prize, Cap'n. I set Murph and Charlie to roundin' up the lads before I got in the boat. They should be on their way here now."

Viktor reached out along the blood link he maintained with his crew to sense their presences. He found Jon-Jon's prediction accurate. "Good; are all the stores aboard?"

"Aye," Grimm replied. "I made sure the lads took care of that before I cut them loose."

Vik bared his fangs in a wolfish grin and turned to the cat. "Lazarus, go find our prey. It is time to hunt!"

☠

Within half an hour, the *Incubus* set sail. In his cabin, Viktor sat on the bed beside the sleeping siren and gently stroked her hair.

"Don't worry, pet," he whispered. "We'll soon give you a proper feed and get you set to right."

He wasn't sure if it was only wishful thinking, but he would've sworn she leaned into his caress and smiled a little.

☠

Viktor addressed his mates about an hour before the *Incubus* would come in view of the three ships they pursued. Lazarus had shown him the small pirate had spooked the treasure ship and escort, causing them to put on more sail.

"I want to fly the Spanish flag and reveal about half the guns. That should calm the Spaniards down and make the pirates think twice. Mr. Grimm, take a boat and ten men with you to request a parley with the treasure ship at dusk. Gordon can go with you. Mr. Brumble, how is your Spanish?"

"Fluent, Captain; my main trade route included Cuba and Puerto Rico."

"Good; you get the escort. Take Thomas with you. I'll take the rest of the cadre and take the pirate. Mr. Jon, you and the crew be ready to help if things get out of hand with the Spaniards."

"Aye, Cap'n; shoot the masts?" Jon-Jon replied.

"Only if you have to. Unmasking the rest of the guns should take any fight out of them, though."

"It'll be good to see some action for a change," Grimm said with a grin.

"Aye!" the others chorused.

The attack went more smoothly than they'd hoped. They came up on their prey just in time to witness the pirate sloop race past the two Spaniards then turn in an attempt to block them. While unable to outrun the sloop, the escort ship's crew quickly shot down the sloop's masts once they realized it carried no cannon.

Viktor saw the Spaniards pulling away from the disabled sloop and had his crew run up the signal to parley. Since he also flew the Spanish colors and had cobbled together enough Spanish Navy uniforms to pass for a warship, the two prizes dropped their sea anchors and waited.

The riggers reefed the sails to allow the *Incubus* to slow to a drift. Viktor had the helmsman position between the sloop and the galleons, both to maintain the ruse and to allow Jon-Jon's gunnery crews to cover all three prizes.

A few small boats launched from the sloop as its pirate crew tried to escape from their disabled ship. Viktor gave the order to unmask all sixty guns on that side and fire over the small boats in warning. The small boats returned to the safety of the sloop.

Grimm and Brumble took their chosen boarding parties and rowed to the galleons. Hidden in the bottom of their boats under some sailcloth, the vampires Gordon Jones and Thomas Brumble awaited the setting of the sun.

When the last sliver of the burning orb slipped beneath the waves, they emerged. Soon, the Spaniards realized the true danger which had befallen them.

At the same time, a third boat lowered from the *Incubus*. Its crew rowed with inhuman speed to the crippled sloop. Screams cut through the dusk as Viktor and four starving vampires attacked the pirates.

Once the cargo, supplies, and survivors were laden and secured aboard the *Incubus*, Viktor gave the order to continue on to Juchitàn.

He next ordered the tub they'd used to force-bathe Sniff filled with sea water. He brought Belle out and placed her in the tub once it was full. He'd remembered to remove her clothes to prevent her transformation from ruining them.

Her body relaxed some when he placed her in the water, but it did not transform, nor did she awaken. He supported her head and gently pried her mouth open. Her teeth remained in their human guise.

This troubled Viktor deeply, but he remained determined. He motioned for Jon-Jon to bring over the prisoner he'd selected. "Hold him," he ordered.

With his free hand, Vik drew one of his knives and carved a small chunk of meat out of the prisoner's leg. He did it so quickly the man didn't react until Viktor placed the bloody gobbet in Belle's mouth. The scream succeeded in waking her.

"Viktor?" she said weakly after she'd swallowed the meat. Her human form persisted in its manifestation.

"Welcome back, pet." He smiled and stroked her hair; glad she at least woke up.

A look of startled pain and fear crossed her face, and she doubled over, clutching her belly. "Oh no," she managed to say before a pitiful, pain-filled moan escaped her lips.

In an instant, her legs joined together to form her shark-like tail. At the same time, a gush of blood erupted from her groin and splashed from the tub as her tail thrashed.

The clot-filled fluid did not stir Viktor's Hunger. Instead, it nearly turned his stomach. Among the clots, he saw a small form with the beginnings of tiny hands and feet.

Some subtle cue from the siren let him know to move. With lightning speed, he stood, yanked the prisoner down to sprawl across the tub, and shoved Jon-Jon back several feet.

Belladonna snarled, her needle-like teeth manifesting; she extended her talons into the frightened man's gut and hurled him over the side. She gave a mighty thrash of her tail and propelled herself out of the tub onto the deck. As soon as she had the rail in her grasp, she flipped herself over the side, as well.

Even with his speed, by the time Viktor could reach the rail the siren had disappeared beneath the waves with her prey. He stood and gripped the rail hard enough to dent the wood.

# Chapter 22

They reached Juchitàn a few days later. While Belladonna did not return to the ship, Viktor sensed she stayed near while she hunted.

He took a single boat to shore and went alone. He didn't want to risk losing any of his crew to Rosalia. He rowed in rather than flew in order to appear less threatening to the Sister. He needed her cooperation.

He noticed the streets seemed more crowded than the last time he'd been here. At first, he thought he might have arrived at market time. That notion soon vanished, however.

Every time he turned in the direction of Rosalia's cantina the crowd grew denser. If he turned back toward shore the crowd thinned out. This told him she knew he was there and felt like being uncooperative.

He grunted in irritation and turned toward her lair. She had to possess one of the puzzle pieces, possibly two; although he realized that hope was probably just wishful thinking.

The crowd thronged about him, and his progress remained slow. He managed to get within sight of the building but could advance no further. The people stood still, no longer making any pretense of just being heavy traffic. They packed themselves body to body and refused to move.

He couldn't shove them aside; they stood so close he had no wiggle room. He thought about testing his will against Rosalia's; he rejected the idea after remembering a similar struggle with her over control of some of his crew. He'd won; but it had killed one of the pirates. At that time, he'd had a blood bond with the subjects of the struggle, and Rosalia's power had been weak. He held no such bond with these villagers, and her power now stood at full strength.

She might be willing to sacrifice her people for such a petty contest; Viktor saw it as a waste of time. Given his recent trials with control of his Hunger, time was not something he could afford to waste.

He decided he'd rather frighten her some instead of playing her game. He could not move forward. He didn't have enough room to even turn around anymore. Still, as pinned in place as the crowd had him, none of the villagers tried to hold or grab him.

He took to flight and shot straight up before the Sister could react and redirect her attack.

He made sure to stay higher than even a gifted human could jump and flew to the roof of the cantina. No one stood guard there, which told him she didn't think he'd use that route.

It took him only a moment to realize his error. Rosalia must have anticipated his move well in advance. The trap door for roof access had been sealed and replaced with an outside stair. Only smooth stucco could be seen where he remembered the trap door to be.

A shuffling sound alerted him to activity on the stairs. He looked over the edge of the roof and saw slow movement among the throng toward the steps. Already, a few forms began their ascent. It looked like Rosalia's strategy would be the same as in the street, though. The people in the fore of the crowd did not try to rush up the stairs. Instead, they moved together like a rising tide.

It felt as if the crowd formed a single entity rather than individuals. If her power and control had grown that much, he couldn't afford to antagonize her by killing his way through to her. He needed her cooperation not her enmity.

He scowled in consternation. The crowd pressed up against the building too thickly for him to access one of the windows. He knew she was inside. He just had to figure out how to get to her. He briefly thought about just hovering above the rooftop until she ran out of air and lost consciousness.

He turned his attention back to the roof area. Given his good blood feed on the small pirate sloop's crew, he'd noticed a considerable sharpening of his senses. The dulling of them during the voyage around the continent happened so gradually he hadn't really noticed at the time. Now, everything lay in hyper focus before him.

He spotted it.

A slight rise in the surface of the stucco beneath his feet outlined a rectangular area. Human eyes probably would have missed it. A wicked smile spread over his lips. He drew his knife and dug into the stucco as he traced the line.

It crumbled more easily than he'd expected. So, she hadn't anticipated him as far in advance as she'd like him to believe. The camouflage couldn't have been applied more than a day earlier. It hadn't been cured properly yet.

He worked at clearing away the crumbling bits enough to get a finger-hold on the edge of the trap door. He had to dig into older, much harder stucco to make enough space to grasp the edge.

A sound behind him distracted him. He glanced toward the stairs and saw Rosalia's tactics changed a little.

Her minions began to reach the rooftop. They no longer stood or moved shoulder-to-shoulder. Instead, they spread apart enough to give a full view of their now naked bodies. Every villager who had topped the stair proved to be a young woman.

Had he been an average male, he might have found this display irresistibly tempting. The nearly constant presence of Belladonna in his life had inured him to the allure of that much female flesh, at least enough to resist it as the bait he knew it to be. The siren went about nude more often than clothed.

He turned back to his digging.

His Hunger flared. The scent of fresh blood filled his nostrils. The scent grew. He turned to glance toward the stairs again and saw the source of the tantalizing aroma.

About fifteen women had made it to the roof now, and more still climbed up. They did not move toward him; they started to form a ring around the perimeter of the roof. The scent of fresh blood came from their arms and legs.

He watched as one freshly bloodied woman passed a pottery shard to the next in line; she, in turn, scored bloody lines down both arms and thighs before passing on the shard. He could tell the cuts weren't deep enough to cause serious blood loss, only enough to drive him to distraction. He ached to take each woman in turn and lick the shallow wounds as he brought her to climax.

He snarled and saw fear in the eyes of those closest to him.

Just like that, his self-control returned, and he clamped down on his Hunger tightly. Normally, the fear would have fueled his predatory nature even more; instead, it told him Rosalia feared him, and her control had been spread too thin. Her minions' sense of self-preservation was trying to surface. Briefly, he wondered if he would have survived this test had he not taken the three prize ships.

He turned back to digging at the stucco. The scent of blood and sex grew stronger. He felt hands on his back. He snarled and turned to face the women again. Three had approached close enough to make any escape for them impossible. His Hunger and lust threatened to break his control when he saw them dip their own fingers in their blood and into their folds. They reached out toward him, fingers dripping with the mingled fluids. Vaguely, he was aware none of the other women approached him, though. He reasoned these three must be especially close to Rosalia, perhaps personal servants. He knew if they touched him again, his control would crumble.

He used his speed to dig the hand hold he needed and ripped the trap door open. He saw the interior ladder had been removed as if that would deter him. He dropped through the opening and used his power of flight to lower safely to the floor.

He found himself in a storeroom. It didn't surprise him. He'd never been beyond the common room of this cantina on his previous visits. Still, he possessed a keen sense of direction. It didn't take him long to find his way to where he wanted to be. Oddly, no one tried to bar his way inside the building.

Rosalia sat on her throne. She wore her braids twined into a crown atop her head. Flower filled bowls surrounded her. Oil lamps suspended from the ceiling beams backlit her. Her black eyes glittered, and her lush lips glistened, moist and inviting.

"Welcome back, Captain Brandewyne."

He gave her a mock bow. "Greetings, Tia Rosalia. I was beginning to think I was unwelcome."

She stood with a smile, her stance seductive, and held her arms open to him. "My followers are a bit overprotective. Come, I will give you a kiss in apology."

He chuckled. "Forgive me, but I must decline. You are clever, Rosalia; but you are not as clever as you think. I smell the honey on your lips, and I know it to be infused with devil's hoof. I don't think you wish me to repeat what I did the last time you tried to trap me with that."

She dropped all pretense of friendly seduction and gave him a look of resentful hatred with a touch of fear. "What do you want here?"

He nodded and got right to business. "One of your Sisters, Circe, has set me to retrieve pieces of a puzzle box which she dispersed among the Sisters long ago. Do you possess one or more of them?"

She blinked, genuine surprise on her face. "I had forgotten about that trinket." She seemed to catch herself and glowered at him. "Did you think you could just walk in here and take it?"

"Hardly, pet; I know well enough these things don't work that way. So, you only have the one, then. What is your price?"

She sat back down. "You refused my favors. You rejected the offer of pleasure and sustenance from my handmaidens."

"I believe you wish to make me your subject and tool, Rosalia. I will not be that. Their flesh and blood would have tied us together. I know you fear me. Do you really want to be trapped in an eternal battle of wills?"

He saw her grow pale at the notion. "No; I will give you what you seek on one condition."

"What is your condition?"

"You will never foot my domain again. If I cannot control you, I cannot allow someone as powerful as you within my territory. Already, the Spaniards and their Church have encroached upon it. I have adapted; I will not give up more to you."

He laughed. "I don't want your territory or power, Rosalia. I already have the portion I need from you. All I seek now is the puzzle piece. Provided no other Sister of Power demands I return here; you have my word I will not visit you again."

She sighed. "I supposed that is the best I can hope for." She clapped her hands. One of the bloodied, naked women from the roof came in with a cloth pouch.

This confirmed to him she'd know all along why he'd returned. He sighed and shook his head. Why should he be surprised the Devil's Daughter could not help but lie?

The woman carried the pouch to Viktor and held it out for him to take it from her hand.

His nostrils flared, and his eyes flashed emerald fire as he fought with his Hunger and natural lust. He forced his gaze to turn to the Sister as he retrieved the pouch. He saw her smirk at his struggle for self-control.

The pouch held something small but heavy. He opened it and took out a carved piece of stone. It was blackish blue in color but flashed green, red, and yellow fire within its depths. He had heard of dark opals, but he'd never seen one before.

He slipped the piece back into the pouch and tucked it in his shirt.

"Thank you, Rosalia; may we never meet again."

He turned, strode to the door, opened it, and took to the sky.

# The Daedalus Enigma

# Chapter 23

Belladonna returned to the ship a day after the *Incubus* turned south. Viktor noticed she'd stopped by her cabin to dress before she sought him out. He also sensed she shielded all but her surface emotions and thoughts from him.

"Welcome back, Belle." He kept his tone gentle. He had a feeling she could easily go feral in her current state. He refrained from trying to get past her barriers.

"You got the pieces from the Devil's Daughter?"

He let her direct the conversation. What had happened to her could wait until she felt ready to talk about it.

"She only had one. It appears I will have to deal with Juma for the final piece."

Belle crossed her arms and raised an eyebrow. "You seemed to finish with Rosalia a little more quickly than with the others."

"She is still afraid of me. She made herself very hard to get to, she tried to entrap me, she tried to seduce me, and when she saw she could not control me, she agreed

296

to give me her puzzle piece in exchange for never footing her territory again."

"What if one of your quests requires it?"

"I made provision for that. She accepted the exception," he reassured her.

"Oh."

He sat at his table and poured a glass of rum. Belle eyed it and licked her lips. He raised both brows in surprise.

"May I have some of that?"

"Do you think that's wise, pet? You got rather — wild the last time you had rum."

She pouted a little, an expression which brought a smile to his lips unbidden. "I just drank it too quickly. I'd never had it before. I promise to sip it slowly this time."

He shrugged and poured a second glass to the halfway point. She took it in both hands and held it to her lips a few moments before she took a cautious sip. She closed her eyes and swallowed.

Without opening her eyes, she said, "Aren't you going to ask?"

Viktor heard the hurt in her voice. "I didn't want to push you, pet. Do you want to talk about it?"

She opened her eyes and looked at him. He recognized the pain in them; pain, he understood. What puzzled him was the shame he saw there. In all their years together, he'd never seen the siren show shame or remorse. Those emotions were alien to her.

"Belle? What is it?"

She dropped her eyes and her shoulders drooped. Her voice came out small and lost sounding. "I'm sorry, Viktor."

She turned partially away from him and hugged herself, the glass still in one hand. Her shoulders began to shake, and he realized she was silently sobbing. Her face remained dry, her species physically incapable of producing tears.

He stood quietly and walked around the table to her. He took the glass from her hand and set it down before he folded her into his arms. She let him. He stroked her back and whispered into her hair, "You have nothing to be sorry for, pet."

"But I didn't carry your child to term."

"Did you even know you were pregnant?"

"I did just before I fell asleep, after we left the straits. I didn't want to believe it, but by then I had no choice. For all intents, I became human. Sirens lose their magic while with child." She looked up at him, a glimmer of anger in her eyes now. "I shouldn't have been able to get pregnant by you. You're not a merman or sea dragon!"

He smiled down at her; relieved she seemed a bit more her acerbic self. "Nor am I human, pet. Correct me if I'm wrong, but feeding you in salt water played a factor, didn't' it?"

"It did." She nodded. "It forced the change on me which made my body reject the pregnancy." She pushed away from him and retrieved her glass of rum. After she had another sip, she turned back to him. "Perhaps it was for the best. I was of no use to you pregnant; and it cost you precious time."

He had a swallow of rum as well before he replied. "Are you at peace with how things worked out?"

"Are you?" she asked cautiously.

He nodded. "I didn't even have time to get used to the idea of you bearing a child of mine, since I didn't know until it was too late. My concern is how it has affected you."

She cocked her head to the side and blinked at him as if he'd grown a second head. "Just when I think I've got you figured out, you say something like that and surprise me. Now that I know you are not upset or disappointed, I am relieved that I didn't have to go through the entire pregnancy. I hate being that weak and at the mercy of others."

He took another drink to avoid the urge to admit he felt relief, too. He had no idea what to do with Belle if she'd not lost the child.

He quickly set his glass down when he saw her down the rest of her rum in one long drink. "Pet —."

She shivered, set her empty glass down, and ran her hands through her hair. She turned her most sultry smile on him, and he felt his body respond despite himself.

She began to strip and said to him, "You have entirely too many clothes on, Viktor."

"Are you sure this is wise, pet? Have you fully healed?"

She pouted up at him as the last of her garments hit the deck. "I am still tender in one spot. Will you kiss it and make it better?"

He smiled and shook his head; in short order he stood as naked as she. He scooped her up and carried her over to the bed.

In only a couple of weeks, they covered twice the distance they'd been able to on the trip north from the Straits of Magellan. The hunting remained just as poor, though. Worse, the weather grew decidedly cooler. This forcibly reminded all aboard how the seasons were reversed in the southern hemisphere.

Viktor called a meeting of his mates to discuss their dilemma.

"Belladonna has read the weather ahead of us," he told them. "Even with the best winds and currents she can provide us, there is a strong chance of getting frozen in the straits. We do not have the provisions to see us through the winter."

"What about raiding one of the coastal villages, or perhaps wintering there?" Zach suggested.

Viktor shook his head. "The crew outnumbers the populations of most of the villages along this stretch of coast and southward. They won't be able to sustain us."

"Nor would they be able to sustain you, Captain; even with the cadre asleep. You'd eventually be forced to feed on the crew before the thaw opened the Straits again," Grimm added.

"Aye, I know. I would prefer to avoid that."

Jon-Jon scratched his head. Cap'n, what say we buy provisions? With the amount of gold we took, I don't think any of the lads will object to pitching in a tenth of their shares. That would be more'n enough to feed everyone well for nearly six months."

Viktor considered the idea. He had to admit it had merit. "If it comes to it, we may do that." He sighed and continued, "I hate to lose the time, but I don't think it wise to try for the Straits now. I propose we sail north and hunt the coast past Rosalia's territory. Even if the hunting remains poor, the ports are more populated."

His mates murmured among themselves for a few moments. Grimm spoke for them all once they reached their decision. "You'll get no argument from any of us, Captain."

"Then it is settled. Mr. Jon, inform the crew. Mr. Brumble, set us a course that doesn't hug the coast. I would like to bypass the Mexican waters as much as possible."

# Chapter 24

Two hours after they'd turned the ship about, a fog began to form. Given their latitude and the season, no one thought much of it. It formed slowly, and they still remained close enough to land for such weather.

It wasn't until they felt the copper-clad hull scrape gently on the bottom that they suspected the fog might not be entirely natural.

Grimm ordered the sails reefed and the sea anchor dropped. He saw no sense in risking damage to the ship while she was run aground.

Viktor and Belladonna arrived on deck close to the same time.

"Hell's Breath?" Vik asked.

"I'm not sure," Grimm replied. "Hard to get good bearings in this fog; but none of our charts show any islands or shoals here. Of course, there's no guarantee they're accurate."

"It's Hell's Breath," Belle said and pointed over the side. "Look."

Both pirates looked and saw a jetty rise from the barely visible island and extend to the ship like a rocky tentacle.

"Definitely an invitation," Viktor grunted. "We might as well go see what the old man wants."

The jetty proved too narrow to do more than walk in a single file. Viktor took the lead with Belladonna behind him, and Grimm took up the rear.

About halfway between the ship and the island, the fog grew so dense they couldn't see each other. They had to proceed forward by feeling the ground beneath their feet.

Both men heard a startled yelp from the siren. Grimm heard Viktor ask her if she was hurt. He heard no answer. Viktor called out again, closer this time. Still no response came from the siren.

"Mr. Grimm, can you see Belle?"

"No, Captain; I can't see anything. I'll crouch down and see if I can find her by touch. Her cry sounded like she wasn't far ahead of me."

He didn't have to say she may be hurt. The thick fog made the jetty very slick.

Grimm crouched on hands and knees and inched forward. Every few moments he swept his hand out to the sides in the hope of making contact with the siren.

"Belle, where are you?" Vik called again. Grimm could swear the Captain sounded both farther away and distinctly downhill from him. He shook his head. The fog must be playing with the sound. With the jetty at sea level, it would be impossible for Viktor to be downhill from him.

"I think you got turned around, Captain," he called. No one answered him. "Captain?"

"Mr. Grimm? Thought you went with the Cap'n," Jon-Jon said and reached down to help him stand.

Only then did Grimm realize the stones of the jetty had been replaced by the deck boards of the ship beneath his hands. "How? Never mind; something happened to Belladonna. I have to get back down there and help the Captain find her."

He ran to the railing to climb down the netting and return to the jetty. What he saw stopped him short. The fog swirled and cleared for a moment to reveal a sea cliff where the jetty had been, perilously close to the ship.

"Clearly I'm not meant to be on the island right now," he muttered in resignation.

The fog swirled again and obscured all visibility beyond the railing.

☠

Viktor wondered what Zeke was playing at with the damnable fog. He couldn't see more than a few inches in front of him. The heightened senses his vampirism afforded him proved nearly useless. Some trick of the fog muffled the sounds around him. He couldn't even hear the heartbeats of his companions, a sound that had been his constant companion for years now.

Suddenly, he heard Belladonna give a startled yelp behind him. He stopped and turned in her direction. "Are you hurt, pet?"

Silence answered him.

"Belladonna, can you hear me?"

Still, he got no answer.

"Mr. Grimm, can you see Belle?" He thought his first mate might be closer to her.

"No, Captain; I can't see anything," Grimm replied. "I'll crouch down and see if I can find her by touch. Her cry sounded like she wasn't far ahead of me."

Viktor frowned. Grimm's voice sounded like he was moving away from him quickly; not only away, but up. He knew Grimm couldn't fly.

306

He couldn't shake the feeling Belladonna was in danger. The fact he could no longer smell her or sense her mental presence did not help.

"Belle, where are you?"

He knelt down and felt along the surface of the jetty. The thought she might have slipped off the side occurred to him. He reached to the side and felt in the water but could not find the siren. When he went to check off the other side, he encountered a cliff face.

"What are you playing at, old man?" he grumbled and stood back up.

The fog lifted to form a low ceiling over him. He saw he now stood inside a stony corridor. No water was visible, nor was the ship. Stone surrounded him on three sides. He growled and turned back toward the main body of the island. It didn't take him long to reach the familiar hollow where Zeke kept his fire. The old man sat absorbed in what he saw in the flames on the opposite side of the fire from him.

Viktor stalked down into the bowl-like depression, glaring at Zeke. "All right, old man, what is so bloody important?"

The Elder looked up from his fire with genuine surprise. The look proved enough to stop Viktor in confusion.

"What are you doing here, boy?"

"Your damn island ran my ship aground and sent out an invitation. Now I've been cut off from both Belle and Hezekiah and herded here. I would like to know what is so damned important."

Zeke grimaced as if he only just realized what had happened. "I do wish she would let me know when she's going to bring you here if I haven't asked her to," he grumbled.

A wave of incredulity washed over Viktor. "You can't possibly be blaming Belle for this."

Zeke shook his head. "Not the siren, no; Hell's Breath. She can be a capricious thing sometimes."

"The island?"

"Pay attention, boy! I told you Hell's Breath has a mind of her own and goes where she will when we first met." The old man sighed and shook his head. "Still, I do need to talk to you and the wild girl. Where is she?"

"Ask the island. She and Hezekiah were right behind me; then they weren't." He stalked over to the fire and sat down. "I can't even sense her presence."

Zeke shot him a knowing look. "Well, that explains your piss poor attitude." He cocked his head to the side as if listening to something only he could hear. Finally, he spoke. "She'll be along shortly. The island has some personal business with her. Female business, she says."

Viktor relaxed a little. He didn't like the fact the island had blocked or could block him from Belladonna; but at least he knew she wasn't in any danger.

Belladonna didn't like the fog which enveloped them shortly after they left the ship. Not only did it render her practically blind, it baffled her sonar, as well.

Without warning, the ground beneath her feet vanished. She gave a startled yelp as she plunged into total darkness. By the time she thought to call out a warning to Mr. Grimm, who'd been just behind her, the hole had sealed itself.

She caught a faint trace of worry from Viktor and tried to reach him through their blood bond. She found the way blocked.

Her back struck smooth stone. The impact knocked the breath out of her. She felt her fall slow as the glassy surface curved under her.

Suddenly, warm sea water enveloped her. She grunted in pain as the transformation of her legs into a tail shredded her breeches. The change at least let her stop her fall. She thought about climbing back up the shaft; she doubted her talons would be able to dig into the stone of the island, however.

With little other choice, she turned and swam downward. Out of the fog and in the water, her sonar functioned properly. The darkness no longer presented a problem.

At about the same time, she sensed an opening beyond the tunnel's end, a soft glow grew ahead of her. Before long she found herself in a large, submerged cavern. A slightly cooler current passed through from another passageway. As her eyes adjusted, she saw several similar passages opened onto the cavern.

In the room's center lay the source of the glow. A giant outcropping of crystals shimmered and flashed with an opalescent light. Slender prisms extended from a central core in all directions. Most appeared clear or milky white, but several radiated multiple shades of blue, green, red, or gold. The colors seemed to shift from one rod to another. Belle thought it resembled a crystalline sea urchin.

She felt compelled to approach it.

*"Welcome, Belladonna,"* a feminine voice said.

"Who are you? Where are you, for that matter?"

The sound of laughter rang around her. *"I am before you and surrounding you, child. You know me as Hell's*

310

*Breath, although I had another name once, long before you were born."*

A sense of awe and dread filled the siren. "I know you."

*"You have nothing to fear from me, child. You have served me well, and you shall be rewarded in time. For now, I have some things to teach you."*

Belle bowed her head. "I receive your lessons, All-Mother." She felt a ripple of loving warmth wash over her.

*"There is something you must understand about your mate."*

"My mate? I have not bound myself to a sea dragon."

*"Your mate is the one called Viktor, child. Already, you have bred with him. I know you lost the child, but you can carry his offspring to term."*

"Why was he even able to impregnate me?" That still bothered her, and deep down, she worried it would happen again.

*"Viktor's mother was my servant. He represents balance. Just as he is a death bringer, so too is he a life giver. The only reason Gloribeau has not borne him a child is she took precautions to prevent it and preserve the magic she has regained."*

311

Belle cocked her head to the side. "Do you mean anyone with magic who bears his children will lose their magic? What about Dorada?"

The crystal cluster seemed to shimmy, and the sound of tinkling laughter filled the submerged cavern. *"Dorada has never been the brightest of my daughters, regardless of her generation. Since all matters of fertility are her province of power, she suffers the least loss of magic. She suffered enough to recognize it, but not enough to realize why. By allowing him to get a son on her who is not to be sacrificed, she has forever forfeited that much more magic for her lifetime. The balance comes from the fact that her next generation will be the most powerful Dorada to exist since the first. The future generations are doomed to diminish, though."*

Hell's Breath continued, *"I sense you fear becoming as a mortal. Such is normal for your kind during childbearing; but you fear the state will be permanent afterward. It will not, although a small portion will be passed on to the child. I think we both know you cannot afford to sacrifice your magic at this time."*

"No, I cannot. Viktor needs my weather magic to help him in his quest. His time is running short," Belle confirmed. "For that reason, I have decided to remain celibate until then." She winced at the memory of recent activities and hoped this decision was not too late. She shouldn't have had that rum. It had affected her judgement. What if she was already pregnant again?

*"Come closer child. Allow me to give you a simple spell to prevent conception. It is the same one Gloribeau uses. Part of Viktor's magic as well as yours is based on sexual pleasure. You cannot deprive yourselves of this and hope to succeed."*

Obediently, the siren swam closer to the cluster of crystals. Without warning, several spines extended and pierced her body and tail. She found herself pinned in place.

Once the initial panic passed, she found the experience not as painful as she'd expected. Comforting warmth flowed through her and numbed the pain. Just as suddenly, the crystal spines withdrew. Knowledge of the spell the island had promised implanted itself in her mind.

Her wounds closed just as a new current struck her and propelled her upwards. She managed to turn just in time to see a passage open in the cavern's roof. Shortly, the current propelled her through it.

Viktor sat up straight. A familiar presence brushed the edges of his perception.

"Belle?"

Zeke looked up from his pipe and nodded. "Island says she's through with her for now, and I'm to hold off on the talk I had for her." He said the last with an indignant snort.

Viktor might have chuckled at the old man's umbrage had he not sensed a growing panic from the siren. Her presence grew stronger by the moment.

A light tremor shook the ground beneath his feet, the only warning before a fissure opened a few yards away. A great gout of water erupted upward. It propelled the alarmed siren high into the air.

Without thinking, Viktor launched into flight. He caught Belladonna midair as the geyser subsided. A quick glance down revealed the fissure had closed.

"Hullo, pet."

She didn't answer. Instead, she clung tightly to him and buried her face in his shoulder. Her tail transformed into legs by the time he landed next to Zeke's fire.

He smiled but refrained from laughing at the now soaked old wizard. Zeke wore a sour but resigned expression as he shook out his extinguished pipe and put it away.

"Old biddy's feelin' saucy today," the old man muttered. "Sit yourselves."

Belle held on tighter, Viktor took it as an indication she didn't want to be put down. He managed to sit while still holding her without losing his balance. She snuggled into his lap, careful to keep her feet from touching the ground.

Apparently, Zeke felt satisfied with the level of compliance. "You've visited five Sisters, yet you only have four pieces of Circe's box."

"Aye; Clarissa had no knowledge of the thing."

"I'm not surprised. Those two never did get along well. Their magic is too similar."

Viktor grunted. "Clarissa said as much. Now I have to go after Juma for the final piece."

Zeke sat up and glared at him. "You aren't ready to deal with Juma yet."

"What choice do I have? It's the only way I can complete the quest Circe set me."

"Boy, you seem to be forgetting something. You know one other Sister of Power."

"I don't —," he started to say; then it hit him. "Celie."

Zeke nodded. "She set you to find her Sisters. That makes *her* one of *them*."

Viktor sighed. "Now I just have to wait out the southern winter."

Zeke just grunted. He nodded at the siren. "Think she fell asleep."

# Chapter 25

The weight of the limp siren in his arms confirmed Zeke's assessment. He worried about this until he heard a vaguely familiar female voice. It seemed to surround him and sounded slightly amused.

*"She feels safe with you. It is time for her to awaken, though. You both need to be on your way."*

He looked over toward Zeke to ask him if the island had just addressed him. He caught a vanishing glimpse of the old man as fog obscured his vision. He felt the rock he sat on dissolve into nothingness beneath him.

The moment he felt warm sea water engulf him, Belladonna reverted to her true form in his arms.

She woke with a start but did not attack. Instead, she took in a mouthful of water and swallowed it. She laughed. "Hell's Breath saved us from a long voyage. We're not far from the Bahamas."

Viktor reached out along the blood ties he kept with his crew and sensed they were close by. "I'm glad she brought the ship as well."

"She likes you."

With the siren's weather magic, the *Incubus* made the voyage from Nassau to Savannah in just over a day. Viktor gave the crew their shares of the treasure ship and turned them loose on the port. He and Grimm headed straight to Celie's.

The two pirates paused in the shadows of the moss-covered oaks which ringed Celie's hut. Although the old marsh-witch wasn't anywhere to be seen, the yard of the little tabby shack was occupied.

Brianna Grimm sat on a stump keeping an eye on a couple of toddlers. Her hands busily worked on a bundle of corn shucks and twine. She obviously didn't see the two men.

Grimm got a mischievous twinkle in his eye and motioned for Viktor to remain quiet. He edged around to be more directly behind his wife. He began to creep forward.

He'd almost reached her, when his son looked up from the mud he played with. The boy pointed a grubby hand and cried, "Mama! Loo' ow!"

Faster than Viktor expected, his first mate's wife whirled in her seat and held a dagger at the man's crotch.

318

"Careful with that thing, woman!" Grimm said and backed up a step.

Brianna looked up at his face in surprise. "Hezekiah?"

Viktor chuckled and stepped out of the shadows. "Your wife is just as dangerous as Belladonna."

"Aye." Grimm still eyed the blade pointed at him.

Brianna seemed to suddenly realize what she'd almost done. She tucked the knife back into the sheath on the front of her apron, stood, and embraced her husband. "I'm sorry. I thought someone was after the children."

He lifted her face to his and kissed her soundly. When he pulled back, she wore a look of longing. He grinned and hugged her tightly. "My children are very lucky to have so fierce a mother."

Viktor cleared his throat and gave them a bow. "I will leave you to get reacquainted; if you could direct me to Mother Celie, Madam Grimm?"

"She was inside last I saw, Captain," Brianna answered, her eyes never leaving her husband. "Mama, doll. Mama, doll!" the little girl insisted as she tugged on her mother's skirt.

Viktor went into the main part of the tabby hut, a smile on his lips.

☠

"Sit down, boy," Celie said curtly. She turned to her special cabinet and closed it. He thought she stuffed something in her apron pocket.

He sat and waited patiently. He'd learned as a child never to try to hurry Celie along. She would deliberately move slower. He strongly suspected she'd subjected him to such treatment to teach him patience.

The old marsh-witch ambled over to the hearth where a small cauldron of stew simmered. He didn't remember there being a hearth before. Celie reached up to the shelf above it and retrieved two wooden bowls. She filled them from the pot, stuck spoons in, and carried them to the table. She reached into her apron and pulled out a small spice box. She opened the lid, took out a pinch of the fragrant powder, and sprinkled it in one bowl.

She pushed the bowl at him and said, "Eat."

"What did you just put in it?"

"I said eat, boy! Now you mind me, or I'll wallop you." She scowled at him, a look he remembered all too well from childhood.

He grunted and picked up the spoon. Before he realized it he'd finished the entire bowl. He eyed the second bowl, which Celie hadn't touched. She snorted and pushed it toward him.

He ate the second bowl more slowly. He noticed a definite difference in the flavor but enjoyed the food just as much. Even as skilled a cook as Trundle couldn't match Mother Celie's cooking.

Once he finished, Celie spoke. "You're looking for the pieces of Circe's puzzle box."

"Yes; do you have the fifth piece?"

She shook her head. She must have seen disappointment in his face, for she reached over and patted his hand. "I do not have it, but I did, once."

"What happened to it?"

"Circe is one of the trickiest of our kind. I knew it would be dangerous for her to regain the locked portion of her magic. Over a century ago, there was another whom we thought was the One. I sent my piece away to make the search for it a test for him. He never survived to even find Circe."

"Of course. It could be anywhere by now."

"I didn't say that, boy. I've kept track of it ever since it left me. Wouldn't want it to fall into the wrong hands after all."

Viktor sat up, a glimmer of hope in his heart. Still, he proceeded with caution. "Can you or will you tell me where to find it?"

Celie cackled at him. "I can see my Sisters have left the marks on you, boy," she said and wiped a mirthful tear from her eye.

"They do have a tendency toward ambiguity," he replied with a wry smirk.

"I can tell you where to look for it. I can even tell you what it looks like. It is a stone ring carved from a single piece of sardonyx. The ornamental side of the ring has a carved image of Janus, the two-faced god of beginnings and ends." She stopped and peered at his hands for a moment. "It would probably fit on your little finger."

Viktor stroked his beard in thought. "Interesting; none of the other pieces resembled jewelry or any specific shape, although all have unusual angles and notches."

Celie nodded. "The ring is the keystone to the puzzle. The other pieces will nest together on the box, but you need the ring to hold them together and activate the lock."

"You sound as if you've seen the completed box."

"I commissioned Daedalus to design it." She sat there with a complacent expression and waited for him to process that bit of information.

"Why do I get the feeling your magic could rival Glory's when you were at your peak?"

She cackled. "It surpassed hers. Glory truly is my sister. We are twins, but I'm the elder by a few minutes. Now stop getting me off topic. When you leave port, you will head to Ireland's western coast. The ring is an heirloom of the O'Malley family."

Viktor perked up at the name. "Are they related to Grace O'Malley, the pirate queen?"

Celie nodded with an amused twinkle in her eye. "She is the one I entrusted the ring to. One of her descendants, by the name of Darcy, holds it now. I would be surprised you know of her; except I know your fondness for books."

"Aye; I don't remember where I came across the book, but I remember reading of her exploits and the lengths she went to in order to protect her lands and people."

"You keep that in mind when you find Darcy, boy. I've watched her for some years, and she has a lot of her great-great-granddam in her. I've no doubt she'll have a dear price for parting with the trinket."

"I will keep that in mind, Mother."

"Good." She pulled the spice box out of her apron pocket and pushed it across the table at him. "You have some idea of who Circe is and what she can do to a man?"

"I saw the poor creatures on her island. Neither Hezekiah nor I ate anything she offered while there. I intend to return to her alone."

"A wise decision; still, I would have more peace of mind if you used this to protect yourself. It is called moly," she said.

He took the box of ground spice and started to open it to sniff it. Celie laid a hand on top of the lid and shook her head. "It is too soon for another dose. You should take it with food no more than twice a day, one pinch per meal only. More than that could make you very sick. You need to use all of it before you return to Circe."

He tucked the latched box into his shirt and asked, "Is this the same substance Hermes brought to Odysseus?"

"It is. You may safely eat anything she offers you once you've finished that off." She held up a gnarled finger. "I would warn against bedding her should she offer, though."

He chuckled. "I've had similar warnings from both Belladonna and Gloribeau. At least I trust Glory's warning. Had it only been Belle, I would have thought it more jealousy than anything else."

He didn't catch the knowing look she shot him. If he had, he would have questioned her about it.

# Chapter 26

They spent three days in port before putting back to sea. Grimm suspected his captain wanted to give him more time with his family, but never questioned Viktor about it.

By the end of the three days, he didn't want to leave. His children had fully captured his heart. He knew they probably wouldn't know him the next time he saw them, and it hurt.

He tried to hide it as he walked up to the helm. Viktor gave him a puzzled look.

"Are you feeling well, Mr. Grimm?" The Captain kept his voice low so only he would hear.

"Is it that obvious?" Grimm kept his voice just as low.

"In appearance, no; but your scent is off," Viktor replied.

Grimm kept forgetting about the man's heightened senses. He cringed just a little. "Just getting old and soft, Captain."

"You? Never."

He felt both grateful for and mildly irritated by Viktor's denial. It was better than pity; but he felt his youthful edge fading away. He knew the day would come when he would have to give up piracy and life on the sea, if he lived that long. For the first time in his life, he had reason to hope he would.

For now, though, he knew he needed to focus on the day to day. Brooding about his age and his family served no good purpose. He turned to the quarterdeck and bellowed, "Mr. Bland!"

"Aye, sir?"

"Are all aboard?"

"All but Belladonna, Mr. Grimm," Bland called back.

"She will be along in her own time," Viktor said.

"All hands make ready to set sail!" Grimm's shout spurred a beehive of activity on deck and in the rigging. In short order, the *Incubus* pulled away from the docks and headed down the Savannah River to the sea.

Viktor felt some relief to see Grimm throw himself into his responsibilities as first mate. It would provide his friend with a needed distraction. He suspected Grimm's melancholy had more to do with leaving his family than his encroaching old age.

The more he thought about it, the more determined he was to see his friend retire with his family once this business with the Sisters was finally concluded.

Grimm had been as loyal as old Zeke's interference had let him. It was because of Zeke that Grimm couldn't leave the crew now. The old wizard's magic bound the first mate to Viktor's quest.

It didn't take Viktor long to realize his definition and Celie's definition of a pinch of moly varied greatly. After the first meal he dosed, he experienced a dull headache and mild disorientation for about an hour. He also felt some weakness during that time.

He didn't like it but figured it a small price to pay for proofing against Circe's wiles. He decided to continue to use the same amount each time. He felt it best to be through with this regimen before they reached Ireland.

For that same reason, he did not ask Belladonna to sing up stronger winds or currents.

Viktor fought the temptation to increase the dosage of moly to three times a day for the next two and a half weeks. He increasingly hated the headaches and fatigue he felt after using it. Instead of discouraging him from taking it at all, it made him want to take it all at once and be done with it altogether.

The longer it took to use up the supply Celie gave him, the greater the chance of one of his mates walking in on him during one of his temporary states of weakness. One of the side effects he'd noticed was a distinct lag and weakening of his blood bond with his crew during those periods. He didn't know if the moly directly affected the bond or if the headaches played more of a role in it.

Either way, he knew he couldn't afford to let that weakness show. He didn't even let Belladonna know; other than his cadre of vampires, the siren shared the closest bond with him. Hiding the effects of the moly from her proved the hardest to do.

Viktor took the box of moly out of the cabinet and took it over to the table where his meal awaited him. He opened it and reached in to get a pinch of the ground herb out. After he sprinkled it over his food, he glanced in the box to see how much was left.

"Looks like just a pinch," he muttered. "Hell, it has looked like just a pinch for the last three days. I am sick to death of this drawn-out torment."

He dumped the last little bit on the food and stirred it in.

To his surprise, he didn't get a headache this time. In fact, he felt remarkably good as he ate. He'd almost finished the meal before he sensed something wasn't right.

Everything around him seemed to grow brighter. It took him a moment to realize his eyes had dilated. He pushed back from the table and stood. He walked over to the window casements and drew the drapes. The cabin's interior dimmed to a bearable level of light.

He turned back to the table and felt a wave of vertigo wash over him. He stood still and let it pass. An odd sense of detachment enveloped him.

He walked back to the table and noted it felt as if he moved his limbs from outside his body. It seemed to take forever for his legs to respond to his desire to walk. He sat down carefully once he reached the table and chair.

The last few bites of his meal sat before him. He debated just tossing it out; his appetite had completely abandoned him. Finally, he determined he would finish it off, solely to finish off the moly. Enough mental coherence remained with him to realize going through all he had with it could be suffered in vain if he left even a small portion uneaten.

The task proved more daunting than he'd expected. Each bite proved increasingly difficult to choke down. He could barely taste the food; something he found both frustrating and confusing. Every time before, the moly had enhanced the flavor of the food and increased his appetite.

Finally, he swallowed the last bite. An overwhelming thirst took him. He started to reach for the bottle of bloody brandy but stopped. The thought of drinking the thick liquid made his stomach want to turn. He decided to opt for rum instead, since he had a bottle of it on the table as well.

The cork proved difficult to pull. He didn't have a corkscrew handy, so he bit into the side of the cork with one fang and pulled. It released with a sudden pop, and he slammed the bottle down on the table before he could stop.

The neck of the bottle broke off in his hand and cut it deeply. It stung, but he didn't think too much of it. He'd gotten used to such wounds healing quickly. He wiped his hand off; fully expecting the cut to already be closed.

He hissed at the unexpected sharp pain this brought. It afforded him just enough clarity to realize his reactions remained sluggish and detached.

He held his hand up to look at the cut. "Huhn," he grunted as he observed that not only had the gash not closed, but it also bled profusely. He wondered if he would have to stitch it up.

*"Mrrrurrr?"* Lazarus hopped up on the table and sniffed at the mess. He purred and butted his head against Viktor's good hand.

He absently rubbed the cat's ears, still lost in fascination with his own blood running down his wrist toward his elbow.

Lazarus sniffed at the blood and began to lick it off his master's arm. Viktor pulled his arm away before the cat could reach the cut on his hand. The ministrations tickled, but he knew they would hurt on the open wound.

He frowned as the cat began to convulse. "Jim? What's wrong?"

In answer, the cat transformed to an amorphous smoky mass. It spread to cover most of the table. Dishes and bottles scattered and clattered to the deck as Lazarus reformed as Jim Rigger.

"Captain?" he managed to croak out weakly.

Viktor watched as the light died in his former first mate's eyes. Sorrow, confusion, and a touch of unfamiliar panic took him. "Jim!"

Before he could do any more than reach for his dead friend's hand, another wave of vertigo swept over him. He blacked out.

*Tamara A. Lowery*

# Chapter 27

Grimm headed to the captain's cabin with the daily report. He raised his hand to knock when a loud clatter sounded behind the door. The Captain's voice called out, "Jim!" shortly after; then no further sound came.

Grimm knocked and called out, "Captain?" he got no answer.

Cautiously, he opened the door and peered inside. It took his eyes a moment to adjust to the gloom. He noted someone had drawn the heavy drapes. He detected no movement.

"Captain?" Still no answer.

He lit the lantern next to the door and entered the cabin. What he saw shocked him. Viktor slumped at the table; blood dripped from his right hand. Pewter dishes and broken bottles lay scattered about the deck beneath the table. On the table lay the ghostly pale body of Jim Rigger.

Carefully, Grimm made his way through the debris to the two men. He breathed a sigh of relief to see Viktor seemed only to be unconscious. He did wonder why, however. It troubled him more when the Captain didn't respond to his calls or a light shaking.

He turned his attention to Rigger. He knew Rigger and Lazarus were the same being; he'd just never been clear on what that was. Clearly, the man on the table was dead. He saw no wounds on the body, but he reasoned its state was the reason for Viktor's outcry.

He returned to the door and called for the cabin boy. The lad arrived right before Belladonna. The look on the siren's face told him she had some idea what was going on.

"Freddy, I need you to fetch Dr. Coffin," Grimm said. After a glance at Belle's reaction, he asked her, "Is there anything specific he should bring, lass?"

"Just have him send some peppermint oil. He doesn't need to come. I can handle this," she replied.

Grimm nodded and turned back to Freddy. "Peppermint oil; got that, lad?"

"Aye, sir; peppermint oil."

Once the boy left, Grimm turned to the siren. "Any idea what happened?"

"I have my suspicions, but I'll have to check if I'm right. The only thing I know for sure is there is some sort of magical interference around him," she replied.

334

He opened the door for her. "Be careful; the place is a mess, and he's still bleeding." He thought he saw alarm in her eyes as she darted past him. He followed to find her already looking at the Captain's wound and sniffing the air around him.

He waited for her to finish her unorthodox examination.

Finally, she looked back at the first mate, partial relief on her face. "He doesn't seem to be in any immediate danger; I don't know about long-term yet. I can heal the cut; but we need to wake him up."

"What about Rigger?"

"He should rise at sunset. He must have drunk some of Viktor's blood and transformed. Luckily for him, the drapes were closed already. I see and smell no burnt flesh. We'll also need victims for both of them. They'll need fresh blood."

Grimm frowned. He knew that meant some of the crew would soon die. They had no prisoners aboard at the time. Still, better them than him. "How many?"

"One each should be enough, preferably healthy."

"Of course." He watched her pull a small flask from her pocket and pour the contents over the captain's hand. She hummed low as she washed the blood away. Slowly but visibly, the cut sealed. By the time she finished, not even a scar remained to indicate there had been a wound.

"Salt water?" he asked.

"Yes."

"I remember you using some on Brumble's hand when he burned it with those peppers."

She nodded. "It strengthens my magic. Thankfully, Viktor had already started to heal; just much more slowly than normal."

"Do you know why it took so long or what caused him to be like this?" He didn't like the fact any kind of weakness could afflict his Captain. Viktor was his friend and the best pirate captain he'd ever sailed with. He took his duty as first mate to head off or prevent any hint of mutiny very seriously. He needed to know what caused this so he would know best how to deflect any worries or doubts the crew may have about the captain if they learned of this.

He knew the best way would be to prevent them from ever knowing, but he wasn't sure if that was possible, yet.

Belladonna picked a small, non-descript box up from the debris. She sniffed it and nodded. "He overindulged in moly. I thought I'd caught a trace of the scent on him a few days ago. At least he didn't take all of this at one time; but I need to find out how much of a dose he took."

336

"Can you wake him?"

"That's what the peppermint oil is for. The aroma is very powerful. I've already tried to reach him through our bond," she said. "He didn't respond; and I can barely sense him."

He narrowed his eyes at her as his mind worked out how things were probably about to go. "How should the oil be applied, and who is going to do it? You've already said he'll need to feed. That means he may bite before he realizes who he has ahold of."

"I see your point. I don't know how he would react to your blood, given your connection to Zeke. My blood is toxic." She furrowed her brows in consternation.

Grimm gave her a look to match his name. "I'll have to pick a victim. He can do it." He stepped out of the cabin to head Freddy off. He didn't want the lad to see the Captain in his current state. Rumors would spread through the ship faster than fleas if he did.

He didn't have to wait long. "Ah, thank you, Freddy; I'll take that to the Captain. I need you to find Mr. Bland and have him send Fox and Davies up here. I've a special work detail for them and need them here as soon as possible."

"Aye, sir," Freddy replied. "Fox and Davies; I'll tell Mr. Bland you said to be quick.

"Good lad."

The boy scurried off, and Grimm returned to the cabin with the peppermint oil. He saw Belladonna picking up dishes and stacking them neatly. She'd already moved Rigger's body from the table to Viktor's bed. He had to admit her human form might be small, but she still held all her inhuman strength.

"Didn't know you were so domestic, lass," he joked.

"The less mess the boy sees when he's summoned to clean, the less wild the rumors will be," she said with a shrug.

"Aye," he agreed and started helping her tidy up the clutter and chaos. "It'll still be a trick explaining Jim. He rarely manifests, and I don't think Freddy has seen him before."

The siren grunted. "I'll leave those explanations to them."

A knock at the door interrupted the conversation. "Hmph, that was quick," Grimm muttered. He went to the door and cracked it just wide enough to see out. The two sailors he'd named stood there with the cabin boy.

"Thank ye, Freddy; that'll be all for now. Fox, Davies, come in. The captain needs to see you."

A hint of fear showed in their eyes, a sure sign Viktor's hold had weakened. "Mr. Bland said you had a special work detail for us," Fox said.

"That I do; now get in here so you can get to it, y'gob," he growled at the man. The two sailors quickly obeyed the first mate's order.

Grimm made a mental note to speak with Viktor about reminding the crew he was the Reaper. Viktor's vampiric magic had made Grimm get lazy, since it kept the crew in line for the most part.

"Bugger, what happened in here?" Davies asked. Grimm closed the door behind them.

"What's wrong with the Captain?" Fox asked, "And who is that?" He pointed at the body on the bed.

"The Captain has been poisoned," Belladonna said. "He killed that man; but there was a magical poison in the blood. We need one of you to give him this." She held out the bottle of peppermint oil.

Davies took it and looked at it. "What is it, and how do I give it to him when he's out cold?"

"Why do ye need both of us for that?" Fox seemed quite suspicious.

"The body over there will need to be moved," Grimm pointed out.

"This is peppermint oil, Davies. I cannot administer it to the Captain because of my magic. Pour a few drops on your fingertips and rub it on his mouth. You may have to do it more than once to wake him up," Belladonna answered.

Davies didn't question any more. He took the stopper out of the bottle and poured some of the fragrant oil onto his fingers. Shortly after he touched his fingers to Viktor's mouth, the Captain awoke.

Viktor sat up and embraced the hapless man before anyone could react. He tore into his victim's throat and gulped down the blood as fast as he could.

Grimm noticed Belladonna stood close to him and the door. Both remained ready to escape if the current victim didn't prove enough to sate the vampire's Hunger.

Fox stood with his back to the bed, the body on it forgotten. He stared, horrorstricken, at the gruesome death of his companion.

Viktor looked up from the dying man in his arms; blood dripped from his beard as he focused on the other sailor. "Jim."

Grimm watched the former first mate's eyes open. In the lamplight, they looked like soulless pools of darkness in the vampire's pale face. Silently and swiftly, he took his prey. As life left Fox's eyes, Grimm watched it fill Rigger's.

By that time, Viktor finished his meal. He arranged Davies' body in the chair. When the siren started to move toward it, he shook his head. "He was a decent sailor. He'll be a good addition to the cadre. You can have Fox once Jim is finished with him. I didn't care much for his attitude just now."

Grimm furrowed his brow. "You heard that? I thought you were unconscious."

Viktor wet a cloth in the wash basin and cleaned the blood from his face and beard. "No, I heard everything said from the moment you came in to check on me; I was merely unable to respond. Having someone more expendable apply the peppermint was a smart move. I was ravenous. I don't think Madam Grimm would've appreciated me turning you," he said as he set the bloody rag down.

"No; nor would I," Grimm laughed nervously. The thought of becoming undead rather than just dead hadn't occurred to him until that moment.

"It's not so bad, Mr. Grimm," Jim said and passed the corpse of his victim over to the siren. "You only miss food for a little while. A blood diet does have some interesting benefits, though." He grinned and indicated his erection.

"Put that thing away, man." Grimm laughed.

341

"I would, but I don't think sweet Belle would let me."

"It would be decidedly unsafe to try," Viktor chimed in. "I thought you had to have human flesh to take this form."

Belladonna looked up from stripping the corpse. "You took too much moly, Captain. When he lapped up your blood, it weakened the spell Celie used to turn him into a cat."

"Will I still be Lazarus? At least it allowed me to endure daylight; and I could spy for the Captain," Jim said with some concern in his voice.

"I would think so. I also believe you should be able to take any of your forms at will now," she replied. "The only way to know definitely is to try it, though."

"Well, since I'm not allowed to play with you —." In a flash, he transformed from man to cat to raven to smoke and back to man. He put a hand to his forehead and sat down. "Now I'm dizzy — and limp," he added after he looked down. He stuck his bottom lip out, and Grimm snickered.

"No staying power, lad," the first mate said with a grin.

"Captain, as amusing as that was, I need to ask you an important question," Belle said. All eyes turned to the siren.

"What is it, pet?"

"How long and how much moly?"

"Mother Celie gave it to me to protect me from Circe's magic. I've taken a pinch with my meals twice a day. I got impatient with the last dose and put two pinches in my food to finish it off," he replied.

Grimm saw her visibly relax. He felt a weight lift simply because of her reaction.

"Good; there should be no permanent damage to you. If you had taken larger amounts, you would have broken your curse; you also would have killed yourself."

"Well, that is comforting," Viktor grumbled.

Tamara A. Lowery

# Chapter 28

Three days later, the *Incubus* arrived on the western coast of Ireland. Given the knowledge that the Irish harbored no love for England, and they didn't want the Royal Navy's attention, Viktor ordered two thirds of the gun ports masked and a French flag run up. The idea was to appear to be a merchantman.

As an added precaution, they anchored well out in the harbor and rowed to the docks. Luckily, Zach had made a few runs from this coast when he'd still been an honest trader in his father's employ. He knew which trading houses in this port to approach; both to keep up the ruse and to get reliable information.

Zach led Viktor and Grimm to the office of a nondescript warehouse not far from the docks. An old, faded sign hung above the door, so weathered the paint flaked off to the point of rendering it illegible.

"You're sure this is the place?" Grimm asked.

"Aye; Father ran some of his more clandestine cargoes through here; shipped a few of them myself."

Viktor and Grimm both stayed very vigilant without seeming to. "The man is expecting us. Eyes have been on us since we set foot on the dock," Vik murmured. "Saw at least two urchins slip this way ahead of us. Just saw one of 'em head back out in the direction of that tavern."

"Aye," Grimm confirmed in a low, casual tone. "Shadow on the rooftop, as well."

"Saw 'em."

Zach gave a cadenced rap to the door. They heard a bolt slide back and the door creaked open slowly. Rather than push on in, the navigator held his hands up and waited for the door to open fully.

"Hullo, Brumble; who are those two?" a gruff voice spoke from the darkened interior.

Viktor's enhanced senses let him see the man hiding in the shadows quite clearly. He smiled in recognition. "Can you even see at all anymore, Harlowe?"

"I know that voice. Bless me if it ain't Vik Brandee!" In a louder voice, Harlowe said, "It's alright, lads; ye can stand down. Come on in, gents."

The distinct sound of a lantern being un-shuttered filled the air, and warm light flooded the cramped warehouse office as the trio entered. A once-burly older man sat at the desk surrounded by logbooks and ledgers. He peered at them from behind thick glasses.

Once the door closed behind them, he took the glasses off and rubbed the bridge of his nose. "Blasted spectacles ain't worth a damn.

Viktor chuckled. "Spend all your time peering at books in the dark; of course, you'll go blind. When did you set up shop here? Last time I saw you was in Charleston."

"Been nearly ten years now," Harlowe answered. "Seems like it's been a few years since I've seen you, young Brumble. Finally gone pirate, I see."

Zach nodded.

Harlowe squinted at Grimm for a while before he put his glasses back on. "As I live and breathe, the Grimm Reaper! I'd heard you and Brandee parted company years ago."

"I've been back with the Captain nearly a year longer than young Brumble here. Got in a tight spot with a dog of a pirate hunter. The Captain found me and set things to rights," Grimm said. "Good to see you're still in business, Mr. Harlowe."

"I didn't know you'd done business with the Captain or Mr. Grimm before," Zach commented.

"It was a few years before you earned your captaincy, lad, and out of a different port." He pointed toward a small cabinet nearly buried in ledgers. "This calls for a drink. Would ye be so kind as to fetch a bottle from there, Mr. Brumble? I'd get it meself, but me legs ain't so spry as they used to be."

"Of course." Zach went to the cabinet and found four glasses and a bottle. "What are we drinking?"

"Ten-year-old Irish whiskey, boy; put some hair on yer chest."

Viktor and Grimm laughed. "Don't come across much good whiskey like that in our waters," Viktor said. "It'll be a nice change from rum or brandy —," as an afterthought, he added, "or that rot-gut gin you and Jon-Jon are so fond of, Mr. Grimm."

Once everyone had a glass of whiskey in hand, Harlowe sat back and asked, "Where's young Rigger at? He's always been with you when we've done business in the past."

"Back on the ship dealing with a new recruit," Viktor hedged.

"He's missing out on some good drink." The old man shrugged. "What brought you to my doorstep today?"

"I'm looking for information on and the whereabouts of Darcy O'Malley." Vik got right to the point. He saw no reason to go through with the ruse of being merchants he'd originally planned on.

348

"O'Malley? Some bad business that be." He gave the vampire a shrewd look from behind his glasses. "I've a business proposal for ye. If yer agreeable, I'll give you what information I have on the lass free of charge."

Viktor gave the whiskey a sniff then a sip. He swished the alcohol in his mouth before he swallowed it. "Not bad; what did you have in mind?"

"First, is that copper clad beauty out in the harbor yours?"

"It was a gift."

"I just bet it was. I imagine she's got more teeth than she shows, too."

"Your point?"

"Ship like that needs a large crew. Lately, this port has been overrun with young hotheads aching to fight the English. I've occasionally arranged for a handful at a time to ship over to the Colonies, since there seems t'be a storm brewin' there that'd suite their temperaments. Currently contracted about twenty of 'em. Trouble is, the captain who was to take 'em got himself conscripted to the Royal Navy. Now I need to get rid of 'em before he shows back up to shut me down. If they're gone, he'll have no evidence."

Grimm spoke up. "What about records of past contracts, man?"

"They don't exist. In fact, I've never dealt with the man before. Chalmsey recommended him to me. If I come through this, I'll make sure that bastard pays for his stupidity," the old man growled.

Viktor chuckled. "I'd almost like to be around when that happens. You've a nasty streak when crossed, Harlowe. I take it you'd like me to take the lads on and spirit them out of this harbor."

"You always were a quick-witted lad, Brandee. It'll also save me having to refund their coin."

"What port do we drop them at?" Zach asked.

The three just looked at him as if he'd grown a second head.

"What?"

Viktor began to chuckle, and the others soon joined him.

"Our young navigator is still a bit too honest for his own good," Grimm said.

"Always has been, to my figuring," Harlowe agreed, but the words held no malice. "Y'can drop 'em off in bloody London, for all I care. They want to fight the English; why not put 'em in the thick of the buggers?"

Vik smirked. "I'll take the lads off your hands. You've no need to worry about them ever returning to this port. Whether or not they get to fight the English will depend on whether or not they survive to meet any that need fighting."

Harlowe extended his ink-stained hand across the desk. Viktor shook it. "Right, then; now, about the O'Malley woman — how much do ye already know about her?"

"Only that she has something I require."

Harlowe sat back and peered at him with a strange smile on his face. "You've no idea who she is, do ye?"

Viktor gave him a pleasantly bland expression but remained silent. Harlowe swallowed hard. He'd dealt with the pirate often enough in the past to recognize the warning signs of when Viktor was his most dangerous.

"Right, then; she's the heir of the O'Malley family, a descendant of Grace O'Malley, the pirate queen. She was wed to Michael O'Connor about a year and a half ago. The marriage was both a love match and a political one. It increased her holdings considerably and united the two most powerful families in western Ireland. Naturally, the English couldn't abide that. Buggers have been trying to get this end of the island under their thumbs for centuries."

"Not four months after the nuptials, young O'Connor met with a tragic hunting accident. One Roderick Brookston introduced himself to the new widow as a friend of the departed. It seems O'Connor was the last of his branch of the family and had befriended Brookston while away at University. More importantly, he'd named the man heir and executor of his estate."

"Interesting," Viktor observed. "An Irish lordling with no immediate successors, unless his widow was with child, picks an Englishman rather than even a distant cousin to inherit; sounds a bit odd to me."

"Aye, it does and did," Harlowe agreed. "Brookston used his mother's Irish heritage as leverage to make his case. He set himself up in the O'Connor estate as lord and graciously made known he would allow the widow her year of mourning before he paid her court."

"Turns out she *was* with child by her late husband. Shortly after she began to show, she returned to one of her own estates and refused Brookston entrance. Rumors are unclear about the fate of the child or even its gender. Some suspect Brookston had it murdered to remove the threat to his claim. None outside of the O'Malley household have ever seen it, and they do not venture out."

"Her estate is self-sustaining, then?" Grimm asked.

"No more than any other. Brookston's men guard it and control who and what passes its gates — in the name of protecting his friend's widow. Her year has passed, he has made his suit, and she has refused him. Now he holds her prisoner in her own home and denies any other suitors access. He means to force a marriage. Had she been a commoner, he might have gotten away with it. Since she holds lands and title in her own right, the courts would not stand for it. The O'Malley's wield too much power."

"Then there's the colleen in question; Darcy O'Malley has the fierce nature of her ancestress. She also has the proof, thanks to me, that the accident which left her a widow was orchestrated by her sole suitor."

"Bet that makes for an awkward courtship," Zach grunted.

Harlowe cackled. "That it does. She hasn't come out and accused him of the murder yet. She wants to regain her freedom first."

Viktor sat back in his chair and crossed his arms. "I am curious, Mr. Harlowe, how and when you got such information of the betrayal to her if she is kept so secluded."

"I am a man who can get things, Captain Brandee, as you should remember. I find it to be in my best business interests if the English do not get such a foothold here, which is Brookston's true purpose. I checked out his story, and my spies revealed although he and O'Connor did attend University together and were friends, they were not that close of friends. He was approached and offered a title to eliminate the political power an

353

O'Connor-O'Malley union would grant. The documents he holds granting him executorship and inheritance were forged and/or coerced."

"One of my spies lives very near Darcy's keep. Brookston gave her a little dog back when he thought she wasn't going to resist him. It has proven useful for getting messages past the guards."

Viktor smiled and nodded. "That is very useful. Do you have any more of this fine whiskey about?"

"I've a few cases."

He reached into his shirt and pulled out a bag of coins. He placed it on the table and asked, "How much will this buy?"

Harlowe hefted the money and grinned. "All but one case, which I'm reserving for my personal use until my next shipment; this will also get you enough fresh victuals to supply a warship for a month."

"Done." He reached across the desk and shook hands with the old smuggler. "Mr. Brumble will see to it the goods find their way to the hold. Mr. Jon should be by in an hour or two to round up our new crewmen. I just need directions to the O'Malley woman's keep."

"I'll have a lad lead you there; but you won't be able to get in."

Viktor laughed and gave Harlowe a wink. "You forget, I learned how to burgle before I learned how to pirate. If there is a way to sneak in, I will find it."

Tamara A. Lowery

# Chapter 29

Viktor only took Grimm and Lazarus with him on his journey to the O'Malley keep. A small village stood nearby to house the families who worked the lands of the keep and owed loyalty to the O'Malley's.

Harlowe's information kept the pirates from being caught off guard by the general disgruntlement among the locals. Brookston and his men were viewed as thugs at best, Englishmen or sympathizers at worst.

Viktor sent Lazarus to spy out the keep while he and Grimm headed to the public house for food and gossip.

The common room grew quiet when the two pirates entered. Given the small size of the village, they'd expected something like that. They were the outsiders. One rough-looking group, in particular, watched them closely.

Viktor caught Grimm's eye and gave him an almost imperceptible nod. He had a feeling the group would soon send someone over to approach them. They took their seats at an open table and motioned for the serving wench.

She, at least, seemed friendlier than anyone else had been. "What can I do for you fine sirs?"

Viktor gave her a devilish smile, careful to keep his fangs hidden. "I could think of a few things, pet, but for now we just want a couple of ales and something to eat."

She returned his smile and cocked her hip. "I'll have that for you in a few moments. Let me know if there's anything else I can do for you, stranger." She turned and headed for the bar and kitchen. She put a very suggestive sway into her hips as she walked away.

"I think she likes you," Grimm teased.

"Aye, and I think those lads don't like that."

They noted the group of ruffians shooting glares their way. One particularly seemed very irate. He chugged down his ale as his companions urged him on.

"Mm-hmm, looks like one is drunk enough to get stupid," Grimm muttered.

"I'm not in the mood to kill him; I don't know his alliances yet."

The belligerent man made his way over to their table. The two pirates sat there and looked at him calmly.

He poked a meaty finger into Viktor's shoulder and tried to loom over him.

"You need t'be leavin' my woman alone."

"Who, pray tell, is your woman?"

The drunkard hooked his thumb in the general direction of the bar. "Moira; she's mine," he growled.

"I don't know anyone named Moira."

"That's only because we haven't been properly introduced," the serving wench said as she returned with a tray of food and drink. "Don't pay any attention to Seamus, here; idiot thinks just because he and his lot work for Roderick Brookston they can come in here and lord it over everyone."

"Quiet woman! You'll show me some respect, by God!" Seamus moved to backhand her.

His hand never made contact with her flesh. Viktor stood next to him and held his wrist in an iron grip. "If you don't mind, I would prefer she not spill my dinner."

"Leggo o' me!" He swung at Viktor's head. The vampire easily caught the fist in his other hand.

"Are you left-handed or right-handed?"

"Whuh?" Clearly the man could not grasp the question.

Viktor repeated it a little more slowly. "It is a simple question: are you left-handed or right-handed?"

"Right-handed; what kind of devil-spawn do you take me for?"

Viktor smiled and squeezed the man's right wrist until he felt and heard bones snap and grind against each other. "One that is colossally stupid. You'd best learn to wipe your ass with your left hand now. I don't think you'll be using your right for very much anymore."

He released his victim and resumed his seat. Seamus fell to his knees cradling his crushed wrist and wailing piteously. A few of his companions eased over and helped him out of the pub.

After some huddled muttering, the rest of the group of thugs left.

Moira frowned after them. "Be careful when you leave here. That lot is looking for trouble."

"They may find more than they bargained for. I see Mr. Brookston hires men who share his disrespect for women. I've heard about his ill dealing with Darcy O'Malley," Vik observed.

She made a growling noise in her throat. "Things have been bad here ever since that Englishman and his lot showed up. You two aren't English, are you?" Suspicion and belated caution crept into her voice.

"I was born in the Colonies, pet. My companion was born English; but he holds no love for, nor loyalty to the Crown."

She laughed. "So, what are you, pirates?"

They laughed with her. Once the laughter died down, Viktor motioned for her to lean in close. "Can you keep a secret?"

Her eyes lit up at the prospect of juicy gossip. She nodded and said, "Better than most." She leaned down to let him whisper in her ear.

"We are indeed pirates. I am Captain Viktor Brandewyne, this is Hezekiah Grimm. I need to find a way into the keep to speak with the young widow. She has in her possession an item I have need of, and I am willing to negotiate for it."

She glanced around furtively and crossed herself. "I don't know of any way to get a man in or out of the keep. Brookston and his thugs keep a close eye on the place. It's hard even to get messages through, but there is a way."

"The dog?"

She looked at him sharply. "How did you know about Ciaran?"

"Will Harlowe and I have had business dealings for years."

Moira sighed and appeared to consider something. "There are wild tales that surround the two of you. If anyone can figure a way into that keep, I imagine it would be you."

Viktor fished out a handful of gold coins and surreptitiously slipped them into her hand. He took care to keep the color of the coins from open visibility to the other occupants of the pub. "I'd like to see where the dog makes contact."

"Meet me at the edge of the village in two hours," she murmured and pocketed the money after a quick glance.

"Moira! Quit yer loiterin' and get back to work," the barkeep barked.

She deliberately straightened up slowly. "Will there be anything else?"

Viktor took her hand, kissed her palm, and gave her a wink and smile which made her blush. "Another round of ale, please."

"Coming right up!" She headed over to the bar.

They saw her slip one of the coins to her employer before she filled two tankards. The man quietly pocketed the gold after testing it and spared her a small smile.

The remainder of their meal was uneventful.

☠

After three more servings of ale, Grimm headed for the back alley to relieve his bladder. A slight brush of shoes against the dirt of the alley gave him just enough warning. He turned and pissed in the face of one of the thugs from earlier.

This had the effect of flustering the man and causing his companions to burst into laughter.

"Di'n' see 'at comin' did 'e, John?" one of the men said with a chortle.

Grimm took advantage of the momentary distraction to tuck himself back into his pants.

John sputtered and spit as he wiped at his face. He turned dark red and yelled, "Don't just stand there, y' buggers! Get 'im!"

"That's enough out of you." Grimm hit him under the chin. Teeth clicked together hard. A chunk of the man's tongue hit the ground with a wet plop. The unconscious man soon followed.

Silence reigned. The five remaining thugs blocked the exit from the alley. Their faces showed varying degrees of shock or drunken anger. Grimm returned their stares with one of calm waiting. He kept his stance loose.

They mistook his readiness for a realization he was outnumbered. Cudgels and knives made their appearance, and the men advanced on him.

He gave them a smile to match his name. It almost seemed a pity how outmatched they were.

"If that's how you want it, I hope you're prepared to pay the price."

"Only one going to pay anything is you, old man."

"Old? Oh, now I really must make it interesting." He let them get close enough for the first two to swing at him. He easily dodged it.

They didn't prove quite as agile. He caught one in the ribs and another in the stomach. He pulled his punches. He didn't want to kill them. Ever since Zeke shared power with him, his strength rivaled that of the vampire he called Captain.

The next two got closer but remained a little more cautious. They tried to circle him. He did his best to keep them in front of him. The two he'd punched recovered and rejoined the fight.

For a couple of minutes, they took turns darting in to swing at him and dodging his blows in return. It gave him a good read on them but not good enough. One managed to slice his arm.

# The Daedalus Enigma

The slice was shallow, but it stung enough to make him change his mind about sparing them.

"I liked this shirt."

He used his enhanced speed to step in and kick the man directly in front of him in the nuts. He used enough force to crack the man's pelvis.

Grimm grabbed the arm of another man, turned his knife hand toward a third, and forced the blade into the man's chest. He broke the knife man's arm and dislocated the shoulder, as well, before shoving him at the last two men standing.

They instinctively jumped back. Before they knew what was happening, a hand landed on the outer side of each of their heads and slammed them together with a loud crack. Both men collapsed to the ground in convulsions.

"Play time is over, lads. Come on, Hezekiah. It's time we were on our way," Viktor declared.

Grimm stepped over the bodies of his assailants and joined his Captain. "You were standing there long enough, Vik."

Viktor laughed and clapped him on the back. "You seemed to have things under control. Shame about the shirt, though."

"Aye; wish I had Brie here."

"You know how to mend your clothes, Hezekiah."

"I do. That is *not* why I wish I had her here right now."

Both men chuckled as they headed for their meeting with Moira.

Lazarus explored the keep in his raven form, or he tried to. It seemed Brookston's men, positioned throughout the keep, had a strong dislike for birds. Several swung at him with whatever was at hand. One fired a crossbow at him.

He decided it would be safer to use his feline form and stick to the shadows. A bird indoors tended to draw too much attention anyway. It meant the Captain wouldn't be able to see through his eyes. He'd give his report later, when they met.

The rest of his exploration went without difficulty. He discovered the routes in and out of the structure and saw how each was guarded. The Captain would be facing quite a challenge. For all intents and purposes, the keep was a fortified prison, complete with a moat. He'd heard about such ancient fortifications, but he'd never encountered one before.

He set about finding the O'Malley woman's chambers. He discovered them on the uppermost floor. He didn't get a very good chance to survey them. A

Spaniel ran at him, claws scrabbling on the stones of the floor. He knew the Captain had plans which involved the dog, so he didn't try to confront it. Instead, he transformed to mist and floated up to lurk in a corner of the ceiling.

The dog yapped incessantly at the spot where he hid.

"Ciaran, stop it!" a female voice demanded irritably. The dog continued to bark and whine.

In his current form, Lazarus could not "see" in the normal sense. Rather, he sensed body heat and heartbeats.

"Hush, you silly dog; it's just some old cobwebs. Now leave it be." The larger heat signature lifted the smaller, hotter one. He heard the woman sooth the dog and sensed its heartbeat calm. The two soon moved to another room.

Lazarus cautiously settled to the floor and awaited his Captain's orders.

*Tamara A. Lowery*

# Chapter 30

Just after sunset, Lazarus felt the brush of Viktor's mind. He sent back the sense he understood his orders and coalesced into his feline form.

Quietly, he padded toward the adjacent room. He figured he shouldn't have too much trouble getting the dog to chase him. He just hoped he didn't encounter any closed doors on the way out. He could get through, but the dog would not be able to.

He spotted the spoiled creature curled up on a large pillow, gnawing on a piece of leather. As he was about to reveal himself, a young girl entered the room.

"There you are, you lazy thing," she said to the dog. "Come on, the mistress wants me to take you for your walk." She put a lead on the dog and led it out of the chambers.

Lazarus quietly followed, careful to remain out of sight. His part in the plan could wait until they were outside the keep.

When they reached the gate, one of the guards stopped them. "Where you going, girl?"

"The mistress instructed me to take Ciaran for his walk." Lazarus noted she didn't seem intimidated by the man's gruff tone.

"Keep him on his lead and stay in sight; no wandering off."

She put her hands on her hips and glared at him. "You know he likes to chase rabbits, Cameron. If you don't let him have his sport, he has too much energy and won't let the mistress sleep."

"Her high-and-mighty can do without sleep, Meg. There was trouble at the pub today. Seamus has a crushed wrist; John's missing a few teeth and most of his tongue; Robbie's arm is broken and out of joint; Ian may never walk again; Corey and Logan have broken skulls and haven't woken up yet; and Marvin is dead."

She gripped the dog's lead tightly. "How many of the gang that fought them did they get?"

Fear shone in the man's eyes in the torchlight. He lowered his voice to a near whisper. "Robbie and Ian say it was only two men they fought. They said they moved too fast to see and fought like demons. It was Robbie's knife that killed Marvin."

He crossed himself and added, "I think they may be Unseelie."

She frowned at him. "You old woman; believin' in faerie stories at your age."

"All the same; you stay in sight."

"I will. I've no wish to encounter brigands. You and your lot are bad enough." She passed him and led the dog across the moat bridge.

Lazarus transformed to mist and drifted behind and over her head. Once sure they were far enough from the light of the torches to not be seen, he settled near the ground and resumed his feline form.

Now, he just had to figure out how to get the dog away from the girl without drawing an attack from the guards.

He ran at the pair, leapt up, and planted all four feet squarely in her chest. He made sure to keep his claws sheathed.

Meg let out a startled grunt as the air was knocked out of her. She stumbled backward and let go of the dog's lead in an effort to catch herself. She sat down hard.

Ciaran locked onto the large black cat, yipped a hunting cry, and bolted after the creature. Meg gave an exasperated cry of dismay and dove for the lead. She just missed it.

Lazarus encountered no trouble staying out of the beast's reach. He kept just far enough ahead of the dog to keep it following. He led it in the direction he sensed Viktor to be.

When he no longer heard the cries of Meg or Cameron for the dog to return, he scaled a handy tree. The dog tried to follow him up and made it nearly five feet up the trunk before it jumped back to the ground. It reared up on the tree and barked incessantly.

He decided he didn't want to listen to that anymore and leapt down to the ground. By the time his feet touched grass, he resumed his human form.

Ciaran gave a yelp and a growl at the sudden appearance of a naked man.

Jim Rigger reached down and grabbed the dog's lead. In response, it tugged against it trying to slip its collar. "I'll carry you, then," he growled back. He reached down to scoop the dog up.

Ciaran nipped his hand and drew a black bead of blood. A moment later, the dog cringed, crouched down with a whine, and rolled to reveal its belly. One brown eye rolled to look up at him.

Jim cocked his head at the dog. He'd had no idea his vampire blood could enthrall an animal like it could a human. He was quick to capitalize on the effect.

He reached down and ruffled the fur on the dog's belly. Ciaran thumped his tail against the ground in pleasure. "Good dog. Come on now, lad. The Captain wants to see you."

The dog jumped to its feet, wagged its tail, and panted in eagerness to be off. Jim took up the lead and headed to deliver the animal.

Moira led the two pirates to a small cottage a good distance from the village. During the trip, she kept looking around to make sure no one followed or watched them.

Viktor found her behavior amusing yet annoying. He and Grimm had been avoiding detection and capture for decades. Moira's actions made it obvious she had not. It was precisely the kind of behavior which drew attention from the observant or merely nosy.

His sense of direction told him she took the most roundabout route possible. At least that was in her favor.

"This is the place. I don't know if she'll send Ciaran or not," Moira said.

"How often do you exchange messages?" Grimm asked.

"At least once a week, but the dog comes most nights, unless it rains, regardless. My sister, Megan, walks him regularly even when there are no messages to pass. She tells the guards he is chasing rabbits."

Viktor heard a sound down the road behind them. Without warning, he clasped Moira and kissed her passionately. During the kiss, he caught Grimm's eye and flicked a look to the right.

A slight nod from his first mate let him know the message was understood.

"Think I'll go relieve myself and give you some privacy, Captain." He turned and walked out of sight behind the cottage.

Moira only stiffened at first. Soon, she returned the kiss with fervor. Viktor lacerated his tongue on one of his fangs.

Within seconds, he felt her will cede to his.

It took her a few moments to recover after he broke the kiss. She blinked up at him with a bemused smile. "What was that for?"

"To throw our shadow off the scent; if they think this is just a tryst, they should lose interest and go home."

"We were followed? But I was so careful." Another kiss quelled her protest.

When he pulled back this time, he kept her in his embrace and whispered in her ear. "You were too careful, pet. It was painfully obvious you were watching for any pursuers. It was bound to draw attention."

She gave him a worried frown and he smiled to let her know he held her no ill will. She relaxed and tried to pull him down for another kiss.

"If only we had the time, pet; I would ruin you for other men," he said with a lustful laugh, "but my companions are about to rejoin us."

On that note, Grimm walked back up from the road, chuckling. At the same time, Jim Rigger strode out of the nearby trees, naked and leading a Spaniel.

Viktor didn't want to deal with incessant questions. He silenced Moira with a thought. "What has you so amused, Hezekiah; besides the sight of our naked friend, I mean?"

"Couple of youngsters just soiled themselves in their haste to escape. They thought some headless apparition had them." He pulled his coat up to hide his head and lurched about comically.

Vik and Jim roared with laughter. Moira's eyes grew wide at the sight of their fangs. Vik had been skillful and careful enough to keep her from detecting his during the kiss earlier. He caught her before she could run far.

"Easy, pet," he soothed. Her fear threatened to override his control and fire up his Hunger. He lifted her gaze to his. "You are in no danger. In the morning, this will all have seemed a dream."

She looked up at him, still mute. A single tear rolled down her face. He wiped it away and gave her a gentle smile. She shot a questioning glance at Jim. Viktor relented and gave her ability to speak back.

"Allow me to introduce my good friend, Jim Rigger. Jim, this is Moira. You'll have to forgive his state of undress, pet; he's usually a cat."

"You mean he's a pookah?"

"What's a pookah?" Jim asked.

Grimm answered, "I think it's some kind of fae that takes on animal form."

Moira nodded. Jim gave her an appraising look which quickly turned to a leer. "I'm not a pookah, but I know how to please a wench such as yourself."

Viktor laughed. "You'll have to feed first, Jim; not on her, though. Hand me the dog and go grab a quick bite."

He handed the lead over to his Captain and said, "I know just the place. Teach those buggers to throw rocks at me."

"Who threw rocks at you?"

"Some of the men on the upper watches of the keep; I had to change from raven to cat because of them."

376

"How many animals can you change into?" Moira's curiosity got the better of her.

"Man, cat, and raven, normally, love; I was a fish once, for a very brief time."

She looked skeptical but said, "If you were a raven, no wonder they threw rocks at you. Early on, Lady Darcy tried to use ravens and pigeons to send messages. Brookston got news of it and made it a standing order to kill or drive off any birds like that."

"Hmph," Viktor grunted. "How is it you came to use the dog, and why hasn't he tried to prevent it?"

She laughed derisively. "He gave her the beast. Ciaran proved to be a very lively, noisy pup. He got loose to chase a rabbit while out for a walk and found his way to this cottage. I fed him and took him back to the keep. My sister is one of Lady Darcy's attendants. We came up with the plan and presented it to her. She approved but cautioned us to establish the dog's behavior before we started passing messages. His lordship doesn't suspect."

The dog whined and scratched at its collar as if trying to get it off.

Moira stooped to ruffle his fur and slipped her fingers inside the collar. "He has a message. We need to take him inside so I can take his collar off and retrieve it."

377

Viktor and Grimm followed her into the cottage. Jim stopped at the door, a puzzled look on his face. Viktor shot him a questioning look.

"Something is keeping me from entering," he said.

"Come on in, then."

Jim nearly fell through the door. He recovered quickly. "What just happened?"

"It would seem the rules for vampires apply to you while you are in this form. You don't have any trouble entering a home when you are a cat or bird, do you?" Vik surmised.

"None at all."

"Remember to get an invitation when you're a man."

"I will."

Moira drew their attention. "She heard about the incident behind the pub and wants to know who did such damage to Brookston's thugs. She also wants to know if you would be willing to help her gain her freedom." She shook her head. "He might be able to get in, but I don't see how a naked, unarmed man can get the Lady out or how the rest of you could get past the guards."

Viktor chuckled. "Don't worry, pet. I have given it thought during our stroll here and have allowed for that."

He began to undress. She stared at him, bemused. He ignored her and addressed Jim, "I only need to hold the shape long enough to get in and to Darcy. How much do I need to eat?"

"Hmm, I'd say no more than a mouthful of blood and some fur. I don't think you'll need to take a bite out of him."

"Good; I admit, the thought of raw dog meat was not appealing." He slipped the chains which held the silver vial and the Elder's stone over his head and held them out to his first mate. "Look after these until I get back, Hezekiah. Jim, you can wear my clothes. I imagine Moira is tired of the sight of you."

Jim stuck his tongue out at him. He chuckled and shook his head at his friend. He finished undressing by taking off the harness which held the sheath for his favorite dagger; the one he kept at the nape of his neck. He laid it on top of the pile of clothes and picked up the dog.

"Don't hurt him! He's a sweet dog." Moira's face twisted in distress.

"Not to worry, pet," Viktor soothed as he retrieved his dagger. "I just need to shave off a little fur and make a tiny prick on his ear. It won't be any worse than a scratch from a thorn."

He found swallowing the fur harder than he expected. It tickled in his mouth and on the back of his tongue and threatened to gag him. As a result, he drew more blood from the tiny wound than he'd originally intended.

A strange, tingling sensation washed over his entire body. He barely had time to set the dog down before a wave of vertigo hit him.

Within seconds, two identical Spaniels stood side by side.

Moira screamed and fainted.

# Chapter 31

Viktor watched Ciaran back away from him with his tail tucked. The dog moved to the unconscious woman and huddled against her side.

Viktor wondered why she looked so much bigger. It took him a moment to process the fact his perspective was now much closer to the floor. Colors seemed muted; his senses of smell and hearing grew even stronger; and he itched.

"Did it work?" he asked or tried to. All that came out was a garbled bark. His mouth felt wrong. All his teeth had grown sharper and his tongue longer. He looked at himself and answered his own question. His ears perked forward as he watched his tail wag. He found it an oddly pleasant sensation.

A chuckle drew his attention. He saw Jim grinning down at him as he put on the discarded clothes.

*"You're enjoying this, aren't you?"* He thought at his friend. Gratification filled him at the surprised expression that crossed Jim's face.

"I understood that," Jim said.

"I'm glad one of us can," Grimm grumbled. He wore a look of unease.

*"You need to wake the wench so she can take me to the keep. I imagine I won't like it but go ahead and put the collar and lead on me, as well. I don't want to raise suspicions. Keep the dog here and out of sight until I get back."*

"He said put the collar on him and wake her up to take him back," Jim relayed.

Viktor almost balked when Grimm slipped the collar around his neck. The fit wasn't too snug, at least. He couldn't shake the feeling of being trapped. He only hoped someone removed the collar before he transformed back to human form. He didn't know if the leather would give before the change in size could snap his spine or crush his windpipe.

"What happened?" he heard a female voice say. He looked over and saw the woman sit up and hold her head. She flinched when Ciaran touched her arm with his nose.

"That's the real dog, lass," Grimm said.

"Oh."

He held Viktor's lead out to her. "You need to keep him here and take the Captain back in his place."

She held her hands close to her body and shook her head. Viktor could almost see the stink of fear on her. It both fascinated him and threatened to bring his more predatory nature to the forefront.

He decided to test the temporary bond he'd formed with her earlier to see if it was still in place. He willed her to not fear him. Her scent instantly changed.

"Blast it, woman; I can't take him there. You have to do it," Grimm growled at her.

"No need to be so snippy," she replied crossly. "Come on, boy. Let's get you home." She took the lead and walked out of the cottage.

He heard the muffled chuckles of his two mates as Moira closed the door behind them. He determined to get both of them back for their merriment at his expense.

The night air sang to him like never before. He'd grown accustomed to the way his vampirism enhanced his senses. This experience far surpassed that. The colors and textures of the new scents and sounds threatened to overwhelm him.

A light tug on the lead made him aware he'd stopped moving.

"You coming or not?" Moira asked with a frown.

He wagged his tail and fell in step. As much as he wanted to drink in the new experiences, he knew he needed to stay focused on the task at hand. He didn't know how long he would be able to hold this form.

He still found his mind wandering due to the constant barrage of new stimuli on his senses. His mental focus returned to the forefront with the scent of fear from Moira. He looked in the direction she did.

A large, armed man approached them. He exuded irritable displeasure. The closer he got, the stronger her fear grew. Viktor growled at him. She tugged lightly on the lead to discourage that.

"About time that damn dog showed back up," the man grumbled. "His lordship never should have given her the flea-bitten beast. More trouble 'n he's worth."

"Oh, he's just a pup, Cam. You know how he likes to chase rabbits."

The guard snatched the lead from her and poked a finger in her shoulder hard enough to push her back a step. "Gimme that. You've caused enough trouble tonight. Because you had to flirt like a common whore with some strangers, we've got men dead or gravely wounded." Her temper flared. "Don't go blamin' me because a bunch of drunken louts picked a fight with the wrong men, Cameron Collins. I don't belong to any of them and wouldn't have 'em, either."

Cameron drew his hand back, prepared to backhand her. Viktor picked that moment to hike his leg and pee on the man's boot.

The distraction drew the man's ire away from the woman but earned him a kick in the ribs. A yelp escaped him. He lay on his side and struggled to breathe for a few moments. He could tell a few ribs were broken and threatened to pierce his lungs.

Moira knelt next to him and stroked his ears, making worried, cooing sounds. As a man, he would have found the noise irritating; now though, he found it comforting. The caresses soothed and distracted him.

"Meg! Come get this damn cur," Cameron yelled back toward the keep's interior.

Viktor felt grateful his rapid healing ability remained with him in his current form. He sincerely hoped the guard was not in Darcy's favor. He determined to make the man pay for his behavior.

A younger woman came out. She ran over to join Moira by his side. "What happened to him?"

"Cam kicked him."

Both women glared at the guard. "Fucker pissed on me boots," he responded surlily.

"That's no reason to kick such a sweet puppy," Meg said. She gently probed Viktor's side. He whimpered a little as her fingers brushed over his bruised but healing ribs. The bones had already reset and knit back together.

Relief colored Meg's voice. "Be thankful nothing is broken, Cameron. His lordship would be very cross if you hurt poor Ciaran. This dog is the only gift he's given Lady Darcy that she hasn't outright rejected."

Cameron made mocking, mewling noises and faces like a child sassing after being scolded by its mother. Meg scooped Viktor up, stuck her tongue out at the guard, and marched defiantly into the keep.

Viktor grinned at Cameron as they passed. His tongue lolled out, and he wagged his tail. Meg's firm but gentle grasp and her warmth and softness felt amazing even through his fur. It brought back subconscious memories of being held and carried by Mother Celie when he'd been an infant.

He also noticed her indignant anger added a tone to her scent he found very arousing. He had to concentrate to keep himself from unsheathing and startling her.

All too soon, they entered a well-appointed set of rooms, and she set him down. She bent down and ruffled his head then went and knocked on a nearby door.

"The scamp finally came back. He ran all the way to Moira's again."

Another woman entered the room. He could tell she had recently washed. The scent of soap almost masked her scent. Her hair hung dark and wet around her shoulders.

She smiled at him. "Did you bring me something from your rabbit chase, Ciaran?"

Meg said in a low voice, "He almost didn't get to have his chase. Some strangers ran afoul of His men in the village and got the better of them. Cam said a couple of the men were dead and a few more badly wounded. He wasn't going to let me give Ciaran a run."

The other woman, Darcy he assumed, knelt and undid Viktor's collar to check it for a message. She found a terse note in unfamiliar handwriting. "I heard about it from Aidan when he brought my dinner up. He was in the kitchen when the bastards were brought in. How did you manage to let him get loose?" she asked absently as she read the note.

"A huge black cat showed up from nowhere and knocked me down. Ciaran took off after it. I've never seen a cat that big. What does the note say?"

"*Help is on the way;* but I don't recognize the handwriting. Moira didn't pen this."

Meg peered over to peer at the missive. "I don't know who did, either."

Darcy pursed her lips. "Ciaran shall have to chase rabbits again tomorrow night. I need to know who wrote this."

Meg gave Viktor a concerned look. He wagged his tail at her. "It might be better to wait a little longer. Cameron was a beast about tonight's escape. He kicked Ciaran hard enough to knock the wind out of him. I checked, and nothing seemed broken; but I think he's bruised."

"Oh, my poor puppy! Tell Cameron if he even touches my dog again, I'll have him flogged," Darcy growled as she gently prodded Viktor's side. He wagged his tail even harder and licked her hands. She tasted sweet and clean.

"With pleasure, milady. Will there be anything else?"

"No, thank you, Meg. I'm going to retire now."

"Goodnight then, milady."

Viktor surreptitiously watched her leave the rooms. He then turned his attention back to Darcy O'Malley.

She stood and headed for the door she had entered through. He glanced over at the pile of pillows that smelled of dog. She stopped and looked back at him.

"Come on, boy. You can sleep with Mama tonight." She tapped her hand against her thigh.

He broke into a canine grin and trotted along to follow her. She led him to her bed chamber. He watched as she disrobed and turned the coverlet back. A strange tingling warned him the magic had run its course.

Just as she turned to call the dog to the bed, Viktor returned to his human form. His vision blurred with the sudden change in height, and his senses dulled back to their accustomed strength, one which still far surpassed that of any human.

The nude vampire stood and looked at the nude woman dumbfounded before him and saw a face he'd never thought to see again.

"Carpathia?"

_Tamara A. Lowery_

# Chapter 32

No, it wasn't her. The scent was wrong. This woman smelled human and very much alive and warm, not the almost reptilian cold of the undead. As his color sight grew sharper in his true form than that of a dog, Viktor also noticed the dark red of her hair, very like Belladonna's.

He made these observations in less time than it took to blink.

He detected no scent of fear from her. She glanced toward her robe but made no move to retrieve it. He smiled, knowing she'd realized it was too late for modesty.

"Is Ciaran unharmed?"

He blinked. That had not been the response he'd expected. "He will be returned to you unharmed, Lady Darcy."

"Who gave you my name?"

Again, an unexpected question; he raised an eyebrow and countered, "You are definitely not what I expected, milady: no fear and full of questions. Most women would be in hysterics at the sight of their pet transforming into a naked man."

"Who gave you my name?" She repeated with some vehemence.

"The woman I call Mother." He took a step toward her and watched her fight not to take a step back. A hint of uncertainty colored her scent. "Know that I intend you no harm."

"Then give me your name."

Her smile and voice told him she thought this would give her some sort of advantage. He saw no harm in it and thought it might help him with his negotiation for her ring later. For now, there was something else he wanted from her.

He gave a shallow bow and said, "Viktor."

She frowned, obviously puzzled. "What kind of name is that for a pookah?"

He laughed, careful not to show his fangs. He didn't want to frighten her. Her frown started to grow angry. He stepped right up to her and pulled her body to his. Her eyes dilated and she gasped in surprise as he caressed the side of her face.

"Yes, I would think Viktor an odd name for a pookah; but I am not a pookah. I'm a pirate." He leaned down and kissed her soundly. When he pulled back, he whispered, "I just happen to know a little magic."

She dug her thumbs into his ribs just below his armpits and pushed away from him. He could have kept her in his grasp but released her with a wicked smile. He watched as she grabbed a dagger from a bedside table and held it like she knew how to use it.

"My, my, pet; you are full of surprises."

"I'm not yer pet, y' filthy bugger," she growled, her natural brogue thickening with her ire.

He held his hands palm outward. "Peace, milady; as I stated before, I intend you no harm."

"Yer pecker seems t' think otherwise." She pointed at his erection with the blade.

He laughed. "Can you blame it when presented with such a glorious bounty?"

She blushed but regained her composure quickly. More and more, he liked the challenge she presented.

"Very well, Viktor, if that is your real name; why are you here?"

Finally, something he knew he could make some progress with, although he still held hope for some sport with her. "You have a ring, a family heirloom that I have need of. I believe I may be able to offer you valuable services in exchange for it." She gave him a shocked look of surprise. "The legend is true, then," she muttered.

He frowned. What kind of story had Celie given this woman's ancestress when she sent her the bauble?

Darcy regained her concentration and met his gaze. "What is your full name? Please, this is important."

"Viktor Brandewyne; though there are some who call me Bloody Vik Brandee." He watched her eyes grow wide and the color leave her face. He only had a fraction of a second to catch her before her legs collapsed under her. He supported her with one arm and gently took the dagger from her limp grasp and placed it back on the table. He swept her up and carried her to the bed.

Looking about the chamber, he spotted the wash basin. He dampened a cloth to wipe her face with. As an afterthought, he tied the drying sheet around his waist to put her more at ease. In short order, he returned to sit beside her on the bed and set about reviving her.

She shuddered when the cool cloth touched her brow. The trembling did not stop immediately. He pulled one of the covers to drape over her, and she sighed. He returned his attention to gently wiping her forehead and cheeks.

Finally, her eyelids fluttered open. "Are you feeling well, milady?"

She scooted away from him, and he gave her time to recover her dignity. Fear, curiosity, and a hint of disappointment colored her scent. It made him want to take her then and there; but he restrained himself.

"You covered yourself."

"I thought it might make you more comfortable. I'd no idea my identity would be such a shock to you."

She glanced down at her lap. "It isn't so much your identity, though that is part of it; it is your very presence here and for the reason you stated."

He began to have an inkling as to why she'd become so suddenly subdued. "I've heard enough talk and whispers from Mother Celie and the other Sisters of Power to realize they have some sort of prophecy about me. Of course, none of them have seen fit to tell me what it is."

She looked back at him, searching his face. "You mean you don't know why you're here?"

He chuckled. "Oh, I know why I'm here. I just don't know exactly what those biddies are talking about when they refer to me as 'the One.' Apparently, there is some ultimate purpose I am supposed to serve; they just remain so damn cryptic about it any time I ask them directly."

"Do you at least know why you need my ring?" She crossed her arms and scowled at him. Clearly, her moods were mercurial.

He mimicked her pose and answered her, "It is the final piece I must collect to complete a puzzle box which belongs to the Sister of Power known as Circe."

Her face flushed and she slapped his arm. "Quit mocking me."

He grinned. He always had enjoyed feisty women. Belatedly, he realized he'd shown his fangs. She stared at him wide-eyed with her mouth open.

"My apologies, milady; I didn't mean to frighten you."

"What are you?" she whispered.

"A pirate and a vampire; I have been cursed to feed on human blood. That is part of the reason I have to finish that puzzle box. It is the requirement placed on me by Circe to exchange for the portion of her magic I need to help break my curse." He watched her carefully. Normally, he did not give out that much personal information.

Oddly, his explanation seemed to put her at ease.

"Your story fits too closely with the legend passed down from Granuille about the ring. This legend has been a closely guarded O'Malley family secret passed

396

down from generation to generation. It has never been shared with anyone outside the family." She looked at him with awe.

He wanted to ask her what the legend was, just out of curiosity; but he expected she wouldn't tell him. He also thought asking would probably cost him the ground he'd gained with her. Instead, his attention began to focus on her body. He wondered if she realized she'd allowed the cover to drop to her waist.

Of its own volition, it seemed, his hand moved up to caress her breast. She didn't try to stop him. He heard her heartbeat quicken. He glanced at her face and saw desire and uncertainty. He thought he knew part of the reason why.

"How long has it been since you've been with a man, milady?"

She blushed. "It has been over a year. If I hadn't been with child after Brookston murdered my husband, I fear he would have raped me by now."

He brushed a tendril of hair out of her face. "What happened to the child? I see no sign of crib or nursery."

"Talia only lived a few days after her birth. She wouldn't eat, and I woke one morn to find her blue and lifeless." She shuddered at the memory and huddled in on herself.

He drew her into his arms and cradled her against his chest. She gradually relaxed into his embrace. For a moment, he thought she had drifted off to sleep; then she spoke softly.

"You said you could offer me services. What exactly did you mean?"

"How would you like to be rid of Roderick Brookston?"

She leaned back and looked up at him. "Can you get me out of here? I have the evidence I need to bring murder charges against him, but I can't do it from here."

"When would you like to leave?"

"How quickly can you arrange it?"

He chuckled. "I can take you now, milady; just get some clothes and the ring, and I will fly you to safety."

She raised an eyebrow at him skeptically. In response, he levitated and hovered near the ceiling. "I told you; I know some magic."

As he returned to stand by the bed, she laughed in delight. "In all my days I never dreamed I'd encounter a man like you, Viktor; family legend be damned. I'd always thought it more of a faerie story and never believed it would come true, let alone come true for me."

398

"I have to admit, milady; though I seem to prove your legend true, I am ignorant of what it is. Mother Celie neglected to tell me about it," he said.

"She's real, too? Oh my, she must be ancient." She gave him a calculating look and seemed to come to a decision. "I will trust you, Viktor Brandewyne, even though you are a pirate and something far more dangerous. The short version of the legend is that Old Mother Celie and a strange old man summoned Granuille, Grace O'Malley the Pirate Queen, to a magical isle. There, Mother Celie gave her a ring. She said it was the key to Circe's puzzle and that a dangerous man known as Viktor Brandewyne the Pirate King would come to claim it from a daughter of her line."

She looked straight at him. "You and your magic were described almost exactly. I think a few details might have been lost over the generations of retelling."

"Interesting; it makes me wonder how much Mother has manipulated me in this. I'll have to ask her about it when next I see her; although I doubt she'll give me a straight answer," he muttered.

Something in her scent drew his attention. He saw the desire return to her eyes as she looked at him. Her previous uncertainty did not return.

"There is one more part of the legend you should know about."

"Oh?"

"It was said the Pirate King would give the daughter of the Pirate Queen an heir."

He smiled his most wicked smile. "And would milady like for me to fulfill that part of the legend, as well?"

She nodded and returned his smile.

He started to move towards her then stopped. He held up his hand in response to the questioning look in her eyes. His enhanced hearing picked up the unmistakable sound of several heartbeats approaching.

"Gather your things quickly, milady. Your guards are coming to check on you."

"Where will we go?" she moved to do as he said even as she asked.

"My ship will offer safe haven until we can arrange a better sanctuary for you." He watched and made sure she got the ring along with clothes. She hung it on a chain around her neck.

"Milady? Is all well? Meg said she heard a man's voice," called a male voice from the next room.

Viktor stood by the window, opened it, and held his hand out to her. "It's time to go." He didn't bother keeping his voice low.

"Who's in there?" the voice called. The sound of a shoulder hitting the door soon followed. It flew open, and the owner of the shoulder tumbled to the floor. No one had bothered to lock it.

Viktor scooped Darcy up in his arms and paused just long enough for the man to recover, and the other guards to enter the room.

"Tell his lordship he has excellent taste in women," he said and stepped out into open space.

*Tamara A. Lowery*

# Chapter 33

Viktor and Darcy watched the keep from far above it as it erupted into an ant mound of activity. The lady's sudden disappearance in such an unorthodox manner threw her household and captors into a panic.

He began to chuckle. He could still hear the conversations of the guards who sought for them. "They think some spirit has stolen you away. No splash from the moat or bodies on the ground beneath your window has them flummoxed."

The woman clung to him, but not tightly enough to indicate fear. "They aren't far wrong. It is clear you are no mortal man, Viktor. Now, where is this ship of yours?"

"Not far; I need to let my mates know to return, as well." He flew to the small cottage.

Grimm sat smoking his pipe on a seat outside the cottage door. He caught a subtle whistle of wind on the nearly breezeless night air. It proved enough to alert him to his Captain's return. He caught sight of the woman Viktor carried, and his blood ran cold.

"Bugger me; how did she get out? I thought Glory said I was the only one who could open that bottle."

"This isn't Carpathia," the vampire replied and set the woman on her feet for the moment.

Her Irish brogue lent credence to Viktor's words. Her tone indicated a mercurial temper. "You're in league with an Englishman?"

"Peace, milady; we are pirates and owe no allegiance to any but ourselves. Allow me to introduce my first mate, Hezekiah Grimm, more commonly known as the Grimm Reaper. Hezekiah, may I present Lady Darcy O'Malley-O'Connor."

Grimm stood and gave a formal, if slightly mocking bow. "Forgive my outburst, milady. You bear a striking resemblance to a troublesome she-devil we dealt with recently. The Captain speaks truth; I am no king's man."

"Now that I know your name, I believe it. I've heard tales of the Reaper."

He noticed she stayed just out of easy reach. He couldn't fault her caution. Under other circumstances, he wouldn't have hesitated to ransom her back to her suitor for a tidy sum.

If not for his vows to his wife and the known cost of breaking them, he'd have charged twice as much to guarantee her return with her virtue still intact. She was a beauty.

Viktor's voice brought his thoughts back to the present. "Where's Mr. Rigger?"

"Inside with the lass; he flew off shortly after she left with you and returned just before she did. Said he got back at one of the keep's roof guards who'd chucked rocks at him."

"Hmph; he was quiet about it, at least." Viktor went and knocked on the door. "Dawn is approaching, Mr. Rigger."

The door opened, and Jim poked his head out. "You know how to ruin a man's sport, Cap'n."

Vik laughed. "There'll be time enough for sport tomorrow night. You and the wench get dressed and bring the dog."

Just then, the animal ran out of the cottage and to his mistress. He proceeded to wiggle, pant, whine, grunt, and lick her hands. She laughed and picked the dog up.

"Time to leave, Captain?" Grimm asked, although he already knew the answer. They needed to leave the area before searchers were sent out.

"Aye."

Jim emerged wearing Viktor's clothes which were a loose fit on the slightly shorter vampire. He pulled the disheveled and hastily dressed tavern wench by the hand behind him.

"Milady! He got you out!" Moira sounded both surprised and happy.

"Yes; thank you for taking care of Ciaran."

"Jim, can you carry two?" Viktor asked.

"Two lovely women? Of course," he grinned, not bothering to hide his fangs.

The Captain laughed at his friend. "I'll be carrying Lady Darcy, the dog, and her things. You can carry Mr. Grimm and the girl."

"Carry me where? Milady, what is he talking about? I'm perfectly capable of walking." Moira looked between her mistress and the three men, clearly confused and a little frightened.

Grimm thought they might have to render her unconscious to prevent panic or screaming.

"Mr. Rigger," Vik said.

Jim lifted her chin and gazed into her eyes with a smile. "It won't be safe for you here for a while, my lovely. You are coming with us back to our ship; but we

406

need to travel fast to reach it before the sun comes up. Are you afraid of heights?"

"What?" She didn't seem to understand what he was talking about.

"Thought as much," he muttered and kissed her without warning. Her eyes rolled back and fluttered shut, and she grew limp in his arms. He draped her over his shoulder and held his other arm open to Grimm.

"Just don't try to be kissin' me, Rigger." He stepped over and wrapped his arms around the vampire's shoulders and the woman draped there. Her body made it a little awkward, but he managed. Jim cinched his arm around Grimm's waist and launched the three of them into the night sky.

Viktor followed closely behind with his passengers.

"Who is she?" Belladonna and Darcy demanded of Viktor simultaneously when he landed on deck. The two red heads glared at each other.

Viktor saw Grimm cringe at the impending storm. Jim's grin grew even wider, for the same reason.

"Lady Darcy, this is Belladonna, a siren. Belle, this is Lady Darcy O'Malley-O'Connor; don't eat her or her dog. She is our guest until better accommodations can be arranged and her unwanted suitor is dealt with."

"So that is the price for the ring," Belle said, her voice suspiciously calm. She shrugged after a brief sniff of the air. "Enjoy your human, but I would advise you do not feed from her: directly or indirectly."

He'd anticipated jealousy from the siren, not this near indifference. "She isn't Carpathia, all resemblance aside; why would her blood pose a danger?"

Belladonna gazed at him as if he were an inexperienced boy, which irritated him. Her words reminded him she was centuries older than him, though. "She smells of selkie. They are both fae and one of the sea folk. I suspect a full blood selkie was one of her forebears."

"I am not food," Darcy huffed. "As for having selkie blood, I don't recall any family legends about it; but it would explain the O'Malleys' love of the sea."

*"It would also explain your mercurial nature,"* Vik thought but kept it to himself. The siren must've picked up on his thoughts judging by the smirk she shot at him.

He decided to continue the conversation with Belle through their mental link. It was quicker and less likely to irritate Darcy.

*"Is she toxic, or is there another reason?"*

The siren responded in kind, *"Not toxic, although selkies are predators in their seal form. I just don't want a repeat of that business with that mermaid. Remember,*

408

*there is a wild element to your magic. It could trigger a transformation, although that's highly unlikely. But that could change if she turned."*

*"I see your point, pet; no blood from her, then."*

"If that will be all, Captain, I'd like to go hunt," Belle said aloud.

"Enjoy your hunt, pet."

He watched the siren stroll away toward the aft of the ship. Once he heard the splash of her dive, he turned his attention back to his mates and two guests. He saw Jim pout, which made him smirk.

"That went smoother than I'd feared," Grimm said with a note of bemusement.

"Indeed."

"Damn, I was hoping for a fight," Jim said.

Viktor chuckled. "Sun's almost up, Mr. Rigger; unless you want a very bad sunburn, I suggest you head below or become Lazarus. Mr. Grimm if you would see to Moira's accommodations, I'll tend to the Lady."

"Aye, Captain." Grimm turned to the woman. "If you'll come with me, lass."

She turned to look at Jim just in time to see him transform into a large black cat. She took an involuntary step back from the creature. Grim touched her arm, and she went with him without question.

Even Darcy seemed mildly disturbed by the transformation. She laughed nervously. "After seeing you turn from a dog into a man, I would think that wouldn't be so unnerving."

"It takes some getting used to," he admitted. "I believe we had some unfinished business, milady; something about a prophecy."

She blushed and allowed him to lead her from the deck.

Darcy yawned and stretched as the afternoon sun shone golden through the windows. Viktor enjoyed the view from his seat at the table. He'd always enjoyed watching a woman sleep; he took equal pleasure in watching her wake and those fleet moments of unselfconsciousness when she is unaware of anyone around her.

He smiled in memory of the pleasure they'd shared only hours ago. He wondered if her resemblance to Carpathia or the trace of fae in her bloodline had enhanced the experience for him. After being with the siren and two of the Sisters of Power, human women seemed bland as lovers. He still enjoyed them, but that touch of mingled magic gave a rush like no other.

All too soon, Darcy became aware of her surroundings. "Where? Oh!" She clutched the cover and ran a hand through her hair. She looked around the cabin, taking in every detail.

He somehow doubted she'd paid much attention to such things when he'd brought her to his cabin that morning. She finally noticed the food on the table.

"I thought you might be hungry."

"Thank you." She didn't hesitate to help herself. She stopped after the second bite, her eyes wide. "This is amazing. I don't think my cooks have ever served anything this good."

"Mr. Trundle was a fortunate addition to my crew. Of course, taking on fresh provisions recently didn't hurt." He only nibbled from the dish at his place. He'd eaten before she woke and had a generous ration of his blood-brandy mixture to keep his Hunger at bay.

She noticed. "Aren't you going to eat? I feel rude eating alone in front of you."

He smiled and shook his head. "I fear I am the one who was rude, milady. I didn't wait for you to awaken to have my own repast. Please, enjoy your meal."

She needed no further encouragement.

Once she sated herself and slowed to nibbling as well, he decided it was time to discuss their plan of action. "We need to lure Brookston to someplace peopled with your supporters."

"The village near my keep; Moira can get word out for my people to gather there," she suggested.

He frowned. "It seemed his men were in strength there."

"I know. The main reason for that was because of my status as a hostage in my own home. Now that I am safely out of his grasp, my people are free to take action. How can we lure him there, though?"

"I'd thought about sending him a ransom letter." He watched for her reaction.

She narrowed her eyes at him then smirked. "He wouldn't pay it. You'd be doing him a favor."

"Oh?"

"He would make a show of trying to ransom me, but he'd eventually spread the story you'd killed me or sold me off and use it to take control of my holdings."

Viktor studies her for a while. Clearly, she possessed a keen intellect to go with her fiery beauty and temper. She recognized Brookston's suit for the power play it was.

"It does not surprise me that the man is more interested in your property than your bed. Most men obsessed with power and position tend to not give the pleasures of life greater priority."

"And you do?"

"What is the point of having great wealth or power if you don't get to enjoy it?"

She smiled. "I like the way you think, Viktor."

"Then you should love this," he said with a chuckle. "I suggest we appeal to his greed." He paused as an afterthought occurred to him. "Before I continue on this course, can you tell me how loyal he is to the Crown? Would his greed override his sense of patriotic duty?"

"Hmm, I'm not entirely sure. I know he came here as part of an effort to cement English control on this end of the island."

Viktor stroked his beard. "I think this plan will still work. We'll just have to be prepped to steer the situation the way we want it to go regardless of which tack he takes."

Darcy sat a little straighter and tilted her head. "What do you have in mind?"

He grinned. "I don't trust his men to be quick to notify him of your disappearance. It wouldn't look good for them. However, I don't need them to report it. I'll send my navigator to negotiate a trade agreement between your family and his father's trading company.

413

He will then send a runner back to Harlowe with word that you are not there. Harlowe will then send word to Brookston, since he controls your husband's holdings."

She considered him for some time before she spoke again. "That just might work, provided the trading company is well known. I take it from Harlowe's involvement that even were this negotiation genuine it would be for an illicit arrangement."

"Aye; thanks to my efforts, Brumble & Sons is in a bit of disrepute. The current state of things back in the Colonies makes honest trade difficult anyway. Blockade running, however, can be quite profitable if you don't get caught."

She crossed her arms and looked at him. "I have heard of Brumble & Sons. They operate out of Boston, do they not?" He nodded. She continued, "Why would a well-known trading house deal in smuggling?"

"Profit, of course," he replied. "Old Brumble's sons, Zachary and Thomas, were smuggling emeralds when I added them to my crew." He walked over to a cabinet and retrieved a small casket from it. He opened it to reveal an emerald encrusted gold cross. "This was among their cache. It has proven quite useful." He took it out and put it on.

Darcy gave him a puzzled look. "How has it been useful? It is gorgeous and probably worth a fortune, but it is just an ornament."

He aimed his most predatory grin at her, deliberately showing his fangs. "It is one of the few things that can curb my Hunger for blood."

She blanched a little but otherwise showed no fear. He liked that.

"I think the ploy will work to get him here. Whether he will be more interested in making money or turning your navigator over to the English to further his position, I couldn't say. He will want to know why he heard of my escape from someone other than the men tasked to guard me, though," she finally answered his question.

He'd already guessed that would be the case. For now, it was something to deal with the next day. He'd gotten the blessed cross out for the very reason he found it useful. He remembered the siren's warning not to feed on this woman. The drawback to using the cross came as an increase of his other appetites.

"I'm not sure I've gotten you with child yet, milady." He gave her a playful smile. She turned bright crimson at the sudden change of subject. He chuckled low and wicked as he advanced on her.

She seemed to notice only then that neither of them had bothered to dress yet. He smiled as he watched her explore his form with her eyes. Her pupils dilated when she reached the part of him which stood ready for her. Her lips parted, and he heard her breathing and pulse quicken. An unmistakable musky tone entered her scent and let him know her body was just as ready for him as he was for her.

Part of him wanted to pick her up and take her where he stood. He knew better than to do that, though. Although she held a trace of magic, she was still human. Her body was too fragile for him to risk being overzealous in his lovemaking.

Besides, he wanted to savor the experience. Their earlier session together had been more of a passionate rut than seduction. Darcy's abstinence during her widowhood had given her a sense of urgency.

Viktor intended to draw things out both for her benefit and his own enjoyment.

He brushed a strand of her hair away from her face and traced his fingertips lightly along her jawline. This brought her gaze back to his face.

"My turn."

He slowly lowered his gaze down her body, taking in every detail. Her dark red hair draped around her shoulders and made her pale skin appear even milkier. Faint freckles dusted her shoulders. Her breasts rounded pleasingly but retained the firmness of her youth. Pale pink aureoles framed delicate nipples. Her belly rounded slightly above the swell of her hips. Dark ginger curls covered the mounded folds of her womanhood. Finally, the soft lines of her thighs and calves marked her as someone unaccustomed to labor.

He knew the lust showed in his eyes when he returned his gaze to hers. He saw it mirrored on her face.

"You look at me as if I were the most desirable, beautiful thing you've ever seen," she whispered huskily.

He only answered her with a wicked chuckle. He stepped closer to her and gently buried his hands in her hair. He massaged her scalp and savored the soft warmth against his skin. Her eyes fluttered shut, and she moaned softly in pleasure.

He leaned down and kissed her. Without breaking the kiss, he lifted her and carried her to the bed. Once she settled, she leaned back with a smile and opened her legs for him.

Her smile turned to a look of confusion when he knelt next to the bed instead of over her. He put his hands under her bottom and positioned her how he wanted her.

"What are you —?"

"Patience, milady," he replied teasingly.

He adjusted her legs to place her knees up and to either side of him. He kissed her right knee and slowly traced his tongue along the inside of her thigh, stopping just shy of her moist folds. He watched her face as he did so and saw both dawning understanding and wonder.

417

"Did you like that?"

She nodded. "Oh yes, but it tickles a little."

He saw gooseflesh had already risen on her skin. "I'm just getting started," he replied with a chuckle and watched her eyes widen. He repeated the process with her other leg. He continued to use the tip of his tongue to draw on her body. He traced a line from one hip bone to the other and back to the middle just above her curls. He proceeded up from there to circle her navel and dipped his tongue in and out rapidly a few times.

She whimpered and squirmed a little.

He continued his path upward between her breasts and traced her collarbones. He blew where his tongue had just passed and raised more gooseflesh. He turned his attention to her breasts. First, he ran his tongue around each nipple and blew on them; then he took one into his mouth and gently closed his front teeth on it. He tugged with just enough pressure to lift her breast a little and felt the nipple harden under his tongue.

She drew in a gasping breath as he continued to tease it.

Satisfied with the effect he'd caused; he released that nipple and did the same thing to the other one. This time she cried out. He dipped an exploratory finger between her folds. It came out very wet.

418

With a growl, he lowered his face to the source of the moisture and began to lap and suckle with ever increasing vigor. As he tortured her nub with tongue, lips, and teeth, careful not to draw blood, she rewarded him with quickened breaths, small chirping moans, and hands flailing at the bedding.

He sensed she was near climax again. Faster than any mortal man, he rose from his position and thrust inside her. He held perfectly still as her back arched, and her body contracted around him. She cried out again.

Once her orgasm played out, he began to slowly thrust. She moaned and gasped. Her face bore a look of helpless abandon. He gradually increased his pace and watched her writhe beneath him.

When he saw she was about to reach that shining moment again, he became vigorous. He did not stop as she convulsed and contracted around him. He allowed the added friction to bring him.

They cried out their ecstasy together.

As they lay side by side in the afterglow, Darcy began to chuckle.

"What has you so amused, milady?"

"I'm just wondering if you were trying to impregnate me or kill me. I don't think I'll be able to walk for some time."

His chuckle answered hers. "Then I did my duty by you."

# Chapter 34

Zachary Brumble fought the urge to ask for whiskey. The ale in front of him wasn't bad, but he wanted something stronger. He knew he needed to be clear-headed, though. If he failed the Captain, there would be hell to pay.

He couldn't help but wonder if the Captain's prey planned to try to turn this into a trap for the pirates. Zach had been with the crew long enough to have been added to the lists. If Brookston held any connections with the Royal Navy, this could go very bad very quickly.

A larger presence of his crewmates would make him feel more comfortable. That was a luxury they couldn't afford, however. He was supposed to be here to negotiate a trade agreement. To have a large part of the crew this far inland would raise suspicions. So, he had to rely mostly on Lady Darcy's people; a thought which did not engender much confidence. He found it difficult trusting people who'd made no real effort to free her from her siege.

"Do y'want me to order us some food, Cap'n?" Jon-Jon interrupted his train of thought.

Zach blinked at the burly pirate and shook his head. It had been so long since he'd held the title of captain, he no longer responded to it automatically. For this ruse, he posed as a sea captain with Jon-Jon as his mate.

"No, Mr. Jon; Lord Brookston might take it as an insult for us to start without him. I don't need to remind you how important it is we broker this agreement with him." At least he could play the role convincingly. He knew a good portion of the tavern's patrons were Brookston's men. Still, the Lady's men outnumbered them; a factor which might come into play later.

A small group of men entered the tavern together. Zach gathered from the attention they drew they were no more local than him. Three of the newcomers came close to Jon-Jon in size and looked well-armed. The fourth man stood much shorter than his guards but wore better clothes. Zach thought he looked quite foppish and took an instant dislike to him.

He didn't let the man's attire, or the presence of bodyguards deceive him about the level of threat Brookston posed, however. The man's stance was that of a swordsman; but pudginess around the middle spoke of a lack of practice and a leisurely lifestyle. Zach doubted the man's reflexes were as sharp as they could be, a possibility which could give the pirates an advantage in a fight.

The assessment only took a few moments. Zach stood and gave a shallow bow. "Lord Brookston?"

He waited patiently while the man gave him a look over. Brookston's eyes narrowed slightly, and his stance took on more of an air of readiness. Zach reassessed the threat level but remained careful not to show it in his body language. He wanted Brookston at ease, not on the alert.

Finally, he nodded. "I am Lord Roderick Brookston; and you might be?"

For a brief moment, Zach had an irrational urge to say, "I might be Bloody Vik Brandee," but he didn't. He'd always hated the affectations of the nobility or even the well-to-do among the gentry. Still, he knew how to play this game; his father had seen to that.

"Allow me to introduce myself. I am Captain Zachary Brumble of Boston. This is my mate, Willoby Jon," he replied with another bow. "It is an honor to meet you, milord."

Jon-Jon only nodded.

Brookston inclined his head to Zach and scowled at Jon-Jon. "Does he speak?"

Jon-Jon opened his mouth to reply. Zach headed him off. "Oh yes, milord, but his language is more suited to the deck of a ship than polite conversation."

"Ah yes, I see; I've a few men like that in my employ as well," the Englishman said with a smile. "I must admit, sir, your manners are remarkably proper for a colonial."

*"And yours are quite lacking for a noble,"* he thought. Aloud, he said, "Thank you, milord. I have my father to thank for that. He insisted all his children be schooled in proper etiquette. He felt it vital to conducting business. Would you join us?" He gestured at one of the vacant chairs.

"Thank you, Captain Brumble." Brookston took the offered seat. His bodyguards positioned themselves accordingly. "Your father sounds like a wise man."

Zach snorted before he could stop himself. "He knows business; but I wouldn't call him wise. You must excuse me, milord. My father and I do not exactly see eye to eye on several things."

Brookston nodded in understanding. "Isn't that always the way of it? Even when one strives for and achieves success, one's father manages to belittle it and make one feel worthless. I know I've dealt with such from my own sire."

Zach smiled and redirected the conversation. "You have my sympathies, milord. Please forgive me for bringing up familial woes; it was not my intention. I came here to hopefully broker a trade agreement. Before we discuss business, however, may I offer you a meal or libation?"

Brookston made a face. "I've never really cared for the local fare. They do offer an excellent ale and whiskey, though."

"Very well; Mr. Jon, fetch us a bottle and glasses." He turned back to Brookston, "shall your men have anything?"

"No, thank you; they are on duty."

Jon-Jon nodded and gave the bodyguards a sympathetic look. "One whiskey and three glasses; aye, Cap'n."

As he headed to the bar, Brookston asked with some incredulity, "You allow your man to drink during business?"

Zach grinned at his consternation. "I've found Mr. Jon to be a far better sailor and mate when he's drunk than most men are sober."

"Odd; indeed, I've heard of such men, but I have never encountered one before."

"You should go to sea, milord. You'll see and do things you never dreamed possible." All too well, Zach knew the truth of that statement.

Brookston laughed. "I think I'm more suited to life on land. What little I've heard of them; sailors are entirely too superstitious."

"That they are, milord. I find it a useful tool for keeping a crew in line at times." He paused as Jon-Jon returned with the whiskey. "Of course, sailors aren't the only ones given to superstitions. I've heard some very fantastical things since I arrived here."

Jon-Jon opened the bottle and poured three brimming glasses. Zach raised an eyebrow at him. He made no apologies. "This was made to drink; so, let's drink. Sorry, milord, but sippin' has never been my style."

To Zach's surprise, Brookston took the proffered glass with a grin. "I begin to like you, sir. This is a man's drink, after all." He proceeded to take a hefty quaff.

Jon-Jon matched him, but Zach restrained himself to savoring sips. He noticed the man's bodyguards exchanged surreptitious glances and wondered if Brookston had a drinking problem. If so, he could work it to their advantage.

"Now then, you say you came to discuss business."

"Yes, milord; with the current unpleasantness, I've been exploring new territory in trade goods."

"Ah yes, that rebellion I've heard of. Really, it is such a shame when politics get in the way of business." Brookston took another drink, and Jon-Jon topped off his glass. "Thank you. So, Captain, what goods did you wish to deal in?"

Zach took another sip to hide his smile. Not only was the man greedy, but he also couldn't hold his liquor. A noticeable slur had already begun to creep into his voice.

"One thing I hope to strike an agreement on is this excellent whiskey. I'm also authorized to negotiate for cattle breeding stock, both beeves and sheep."

"I see. Are there any goods you propose to bring here?" Brookston got an avaricious gleam in his eyes, which were beginning to grow red. His face took on a flush, as well.

"I had hoped to get a tobacco contract, but that trade is too closely controlled and watched right now. What I do have to offer is indigo, rice, and cotton."

Brookston rubbed his chin, took another drink, and looked like he was trying to concentrate. After a considerable lag, he said, "Yes, I think I could find a good market for those commodities. What about wheat or wheat flour?"

Zach blinked. He'd been with the pirates long enough to forget what a valuable commodity those could be, especially if traded duty-free. The question made him wonder if this was a trap for smugglers. "I do not currently have a supplier for that. I could make inquiries."

Abruptly, Brookston changed the subject. "I notice you've only been sipping your whiskey."

"I intend no insult, milord. It is quite excellent. I just don't have a very high tolerance for it," he replied.

"I see. You strike me as a prudent man. Your father must be very proud of you doing your part to grow his business." Brookston paused and his gaze darkened. "You say you came to broker this trade agreement with the O'Malley family; you didn't hope to marry into Lady Darcy's wealth, did you?"

Zach held up his hands. "No milord; my profession does not lend itself to taking a wife, despite the number of sea captains who have. Before she passed, I saw how my father's absences affected my mother. I couldn't bring myself to do that to a woman I'd pledged to cherish."

"My father, on the other hand, wouldn't hesitate to force me or one of my siblings into such a union if he thought he could profit from it. That is one of the reasons I have set out to build up my own trading business. I haven't worked for Brumble & Sons for a few years now."

As an afterthought, he added, "I was a bit dumbfounded by the accounts I heard when I arrived here and made my inquiries about whom to speak with concerning business with the O'Malley family."

Brookston frowned, his face darkening. Zach spoke quickly to put him at ease. "I meant no insult, milord. It is quite common, even in the Colonies, for a family to use a business proctor; especially so if the current head of the family is not business-minded or is a woman. No, I meant the wild stories that the Lady had been spirited away from her home by the fair folk."

He saw the man shoot a glare toward a group of men near the bar. They shifted about nervously.

"This is the first I've heard such a fanciful tale. I see what you meant by an earlier statement about sailors not being the only ones to hold to superstitions," Brookston said. "To my knowledge, Lady Darcy remains sequestered at one of her homes for an extended period of mourning."

Zach acted as if he hadn't already known this. "Oh, I am sorry to hear about that. A death in the family always makes for a chaotic atmosphere. It was indeed wise of her ladyship to appoint someone to handle her affairs."

Brookston snorted and chuckled. "In truth, she didn't. I am the executor of her late husband's estate."

"She is a widow? How tragic. Is that why you were worried I was here to court her?"

The Englishman took a couple of swallows of whiskey. One of his guards put a hand on his shoulder and leaned down. "Milord, perhaps it would —."

"Get your hand off me! How dare you presume, Montcrief. I should have you whipped for such effrontery," Brookston snarled with a very noticeable slurring of his words.

The man released him. Zach noticed a brief look of surliness cross the guard's face. The other two, out of their employer's line of sight, rolled their eyes in resignation. Plainly, they were used to Brookston's behavior and its consequences, for they also scanned the room quickly and checked their weapons.

Brookston took another drink and leaned forward. His attempt at a conspiratorial whisper was far louder than he thought. "You should be glad you're not here to court her. That woman will drive a man to drink. You should count yourself lucky."

"Oh?" Zach took a sip of his drink.

He nodded. "I made my suit after Lord O'Connor passed. She requested her year of mourning, and I honored that. I realize a certain amount of propriety needs to be maintained. Before the year was up, she holed up in that keep of hers and refused to see me."

Zach frowned in sympathy. "Women can be frustrating creatures. Still, you are in charge of the family finances and business interests."

Brookston made a sour face. "Only until she takes a husband; that needs to be me, or she will challenge me in the courts over her late husband's holdings. If that happens, all my work to get this position will be for nothing."

Zach maintained his silence. He felt as if their prey was close to springing the trap, but he knew he could just as easily slip it.

Brookston didn't seem to notice the silence. In fact, he seemed to have grown oblivious to his surroundings entirely. "I won't let the old man have the last word. Bloody bastard: he married into wealth but has the gall to frown on me to do so? He cut off my allowance three years ago! Worse, most of my friends were no better off than I was."

Zach nodded sympathetically but remained silent.

Brookston continued, "I tell you; I was lucky to meet O'Connor at University. He and I hit it off, and he was more than willing to support me until the old man dies and I can get my inheritance. Would have been happy with that arrangement; my father couldn't live forever, right?"

Zach shook his head. "No, milord; death comes for us all, eventually."

"Then the bloody bastard writes to notify me he's disinherited me! Said he'd rewritten his will to leave his entire estate to one of his bastards by a mistress younger than me. Said the whelp showed greater potential than I did." He gulped the remaining contents of his cup and held it out to be refilled. Jon-Jon obliged. Refortified, he continued his tirade. "To top that, O'Connor went and married Lady O'Malley. The two richest families in all of western Ireland had united, and I was left with nothing but a useless title; penniless and dependent on the charity of others."

He took another swallow and moped silently for a moment. Zach asked, "What did you do, milord?"

"I'll tell you what I did. I determined I would ensure I was poor no longer. O'Connor never could hold his liquor, but he didn't have the sense you do to partake in moderation. I was already in his confidence; it didn't take much to get him to sign documents without reading them while he was in his cups. He thought he was signing a loan for me, not a new will naming me executor. A few weeks later, we went hunting. He was in his cups again, and I saw my opportunity. It didn't take much to make him lose his footing on that bluff."

Zach took a hefty swig of his own whiskey and sprang the trap. "You mean you did away with Lord O'Connor and took his holdings?"

Brookston, drunken enough to not think of what he was saying, replied, "I did, sir. It worked wonderfully or would have if Lady Darcy had been more cooperative. I'd always heard widows, especially young widows, were eager to get someone back in their bed. She's an odd one, though; temper of a shrew, but as frigid as a nun. Maybe she suffers from some madness restricted to gingers."

# Chapter 35

Zach and Jon-Jon pushed back from the table and stood without a word. The bodyguards went on instant alert; but the two pirates made no move toward their weapons.

A door at the back of the room opened and several people emerged. Darcy O'Malley led the group accompanied by several burly men and one scrawny, bookish looking man in a barrister's powdered wig.

"Roderick Brookston, I accuse you of the murder of my husband, Michael O'Connor and of defrauding his estate," she declared.

He threw his cup across the room and lurched drunkenly to his feet. "You are mad, woman. Obviously, your grief has addled your brain."

The clerkish man cleared his throat. "As Director of Public Prosecutions of Mayo County, I bear witness to your confession, Lord Brookston. Take him into custody." He stared pointedly at the bodyguards and the thugs at the bar. "I need not remind those here that any attempt to remove Lord Brookston by force will result in charges of accomplice to murder."

Brookston's men soon realized they were outnumbered and backed away from the situation. Darcy's men put him in irons and led him out, screaming obscenities at his lackeys for failing to protect him.

Lady Darcy turned to face the lackeys and proclaimed, "You — gentlemen have until nightfall tomorrow to be off my lands. Any who remain past that will be charged with trespass and shipped to a penal colony."

They quickly exited the tavern.

Viktor watched from the roof of the tavern. He heard everything that took place inside. Instinct told him things had gone too smoothly. He held no doubts Brookston's men would try something; maybe not free their lord, but definitely try to hold onto their power in the county. They'd bullied the locals for too long and didn't want to give that up.

They seemed to scatter upon leaving the tavern. He launched into the air, careful not to let his shadow give him away. As he suspected, several of the hired thugs met up in a wooded area outside the village.

He landed some distance away and crept closer to eavesdrop.

"How many men are still at the keep?" one of the bodyguards asked.

"We've got about twenty on duty and another ten sleeping, Montcrief."

"How in hell did that crazy bitch get out?" he growled.

"She jumped out her window with some half-naked man. We still haven't figured out how he got in or how the fall didn't kill them," one of the men said. "Her window opens on the courtyard; but we found no bodies or a grapple and rope. It was as if they vanished or flew away. Then she turned up here, waiting for that idiot Brookston to hang himself."

Montcrief scowled. "I expect these Irish bumpkins to be superstitious and backwards; but you are Englishmen!"

The man held up his hands. "I am only reporting what we saw and what we found when we investigated, Montcrief."

"Awfully peculiar that this sea captain shows up just a few days after she disappeared. Did he or his mate look anything like the man you say she left with?"

"No, those two didn't; but now that you mention it, there were two other strangers who caused some trouble the day before. Seamus said the man who crushed his wrist had a black beard and hair and striking green eyes.

436

The man I saw jump out the window with Lady Darcy did as well."

"Crushed his wrist?" Montcrief asked. "I didn't know anyone still used a war hammer."

"He didn't, Monty; he crushed it with his grip. Uncanny, it was," another of the men said. "Sure an' he was a tall one, but he didn't look brawny enough for that. The man looked like he wasn't even trying."

"You saw this, Robbie? Is this the mystery man responsible for your arm in that splint and sling?"

"No," the man in the sling said. "The older man with him did this when he forced my knife into Marvin. The man had to be a demon. I've never seen anyone move that fast. He kicked Ian so hard he'll never enjoy bedding a lass again; broke his pelvis, too. He may be crippled for life. The black-haired man slammed Cory and Logan together hard enough to break their skulls. The whole fight was over before any of us knew what was happening." A lingering horror showed in his eyes.

Montcrief frowned incredulously. "If I didn't know you aren't the fanciful sort, Rob —. Did any of you catch the names of these men?"

The men before him shook their heads.

"Hmph; be that as it may, we've got a sweet spot here. I've no wish to give it up just because of a drunken

"Listen up, lads. I know you signed on to fight the English; I know you thought that would be in the Colonies. Right now, there is a chance to fight the English right here."

They perked up at that.

He smiled grimly and continued, "It seems there is a group of English thugs determined to keep control of this county. They tried to use a minor lord to gain control by fraud. That has been defeated, and he faces the gallows for murder. The men he thought were underlings turned out to be organized spies for the Crown. They plan to take this keep and hold the county and Lady O'Malley by force. You have the opportunity to thwart that plot."

This information got an enthusiastic reception. He felt any residual resistance to his will melt away. He felt grateful for that. He knew his next words would lose them otherwise.

"If possible, I want to take them alive."

They looked at him in silence, but none raised any protest.

He divided them up into groups of six, assigned each group to follow a vampire, and sent them to sweep the keep. Meanwhile, he and Rigger flew to the nearby cottage to meet with Grimm.

Jim Rigger headed straight for Moira and soon had her in his arms and looking disheveled.

"Belay that, Mr. Rigger. We don't have time. Mr. Grimm, I have the cadre and our new recruits started at the top of the keep. We three need to get there to start from the bottom. I don't want to risk the Lady getting caught in the skirmish."

Jim stuck his bottom lip out, but left Moira standing where she was and joined his Captain.

Grimm tapped out his pipe and followed them outside. Once they were out of hearing distance of the cottage, he asked, "You already got the ring, Vik. Why are we still meddling in this affair?"

The vampire stopped and looked at his first mate. "I gave Darcy my word I would free her. Brookston is dealt with, but she isn't going to be free so long as these men remain here."

Grimm held his hands up and took a step back. "It wasn't my intention to offend."

Viktor just nodded silently.

Jim broke the tension. "Don't know about either of you, but I'm Hungry." He grinned and showed his fangs when they turned to look at him.

Viktor smirked, shook his head, and put an arm around both men's shoulders. "Trust you to have your

440

priorities straight, Jim. Once a pirate; always a pirate. Come on, Hezekiah, let's have some fun."

Grimm smiled and nodded. "Aye, guess I should prove to the Irish not all Englishmen are total bastards. Not that I'm not; but they don't need to know that."

With a chorus of male laughter, the three sped toward the keep faster than any mere mortal could follow.

Montcrief's men put up a good fight, but they were doomed to failure. The vampires were too quick for them. The attack from the upper levels caught the English completely off guard.

In a desperate attempt to regain control of the situation, he and half of his fighters took Darcy hostage.

Viktor and his mates found them hiding in the cellars. Montcrief held Darcy around the waist with her arms pinned to her sides. He held a blade to her throat with his other hand. Four of his burliest men stood between him and the pirates.

"I don't know who you are, but you need to turn around and leave now."

Viktor gave him a tight-lipped smile. "No."

"Dammit man, I will slit her throat."

441

"No, you won't. You need her alive to have any hope of holding this territory."

Montcrief scowled fiercely. "Kill them!"

His men never got past their second steps. Viktor and Jim moved faster than the eye could see to knock them unconscious. The four English thugs dropped like rag dolls.

"Actually, I prefer to take them alive, if you don't mind. I have a use for them aboard my ship," Vik said with a pleasant smile.

"Who are you? What are you?"

With a sinister chuckle, Grimm asked, "May I do the introductions, Captain?"

"I don't see why not."

"You have the unfortunate privilege of addressing Bloody Vik Brandee." Grimm paused, and Viktor inclined his head. "I am the Grimm Reaper, and this is Jim Rigger."

The three pirates watched the color leave the man's face. His knife hand trembled a bit, and the blade nicked Darcy's skin. A thin runnel of blood slid to her collarbone. She hissed at the sting.

"Hold Rigger," Viktor ordered just before he turned into a blur.

442

Grimm barely had time to react. Jim's eyes flared with reddish-brown light, and his lips pulled back in a feral snarl, baring his fangs. Grimm had to use every bit of his enhanced speed and strength to put the vampire into a headlock and keep him from attacking the woman.

In the next instant, Viktor returned to his previous spot. He wiped his dagger and returned it to the sheath at the nape of his neck. "Drop your weapon, Mr. Montcrief."

The man started to reply but never got more than a slight gurgle out. A startled look of confusion crossed his face. His head tilted to the side slightly, and a thin red line appeared. It quickly grew wider, and arterial blood began to spurt out in a rhythmic spray.

The knife clattered to the floor as both his hands flew to his throat in an effort to stem the flow.

Viktor flew Darcy to the other side of the cellar and held a cloth to the nick on her throat. "You can let go now, Mr. Grimm," he called from behind the safety of some wine casks.

The first mate obediently released the vampire in his grasp. It had been all he could do just to hold him.

Jim latched onto Montcrief's throat with a growl. The dying man managed a weak scream. The vampire ripped the neck wound even wider. Blood sprayed all over him, as much going on him as in his mouth.

Grimm stood transfixed by the sight. He'd seen Viktor and the other vampires feed before; none of that compared to the animalistic ferocity he witnessed now.

Something hit him very hard. The next thing he knew, he landed outside the door of the cellar. He stood up and saw Viktor slam the door shut and hang his gold and emerald cross on it. A second later, a blood-covered, snarling face appeared in the small, barred window. He barely recognized Jim Rigger.

A claw-like hand reached through and grasped the chain the cross hung from. The smell of burnt flesh filled the air and a piteous scream emanated from the creature in the cellar. The hand retreated, smoking.

Jim's face returned. His eyes showed pain and returned sanity. "Captain, please get her out of here. I don't know how much longer I can control myself."

"I feel its pull, too, Jim," Vik said. "I'll be back shortly. Mr. Grimm, do not approach that door until I return."

In a matter of minutes, Viktor returned Darcy to her chambers. "I apologize for the abruptness, milady, but I need to know if there is another way out of that cellar, even if it's only big enough for a cat to pass through."

She shook her head. "No; there used to be an old drain. Father sealed it up years ago after a rat infestation, though."

"Good." He kissed her hand. "Now I must leave you. Be glad Belle warned me against feeding on you, for the scent of your blood is maddening. You saw what it did to Mr. Rigger. Without that cross on, my own control is eroding by the minute."

"Thank you for all you have done for me, Viktor Brandewyne. I only ask that you take those English bastards with you when you go," she replied with a warm, if shaken, smile.

"Gladly."

He found Grimm smoking his pipe a few yards away from the cellar door. The cross still hung from it. A pall of tobacco smoke filled the motionless air. Jim no longer peered through the bars.

"Comfortable, Hezekiah?"

"No; he kept whining he could still smell her and begging me to let him out." Grimm paused to cough and wave at the smoke.

"Ah, good thinking; use the smoke to mask the scent of the blood." Viktor nodded his understanding. "How fare you, Jim?"

"Better, Cap'n," the vampire's voice came through the door. He sounded tired and in pain. "Hand hurts like the devil, though."

"I'll see if Belle can fix it for you. Are you in control of yourself?"

"Aye; I don't think you have to worry about me drinking Mr. Grimm, now."

Viktor could sense the truth in his friend's voice. He removed the cross from the door and hung it back about his neck. "I am coming in."

He heard movement behind the door. He opened it and stepped through. Jim Rigger stood facing him, holding one hand cradled to his chest. Viktor held his hand out to his friend, and Jim showed him the burn.

An almost perfect impression of the cross in raw blistered flesh marked the vampire's palm.

"I am sorry about that, Jim," he said low. He knew Grimm could still probably hear him, but he wanted to maintain the illusion of privacy for his friend. He reached out to the siren through their link. *"Do you think you can heal this?"*

He felt an unfamiliar gentleness in her mental reply. *"I cannot. Were it an ordinary burn, I could, but it is a holy burn. The best I can suggest is to let him feed. That will heal the raw flesh; but he will always carry the scar."*

446

*"Thank you, pet."*

He broke the connection and frowned. "Belle says she cannot heal a burn like this —." He trailed off as an idea occurred to him. Looking about, he soon saw what he wanted. He picked up the cup and drew his dagger. He rolled up his sleeve and drew the blade across his forearm. He held the knife in the wound to keep it open until he'd caught a good amount of blood in the cup.

The cut closed and healed as soon as he removed the blade. He handed the cup to Jim.

"You need to feed again. This will hold you over until we get back to the ship. You can have a couple of the prisoners then."

"Thank you, Vik. I'm sorry I lost control of myself." He drained the cup.

Viktor clasped him on the shoulder. "Don't blame yourself, Jim. It was all I could do not to attack her myself. I'd hate to meet a full-blooded selkie if a mix-breed smells that good."

Jim dropped the cup to the flagstones and gasped at his hand. Before their eyes, the damaged skin sloughed away. New skin soon covered the raw wound. Within minutes, not even a scar remained.

Viktor raised an eyebrow. "Interesting."

# Chapter 36

They sailed southwest to skirt around British waters. If not for the need of Darcy's ring, Viktor wouldn't have gotten as close as he had. While the *Incubus* could hold her own in a one-on-one battle; he didn't want to risk encountering a fleet.

Once he felt they'd sailed far enough south, he ordered a course change due east, toward Gibraltar.

"Enter, pet," Viktor replied to the knock at the cabin door. He glanced up from the puzzle box on the table.

Belladonna closed the door behind her and walked around behind him. She began to massage his shoulder. "You are very tense. Try to relax some."

"It's this damn box; I think I've figured out how all the pieces fit together; but something is still missing. Do you think one of the pieces was damaged and a part lost?"

She looked over his shoulder, and he could almost detect a low thrum. A moment later she said, "Circe must have the keystone. I can detect no damage to any of the pieces you've gathered. They all mesh; but they combine to make a distinct cavity. Once the missing piece is added and turned, the box will open."

"Of course." He sighed. "A wise precaution, I guess, to ensure I bring the thing back to her. Still, even I know stolen magic will turn on the thief."

She walked around him, leaned her hip against the table, and crossed her arms. "That is true. I am curious; how did you learn that fact?"

He chuckled at the memory. "I picked the lock on Mother Celie's cabinet."

"You tried to rob the Sister who raised you? Are you mad?"

"Peace, pet! No; I didn't try to rob her. I was just too curious for my own good."

"Oh? What happened?"

"I saw all sorts of oddities and boring herbs; but what drew my attention was a large gold coin. It was easily the size of half my palm and had strange images on the face I saw. I made the mistake of picking it up for a better look." He absently rubbed his hand at remembered pain. "Dropped it right away; it gave off an odd, strong tingle which made my hair stand on end. My hand turned blood red and itched like mad. Worse, the coloring and itch spread to any part of my body I touched. I looked like a boiled crab before Celie had pity and lifted the spell."

"Hmm, that sounds familiar. I wonder if she placed the coin there as bait," Belle mused.

"Oh, I know she did."

She raised her eyebrows questioningly at his declaration.

He grinned and explained, "I'd already gotten a couple of beatings for being nosy about that cabinet. Of course, that only made me more determined to see what was in it. Old Celie knows me and my nature better than any other living being in this world; sometimes even better than I know myself, it seems. She put that coin in my path, knowing I would go for it before anything else."

"So, you're saying it takes harsh measure to teach you."

"In my youth, yes. She did me a favor with that minor curse, though. I suspect there were far more dangerous things in that cabinet I could have gotten ahold of had I not been distracted by gold. The Elder's Stone was in there when she gave it to me."

"You have a point."

He got up and put the puzzle box in a cupboard. He stayed facing the shut cupboard and mentally prepared himself for what he knew he had to do. When he turned around, he saw the siren watch him patiently. He could feel her gently probing his consciousness, though.

"When we reach Gibraltar, you need to leave the ship."

"What about the navigational hazards which surround Circe's island?"

"I don't intend to take the ship that close. I can fly the box to her," he countered. "I don't want to put you at risk, pet. Just because one sea dragon with an ancient grudge thinks he's entitled to you doesn't mean I'll let him have you. You are mine, and I protect what is mine."

Whatever response she was going to make was lost in the scramble to remain upright as the ship came to a sudden stop.

"If he's put a hole in my ship —," Vik growled. They currently sailed in deep water. He knew the only thing which could have stopped them that quickly was Hell's Breath Island manifesting in their path.

"Might as well head topside and see what the old man wants."

Belle followed him silently out of the cabin.

452

# *The Daedalus Enigma*

Zeke sat on a rock by his fire. Three empty rocks ringed it. Viktor took this as a sign the Elder wanted to see Grimm, as well. He sent a thought to Lazarus before he and the siren took up seats by the fire. They waited in silence for the first mate.

*"Luckily the sun just set,"* Jim Rigger thought as he headed to the helm in search of Grimm. He found him puffing on his pipe, leaning against the railing.

"Ho, Mr. Rigger! Come to relieve me?"

"Cap'n says the old man wants to see you, too, Mr. Grimm."

"Better get my extra tobacco pouch before I go ashore, then. Zeke'll want a smoke." Grimm pushed off the rail and headed for the hatch.

"I hope this doesn't take long. I'm Hungry."

"I'll be sure to let the Captain know, Mr. Rigger." Grimm's tone let him know he fully understood the danger inherent in leaving the vampire unfed for too long.

Grimm arrived at Zeke's fire shortly after. He walked over and handed the old man a pouch plump with tobacco and took the final empty stone seat.

453

"Much obliged, Hezekiah Grimm," Zeke said with a nod. "Now that I have all three of you young 'uns here, we can begin."

Grimm held up his hand. "A moment, Elder; Vik, Jim warned me his Hunger is up. You might want to send him down to the larder and have Mr. Jon relieve him."

Viktor nodded. His eyes grew unfocused for a moment. "Done; good thinking, Hezekiah. I'm still not sure how good his control of it is, now that he can hold his true form again."

Zeke seemed to perk up at that revelation. "What's this?"

Grimm hid his surprise that the old wizard didn't already know about it. He had to remind himself that Zeke was not truly omniscient, despite enough instances to make one think he was.

Viktor explained the situation. "Celie gave me some moly along with instructions to give me some protection against Circe's spells. I got impatient and took the last two doses at the same time. I cut myself, and Lazarus lapped up the blood."

"So, it broke her spell on him and now he's just a vampire," Zeke surmised.

Viktor waggled his hand. "Not exactly; he can take any of Lazarus' forms at will now. He doesn't have to eat

454

human flesh to become Jim anymore. He can still move freely in daylight as Lazarus, also."

The old man didn't say anything. He filled his pipe and lit it with an ember from his ever-present fire. For several minutes he smoked in silence and stared at the flames. When he finally returned his attention to them, Grimm noticed a sadness in his eyes.

"That was wise of her. She foresaw something I was blind to."

Just as suddenly, the sadness vanished. He fixed Belladonna with an intense gaze. "You have earned a pardon, girl. I hereby lift the ban placed on you from entering the Mediterranean, and I revoke Xandricus' claim to you. If you should cross his path, you are free to defend yourself."

She blinked at him. "Thank you, Elder."

"Will you inform him of this change?" Viktor asked.

Zeke snorted. "Wouldn't do any good; he'd still try to claim her. It's in his nature. Would you give up claim on something simply because you were told it was no longer valid?"

"No; I guess I wouldn't."

"You have a trial ahead of you, boy." Zeke stared at Viktor as if Grimm and Belladonna did not exist. "It will test the very core of your being and resolve. I am not free

455

to tell you what this trial is; it is partially clouded to me, and to tell you what I *have* seen could alter the happening of it. The only thing I can tell you is it is coming soon; possibly before you reach Circe; possibly after."

"Wonderful," Viktor growled. "Can you at least tell me if I have missed something?"

Zeke cocked his head. "What do you think you have missed?"

"Circe sent me to find five pieces of a puzzle box, pieces she had scattered among the Sisters. I have done this and assembled them in their places on the box. There seems to be a sixth piece still missing, though."

"There is: the keystone."

Grimm asked the question. "Do you have it, Elder, or does the witch?"

"She has it."

"Of course," Viktor said and pinched the bridge of his nose. He sighed and asked, "Is there anything else we need to know before we continue our journey?"

Zeke took a few puffs on his pipe before he answered. "For now, no."

The smoke from the old man's pipe seemed to dance. Grimm felt mesmerized by it. A fog formed and swirled with the smoke until it obscured his sight. He thought he heard Zeke telling him things; but the sound was muffled. He couldn't quite make it out other than a deep sadness to the tone.

Just as the fog began to dissipate, he got a sense of hope to brighten the sorrow.

His vision cleared, and he saw they once again stood on the deck of the *Incubus*. No sign of Hell's Breath Island could be found.

*Tamara A. Lowery*

# Chapter 37

Brookston's lackeys alleviated the lack of good hunting during the traverse of the Mediterranean. Word had apparently spread among the Barbary corsairs about the *Incubus*. Any ships which came in sight of her fled as quickly as possible.

Belladonna kept the winds and currents favorable. They made good time to the eastern islands.

Xandricus caught the scent on the westerly breeze. Not only was she returning to him, she was bringing a meal as a peace offering.

Soon, very soon, he would once again have a mate he could breed with.

"We're close enough, pet. I don't want to risk the ship or crew to that rocky maze or the whirlpools again," Viktor said. "Calm the winds."

Belle changed a single note in her melody, sang one more bar, then stopped her song altogether. The wind died down, and the sea around the ship grew glassy calm.

Once the sails drooped limply, he called out, "Riggers reef your sails! Mr. Bland, drop the sea anchors."

A chorus of "ayes" answered him as the crew set about fulfilling the order.

Viktor watched the activity with an approving eye. A sudden stiffness in the siren drew his attention. "Pet, is something wrong?"

"He is here." Her voice came out low and tense. Her scent spoke of apprehension which bordered on fear.

"The dragon?"

In answer to his question a cry came down from the lookout. "Rogue wave from starboard!"

Every eye turned that way. A huge mound of water at least two hundred feet wide rushed straight at the ship.

Viktor turned to the helmsman and shoved him out of the way. He spun the wheel hard to starboard and yelled, "Cut the anchor lines!"

Crewmen set to the thick ropes with hatchets, chopping furiously. "A little push of wind to help us swing around, pet," he growled, fighting to turn the becalmed vessel.

"Oh, right." She seemed to come out of a daze and sang a few quick notes. A gentle breeze blew against the prow on the port side. The ship, now free of her anchors, pivoted to face the wave head on, seconds before it reached her.

"Brace for impact," someone yelled.

The mound sub sided just as it reached them. The ship only rocked a little. Sailors looked around nervously.

"What just happened?" Vik demanded quietly.

"He dove under. He could come up and engulf the ship; he's big enough in this form to swallow it whole," Belle answered.

"That is not comforting, pet."

"I know; but I don't think he will; at least not while I'm aboard. It would be difficult to claim me as a mate if he's digesting me."

"There is that." He snorted. "Do you think he'll try to board?"

She shrugged in response. "That or capsize us."

He found the situation a little more than frustrating. *"How do you fight something like that?"*

Belle must have caught the thought. "Maybe if we can get him to take human form," she suggested. "But be careful; he'll be just as fast as you or I am, and he's physically stronger than me."

"Wonderful."

"He's coming back up."

A new mound rose up in the water on the port side. It grew to nearly forty feet before the dragon erupted through. The water crashed back down and nearly capsized the ship. The great beast continued to rise.

Greenish black scales with a pearlescent sheen covered his body. Just as Belladonna told him, the dragon's head and maw were nearly twice the size of the ship; easily capable of swallowing it whole. Viktor saw he had forelegs or arms which ended in grasping, clawed fingers.

The creature propelled upwards completely out of the water. He had no legs. Instead, his lower half consisted of a long serpentine tail with a dorsal fin along its crest.

The dragon flipped in mid-air, a surprisingly graceful movement for such a gargantuan creature. During his descent, he transformed; first to a very male version of Belladonna's half-human/ half-shark form; then to a fully human form.

The siren landed in a crouch on the deck hard enough to make the boards creak and the ship rock. With inhuman grace, he stood and looked at Belladonna with a cruel gleam in his amber eyes and a triumphant smile. He completely ignored Viktor and his crew.

*"Welcome home, Belladonna. I see you have finally accepted your fate."*

Viktor realized the siren male spoke the same language he'd heard Belle use with Bonobibi in the Bengali saltwater swamps. He understood it because of his blood and flesh bond with her. He feigned confused incomprehension to hide this from the male.

Belle maintained her silence. Viktor could feel her drawing on their bond to resist the mating scent the male exuded and to keep her temper in check. He could tell she wanted very much to blast her nemesis with the full force of her powers; but she did not want to destroy the ship and crew in the process.

The male held out his hand to her, not so much as an invitation as a summons. *"Come to me now. It is time to take your place as my mate."*

She laughed. *"I am not your mate, Xandricus; not now, nor ever."*

463

*"You are mine! You forfeited your freedom by your presence here. Come!"*

*"No."* She smiled serenely. *"The Elder lifted my exile and nullified your claim to me. I have earned my redemption."*

*"You lie! If that were true, I could have followed you beyond Gibraltar's gate when you last invaded my territory,"* he snarled.

*"The ban had not been lifted at that time. I only invaded because my master needed my aide and knowledge of these waters."*

Xandricus tilted his head in puzzlement. *"Your master? If I could not tame you, who could?"*

Viktor stepped forward between the two sirens. *"I could. She is mine."*

Xandricus snarled and sniffed the air. Apparently, what he smelled did not improve his mood. *"You dare challenge me, human?"*

This time Viktor laughed and made a point to let his fangs show. *"Who said I was human?"*

The male lunged for him. A split second later, Grimm's blade across his throat brought him up short. Only quickly manifested scales prevented the sword from biting into his flesh.

464

He turned his attention to the first mate. *"You stink of that old bottom feeder who imprisoned me in these waters!"* With no further warning, he extended his talons and plunged them into Grimm's chest. The siren picked him up with his talons still in his body and flung him over the railing.

"Hezekiah!" Viktor felt a white-hot rage consume him. He retrieved his friend's sword from the deck and swung with all his might.

Xandricus gave a strangled scream and stared at his hand where it lay on the deck. The talons bubbled and smoked. The skin and flesh sloughed away to reveal bloody bone.

*"The Elder's magic."* Viktor heard Belladonna's theory in his head. He reacted quickly and pulled out the Elder's Stone. The milky white crystal flared to life with a blinding light.

Xandricus flung his arms up to protect his eyes. Viktor swung the sword at his exposed belly but missed. The siren vaulted over the side with inhuman speed.

Grimm couldn't breathe. He couldn't move. Every muscle in his body felt rigid with paralysis. A crushing sensation in his chest told him his heart probably wasn't beating either.

His body hit the water. He barely felt it. He began to feel detached from his situation. He wondered how he wasn't already dead and thought perhaps he was; probably not, though. He could still see the hull of the ship above him as it shrank away, and he sank deeper. He felt no fear. He only felt regret that he couldn't see Brianna again.

His vision began to cloud. It cleared for a moment, and he saw her face. She wore a look of confusion and worry. Her mouth moved, but he could hear nothing. She seemed to place a hand to his cheek, but he felt nothing but the paralyzing pain. She slapped him; again, he felt nothing of it. He saw her face grow red with fear and anger and saw tears stream down her cheeks. He tried to reach out to her. He wanted to tell her how much he loved her and how much he hated leaving her alone. It tormented him that he still could not move or speak, even in this final vision.

Her image dissolved into a blinding light, and he felt his pain vanish and his muscles relax.

Everything went dark.

Belladonna thought she would have to keep Viktor from diving in after Xandricus. She could sense he wanted to. She opened her link with him completely and hoped he would not shield himself from her.

466

It must have worked. He pushed away from the rail and turned to face the quarter deck.

"Riggers to the deck! Man the guns, all ports open! We don't know which side the bastard will come up on," he ordered. The crew rushed to obey.

Belle shot him an image of the dragon's claws and the masts. The imagery proved much quicker and more efficient than spoken words could have.

"Lower the masts!"

The riggers got the collapsible masts to a horizontal position just as the dragon surfaced to the port side. He roared and swiped at the ship. The single clawed hand passed yards above their heads. The other arm terminated in a scaly stump.

"Gun crews at the ready — fire all port-side guns!"

All sixty guns on that side let loose with a thunderous volley. Despite the cannon smoke, Belle could see the projectiles bounce off Xandricus' scales like pebbles off a rock wall.

Viktor saw it, too. "Damn; you could have told me cannon fire wouldn't work on him."

"I didn't know. No one has ever tried to battle a sea dragon before to my knowledge."

The dragon swung at the ship again. Once again, he missed.

"Can he not see us?" Viktor asked with surprise.

Belle blinked. "That does seem odd. Maybe his eyesight is weaker in this form. The dragons usually stick to the deeps. This sea is much shallower than he would choose. There's not much light at his normal depths."

A swat hit the surface close by. The resulting wave rocked the ship badly.

"That was too close." Vik turned his attention back to the crew. "Reload and aim for his eyes!"

Only the deck guns could comply. The lower gun decks couldn't get enough of an angle. They let fly with the volley. Some of the shots might have made it to their target; but the dragon swatted them away.

Belladonna felt a deep thrum in her bones. "He's using his sounding to see!"

"How do you kill this thing?"

She could hear the frustration in Viktor's voice and feel it in his mind. He needed very badly to destroy Xandricus; both to protect the ship and crew and to avenge Hezekiah Grimm.

"Sirens are hard to kill; dragons are damn near impossible. The only sure way is to behead him; and no blade can pierce those scales."

She sensed his plan a split second before he blocked her out.

"Viktor, no!"

He took Grimm's blade and drew his own sword. He leapt into the air and took flight. He knew Belle would try to stop him if he gave her the chance.

He flew an erratic pattern as he ascended. The beast swatted at him but was unable to make contact. The winds generated by the passage of the great claws did cause him some trouble. The turbulent air currents sent him tumbling, and he nearly lost his grip on the swords.

He focused and regained control of his flight. Determined, he flew straight up until he hovered several feet above the dragon's head. This gave him time to rethink his plan. He needed to lure Xandricus away from the ship first.

He flew down and flitted around the dragon's face. Memories of the sand gnats from his native salt marshes gave him an idea.

He darted around to the back of the creature's head. With the longer of the two swords he pried in between scales, jabbing as hard as he could. He pulled it back out and saw blood on the end. With lightning speed, he repeated the process several times in various areas.

Xandricus roared and swatted at his head and neck. Clearly, he wasn't used to such a nuisance. Viktor flew around to his face then off to the side.

*"Catch me if you can, beast!"* he taunted.

The creature blew a gust at him. Forced back by the foul-smelling wind, he flew straight up to escape the current. He quickly returned to jab at the dragon again.

Just as quickly, he darted away again. Xandricus still didn't follow.

Viktor wondered if male sirens were as prone to jealousy as females were. He decided to find out.

*"She doesn't want you, Xandricus. I keep her more than satisfied, and I feed her well."*

*"I can do the same, human."* The words sounded surprisingly clear coming from his draconic maw.

*"You forget I am not human."* He thought of one more taunt to throw at the dragon. *"I also sired a child on her."*

That did the trick.

Xandricus roared his fury and turned away from the ship to charge at him. *"You lie! You are not a dragon. You could not sire a child on a siren."*

*"Use your senses. Surely you can smell the truth of my words."* Viktor didn't see any need to tell him she had miscarried. He spoke strictly truth. Belladonna had carried his child in her womb.

The dragon moved faster than he expected for a creature so gigantic. He barely escaped the next blow directed at him. He checked to be sure they were a safe distance from the *Incubus* before he stopped taunting and jabbing.

*"Now we end this, dragon."*

He dove at the creature's head and managed to blind one eye. He leapt away as Xandricus slapped at the ruined orb. The dragon screamed in fury and pain.

Viktor flew into his maw and straight down his throat.

# Chapter 38

"No!"

Belladonna's scream of protest barely registered on the shocked crew. They all paused in the process of raising the masts. Their captain sent the silent order to make sail as soon as possible just moments before the dragon ate him.

The pause only lasted a moment. The compulsion still lay on the pirates.

Viktor knew he had no hope of beheading the beast from the outside. Even though he could penetrate the flesh between the scales, he couldn't pierce deep enough to cause real damage.

He thrust his arms out straight from his shoulders, a sword in each hand. He began to spin in the dragon's throat with all his might. He had to do this before the creature could swallow.

The theory behind the move proved sound. Impenetrable scales could not protect from an attack within. The spine almost stopped him. Rather than try to hack through the bones, he did his best to keep the blades to the softer tissue between them.

His lungs and muscles burned. What little air he found in the dragon's throat proved too fetid to breathe. The tissues around him constricted and twitched. Blood and other fluids coated and soaked him, making the swords difficult to hold onto.

He got the sense Xandricus was trying to heal himself and knew he must finish this quickly. He redoubled his hacking.

Just as he thought his lungs would burst, he reached the skin and finally severed the dragon's head.

He saw the head crash into the sea as it fell away from the body. He could have sworn it shrank and transformed back to its human visage.

The body began to collapse toward the water, and he realized he was still lodged in the creature's throat. He struggled to get free as Xandricus' body began to constrict and change around him. He noted that the flesh did not tear as it shrank, and the pressure on his waist and legs became painful.

He'd lost one sword somehow. The other proved too awkward to use for fear of cutting his own legs. He desperately retrieved his dagger from the sheath at the nape of his neck. He found himself forced to cut from the inside outward to pierce the dragon's skin.

474

He won the race, but not without cost. A scream escaped him as the shrinking neck muscles crushed his pelvis. One of the severed arteries chose that moment to hit him with a high-pressure spray from the creature's final heartbeats.

He hit the water hard and lost consciousness.

Belladonna didn't bother undressing. She dove over the railing as soon as she saw Xandricus' head part from his body. Viktor would need her help to survive.

Her breeches shredded as her legs transformed into a shark-tail.

She still sensed Viktor's presence, but it felt weaker by the minute.

Xandricus' head sank past the siren as she sped to aid her captain. It wore a surprised expression. She briefly imagined her erstwhile sister's mate had believed he was immortal.

She was grimly aware immortality was only an illusion. Viktor was a vampire, a supposedly immortal being; and he was now covered in one of the few substances which could truly kill him: siren's blood.

She only hoped she could reach him before he accidentally swallowed any.

475

A stab of anguished pain hit her followed rapidly by a chilling numbness. She could no longer sense Viktor's presence. Fear shot through her, and she darted toward the last place she had sensed him.

Two bodies sank toward the murky depths, one clearly headless. She swam to the clothed, intact one.

Viktor's eyes stared sightlessly ahead. His features hung slack. Something about his hips and legs looked disjointed and deformed. Blood clouded the water around him; she knew it was Xandricus'.

She grabbed him around the waist and swam toward the ship and the surface. He remained limp in her arms. She gave a mighty thrust of her tail and launched them out of the water. She turned in mid-air to take the brunt of their impact on the deck.

"Fetch Dr. Coffin!" she yelled at the nearest pirate. He hesitated, and she growled, "Now, or I'll gut you where you stand!"

The man quickly scurried away.

Jon-Jon ran to where they lay on the deck. He stopped short when he got a good look at his captain. "Is he —?"

"No," Belle answered the unfinished question. "His heart still beats. He was crushed from the waist down, though. Hold some slack on his breeches. I don't want to nick him with my talons while I cut them off him."

476

The second mate's face darkened, and he frowned. "Now is not the time for sporting, lass."

"Do as she said Mr. Jon. Those bones must be set properly." Matthew Coffin knelt beside them. "Can you tell how badly he's broken?"

Belle felt gratitude for the ship's surgeon's grasp of the situation. "His lower legs and feet are only bruised. Both legs are broken above the knee. His hips are broken in three places, and his back is broken." She gave the assessment of what her sonar had shown her while she'd cut his garments away.

Coffin shook his head and helped her ease the sodden cloth away from Viktor's body. "He already feels cold. I don't see his chest move. Are you sure he's still alive?"

She nodded. "I can hear his heart. It's very weak, but the pulse is there. The broken back is the cause of the coldness is his legs."

"I know he can heal rapidly, but I don't see how he can heal an injury like that. I doubt he'll ever walk again."

"He will if I can act in time. The bones are crushed, but his spine is intact. It's just very compressed. Already, the bones are re-knitting; they're mis-positioned and keeping pressure there. I've got to get them realigned."

"How, in God's name, do you propose to manage that?" The doctor displayed his familiar incredulity.

"The same way I can 'see' the broken bones," she answered tersely. She gently eased one hand under Viktor's lower back and began a low thrum. Jon-Jon grew glassy-eyed. Even Dr. Coffin had to shake his head to stay focused on making sure the captain's legs were properly aligned.

After about five minutes, Belladonna grew silent. She looked up at Viktor's face and eased her hand out from under him.

"Did it work?" Coffin whispered.

"I hope so."

"You don't sound entirely sure of your abilities, pet."

"Viktor! You're alive!"

"Aye." He opened his eyes and smiled at her. "I may need to lie here a few more moments. My legs feel like they're covered in sand gnats."

"They're waking up," Dr. Coffin said with some relief. "That you can feel anything at all below the waist is a miracle. Had it been any other member of the crew, I'd have been compelled to take both legs while you were still unconscious."

478

"Be glad you didn't, Dr. Coffin." Viktor's voice held a dangerous note.

Coffin shook his head and got up. "I knew better. You have an uncanny ability to heal yourself. I didn't want to face your wrath for what you would view as unnecessary mutilation."

"Wise man."

"Thank you for your help," Belle said. "Jon-Jon, are there any prisoners left in the larder hold?"

The second mate blinked but quickly grasped her intent. "Aye, I think there be a small handful yet. I'll look 'em over and fetch the strongest lookin' one."

"Thank you."

"Good thinking, pet. A fresh feeding will help me finish healing. I'd like to be able to return to my cabin under my own power."

After draining the man Jon-Jon brought to him, Viktor gave the body to the siren for disposal. He stopped her before she could dive over the rail with it.

"Pet, see if you can find Mr. Grimm's body. I'd like to return him to his wife."

She paused for a moment. With a nod, she slipped over the side with her meal.

He noticed Dr. Coffin still lingered nearby and seemed a bit perturbed. "Out with it, man."

To his credit, Coffin kept his voice low. He stepped in close before he spoke. "Do you think that wise, Captain?" Given how long the trip will take, Mr. Grimm's body will bloat and begin to rot before we're halfway across. I doubt Mrs. Grimm would wish to see him in that condition; and there is the risk of pestilence among the crew."

Viktor admired the fact the man was brave enough to question him yet cautious enough to do so without broadcasting it to the entire crew.

"I did take those factors into consideration, Stitches. I will have his body cleaned and sewn up in a hammock then secured in one of the small boats to be towed well behind the ship. I have no intention of letting Brianna see him in any but a perfect state, regardless of his actual condition."

To prove his point, he caught Coffin's gaze and planted a brief image of himself rotting before the man's eyes and returning to perfect health. The shaken look on Coffin's face gave him a little gratification as well as an unfamiliar touch of remorse. He reached out and placed a hand on the doctor's shoulder. The man's flinch reinforced the remorse.

"Easy, man; it was only an illusion."

Coffin gulped, nodded, and offered a weak smile. "Quite right; of course it wasn't real. It's just, recent events and all being what they've been, I wonder about my sanity sometimes."

"As I do mine, Matthew; I've no further need of your services at present, and I don't think any of the crew sustained any injuries. Head below and have Mr. Murph draw up a bottle of the good brandy. I'm sure he still has some he hasn't mixed for me."

As the doctor headed below, Viktor turned his attention to the rest of the crew. "Mr. Jon!"

"Aye, Cap'n."

"Have a few lads rig some new sea anchors. I don't want this ship any closer to Circe's island."

"Aye, aye; Gordon, Collins, fetch some ballast bags and some rope. Cap'n wants new sea anchors!"

The two pirates tapped a handful of their mates to help and headed for the ballast hold.

Satisfied with the level of activity, Viktor returned to his cabin.

He was halfway through a bottle of gin by the time Belladonna returned. He looked up to see a look of defeat on her face. He took a long pull on the bottle.

"You hate gin," she observed.

"Aye."

She sighed. "I couldn't find him."

He took another pull and frowned. "Do you think that scaly bastard ate him?"

"Possibly; if he did, the transformation destroyed his remains." She sat down across from him. "Does that stuff help?"

"Not really."

She reached over and took the bottle from him. He tried to take it back, but she held it just out of reach. "I only want to taste it."

"After how you reacted to rum? I don't think so, pet. Give it back."

Rather than obey, she held the bottle to her lips and tilted it up. She quickly turned her head to the side and spat it out. "How could he drink this filth? Bilge water tastes better."

"It is vile, isn't it?" He took the bottle back, upended it, and finished it off. He made a face and shuddered.

482

"*Eaugh*; in Hezekiah's defense, I would say Jon-Jon likes this stuff, too."

"Jon-Jon would drink his own piss if he couldn't get liquor. It certainly smells fermented enough most of the time."

"There is that."

They sat in companionable silence and sorrow for a while. Viktor still felt numb. Grimm's death seemed surreal, like a bad dream. It had happened so abruptly.

The emotion he sensed from Belladonna drew his curiosity. To distract himself, he gently probed at her mental shields. What he found surprised him.

She felt responsible for costing him his friend's life. If she hadn't returned to these waters, Xandricus wouldn't have attacked. She also had liked Grimm, even if they hadn't always gotten along. She had trusted him to watch out for Viktor's best interests.

"It's not your fault, pet."

"Isn't it?"

"No; it was a risk of our chosen life. That it came at the talons of a sea dragon rather than a blade, gun, or the hangman is inconsequential. He could have stayed out of it. He chose not to."

She narrowed her eyes, and he felt the heat of her anger.

"You blame him," she stated. "You are angry with him!"

He shook his head. "You misunderstand. I don't blame Hezekiah for anything. He died the kind of death he chose, doing what he wanted to do. Not many men get that privilege. They live and die on the whims of another. Remember, he was the only man on this crew not bound to obey my will."

"As for being angry at anyone, the dragon is dead. I'm still finding it hard to believe Hezekiah is gone. I know the anger is there; but I'm just too numb right now for it." He looked at the bottle, now empty, and smiled. "He really did have rotten taste in liquor, though."

"You wanted to see me, Cap'n?" Jim Rigger closed the cabin door behind him.

"Aye, Jim." He looked at his old friend. He would always have Jim by his side; as his first mate by night and Lazarus by day. "I should have turned him."

"Vik?"

"Never mind; Zeke's magic probably would have interfered anyway."

"You mean make Grimm a vampire?" Jim gave him a look he knew all too well; the one that said he thought Viktor's idea was not a good one.

"I said it probably wouldn't have worked," he replied testily.

"No; it definitely wouldn't have. You saw what his blood did to that dragon's claw; melted the flesh right off it."

Viktor blinked at him. He'd always kept Grimm off his menu out of respect and friendship. It had never occurred to him that Zeke's magic would make his blood toxic. It should have.

"Look after the crew. Jon-Jon will help. I've got to take this damned box back to Circe."

"Aye, Cap'n. Be careful around that tricky bitch."

"Always."

*Tamara A. Lowery*

# Chapter 39

Viktor arrived at Circe's island at dawn. He saw the rocky maze and whirlpools remained gone. He still felt glad he hadn't brought the ship in close. Anything which could be removed like that could just as easily be conjured again.

A dense fog surrounded the island and obscured the wrecks he knew ringed it. Odd that she'd brought that back but not the outer defenses.

He heard a single note sung and recognized Belladonna's voice. She sent him a quick notice she was going to hunt. The fog evaporated in a matter of minutes.

*"Thank you, pet. Enjoy your hunt."*

He landed at the top of the stone stairway he'd climbed when he first visited this island. A few animals roamed near the path, but not as many as previously. He wondered if the witch had been eating alone or entertaining a fresh batch of victims. He hadn't surveyed any recent wreckage; but he hadn't surveyed the entire coast, either.

He headed for her villa.

☠

"My fog! What happened?"

Viktor heard the feminine shriek from a few yards outside the villa. He smirked. It told him Circe was probably unaware of his arrival. The *Incubus* lay at anchor beyond the horizon.

He gave a perfunctory rap at the doorway and entered unbidden. Her tirade grew louder as he moved through the dwelling. He used it to guide him to her. No one seemed present to bar his way or question his presence. The range of languages she used impressed him.

Shortly before he reached her, he caught the name Xandricus inserted liberally in the rant. His rage began to bubble under the surface; it finally had another focus. He quickly connected the unnatural fog she now missed to the sea dragon.

He used his vampiric speed to close the rest of the distance. He stopped directly in front of the Sister of Power, giving the illusion of just appearing there. Her startled squeak and sudden silence gave him a small sense of satisfaction.

He loomed.

"How? Where?" she sputtered. Her eyes darted about nervously, as if seeking an escape.

"Does that really matter?" He gained control of his anger. He still needed to complete his transaction with her. He decided any vengeance could wait. He pulled the nearly completed puzzle box from inside his shirt and presented it to her. "I have completed your request."

She recovered from her initial shock and took the relic from him. She examined it and smirked. "It is not complete. You have failed."

He kept his voice calm and pleasant. He'd expected this response and refused to rise to her bait. "You required that I recover five pieces from the Sisters; I have done so and assembled them. They only fit together one way. I noticed the small gap and had Belladonna examine the pieces for any damage which might indicate a fragment broken off. She found them to be sound and whole. The only other conclusion I could reach was there had to be a sixth piece missing."

She raised an eyebrow, obviously impressed. "You surprise me. Very few would have gotten past that puzzle; but then, how many would have the cooperation of a siren?"

He smiled and knew it wasn't friendly. "I can only think of one other. Where is the keystone, Circe?"

"You only found five then returned here. Perhaps it is with one of the Sisters you didn't visit."

He shook his head slowly. "The only Sister I did not visit was Juma. She has not had her power long enough to have received a piece from you. For that matter, she is not a true Sister of Power; her magic is stolen."

Circe opened and closed her mouth a few times, at a loss for words. Clearly, she hadn't expected him to have that knowledge. He wondered if she had even known about Juma's existence.

Finally, she spoke. "Fine; yes, I have the keystone and the key to the box. I will have to retrieve it tomorrow."

He frowned, and she continued quickly, "I hid it in a place that can only be accessed at dawn. The spells on it keep even me out at any other time of day."

He smelled the simple spell which hid her lie and recognized it for what it was. He debated whether to call her on the lie or ride it out to learn her purpose.

She didn't catch the subtle change in his body language and continued. "Dine with me tonight. A good meal and a night on dry land is the least I can offer to make up for the delay."

*"And the trap is set,"* he thought. Still, he nodded. "I accept your hospitality, Circe."

He allowed her to lead him to a room with a bed and wash basin in it. She left to prepare the meal as he surveyed the room. First, he investigated the wash basin

490

and the ewer of water nearby. He fished the Elder's Stone out and held the milky crystal close to the water.

The lack of any glow assured him she'd placed no enchantment on it. The bed and other sparse furnishings proved magic-free, as well. The crystal only glowed near the window and door. He closed his eyes and opened his other senses. The spell on the room's exits seemed to be a simple aversion or containment spell. He'd encountered similar before and knew he could easily break them if he wanted or needed to.

He turned his attention to the room's decoration. Gauze drapes covered one wall. Vague figures could be seen through it. He lifted the thin fabric to reveal a detailed mosaic. He couldn't help but smirk at the theme.

Nude figures and animals frolicked about in various erotic poses. The artistic style reminded him of Grecian potter he'd seen occasionally. He particularly found the exaggerated breasts, hips, and phalli humorous. He wondered if the mosaic was supposed to arouse him.

He shook his head and made use of the wash basin.

Circe came to call him to dine a couple of hours later. She seemed disappointed to find him clothed and unaroused. She glanced at the now revealed mosaic. He caught the unmistakable muck of her arousal as well as the increase in her heartbeat and breathing.

He noted the change and decided to include that knowledge in his plans to torment her. He fully intended to make her suffer for the loss of Hezekiah.

He reached out along his blood tie to Belladonna and mentally whispered. *"Pet, can you read Circe through our bond? I need to know how powerful her magic is."*

He kept a careful eye on the Sister; she showed no sign of sensing the flux in his power.

*"You are playing a dangerous game, Viktor,"* Belle replied. *"What if she catches you and takes it as a threat?"*

*"She hasn't noticed this exchange. I know you can keep your magic very subtle. If she is as weak as I suspect, it won't matter if she catches me or not."*

*"I would still advise against it. You've completed her quest. Just get the portion of magic she owes you and get out. Regardless of how strong or weak she is right now; once that box is opened, she'll be restored to her full power."*

He sensed the siren's worry. He told her the one thing he hoped would gain her cooperation. *"She had dealings with Xandricus to maintain the protective fog around her island."*

He felt his skin grow hot with the siren's rage. *"Keep her distracted."*

He made a point of inhaling deeply. "Mmm, the food smells as delicious as you look, Circe." He gave her a hungry, almost lascivious look.

She stopped just shy of the doorway to her banquet hall and gazed at him, sweeping her stare down his tall frame. She lingered at his crotch and smiled.

He returned the smile and stepped in close. "Perhaps I shall have you for dessert." She blushed, and he chuckled wickedly; her deepened blush told him she hadn't detected the lie.

She tried to close the distance; he stepped back and waggled a finger at her. "Patience, Circe. The anticipation is half the pleasure; food first."

She pouted in frustration and whimpered. He remained unmoved. She pursed her lips and sighed. With slightly slumped shoulders, she turned and led him into the banquet hall.

He heard Belladonna's chuckle in his head. *"She has a sex drive to equal yours or mine, but a severe lack of partners. Her magic potential is strong. From what I can sense, she has grown lazy in practicing it. She could control all domestic animals as well as the men she has transformed into animals. She lacks the control to do so, though; she is too long out of practice. She's also not very observant."*

*"I think she sees only what she wants to see,"* he replied mentally.

*"What do you plan to do?"*

*"For now, drag this meal out as long as possible. She's in heat; I want to build the anticipation and desire until she can't stand it, then deny her. After I've received what she owes me at dawn, I will put the fear of the Elder in her."*

*"Why is she waiting until dawn?"*

He picked up a piece of meat and saw Circe get an almost panicked look in her eyes. He paused. *"She said the key and keystone are hidden with a spell and can only be accessed at dawn."*

"Please, try the hummus first. I fix it more often than meat, these days," the witch protested. "I'm afraid the meat might be underdone."

*"She's lying about the spell, and I think she's having second thoughts about trying to transform you. That spell is only on the meat,"* Belle informed him.

*"I know about the lie. As for the meat, I'm protected by the moly, pet. I'll let her have her delusion. It will be that much sweeter to shatter it."*

He set the meat back and spread some of the tannish paste on a piece of flat bread. The flavor surprised him. He'd expected something bland, given the color of the

494

stuff. Instead, he detected a hint of garlic underlying the nutty flavor and smooth texture. He would have to stop by one of the eastern Mediterranean seaports and get a good recipe for it to give Mr. Trundle. He didn't trust Circe to get her recipes, but he decided to ask about it to keep her off guard.

"I've never had — what did you call this?"

"Hummus."

"I've never had this before. It's quite good. What's it made of?"

She seemed to perk up at the question. He wondered how long she went without human interaction between victims.

"The base is made of ground chickpeas. I use various herbs to flavor it and olive oil to bind and give it the smooth texture."

"Oh, so it is something you can experiment with for a variety of flavors." He helped himself to some more.

She nodded. "Yes; sometimes I make it savory, like this batch. Sometimes I opt for something spicier. Occasionally, I even make up a sweet batch by adding honey to it."

He put a surprised look on his face. "Damn, that is versatile. So, do you cook the chickpeas first or grind them raw?"

"I cook them first." She gave him a pleased but curious look. "I don't think I've ever encountered a man so interested in cooking before. You are quite unique, Viktor Brandewyne."

He inclined his head to acknowledge her compliment. He opted not to tell her about his cook. "Thank you. I paid attention when I was young to Mother Celie's cooking. I knew there would be times I would have to feed myself; I wanted to make sure I could eat well."

He reached for the meat and popped a bite in his mouth before she could protest. She made a small cry of distress. Inwardly, he smirked; outwardly, he smiled reassuringly. "Don't worry so, Circe. This is delicious and cooked just right. Did you use sage?"

Flustered, she replied, "Uh, oh, yes; yes, I used sage and sea salt."

He ate some more of the meat and savored both the flavor and her growing agitation. He noted that she no longer tried to prevent him from eating it. He guessed one bite was enough to activate the spell. He wondered how long it took before the transformation happened.

When he swallowed the bite and had some wine, Circe blurted out, "Would you like your dessert now?" She tried to strike a seductive pose which looked more awkward than anything else. Viktor almost felt sorry for her; almost.

He smiled, picked up another piece of meat, and popped it into his mouth. "Not just yet, pet," he said around the mouthful. He chewed slowly and watched her squirm.

When he finally swallowed, he said, "Meat, fresh meat at least, is a rarity aboard a ship. You are too good of a cook, Circe. There is plenty of time before dawn to enjoy dessert."

She smiled, but some anxiety showed in her eyes. It added a slightly sour tone to the scent of her arousal. It served to steel his resolve to show no mercy.

He continued to eat slowly. Circe's agitation continued to grow. She kept glancing at an elaborate water clock against the far wall. Eventually, she reached some breaking point.

She reached out and clutched his arm as he lifted another piece of meat. He stopped and looked at her questioningly under the pretense of not knowing why she was so anxious.

"Viktor, please! You have to make love to me!"

He arched an eyebrow; the faintest of smiles tugged at his lips. "Have to?"

"Yes; there is not much time left. You have to make love to me before midnight." Her grip tightened in her desperation.

497

His smile spread; but his eyes remained icy. He very deliberately disengaged her hands from his arms as if her touch disgusted him. He spoke with a pleasant, deadly calmness. "So, midnight is when the transformation spell you placed on the meat takes effect. What am I to become, Circe; a pig, a goat, what?"

She cringed away from him; her eyes filled with horror. "How did you know? Why did you eat it if you knew? I tried to stop you."

"I read. Why do you think I refused your hospitality on my first visit? Just as I did not allow my crew to foot your island."

"But why now?"

"I have my reasons."

"Please, Viktor, please forgive me. If you make love to me, I can save you."

His smile slowly dissolved and left a stony, emotionless visage in its place. "No."

"But —."

He held up a hand to stop her. "If you could 'save' me, you'd have done so already. We shall just sit here and wait for midnight to pass."

She bit her bottom lip and scowled in concentration. He remained impassive and sipped his wine.

After a few minutes, she spoke again. "At least let me try to save you and counteract the spell. You cannot complete your quest if you lose your humanity."

He laughed long and hard. When he finally wound down, he said, "If I become an animal, my quest will no longer be a concern to me. As for my humanity, I lost that when Juma cursed me. I do not believe you have the power to counteract the spell, anyway."

"I can once I am restored to my full power," she countered.

"Which will not be possible until just after dawn; while the transformation will happen at midnight," he pointed out calmly.

She made a fist and struck her thigh several times. With a frustrated, strangled cry, she said, "I lied! Are you satisfied? I lied about the spell. I will get the keystone and key now."

"I would appreciate it."

She got up and hurriedly left the room.

Once he heard her leave the villa, he summoned his first mate. "Lazarus, come forth."

Instantly, the black cat materialized before him. Just as quickly, it transformed into Jim Rigger. He looked around at the remains of the meal. "Smells good; makes me wish I could still eat food in this form."

"It's as good as it smells, even if the meat is ensorcelled. I need you to fly Jon-Jon here. Circe has gone to fetch what she needs to open the box and restore her magic. I need him to make the exchange."

"Aye, Cap'n. I'll be back with him soon."

"No."

"Cap'n?"

Viktor smiled. "Circe is convinced her spell will turn me into one of her animals at midnight. I am not happy with her at the moment. First, I need to know if you can take the form of an animal you have eaten in the past or if that only applies to once per meal."

Jim cocked his head to the side, a mannerism which reminded Viktor of his friend's raven form. "I first transformed into a fish when Zeke taught me the trick. I've never tried to take that form since then."

He wore a look of concentration for a few moments then seemed to vanish.

"Jim?" Viktor looked around for his friend. A flopping sound drew his attention to the floor. There, a silvery fish twitched and gasped. A few seconds later, Jim stood before him again.

He shuddered and said, "That was unpleasant, Cap'n."

"Was it painful?"

Jim shook his head. "No, but it's not a comfortable shape to wear in the air. I couldn't breathe." He held up his hand. "I know I don't need to breathe; but the instinct is still there."

Viktor nodded his understanding. "Very well, Jim. You can go fetch Jon-Jon; but don't deliver him until after midnight. I'm not through with Circe. She still hasn't suffered enough for my satisfaction."

"Aye, Cap'n. I'll be back with him later." Jim morphed into raven form and flew off.

To be sure he had control of his own shape and was not a victim of Circe's spell; Viktor changed into a hog before she returned. He briefly morphed into a dog and back to a hog to double check. He returned to human form and put his clothes back on.

Before long, he heard the Sister return to the house. She entered the room at nearly a run and a bit out of breath.

"I finally found it," she gasped. "It was hidden better than I remembered." She glanced at the spot where she'd left the puzzle box only to discover its absence. "What happened to the box?"

Viktor feigned concern. "I thought you took it with you."

"No; I left it here! What could have happened to it?" She began to tear around the room looking under pillows and behind wall hangings. He watched her frenzy with hidden amusement.

"Perhaps you left it in another room," he suggested.

She shook her head. "No, I don't think so."

He shrugged. "You won't know until you look."

She gave him a frazzled look. "I'll check, but I'm pretty sure I didn't." She let out a frustrated growl. "There's not much time left."

As soon as she left the room again, he took the puzzle box out of his shirt and set it back where Circe had originally left it. He then undressed and carefully folded his clothes on top of his boots. He tucked the Elder's Stone and the silver vial into one of the boots.

Satisfied with his preparations, he reclined at the table again, comfortable in his nudity.

Circe returned to the room, clearly frustrated. She stopped, dumbfounded at the sight of him. He smiled and waved a hand at the puzzle box.

"I found it."

She shook her head. He saw it took her a while to process what he'd just said. His nudity seemed to be extremely distracting to her. The scent of her arousal deepened.

Circe practically ran to the table. She fumbled hurriedly with the small piece of carved cat's-eye in her hand and almost dropped it before she could get it into the vacant cavity on the puzzle box. She then inserted a delicate-looking golden key into the resulting slot. With a trembling hand, she turned the ring portion and key half a turn to the left.

A soft click preceded the appearance of a fine crack all the way around the lid of the box. The lid raised and slid back to reveal a fine, silvery powder inside.

Circe carefully poured the contents of the box into her wine cup. She stirred it and lifted the solution to her lips, careful not to spill any of it.

Viktor waited for her to finish. He felt the rush of magic as she was restored to her full power. His body reacted to it, and he grew rigid and ready. He knew sex with the Sister at this moment would be glorious beyond description.

He had no intention of giving in to that urge, however. Just as she set the empty cup down, he transformed into a hog. The transformation had the dual effect of reversing his erection and thoroughly disconcerting her.

"No! How can this be? It's not midnight yet! No, no, no, no," she sobbed. She got a grimly desperate look on her face. "Stop it, Circe. You have your power back; you can restore him now; and you will have control over him. The One is yours, you silly sow."

Viktor cocked his head at her. He'd no idea she talked to herself like that. Still, he supposed isolation from regular human contact would make anyone a little daft.

It also put him on the alert. He'd felt the full strength of her magic. Her apparent madness made her dangerous. He hoped Belladonna was right about the Sister's skill level at wielding that power.

A wave of magic washed over him, and he felt the need to return to human form. He resisted. Circe frowned, and he felt the magic increase. He continued to resist, grateful for the moly.

"Why aren't you changing back? I know I'm doing this right." Circe's frustration gave her voice a whiney quality.

He felt the magic increase again and decided to change for her. In a blink, he turned from a hog to a dog.

She looked completely confused and let out a little shriek. "How did that happen? I've never turned anyone into a dog before." She pulled her hair, at a loss for what to do.

He couldn't hide his canine grin at her discomfort.

"You dare mock me? Back to a pig with you!"

He felt the full force of her magic and knew it would not work on him. He defied her spell and returned to human form.

"Really, Circe; you need to get out more." He turned and began to put his clothes back on.

"What are you doing?"

"Getting dressed; what does it look like?"

"But why? I command you to make love to me."

He laughed. "You command? I am not yours to command, nor will I ever be."

"But you fell to my spell," she whined.

"No; I transformed of my own will and at my own choice of form. It has no bearing on your spell or your power. I did it to prove you have no power over me."

He let her digest that information.

She hit him with a blast of magic. He just stood there and let it wash over and past him.

Finally, she seemed to accept the truth of his words. "How have you escaped me?"

"Can't you figure it out?"

"Tell me!"

"If you can't figure it out, you don't deserve to know," he replied calmly. He heard Jim and Jon-Jon arrive and gave them mental directions to enter. He specifically put a compulsion on Jon-Jon not to eat anything there.

She turned, a touch of fear in her eyes, as the two pirates entered the room. "Who are you?"

"Allow me to introduce my first mate, Jim Rigger, and my second mate, Willoby Jon. Mr. Rigger is one of my vampires. I had him fly Mr. Jon here from the ship to facilitate the conclusion of our transaction. He is magically null." Viktor slipped the Elder's Stone back on and tucked it into his shirt while she was distracted.

"Our transaction —," she said reluctantly.

"Yes, Circe; I have fulfilled the requirement of me to retrieve the scattered pieces of the puzzle box. It is your turn to grant me the portion of magic I require," he reminded her.

"You must make love to me to receive it."

"I don't think so. That would involve sharing my power with you, which was never part of our bargain. Try again."

"Fine; do you have a vessel to receive it in?"

"I do." He held up the silver vial by its chain and passed it to Jon-Jon.

The tall, tattoo-covered pirate closed the short distance to Circe and held the vial out to her. In response, she untied her belt and undid the shoulder clips of her dress. The filmy garment spilled to the floor. Jon-Jon leered down at her.

"I must transform. When I do, milk a single drop from my teat," she instructed.

"With pleasure, love."

Without further warning, the witch turned into a huge sow. She seemed to ignore the men and began to root about at the table.

It took Jon-Jon a few moments to get in a favorable position to milk the sow. He finally managed to grab a teat and held the open vial under it. He gave a gentle squeeze, and a single drop of milk fell into the vial with a brief flash. He closed the cap and returned the vial to his Captain.

Circe returned to her human form. She walked to Viktor and gazed up at him. "Do you want me to beg? I will beg. I need you to make love to me, please."

He stared down at her and let the cold loathing finally show to her. "Never; nor will I permit any of my men to service you, Circe." He'd seen her eyes cut to Jon-Jon in speculation. "You have already cost me greatly. I will not lose another man to your machinations."

"I have not touched any of your crew," she protested.

"Your dalliance with Xandricus resulted in the death of my former first mate, Hezekiah Grimm. I must delay the completion of my quest to inform his widow and their children of what happened."

"I have no control over the sea dragon. He is just an occasional lover."

"Not anymore; I killed him."

She grew pale. "You managed to kill a sea dragon? How? Never mind; I do believe you. Still, your mate's family is of no consequence to me. I have created countless widows and orphans." He noticed her demeanor grow considerably colder once she accepted the fact her desire would go unfulfilled by him or his. "You have what you came for. Be gone."

He nodded, and Jim and Jon-Jon left. He turned to follow them, stopped, and turned back to face Circe. She stood naked, glorious, and clearly angry.

"Perhaps you have forgotten, Circe; so, I will remind you. Mr. Grimm was my companion on my first trip here. He was the man who refused you in favor of his

508

wife and children." He saw the realization dawn in her eyes. His smile was anything but friendly. "He was the man who carried the Elder's magic; and it is the Elder you may have to answer to for his death."

*"Let the bitch worry on that bone,"* he thought with small satisfaction.

He turned and strode out of the villa.

Celie sat and stirred her fire. The dancing flames and the images they portrayed held her rapt. She never noticed the thick, unnatural fog which sprang up around the two small tabby huts.

Just as quickly as it came, it melted away.

Sometime later, the old swamp-witch stood and stretched. She turned and went back into her hut. The fact it was the only one there had no effect on her. She gave no thought at all to what had happened to the second one.

*-fin-*

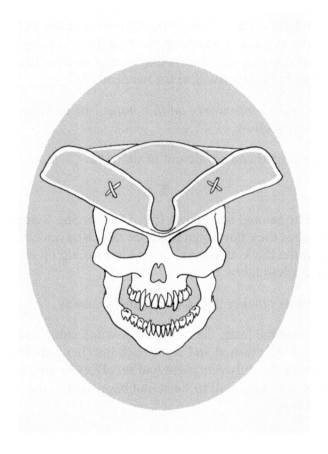

# *Here Be Spoilers*

### Blood Curse

After being shipwrecked by a British Navy ship and a killer hurricane, Bloody Vik Brandee and the survivors of his crew make shore in the fishing village of Terra Beau on the north coast of Hispañola. While waiting for a suitable ship to steal, he kills a local boy over a tavern wench, incurring the wrath of *Mamaan* Juma.

Juma sends her zombies to fetch the pirate. She curses him to become a living vampire. The tavern wench, Carmella, becomes his first victim.

Vik returns to his home port, Savannah, and learns from his foster mother Celie, aka the Thunderbolt Witch, just what has happened to him and how to break the curse before it destroys him. While there, Jim Rigger, his first mate, becomes his second victim. Celie resurrects Jim as a black cat which can take the form of a raven.

Celie sets Vik to find the seven Sisters of Power and sends him to Hell's Breath Island to Uncle Zeke, an ancient wizard of sorts. Zeke sends the siren/sea witch Belladonna with him to locate the Sisters using her visions.

511

She pinpoints *Madre* Dorada on the Isle of Youth. En route, Vik learns an old friend, Hezekiah Grimm aka the Grimm Reaper, has been taken by pirate hunters in Havana. He detours to rescue Grimm despite warnings from Zeke and Belladonna not to stray from his course.

Manages to find and rescue Grimm but arrives at the Isle of Youth only to find Dorada fled. With the aid of Paella, a local girl, he manages to track the Sister down and brokers a deal with her: one of her golden tears in exchange for an opal pendant called the Mermaid's Tear.

After some misunderstanding of what the Tear actually is, he finds it, helps Dorada regain her magic, and makes the exchange.

## Demon Bayou

Viktor tracks the next Sister, Granny Glory, to the bayous north of New Orleans. When he finds her, she sets him to capture the demon Tulimanchulo, who possesses the body of a white alligator. He finds and captures the beast with a magic cast-net but is wounded in the process.

Glory slaughters the demon gator, collects its blood in a cauldron, and has Viktor remove all its teeth. She throws them in the blood and pulls them out as a necklace. Viktor must take it to Zeke. She warns him not to wear it at any time. She then has him toss her into the boiling blood. The hag emerges as a beautiful woman.

512

On Hell's Breath, Zeke burns the alligator teeth, releasing the demon's spirit. He fishes out a coal from his fire and puts it in a conch shell for Vik to return it to Glory with instructions no one else is to touch it and not to let it extinguish.

Vik returns to New Orleans and discovers a storm has altered the paths through the bayous.

While waiting for a guide back to Glory, he encounters true vampires for the first time. He ends up tangled in the local vampire politics because of attacks on two of his favorite brothels, one by agents of the Church, and the other by vampires curious about him. To get out of this predicament, he must kidnap the daughter of the Lord Mayor and make her vampire. This gives Jeorge, king of the local vampires, a means to spy on him.

On his final return to Glory, Belladonna begins to grow weak as the Sister's black water magic wars with the siren's salt water magic. She falls unconscious into the swamp but does not change into her true form. Vik must remove the coal and place it in his mouth to protect it before he can dive in after Belladonna. He knows she'll drown if she remains in human form. When he surfaces with her, the boat with his other companions is no longer in the area. He climbs out onto a hammock of land and Glory appears to him. He passes the coal to her via a kiss, returning the powers the demon stole from her ages

513

earlier. She adds her spit to the golden tear of Dorada in the silver vial Vik carries for that purpose.

He returns Belladonna to the sea and sacrifices several of his crew to her appetite to restore her. He then abducts a couple of unwary sailors from port to swap for Grimm and Jon-Jon, rescuing them from Glory's amorous clutches, as he's learned she now has the nature of a succubus.

## Silent Fathoms

The search for the third Sister, *Tia* Rosalia, takes Viktor to Mexico. He lands on the Gulf coast and must travel over the central mountains to the Pacific coast to reach her. She first tries to deceive and enslave him. Her spell manages to control his crewmen traveling with him, but his power proves stronger at the cost of one pirate's life. The Elder's Stone proves to her he is the One, and she gives him the quest of procuring Devil's Hoof, a key ingredient in her spells. She deliberately doesn't tell him where to look or what it actually is.

He follows rumors of a cave in the mountains where the Devil is said to live. Instead, he finds an old *brujo* (male witch) who was once Rosalia's lover. He tells him Devil's Hoof is an extremely hot pepper said to cause hallucinations with its spiciness. The pirates return to the ship. Navigator Zach Brumble tells Vik about such a

514

pepper his father once dabbled in trading found in the northern part of the Bay of Bengal.

When he tries to contact Belladonna to sing up favorable winds to speed the voyage halfway around the world, he cannot reach her or even sense her presence. Unbeknownst to him, Zeke and Hell's Breath Island have sent her to hunt down the mermaid Alyssa, whom Viktor impregnated while seeking for the Mermaid's Tear. He'd also fed on the creature, and she began to turn while still alive. Belle must kill the mermaid but return the child to the island and Zeke's care. To prevent Viktor's interference, Zeke blocks them from any mental contact until her task is done.

The siren is finally able to rejoin Viktor as the ship is caught in the doldrums near the middle of the Indian Ocean. They make their way to a Bengali village near the Sundarbans, a salt swamp jungle. After warnings from a local elder not to anger the jungle goddess, Bonobibi, or the tiger god, Daskin Rey, they enter the swamps to find the pepper (known locally as the naga pepper). They must also harvest honey to safely transport the peppers in. One of their guides harvests more honey than they need, hoping to profit enough to laze away the wet season. This leads to an encounter with the local deities and the man's death.

With Devil's Hoof acquired, Viktor opts to cross the Pacific directly to Rosalia's home port.

Once back in Mexico, she tries her best to enslave him using fresh ingredients for her spell. He proves his power is stronger than hers, and she begrudgingly agrees to give him the portion of her magic he requires for his quest to break his curse.

After he returns to his ship, Hell's Breath manifests. Zeke introduces him to his son by Alyssa and orders him to get the child off the island. When the island vanishes again, Viktor finds the ship has been transported back to the Caribbean.

### Black Venom

Viktor and his crew find themselves deposited close to Havana by the disappearance of Hell's Breath Island. Grateful for not having to sail around South America, they make for New Orleans. He must find a home and guardian for his merchild son, Robert, and wants to see if Gloribeau will take the boy on.

Glory agrees in exchange for Viktor in her bed for one night. The sheer magnitude of magic released by their climax alerts Jeorge, king of the New Orlean vampires, to the child's presence. He also becomes aware of Viktor's increasing powers, growing far faster than those of a truly undead vampire.

Jeorge "summons" Viktor to join him in a hunt. Because he needs to arrange protection of his son from the vampires, he agrees. They attend a reception at the

Lord Mayor's for the new governor. Jeorge uses it as a fishing expedition to learn more about the boy and to put the new governor in his pocket.

Samantha Brumble and Captain Bainbridge arrive at the Islas de los Roques and encounter *Madre* Dorada. They learn that the lead which led them there is nearly three years old but gain valuable information about the nature of what Viktor now is and who sails with him.

After dealing with a small British blockade of the entrance to Lake Pontchartrain, Viktor heads for the Florida Strait. Belladonna rejoins the ship there and is given a victim to induce one of her visions to locate the next Sister of Power. *Mere* Venoma Noir directs a psychic attack back at the siren, revealing her power over all things venomous, even over Belladonna.

Jeorge's curiosity gets the better of him, and he sends a couple of his vampires to investigate Viktor's son. Gloribeau's dealing with this invasion of her bayou costs him both his minions and convinces him to leave it alone.

As the pirates near Venoma's territory, she uses her power to attack through the siren. Only the Elder's Stone and Viktor's blood can override the sister's magic. After landfall, she actively tries to kill him and the crew remaining aboard the *Incubus* with hordes of venomous creatures. Once he succeeds in reaching her, she relents and instructs him to retrieve an amulet imbued with her power which was stolen by a notorious slave trader,

Quentin LaForte. They make for the west coast of Africa to search for him.

Commodore Critchfield encounters Lady Carpathia and Captain Wormsloe when they return Commander Turlington to the *HMS Quicksilver.* He has a dalliance with the vampire, never realizing what she truly is. They exchange information about Viktor, and she directs him to sail to Amherst in search of a vampire expert and hunter.

Venoma warns LaForte in a dream that Viktor is hunting him. He doesn't trust the old witch, but makes plans to protect himself nonetheless, especially since she alerted him to the possibility of using Belladonna against Viktor.

Close to the Azores, Viktor pirates a pirate which just took a packet ship. In a bid to thwart Viktor getting ransom for a promised bride taken prisoner, the other pirate kills the woman he believes to be her. The victim was actually the handmaid who'd changed places with her. The true bride, Brianna Belmont, stabs the pirate at the same time Viktor does. Grimm claims her as his share of the spoils and lets her know her intended husband was actually a pimp who specialized in well-bred virgins.

Samantha and Bainbridge arrive in Havana looking for fresher news of Viktor and Grimm. At the Crescent Inn, Luz passes a message to Sam from her brother Zach to abandon the hunt for her own safety. They learned the likely next port Viktor went to was New Orleans.

Lady Carpathia and Captain Wormsloe follow an old lead to the slaver, Delacroix. She learns about Samantha's hunt but nothing else of value. She kills the slaver and a priest looking to buy some new altar boys. The remaining children there, she takes for blood stock.

Viktor gets a lead on LaForte in Tenerife which sends him to Abidjan. They arrive in port and find the man in the process of exchanging a trader's hobbles for his own on a young female slave. She gets loose and provides enough distraction for LaForte to use his black magic to teleport away. They take the woman back to the *Incubus.*

Viktor learns she is called Nahila, and she is LaForte's daughter. She agrees to lead him to the slaver in exchange for her freedom. She leads them to a nearby river. As Viktor takes a small group upriver, LaForte teleports back to his shore camp. He uses the power of Venoma's amulet to ensnare Belladonna and sends her to kill the crew still on the ship.

Grimm's portion of the Elder's magic frees her from the spell. They stage the ship for the slaver and his crew. Viktor gets word from the siren and flies back to the ship. LaForte falls for the trap. Nahila is brought back and kept captive for her part in helping her father try to trap Viktor.

Viktor nearly kills Grimm for keeping the Elder's magic a secret. Brianna's intervention saves the 1st mate.

They learn Nahila serves as a familiar for her father's black magic when the ship is mired midway across the Atlantic in a mass of jellyfish. Viktor has her drugged, and Belladonna creates a current to clear the obstacle and speed them back to South America.

Venoma requires Viktor and LaForte to fight to the death. Only the slaver's death can release the amulet's magic back to her. When Viktor is victorious, but the magic doesn't return, they tell her Nahila holds part of it. She makes the dead man's blood flow onto the slave and turns her into a scorpion. She gives Viktor a drop of the venom as her portion of magic.

The scorpion stings itself, turns back into Nahila, and dies, leaving Venoma forever magically crippled. For good measure and a bit of payback, Belladonna calls a lightning bolt and fuses the sand around Venoma's feet into glass, trapping the witch.

### Hell's Dodo

The revelation that Brianna Bemont is pregnant with twins by Hezekiah Grimm temporarily interrupts Viktor's quest. The *Incubus* travels to Savannah to deliver her to Mother Celie's care. Grimm officially marries her and swears faithfulness to her alone. Celie pulls Viktor aside and warns him the unborn children carry part of the

520

Elder's magic due to Grimm's connection with the old wizard. If he ever breaks his vow, the children will die, and that portion of magic will be forever lost to the world, possibly destroying it in the process.

Viktor tries to release Grimm from his service and the crew, but the first mate won't hear of it. As they clear Tybee Island, heading back to sea, they encounter and take the *Georgia Belle* and her captain, Chadwick Harris. One of the prisoners manages to shoot Viktor in the neck, rendering him mute temporarily. He gives the man to Belladonna to torture and eventually eat.

The vision she has as a result confuses her with its vagueness. After describing it to Viktor and his officers, Zach Brumble realizes she's seen the kitchen at a tavern in Salem, Massachusetts, called The Dragon and the Dodo.

Commodore Critchfield finds Britt Westin in Amherst and proceeds to learn as much as he can about vampire hunting. During the voyage back across the Atlantic to Caribbean waters, the younger man tells him of his quest to hunt down Lady Carpathia and exact revenge for the murder of his family. Britt remembers his father accidentally killing his mother over believed unfaithfulness and abandoning his little brother, Jim. However, he thinks these were false memories implanted by the vampire who later turned his father.

Viktor and crew make use of a newly acquired Colonial Navy flag to get into Salem's harbor. They learn the Sister fled months earlier by turning into a bird and flying away. Instead, they find an excellent cook in Nathan Trundle, the owner of the tavern who uses a trick she taught him to addict customers to his egg pies: add a drop of blood to the custard before cooking it.

Samantha Brumble and Captain Bainbridge arrive in New Orleans looking for news of Viktor Brandewyne. The revelation of her last name, but not her true gender, lands them in custody of the *gendarmerie*. The Lord Mayor has them released when he sees she is not male and learns her brother Thomas is innocent of the kidnap of his daughter, Melanie. Later, Jeorge has one of his vampires abduct Sam and questions her about why she seeks Viktor. He erases the memory of his interaction with her and returns her to her ship.

Back in the Caribbean, Viktor and crew take a Brumble & Sons convoy. In the process, they acquire an old salt by the name of Leland Stoud who once sailed with Billy Black, Viktor's former mentor.

In Cartagena, Viktor encounters Lady Carpathia for the first time. He finds himself unusually attracted to her, much to Belladonna's consternation. The siren warns him this is the vampire sent to hunt him. During the encounter, however, he leaves a few drops of his blood on Carpathia's blade. Neither vampire thinks much of it at the time.

Britt Westin inadvertently discovers his bunk mate aboard the *HMS Quicksilver*, Commander Turlington has been bitten by Carpathia. He tries to warn Commodore Critchfield. Not long after, Britt is cudgeled and set adrift. Critchfield has the information he needed from him and sees him as a liability now.

Having no luck on finding Auntie Clarissa, Viktor sacrifices two crewmen to the siren for a clear vision. She returns to the ship just in time to keep him from killing Grimm when the vampire's Hunger takes control. The truly blessed emerald cross brings Viktor back to his senses, but Belle has to seal herself in the cabin with him to protect Grimm and the crew before the power drains from the cross.

She directs Grimm to make a course to Tierra del Fuego, south of the Magellan Strait. Days later, Viktor and Belle both wake from the sleep spell she used to dampen his Hunger.

The *Shining Star* came across Britt Westin adrift in a small boat. Sam is struck by his close resemblance to the dream man who ravaged her and left her severely weakened. She nurses him back to health. They bond over their hatred of Commodore Critchfield and compare notes in their respective hunts for Carpathia and Brandewyne.

Viktor reaches the previously uncharted Tierra del Fuego. He, Grimm, and Zach Brumble go ashore to seek Clarissa, while Belladonna goes hunting and takes a leopard seal as prey. The pirates find the Sister. She names three different prices she'll accept in exchange for the portion of her magic Viktor needs. The first two, he recognizes as traps. He has no choice but to agree to the third: the eggs of a dodo and a dragon, and a drop of blood from the Daughter of the Dragon. She then turns into a hummingbird and flies away.

Not knowing what a dodo is but remembering Jeorge's extensive library of ancient texts, Viktor decides to make for New Orleans. It takes much of Belle's weather magic to race the ship north ahead of the southern hemisphere's winter and sea ice.

During the voyage, Stoud tells of once bedding the siren when he was a young man. Jon-Jon refuses to believe until Belladonna confirms it and reveals she is a few millennia older than she looks. The old salt regales the crew with tales of encountering a kraken and even of the existence of dragons. This last draws Viktor's attention, and he finds out he needs to hunt that egg in the islands between Asia and Australia.

Lack of ships to pirate forces Viktor to put in at Port-of-Spain, Trinidad to hunt. He again encounters Carpathia. They hunt together, then she has him as a guest in one of the local vampire kiss' safehouses. During their tryst, he spots her tattoo of a dragon twined around a scythe and learns she is the leader of the Daughters of the Dragon. When she dies for the day, he steals some of her blood and places it in the vial Clarissa provided him. He returns to the ship and sets sail for New Orleans.

Carpathia pursues the next night aboard the *Lorelei*. Belladonna becalms her ship and delays the pursuit to the point that many of the crew fall prey to the vampiress before the wind returns. Still, she knows where he's headed.

Critchfield arrives in Savannah and heads to the Black Flag looking for news of Brandewyne. A drunken Chadwick Harris gripes about his treatment by Brandewyne. Maggie, now owner of the Flag, bars him from her establishment and has him abducted and shipped from Savannah to protect him from both the Navy and Viktor. Critchfield has Turlington take Harris' ship, the *Georgia Belle*, to act as bait for the pirate-turned-vampire, since Viktor seems to bear Harris some grudge.

Critchfield seeks out the Thunderbolt Witch to verify rumors of the pirates delivering a pregnant girl, supposedly the reaper's bride. Celie keeps Brianna hidden. She proves to the Navy man he has no power to truly threaten or harm her. After he leaves, Brianna goes into premature labor from the stress.

Viktor learns from Jeorge only what a dodo is and where it was discovered. The vampire king of New Orleans does not try to prolong the visit this time, catching Carpathia's scent on the pirate.

*En route* from New Orleans to Savannah, the *Incubus* encounters the *Quicksilver*. When sent to spy on the Navy man, Lazarus finds himself instead transported to Mother Celie. She shows him the twins and sends him back to Viktor with the message to avoid Savannah until he finishes with Clarissa. Having escaped the pursuer in a fog of Belle's making, Viktor takes the advice and sets course for Africa.

Carpathia arrives in New Orleans and proceeds to make Jeorge's unlife miserable. When she learns Viktor delivered his merman son into the old swamp witch's keeping, she sends men in to find the child. Gloribeau uses her succubus powers to deal with them but leaves one man alive to carry her warning back.

Carpathia finds dried blood on one of her blades from her first encounter with Viktor months earlier. She consumes it and forms a bond with him instantly but tries to hide her presence. He picks up on it and gets Belladonna to help him distract the vampiress. The build-up of pure power from his and Belle's passion proves enough to force Carpathia to vomit up the blood and break the bond.

In Mauritius, Viktor learns from a local teacher and historian, Jean Beaujolais, that the dodo has been extinct for over a century. He continues to the East Indies to try to acquire a dragon egg. The encounter with a Komodo dragon costs one crewman a leg. The siren, well fed from a mermaid hunt, uses her healing magic to regrow it.

Hell's Breath Island intercepts them on their trip back to Clarissa. Viktor is grateful for the encounter after learning that dodos still exist on the travelling island.

Zeke agrees to give him an egg in exchange for the vial of Carpathia's blood. The old man then reveals that the siren is branded by the Daughters of the Dragon and that, as a siren, she is the daughter of a sea dragon. Her blood will fulfill the Sister's requirement.

Viktor completes his journey to Clarissa. She uses the ingredients to make a pie, which she then consumes. She transforms into a bird and lays an egg. This, she breaks and crushes into the vial with the magical tokens from the other Sisters of Power. Too late, she realizes her plan to gain control over Viktor with the blood in the pie has actually enslaved her to the source of the blood. Zeke knew what a disaster it would've been to give control of one of the Sisters to the second oldest vampire in the world. Belladonna has no desire or need to control her.

As a parting gift, Viktor leaves Nathan Trundle with Clarissa, since she acquired some of the siren's sexual appetite, and the cook was prone to seasickness.

*Tamara A. Lowery*

# About the Author

Tamara A. Lowery, who once considered herself close to becoming a Crazy Cat Lady is now down to three cats. She lives with them and her husband in Tennessee and builds cars to pay the bills when not writing. She's been writing since the early 1980s but only published since 2011.

In addition to the Waves of Darkness series, she is the author of a steampunk episodic serial, The Adventures of Pigg & Woolfe.

She hopes to release a short story collection sometime in the near future, as well.

Website: talowery.wordpress.com

Facebook: facebook.com/Waves.of.Darkness

Instagram: Instagram.com/talowery_author

Plurk: plurk.com/Viksbelle

YouTube: youtube.com/user/Viksbelle

**Waves of Darkness**

_Tamara A. Lowery_

## Sisters of Power arc

Blood Curse

Demon Bayou

Silent Fathoms

Black Venom

Hell's Dodo

The Daedalus Enigma

Maelstrom of Fate _October 2024_

## Daughters of the Dragon arc

Hunting the Dragon _2025_

## The Adventures of Pigg & Woolfe

## Season 1

The Girl Who Fell from the Sky (S.1 omnibus)

### Episodes

A Chance Encounter

The Truce

530

# The Daedalus Enigma

In the Woolfe's Den

Chase the Lightning

Peril in the Philippines

Rendezvous in Hong Kong

Double Jeopardy

Chance and Fortune

The Italian Connection

Rescue at Sea

Ghost Riders in the Sky

Castle in the Clouds

## Season 2

Turmoil in Tunilia (S.2 Omnibus)

### Episodes

Airborne Alliance

Under the Mountain

Reversal of Fortune

Frustrations

Going Underground

Tamara A. Lowery

Evade and Elude

Escape

Sanctuary

Message in a Bottle

Strange Bedfellows

Family Reunion

Berthing Assignments


**Season 3**

Pathway to Downfall (S.3 Omnibus)

**Episodes**

The Canary Has Flown

Truth and Consequences

Detective Work

Family Secrets

Organizing a Fox Hunt

Divided Forces Part I

Divided Forces Part II

Queen of the Nile

Foiled Again

# The Daedalus Enigma

Doom in Khartoum

Fly Me Away

The Fall of Tunilia

**Season 4** *2024/2025*

*(Publication dates subject to change)*

Diamond of the Mind (S.4 Omnibus) *TBD*

**Episodes**

Aftermath

Laying Low

Regroup *June 2024*

The Cost of Salt *August 2024*

Across the Sea *October 2024*

The Forgotten Kingdom *December 2024*

Staying Afloat *February 2025*

Black Sea Resort *April 2025*

The Italian Connection Redux *June 2025*

Peace Talks *August 2025*

Forces Reunited *October 2025*

The Canary's Eye Conundrum *December 2025*

**Season 5** *(TBD)*

Milton Keynes UK
Ingram Content Group UK Ltd.
UKHW020909140524
442690UK00015B/548